THE YELLOW PACKARD

Center Point
Large Print

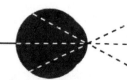

**This Large Print Book carries the
Seal of Approval of N.A.V.H.**

THE YELLOW PACKARD

Ace Collins

CENTER POINT LARGE PRINT
THORNDIKE, MAINE

This Center Point Large Print edition is published in the year 2013 by arrangement with Barbour Publishing, Inc.

Copyright © 2012 Ace Collins.

The text of this Large Print edition is unabridged.
In other aspects, this book may
vary from the original edition.
Printed in the United States of America
on permanent paper.
Set in 16-point Times New Roman type.

ISBN: 978-1-61173-803-2

Library of Congress Cataloging-in-Publication Data

Collins, Ace.
The yellow Packard / Ace Collins.
pages ; cm.
ISBN 978-1-61173-803-2 (library binding : alk. paper)
1. Kidnapping—Fiction.
  2. United States. Federal Bureau of Investigation—Fiction.
  3. Large type books. I. Title.
PS3553.O47475Y45 2013
813'.54—dc23
                                                    2013002770

Dedication

To our sons Clint and Rance

Prologue

From a balcony on the second floor, Helen Meeker, an auburn-haired, slender, attractive woman with piercing blue eyes, dressed in a gray business suit and black pumps, glanced out toward the line workers below. Things in the three-decade old, Albert Kahn-designed Packard automobile plant appeared to be running smoothly. And why shouldn't they be? After all, John G. Graves, second in command at the company's public relations department, had just assured Helen Meeker that thousands of craftsmen simultaneously practicing over eighty different trades within the reinforced concrete walls of the 3,500,000-square-foot building combined their unique skills to create the finest cars in the world. He had then added, "If you don't believe me, ask the man who owns one."

Meeker had expected Graves to trot out the company's time-honored motto at some point, and she gave him high marks in restraint for at least waiting until the moment she got to see the assembly line in action, which was three full hours into their tour.

"So, Miss Meeker," Graves yelled over the factory noise, "you can tell President Roosevelt that while the dismal economy has hit even our company to some extent, we feel confident we are once more on our way to solid financial footing. I fully expect 1936 to be a profitable year and by next year, I think we will be hiring hundreds of new workers. That has got to make the folks in Washington happy!"

With Graves hovering at her shoulder, a still mute Meeker continued to study the rapidly moving assembly line that sprawled in front of her. The smoothly working operation could not hide the fact that the Depression had struck a mighty blow to the motor vehicle industry. Some of the best-known manufacturers in the world were hanging on to life by a thread while others had already shut their doors. Even Packard had been hemorrhaging so much red ink that it had been forced to produce a line of cheaper cars for folks whose names were not Rockefeller or Vanderbilt. In these unsure times, adaptation was a part of survival, and it appeared in this case that adaptation had come at precisely the right time, even if that meant giving up a bit of company prestige. Still, the cars she was watching below, with their dynamic styling, managed to create a sense of class and refined quality even if it was at a cheaper price.

"It is an impressive sight," Graves shouted, a high degree of pride in his voice.

The young female attorney nodded. This was her third day in Michigan and her third company tour, having visited Ford and General Motors. While she was examining the companies' books and production operations, that was simply a front. She had been given a much more important mission—looking for ties between crime and organized labor. The theory made some sense. Criminal elements always searched for weak points to get their hooks into legitimate business. But if it was happening in Detroit, Meeker had found no evidence. Just like Ford and GM, Packard seemed as squeaky clean as the company's state-of-the-art plant.

"Miss Meeker," Graves's voice pulled the woman from watching a myriad of cars being assembled back to her host, "do you have any questions? Is there anything else the President might want to know?"

It was evident from his hopeful expression that the tall, lean, balding Graves was expecting a quick reply, but rather than offer even a token response, she just shrugged. Packard had been told Meeker was on this Detroit assignment to ascertain the effect of the President's programs on the auto industry, thus they had rolled out the VIP treatment including this tour to fully impress her as to their fiscal stability. Yet for this White House–based assistant to the President, observing industry at work, even as a cover for something else, was simply not her cup of tea. What she really wanted was to be working in law enforcement out in the field, but the sad fact was the FBI was simply not interested in bringing in women as investigators, no matter how bright and well educated they were. Therefore, until she found a way to crack J. Edgar Hoover's men's club, she would play the role of free agent for Roosevelt. And for the moment, that meant pretending to be interested in the goings-on at the Packard Motor Car Company. She glanced at the cars coming through the production line, noting one in a canary yellow. Its bright, cheery color seemed out of place in the otherwise mundane lineup.

"Mr. Graves," Meeker finally broke her long silence.

"Yes."

Yelling over the noise, she pointed. "There seem to be five main colors, all pretty conservative, but that bright yellow car body out there doesn't seem to fit in."

He nodded, "We get special orders from customers from time to time. If you look to your far right you will note a bright blue coupe body about to be assembled onto a chassis. That is a departure from the norm as well."

Meeker's eyes darted to the bright blue paint. In the world of drab creams, maroons, navies, and blacks, the color did stand out. She followed the Carolina blue body as it was lifted above the line until a point where it would be dropped down onto its chassis. It was still hanging in the air

10

when alarm bells, unexpectedly ringing from every corner of the plant, brought the long assembly line to an unexpected and sudden halt. As she reached up to cover her ears she yelled, "What does that mean?"

Graves, his dark eyes now as large as saucers, scanned the long line until he finally locked onto a spot about a hundred yards to his right. Meeker followed his gaze and saw a crowd of men gathering around the brightly painted yellow car she'd noticed a few minutes earlier. It was obvious that something was wrong. When the clanging stopped and the huge plant became as hushed as a church during prayer, the gravity of the issue was fully revealed. Every one of the thousands of men in the plant was standing perfectly still looking down to where that car had stopped the well-oiled machinery of one of the world's longest assembly lines.

The forty-year-old public relations employee moved quickly to a flight of metal stairs leading to the plant's floor. Meeker, her heels echoing on the steps, followed him stride for stride. Within two minutes the pair was a few feet from where a group of eight workers was trying to lift the sedan's body off one of their coworkers. The man trapped face down between the yellow body and the car's frame was still. His chest didn't rise and fall. Blood oozed across the cement floor.

After noting the victim's most obvious injuries

Meeker's eyes moved to a dangling cord just above the car. A quick examination revealed that one of the straps used to lower the body had broken, causing the main part of the almost completed Packard to fall forward, pinning the man where he had been working. Her investigator's senses told her this was nothing more than equipment fatigue. After lifting thousands of cars, the belt had worn out, and in the process a man working below a car body had had his life snuffed out in the time it took to make one turn with a wrench.

"Miss Meeker," Graves's voice pulled her attention back to her tour guide, "we need to move away." Just then the company doctor arrived. Graves added, "There is nothing we can do here; we'd just be in the way." Grabbing the woman by the elbow and turning her back toward a wall, he whispered, "Let me assure you things like that never happen at this plant. It has been months since we have had any kind of accident. We take our workers' safety very seriously here. Make sure the President knows that."

Meeker glanced back over her shoulder. She had read enough about the company to also know that Packard's record was exemplary in this area, but those facts weren't going to mean much to the family of the man who'd just been killed by that bright yellow Packard. Nor would it improve the spirits of the eight grim men who had now managed to lift the car body from their fallen comrade.

Chapter I

As she lay on the floor struggling for breath, she knew her time on earth was numbered in minutes. Accepting that fact was much easier than Abigale Watling had imagined. Death, after a life well lived, was not something to fear. So there were no tears in her blue eyes, nor was there a frown drawn on her thin lips. She was ready to see what was next. If it was anything like her adventures on earth, it was going to be a wild ride. Yet as her mind began to cloud and her body started to shut down, the irony of dying in the same room with her beloved books was not lost on her. Those volumes that gave her so much enjoyment in life —that took her to so many places and introduced her to so many people—were now watching over the last chapter in her life. And that chapter would never be finished to her satisfaction.

As she quietly waited for the inevitable, she considered all she'd done in her almost eight decades of life. She'd seen the world. She'd been all over Europe and Asia many times and even trekked to Africa once. How many people could say they heard Big Ben chime, climbed up the Leaning Tower of Pisa, and jumped on a pachyderm named Sally all in the same trip? She'd met three presidents, including the one currently in the White House and even flown once with Amelia Earhart as her pilot. She'd seen Babe Ruth hit a home run in Yankee Stadium and watched Red Grange roam the gridiron in Champaign. And while she'd never had children, she had been the guardian angel of more kids than she could count. And of course she'd become like a mother to her niece, and what a wonderful experience that had been. So there were really very few regrets—very few at all!

Even the way she was dying was something she could fully embrace. While most of her deceased friends had gone with a heart attack or cancer, she was greeting the grim reaper through very unnatural circumstances. The man digging through her desk drawers at this very moment had seen to that. And she had to admit he'd been clever, much more clever than she would have predicted. So there was a very good chance no one would ever know he'd been responsible for her untimely exit. Yet, by the same token, she doubted he'd find what he so badly wanted to find. Thus he would likely spend the rest of his days frustrated, knowing he'd murdered someone for nothing. So all things considered, there was a bit of justice in it.

As her vision dimmed, she smiled. Maybe her memory would haunt him. Maybe he'd see her face everywhere he went. Maybe he'd hear her death groans in his sleep and they would drive him mad. Yet there was a problem. She hadn't moaned, much less groaned. In fact when she'd figured out what he'd done, she'd just smiled the same smile she was smiling right now. So haunting him was probably out of the question.

Now with the mantel clock ticking out her final seconds, what was left for her to do? What kind of clue could she leave as to why she was killed and by whom?

Then just as if Raymond Chandler's pen had scribbled it into the deep recesses of her mind, it came to her. Taking a deep breath, she used what little focus she had left to slowly and silently raise her right hand from the floor. Concentrating as hard as she could, she moved it inch by inch to the right-side pocket of her yellow, floral-print dress. Finding the pocket, she pushed two fingers in and felt what she needed. Would she have the strength for one final act?

Pulling her hand, she lifted it for the final time. It hovered in the air just above her body for a moment then fell gently to the place where her heart had just one beat left.

He looked down at the woman. Smiling, he bent over and plucked the one-hundred-dollar bill from her hand. He studied it for a few seconds, grinned, and slipped it into his pocket. He turned then and walked out of the room and into the night without even noticing the keys that she still clutched in her fingers. A second later the air rushed from her lungs for the very last time.

Chapter 2

July 7, 1937

Stepping off the 1936 Packard's wide, rubber-ribbed running board, Janet Carson swept her auburn hair from the side of her face and lifted her blue eyes to the familiar three-story Victorian home. In a block filled with small, cookie-cutter houses, it was as imposing as it was unique. Even though the paint was beginning to peel from the faded yellow clapboard siding and the windows needed a good cleaning, with its myriad of gables, stained-glass windows, upper and lower porches, and more than six thousand square feet of living space, the house seemed to have jumped directly off the pages of a child's fairy tale. In fact, it was so unique that just seeing it once brought back a lifetime of memories.

As her gaze slid from one window to the next, the memories of time in the Watling home so many years before poured through Janet's head like water from a pitcher. She was unable to completely focus on any of them until her eyes locked onto the round, three-story tower on the house's far right corner. It was then that one memory drew suddenly into sharp focus, and for an instant time stood still. Two decades may have passed, and during those years Janet had grown into a woman, gone away to college, and launched a career, but now that long-dismissed moment in time was as fresh and alive as the summer breeze that pushed her shoulder length hair once more back onto her cheek. For a second she was an energetic six-year-old, pigtailed girl playing with dolls inside that glorious round turret. That was the room where her aunt kept her doll collection and the one place in the home that was reserved just for fun. It was a magical place, a place where time stood still and where childhood wasn't measured by age, but by games. And anyone of any age could be a child again if she just stopped to play. Aunt Abbi had taught her that and so much more.

"She was a really strange woman. I mean just plain weird."

Her cousin's words tore Janet from her long lost recollections and to the tall figure sliding out from behind the Packard's steering wheel. Though Abigale Watling had also been Jim's aunt, he'd never been close to the woman. His eyes were not filled with wonder or nostalgia; his was the grim, impatient, almost nervous glance of a person who couldn't wait to be somewhere else.

Janet had little in common with Jim. She never had. So talking to him always seemed to be an ordeal. Still, in order to take the raw edge off the moment, she posed a question that demanded a response.

"When was the last time you were here?"

"I don't know," he replied, his tone as flat as the Illinois prairie that surrounded the old place. "Maybe ten years. What about you?"

"About three weeks ago." Her voice lifted with the thoughts of that recent visit. "Aunt Abbi and I got out the old dolls. As we talked about the days so long ago, we played with them, sitting in the turret over there. We also spoke about all the summers I spent here and all the times I drank lemonade under the old sugar maple." She paused for a moment, relishing another memory, before adding, "I've never known anyone who was kinder. She so wanted to make everyone's dreams come true."

"To you she was a fairy godmother," the heavy-set, pasty-faced man cracked, "but to me she was just a weird old lady. She was always prying into my life. Always asking questions! Poking her nose in places it didn't belong."

"She wasn't strange," Janet shot back, "just different. I liked that about her. She didn't feel the need to be just like everyone else. And she was never boring or predictable. And if she was asking questions, it was just because she wanted to know what was going on in your life."

As he strolled up behind her, Jim groaned, "Whatever stirs your drink! Why don't we just compromise and call her eccentric?"

Ignoring the jab, Janet walked slowly through

18

the gate of the yellow picket fence that separated the yard from the street. With a quick, determined stride she stepped up onto the eight-foot wide wraparound front porch. She was studying the gingerbread railing when she heard Jim's footsteps behind her. Without turning her head, she sighed. "I think she would have loved the funeral."

"She's dead, so what difference does it make? Personally, I thought it was too long. We should have just had a graveside service. After all, she never married, and you were about as close to a kid as she ever had. What a waste! I wonder how much she dropped on that fancy coffin. And why did everything have to be yellow? Yellow casket, yellow flowers. They even dressed her in a bright yellow dress. Who does that? Her friends died years ago. So who was really left to care?"

Janet twisted to stare deeply into her cousin's frigid, gray eyes. She'd never really understood him. He'd always been so bitter and aloof. Now, even in the minutes after they placed Aunt Abbi in the ground, he was as cold as a gravestone. Pushing sincere words from the depths of her heart, she whispered, "*I* cared. And you know how she loved yellow."

"Well that's your loss then," came the terse reply. "And I hate yellow because whenever I came here it is all I ever saw! If something wasn't yellow, she painted it yellow."

Janet shrugged. Not only did she not understand Jim, she didn't like him. At this moment she felt like telling him that, too, but his words stopped her before she had the chance.

"What tees me off is her will. She left everything of any value to that orphans' home downstate. All she gave me was a stupid old desk. All the stuff she had, and she gave me one worthless hunk of wood."

"Well it did belong to your father," Janet argued as she lowered herself to the porch swing. She was already gently rocking by the time he answered.

"And he's dead, too, so what good does that do me? I don't want it. It's just an old piece of wood. I mean who uses rolltop desks anymore? Not me. They just take up space and collect dust. I told her attorney—what was his name?"

"Johns."

"Yeah, old man Johns. Anyway I told him he could put it in the estate sale and send me whatever it brings. She could have at least given me that Packard. Don't like that yellow color, but it still would have made an impression when I drove up to work."

"Sounds like you," she quipped. Wrapping her hand around the swing's support chain, she added, "It's not like she didn't give you anything. After your folks died, she was the one who paid for your college. You wouldn't have a degree if it weren't for her."

He shrugged. "I'd a figured out a way. I never needed her. Besides, you've got nothing to complain about. She left you all her cash."

Janet almost laughed. "Well don't feel like she shortchanged you too much. I got $75.04. That was all there was in her checking account. Her savings account was empty. So when they sell that desk, we'll be about even."

He leaned his full form into the porch railing, a look of astonishment framing his face. "Then what happened to the old bat's money? When we were growing up she was loaded. She paid cash for everything. She never had a loan in her life."

Janet shook her head. "Mr. Johns said she was heavy into the stock market when it crashed."

"Doesn't that just beat all," he snarled. "Our aunt has to be the one woman in the state who played the market. If I didn't have bad luck, I wouldn't have any at all. I hated her and I hate this town!"

Shoving his hands into the pockets of his gray wool slacks, the tall, rotund thirty-year-old ambled back across the yard, out the gate, and to his light blue, 1931 Plymouth coupe. Without a word he opened the door, slid in, and hit the starter. As the flathead roared to life, he hollered out the window, "I'm headed back to Springfield. No reason to stick around. Don't spend all that money in one place."

Janet casually observed the car as it swept

around a corner and headed out to Highway 150. He had never cared about anything but himself. It was as though he'd been born without a heart. Yet rather than hate him for his selfishness, she pitied him. He'd probably never known a truly happy day in his life.

Pulling her lithe sixty-two inches off the swing, she resolutely walked to the front door, turned its old brass knob, and strolled into the old home's parlor. The house was crammed with antiques. Her aunt simply couldn't resist adding more and more fine pieces. They were arranged in a semblance of order, but the house was so crammed full it was difficult to slide between the chairs, couches, love seats, and tables just to get to the library. And it was the library, complete with its floor-to-ceiling, twelve-foot-high bookshelves that contained Abigale Watling's most prized treasures. This was the room where she'd spent most of her time. Sliding open one of the oak pocket doors, Janet smiled and stepped into a place that smelled of lilac perfume and musty pages.

"She did love to read," Samuel Johns announced from behind the room's large center desk.

His deep voice caused her to stiffen in shock. He must have noticed because he immediately lowered his tone and said, "Sorry, I didn't mean to startle you."

After regaining her composure, she took

another step into the room. "I thought I was alone."

"I came over right after the funeral to do some looking around. In fact, the sheriff is here, too. Our cars are out back, so guess you didn't see them."

Janet walked over to a chair beside the walnut desk, her pumps clicking on the wood floor, and sat down. As she felt the breeze blowing into the room from an open window she pondered what she'd just been told. *The sheriff? Why would he be here?*

Just a few feet away, Johns rested his elbows on the desk and pushed his hands together, his fingers interlocked. The large brown eyes peering through the attorney's round, thin-framed glasses indicated a contemplative air. As his two chins came to rest on his hands, he took on the look of a French bulldog. Taking a deep breath, he noted, "Your aunt was a very meticulous woman. As eccentric as she was, she was also a creature of habit. I'd come to visit her on a business matter, and we'd always end up in this room where she'd serve me a cup of tea and some shortbread cookies. It was that same routine every trip. Never changed. I always took what she served, but I hate hot tea, and if I never see another shortbread cookie in my life it will be too soon." Janet wasn't sure what to make of the comment.

Leaning back in the high-backed desk chair,

his eyes roved from one shelf to another as if he was taking inventory. After several minutes of silence, only interrupted by the songs of birds and sounds of traffic coming in from outside the open window, he noted, "There are over six thousand books on these shelves."

Janet grinned. "She probably knew the exact number."

"Not only that," he instantly returned, his fingers tapping a book on the desk, "but she has each of the titles listed right here in this journal. She even wrote down what she paid for each book, when and where she bought it, and she rated its literary value. I'll be honest, in looking through her notes, I'm a bit surprised by her taste. Though she owned all the major classics, it seemed she was decidedly fond of detective yarns and mysteries."

Janet nodded. "She was a big Charlie Chan fan; I knew that. She read all the Sherlock Holmes stuff, too."

The attorney nodded. "I know in real life she did love a mystery. She followed the crime beat in the *Commercial-News* much more closely than she read the society pages. She constantly talked to me about criminal trials from all over the nation, always looking for hidden clues—those the cops had missed."

"She had files on unsolved cases," Janet chimed in. "She told me tales of lost treasures and shipwrecks for my bedtime stories. Not exactly the kind of thing a kid needs to hear before the lights are turned out."

"I heard some of those stories, too." Johns laughed. "What always amazed me was that she could mention a book and immediately walk over to its place on the shelf and pull it down. She was that way about everything. This old house is filled with all kinds of stuff, and she could still tell you which drawer in which chest in what room was a thimble she bought in 1922."

"No doubt," she agreed, "she had a mind like no one I ever met."

Johns's tone suddenly grew even lower and more serious. "And that's why the sheriff has been going through this whole house from top to bottom the past two days. There's something wrong, Janet."

"Wrong?" Her puzzlement resonated in her tone.

"As executor of her estate, I quickly went through her records. It seems that about six months ago Abigale withdrew just over $100,000 from the bank. That was practically everything she had. I made some calls and discovered she had them give her the cash in one-hundred-dollar bills. Now I know she's been fixing up a few things around the house—she bought that new Packard; she made a trip to Chicago, too; and it was well known she constantly gave out cash to those going through tough times. Did you know that just last week she paid for a ten-year-old boy's cancer surgery? It was somebody she'd never met. Just read about the family and their need in the newspaper. She probably did a few other things like that in the past half year, but I seriously doubt she could have gone through all that money."

Janet folded her hands over her dark blue skirt. The single schoolteacher carefully considered her aunt's habits and the lawyer's words before speaking. "So what are you saying?"

"I don't want to alarm you, and I hope I'm not jumping to any conclusions, but I believe she might have been robbed. In fact, she might have been murdered for that cash."

Janet's gaze shot to a photo of her aunt on the desk directly in front of her. As she looked into the woman's kind eyes, a chill ran down her spine.

"Janet, I've got no evidence. She'd been dead for at least a day when Mrs. Clawmind found her. The coroner ruled that she died of a heart attack. That's logical. She was seventy-nine, but to me she seemed to have more energy than most college kids. She was always out, going places in that Packard. When I saw her earlier this week, she seemed as healthy as a horse. Yet even with that in mind, I'd buy that she'd died a natural death if at least some of the money were still here. But it's not. We've looked in every drawer, under the beds, in the attic, and everywhere else she could have hidden cash. We found nothing but the change in the living room couch!"

The sadness that had tugged at her heart over the past few days now overwhelmed her. And it wasn't the money. She didn't care about that. It was the picture of Aunt Abbi being murdered—she couldn't bear the thought of the woman she so loved dying in fear.

"So what do you think might have happened?" Janet asked, the words tugging at her heart even as they spilled from her mouth.

"There were no signs of violence," he assured her. "If she was murdered it wasn't in a traumatic fashion. Maybe someone poisoned her. My guess is that someone found out where she kept her money, devised a scheme to kill her in a manner that wouldn't attract immediate attention, and then took the cash. By the time I suspected foul play, the undertaker had already embalmed her and pitched the fluids that might have told us something."

As the color drained from Janet's face, a sick feeling twisted her stomach into a thousand knots. This couldn't be true. Aunt Abbi, the kindest woman in the world, never had an enemy in her life. She spent her days helping everyone. She was the living embodiment of the charge to reach out to the least of these. No one could have hated her enough for that. She just couldn't have been murdered! Janet's unexpected plunge into a darkness she'd never known or expected was interrupted by the attorney's words.

"Sheriff Akins and I figure it has to be someone who knew her pretty well. Unless Jed finds something out back in the carriage house, the money is gone. With that in mind we'll have to wait until the thief shows his hand."

"I don't understand," Janet replied. "What do you mean shows his hand? You said you had no evidence, only suspicion."

He forced a smile. "We aren't completely lost in a fog. You don't see a lot of hundred-dollar bills being tossed around here or even in Danville. Thus we'll alert store owners, banks, and businesses to watch out for someone flashing a lot of C-notes."

A knock at the front door caused Janet to glance out the window to the porch. Through the sheer curtains she spotted a man waiting by the door.

"Come on in," Johns yelled.

Within a few seconds he joined them in the library. Janet had known the law officer for more than twenty years, and during that time he had never been one to waste words. He said what he had to say, and he did it succinctly. This moment was no exception.

"Found nothing."

"Then," Johns announced as he rose from his

chair, "we'd better quietly get the word out that we're looking for a big spender."

"On it," Atkins answered. A few seconds later he was out the door and headed to his car.

"I can't believe it," Janet whispered, pulling herself to her feet and moving over to the front window. Glancing out toward the street she noted a solitary figure walking slowly past the house. She had never seen him before. Of course that was nothing unexpected. She hadn't lived in Oakwood in five years. But there was something about the way this man stared at the house—almost like he was taking inventory—that sent chills up her spine. With one look from the scruffy stranger's dark eyes, all the bittersweet, heartfelt memories that had flooded her soul over the past few days were replaced by fear's cold reality.

Chapter 3

It was twenty degrees warmer than it should have been as a high-pressure system took root over the Midwest, pushing people and machinery to the limits. For the last week countless cars had overheated, icehouses had sold through their blocks of frozen liquid, and department stores were completely out of fans. During that time, Janet and the sheriff carefully observed Janie Timmons and her workers deftly remove and catalog every piece of furniture, dish, glass, and painting in the old Watling place. Even her aunt's clothes were tagged and hauled away to the auction barn. By early Friday afternoon the home was nothing more than empty rooms and bare walls.

Atkins began a final exhaustive inspection of the premises. After finishing his duties at the law office and changing into work clothes, Johns joined the sheriff about five thirty.

Over the course of several hours the men searched every corner of the home for hidden passages, loose boards, and false walls. Sadly they found nothing. It was just past nine when they completed that work, and a disappointed Johns and Atkins joined Janet on the Elm Street mansion's front steps. It was still so hot the mosquitoes had called off looking for human targets.

"We can be sure of one thing," the weary attorney noted, sweat dripping from his brow, "she didn't hide any cash in the house. Every place it could have been stashed has been checked and rechecked. And if any false walls were in that old place, we'd have found 'em. The money is simply not here."

An exhausted Atkins plopped his lanky form onto the steps and ran his right hand through his short-cropped brown hair before adding, "This has proven to be a colossal waste of time and energy."

The heat, combined with their hard work, had done the trio in. It was an exhausted and frustrated Janet who moved away from the men to the one familiar thing still remaining at the now empty old house. After taking a deep breath, she eased down onto the swing. Even as she rocked back and forth, the hot, damp air all but smothered her.

"So," Johns mumbled from a spot he'd taken leaning up against the porch railing, "I think my gut feeling was spot-on. Someone knew where she kept that cash, and they took it."

Pushing off the railing, he ambled over to Janet and asked, "Do you mind if I sit down?"

"Plenty of room," she assured him while stopping her slow, rhythmic swinging long enough for the middle-aged attorney to ease onto the wooden slats. As the pair began to swing, he took a hand-kerchief from his pants pocket and wiped his receding brow.

"So," Janet said, "you've got banks and stores on the lookout for folks with a wad of hundred-dollar bills?"

Johns nodded, "Have had since you and I talked in the library right after Abbi's services."

Janet didn't answer; there was no need to. She had nothing to add. She was convinced that someone had not only robbed her aunt, but murdered her as well. It would have been so much easier to handle if they had just found the money. Then she would have known Aunt Abbi died a natural death. Now, much more than anything else, she needed to be assured the old woman didn't spend her last few moments consumed by fear.

"You lost a lot of money in this deal," Johns noted, breaking a silence that had fallen over the trio like an unwelcome fog. "I'm sorry about that, too."

It was too dark to see his face, but she heard in his tone a sincere regret for her loss. His tone also seemed to hint at a bit of guilt on his own part. Maybe as her attorney he sensed he should have watched Aunt Abbi more closely. Maybe he should have been aware that she'd withdrawn cash from the bank. But in truth that wasn't his job. The old woman made those moves on her own, and she was sound enough mentally to conduct her own affairs. If there was fault to be given, it was Abbi's. She wasn't careful enough. Yet that didn't make her death any easier to swallow.

Johns's deep voice once more filled the darkness, "You know I was there the night your parents died in that car wreck two years ago. I was looking out my window when the drunk ran the stop sign and hit them. Such a senseless tragedy! Not only do I wish it hadn't happened, but I also wish I hadn't witnessed it. Still keeps me awake at night."

"You were the one who called me," Janet quietly

replied. "I'll never forget that call. Changed my whole world. Turned it upside down."

"And you came immediately back and stayed right in this old house for those three weeks while we got things straightened out."

"Aunt Abbi made those days a lot easier for me."

"And that's why I feel so bad now," Johns admitted. "Your folks barely left you anything. You don't make much as a grade-school teacher. Now, just when you could have had a real break, put together a nest egg of sorts, there's nothing here for you."

"I'm not worried about that," she quickly assured the man. "I'm not like my cousin. I never planned on getting any of Aunt Abbi's money. For me that was never important. I've got a job and an apartment, and that is more than a lot of folks have in these hard times. My parents always told me it wasn't what a person has, but what a person is. I think they'd be proud of the kind of person I have become. And they'd have been proud of Aunt Abbi, selling everything for the orphan's home, too."

"Yeah," Johns sighed, "but that missing cash still should have been yours."

"It was the car," Atkins matter-of-factly announced as he steered the conversation in a direction that Janet couldn't have predicted. "If she hadn't bought that blame car she'd still be alive."

"What do you mean?" Johns shot back.

"That Packard was bad luck," the sheriff quickly replied. "You surely heard the story about what happened when it was delivered?"

"Now, Jed," Johns argued, "you don't believe in that kind of nonsense. You go to church. Where's your faith? What you're mentioning is nothing more than stupid superstition. Now tell me, do you believe a black cat is bad luck? Or what about walking under a ladder?"

"I'm not stupid enough to walk under a ladder," the sheriff explained, "and as for cats, well no, I don't put much stock in that either. We own a black cat, and I named him Lucky. But that car is something else altogether."

"What happened?" Janet asked. "What's this about Aunt Abbi's car?"

"It was nothing," Johns quickly answered. "It was just an accident."

"You can call it an accident," Atkins barked, "but those that were there know it is something more."

"What do you mean?" the woman demanded.

"Well," Johns explained, "the car came in from the factory by rail. When they brought it out of the boxcar, the guy backing it out didn't see one of the other men who was working for the Illinois Central. The driver accidentally drove into him, knocking him off the dock and onto the rails. He hit his head and died. But it was nothing more than an accident."

"Maybe," Atkins chimed in, "but how do you explain what happened at the dealership?"

Janet looked from the sheriff to the attorney. Even in the darkness she could sense the man's impatience.

"Just another freak accident," Johns said. "That's all it was!"

"What happened?" Janet again demanded.

"The car body was being lowered onto the frame," an exasperated Johns sighed, "and the lift's hydraulic failed. Everything suddenly came down on top of the mechanic."

"In the span of three days," Atkins chimed in, "that car killed two people! And the man who ordered it refused to buy it after that, even though he paid a deposit to have it painted that hideous color."

For the next few seconds no one spoke, and the warm air grew even thicker. It was Johns who finally tried to bring some logic back into the discussion.

"Jed, you sound like some crazy child. Cars aren't cursed. It was nothing more than just bad luck."

"You can believe that," the sheriff muttered, "but you and Abigale were the only ones who did. No one would buy that car. The dealer kept discounting it and discounting it. Six months after it arrived in Danville, old Abigale paid less for that fancy Packard than she would have a

35

Ford. And now she's dead. That just proves it to me. That car should be destroyed!"

"You can't blame a car for that," Johns argued. "It's not like she died in it."

"I can," Atkins firmly answered, "and you watch that sale tomorrow. There aren't going to be any locals who will buy the Packard. No sir! Anyone who knows that car's history won't touch it with a ten-foot pole. Gives me the spooks talking about it." The sheriff wiped his brow with a handkerchief as he stood. After taking a deep breath, he glanced over to the other two. "I'm heading out. Mabel's been waiting long enough. I'll see you at the sale tomorrow. I want to look pretty closely at everyone who's there; I might just spot a killer. I also want to know who buys that car. Mark my words, whoever it is will be dead by Christmas."

" 'Night, Jed," Johns muttered as the sheriff climbed off the steps and strolled resolutely toward the street.

"Thanks, Sheriff Atkins, for your help," a still rattled Janet added.

The law officer didn't look back, just raised his right arm in a halfhearted wave. Folding himself into his Ford coupe, he hit the starter, pushed the sedan into first gear, and eased down Elm Street and out of sight.

"It's eating him up," Johns announced.

"What is?" Janet asked. "The story of the cursed car?"

"No, though he might just come to blame the car for her death. What's eating on him is that this crime is too perfect. He doesn't have a suspect or even a ruling of suspicious death. All he has is a motive. And as we don't know how much money she had left from the hundred thousand she withdrew, he doesn't even know how he is actually going to prove a crime happened. Even if he finds someone spreading around hundred-dollar bills, he likely couldn't tie them to your aunt. So he's going to blame the yellow Packard. He has got to blame something!"

Janet couldn't help but smile. Her aunt, the mystery reader, would have appreciated this ironic twist. She'd had hundreds of whodunits lining the shelves in her library, and few of those authors had scripted a perfect crime. Yet it seemed the final chapter of the old woman's life ended with a crime that could not be solved and a murderer who would never see justice. Compounding it all was a car that no one would dare buy.

Somewhere in the darkness she heard a neighbor's clock chime. It was ten o'clock, time for her to step off the porch for a final time and head back to Becky Hammer's home. Tomorrow afternoon she'd be on a bus bound for Carbondale with $75.04, a head full of memories, and a lot more questions than answers.

Janet moved her gaze from the familiar porch to the street. There, almost completely hidden in the shadows, was a man. She felt his eyes on her even before she spotted him.

"Who's that?" she whispered.

"I don't see anyone," Johns quietly answered.

"Across the street, in front of the Balts' house. His hat is pulled down, and he's leaning against that elm tree. If you look closely, you'll see him."

Johns stared out into the darkness finally spotting the object of Janet's concern. "That's Mitchell Burgess."

"I don't recognize that name," she replied. "But I saw him a few days ago staring at the house when we were in the library. He gives me the spooks."

"Don't worry about him," Johns quickly assured her. "He moved here a few years back from Missouri. Lives in one of the shotgun houses on the other side of the tracks. He did a lot of work for your aunt. Mowed her grass, tended her garden, that sort of thing. He's probably just hanging around lamenting the fact he's going to have to find another way to make ends meet. And we know that's not easy during these tough times."

Johns waved and called out, "Hey, Mitchell, you all right?"

"Yes sir," came the reply. "Sure is a shame about Miss Watling."

"Yeah," the attorney replied. "If you could use some work, why don't you come by my office on

Monday. I have some things I need done at my house."

Stepping from under the tree and into the glare of the street lamp, Burgess nodded. As he did, Janet sized him up. He was likely in his forties, barrel-chested, and average height. There was an apelike quality in the way he stood, his shoulders hunched forward, his hands hanging at his side. He wasn't the kind of person she would want to meet on a city street at noon much less in the shadows of a lonely night. "I'll do that," he replied, "and by the way, do you think I could still do the gardening around here until they sell the place? I'd hate to see it go to seed."

"I'm handling the estate," Johns informed him. "You just continue to do what you were doing, and I'll pay you the same she did until we get the property sold."

"Thanks. I appreciate it."

"Let me give you a ride," Johns said to Janet as Burgess ambled down Elm Street toward the tracks.

Janet didn't answer, her eyes never leaving Burgess. Though she had no logical reason, there was something about the man that bothered her.

"You ready?" the attorney asked.

"Yes," she finally replied, suddenly glad not to be walking the five blocks to the Hammer's.

"And, Janet. Don't worry about what Jed said about the Packard. The six months the dealership had the car they saw the best sales in their history. In fact your aunt even called the car her *good luck charm*. She loved it so much she said it was worth more than anything else in her life. That Packard had nothing to do with her death."

"I wasn't worried," Janet assured him. After standing and smoothing her skirt she added, "I know it wasn't a car that caused her death or took her money. But I'd sure like to know who was responsible."

Getting out of the swing and moving toward the porch steps, Johns solemnly said, "So would I."

Chapter 4

The six-foot-tall, dark-headed young man had shed his suit coat more than two hours before. Now his blue-and-red-striped tie loosened around his thin neck, and the sleeves of his wrinkled white shirt pushed up almost to the elbows of his long, athletic arms, George Hall was wearing out his brown wing-tip shoes as he paced from one end of the eighteen-foot-long waiting room to the other. Another, much more seasoned, veteran of the childbirth experience sat in a far corner chair, his feet casually propped up on a table, a smirk on his face, and an eyebrow raised at Hall's nervous energy.

"You're going to wear out the floor if you keep

that up." The stranger laughed. "And your shoes aren't going to last long either."

"Yeah, I know," the expectant father admitted while continuing his trek toward the far wall. "But this waiting is just too much. I've never been through anything like the last five hours. I wish she'd hurry up."

"I'm sure your wife is doing all she can to accomplish your objectives. So why don't you just sit down and read the paper or something? Of if you need to walk, take it outside. The sidewalks are probably lonely this time of the night, and they might enjoy your long steps a bit more than the nurses and I do."

George stopped momentarily and glanced up to the wall clock. Three thirty! Why did the baby have to pick the middle of the night to be born? Surely midmorning or even late afternoon would have been much better for everyone. Then a cold chill ran down his spine. If this long, unpredictable night was any indication, raising this child was not going to be easy! What had he gotten himself into? Suddenly thoughts of dealing with a troubled teen restarted his involuntary exercise program. His walk across the room was stopped in midstride when a middle-aged nurse sauntered down the hall and into the room. George quickly looked her way, his nerves taut with anxious hope, but her eyes didn't catch his nor were her words the ones he wanted to hear.

"Mr. Sims," she announced with a smile as she looked at the other man, "congratulations. You have another daughter. I think that makes five if I remember correctly."

The small man with the thinning blond hair grinned, uncrossed his legs, stood up, and stretched. "Just can't seem to get this right. Keep trying for a son and always end up with another girl. Guess I'll have to take that Babe Ruth baseball glove back to the store for a doll. Again!"

"That's the way things often turn out," the woman teased. "And there's nothing wrong with girls. I used to be one."

Ignoring the woman's joke, George quickly moved toward her and chimed in, "Excuse me. Is there any word for me?"

She nodded and grinned. "Yes, the word is *patience!*" The nurse shook her finger at Hall before smiling and turning toward the other man. "Now, Mr. Sims, why don't we walk down the hall so you can meet your latest. Do you have a name picked out?"

"What's your name?" he inquired.

"Elizabeth."

"That sounds all right to me."

A deeply disappointed George didn't hear the woman's response. Exhausted and alone, and now overcome with fear that he might not be up to being a parent, he gave up his pacing and collapsed into a wooden chair. He needed sleep, but he knew his nerves wouldn't let him nod off, so he picked up the newspaper. It was opened to an advertisement for an estate sale and auction in the same town where he and Carole lived—Oakwood. Though he had no interest in the event, he scanned the long list of furniture, jewelry, kitchen items, and books. Nothing captured his attention until his deep-set, hazel eyes neared the bottom.

1936 PACKARD FOUR-DOOR SEDAN, 6,200 MILES, EXCELLENT SHAPE, YELLOW EXTERIOR AND GRAY INTERIOR.

He reread the listing three more times, the last time out loud. Tossing the paper into the chair beside him, he grinned and stretched his arms above his broad shoulders. Wouldn't it be something to take his baby home from the hospital in a grand, eight-cylinder car like that Packard! What a way for his little man or little gal to start life! Style, that's what it would be. He could see himself behind the wheel, sporting to work or taking his family to church. They could even go to Kickapoo Park in the summer and picnic on the wide running boards. Carole and the baby deserved a car like that. So much better than his third-hand, beaten-up Chevy coupe with brakes that worked sometimes and with an old Indian blanket covering tears in the front seat's upholstery.

Twenty minutes later George was still in that same chair, lost in visions that mixed fatherhood and automotive grandeur, when the plump nurse returned to the room and announced, "Mr. Hall, your wife is fine and you have a little girl!"

All thoughts of the car suddenly evaporated. In fact everything evaporated from his head.

"Oh, thank God!" he shouted. "This is all the answer to prayer I needed. She's healthy. . . . They are healthy. Amen!"

Leaping from the chair, a rejuvenated George raced up to the nurse, threw his arms around her, lifted the woman up into the air, and spun her around like a rag doll. If she was surprised or put off by his actions, she didn't show it. Without complaint, she took the unscheduled ride, circling the room four times and then, without as much as a thank-you, was plopped down on the wooden floor. Once back on the ground, she straightened her uniform and hair before asking the obvious, "Would you like to see your daughter?"

"Would I?"

"I take it that is a yes." She laughed. "You just follow me. Do you have a name picked out?"

"Rose, you know, like the flower."

"Yes, Mr. Hall, I've heard of the name. This may come as a shock to you, but I know it's a flower." She added, "It seems I recall they come in a variety of colors."

"By the way," he asked, "do you want a cigar? I've got some in my coat pocket. I can go back and get one. My jacket's in the waiting room."

"Ah, no," she replied. "And don't you dare light one of those nasty things up in my hospital. You hear me?"

"Yes," he almost sang out. "I don't smoke anyway!"

"Yeah," she groaned, "that's what they all say before they see their new kid. Then they all light up like a five-alarm fire. But not in my hospital! If you do I'll ring your scrawny neck."

"Sure," he laughed, "not inside the building. I've got it."

"You'd better!"

The pair rounded a corner in the wide hall and quickly made their way to a large plate-glass window. On the other side was a nursery containing ten tiny cribs. Seven of them were serving as the resting place for newborns. A white-clad, older nurse sat to one side of the room keeping watch on each of these welcomed additions to the world. For a few minutes George's eyes roamed from one infant to the next wondering which one of the little ones was his Rose. He was about to pick one on the far right when the nurse elbowed him in the ribs.

"She's not one of those. Look toward that door in the back."

George lifted his gaze to the oak entry. Just as

he did it swung opened and another nurse, this one thin, redheaded, and not more than thirty, carried a tiny bundle into the room. Looking their way, she smiled. Several quick but gentle steps later she was on the other side of the glass from the new father and the veteran nurse.

"There, Mr. Hall, is your Rose."

As he took in the wonder of the moment, studying the hairless head, the wrinkled, red face, and the tiny hands, he sighed in wonder. "She's so small."

"And your wife is more than glad she's not bigger," the nurse added. "Now, take one more good look, and then I want you to go grab your suit jacket and those nasty cigars, get into your car, go home, and get some rest. And that's an order!"

"Can't I see my wife?"

"Not now," she barked. "She needs to get her rest, too. Now go home!"

Like an obedient child, Hall nodded, and, after watching his baby placed in her crib, he waved his hand, whispered, "I love you," and moved back down the hallway to the waiting room. With a hundred different emotions flooding his soul, each of those varying and often conflicting feelings pointed out to him that his life would never be the same, he slipped on his suit jacket and headed toward the exit. He was almost to the door when he yanked a cigar out of his pocket, hurriedly unwrapped it, grinned, placed it in his mouth, struck a match against the wall, and lit it up. From the hallway behind him a woman's voice yelled, "Mr. Hall, I warned you!"

Chapter 5

George only slept a couple of hours. To save time the next morning, he opted to skip breakfast before driving the twelve miles from Oakwood to Danville. Though there was a new and special kind of sunshine in his life, the trip was made under cloudy, threatening skies. It was misting when he arrived at Danville City Hospital at nine thirty sharp. After parking his car in the visitor's lot, he sprinted up the sidewalk and to the old brick building's entrance. He took the dozen steps two at a time and jogged down the hall to room 134.

George was hoping to hold Rose the moment he arrived, but that wasn't to be. Thus it was an anxious Hall who was forced to wait in Carole's room enduring a seemingly endless delay to what he sensed would be the biggest moment in all his twenty-six years of life.

"George," his wife scolded, "you need to quit pacing. You're going to wear those shoes out."

"I know, honey," he answered, his excitement shooting his words out like machine gun fire.

"You're not the first to say that. But I just can't settle down. I barely slept at all. I can't eat. Why haven't they brought her in? You don't think there's something wrong? I don't know if I can take anything being wrong!"

Carole laughed. "No, Rose is fine. I saw her a few hours ago. She is strong and healthy. You just got here a bit too early. Now sit down and talk to me. I'm a part of this, too, you know."

He nodded, took a deep breath, and pulled a chair up to his wife's bed. But rather than saying anything, he just stared at Carole as if he were seeing her for the very first time. Childbirth had done something to her, and whatever it was she wore it well. She still had the same round face, pug nose, blond hair, and gentle green eyes, but she looked different to him. Almost angelic. She seemed stronger, too. Finally, his words carefully measured and dripping in sincerity, George stammered out what his eyes had just stamped on his heart. "You are the most beautiful mother in the world."

Carole demurely smiled.

After studying her for a few more seconds, Hall gently touched her cheek and traced her smile. Three years of marriage and things were even better now. He was more in love than he'd ever been. He felt like a schoolboy as he leaned closer and whispered, "I don't know why you fell for me. You're out of my league."

"That goes double," she laughed. "Just remember I wasn't the prize catch. Before me you went with Mary Cole, and she was not only the homecoming queen at Oakwood High, but she took that crown in college, too."

After patting his hand she added, "Maybe in your eyes I seem beautiful, but I'm really just another mousy, washed-out blond. My nose, with this bump, is too small, and my face too round. And look at my lips, they are too thin, and my teeth are not as large or white as the models in the magazines. And of all the girls you dated, I was the one who was not the prom queen. I wasn't even considered for the court. So I don't see what you ever saw in me."

He smiled. "A great deal more than you see in yourself." He placed his hand on hers. As he did, a memory flooded his mind, he pushed out his lips. "That first moment I walked into the Methodist Church and saw you singing in the choir, I was smitten. When you sang it was like God was speaking to me. And when you've heard God talk, or sing in this case, you aren't satisfied with just any girl. I wanted *the* girl, and that was you."

Carole shook her head incredulously. "You heard God speak through me?"

"Oh, Carole, I see Him in you everyday. The way you reach out to help others. The concern you show for your parents or even that brat of a kid who lives next door. The way you put up with us living in an old, drafty rented house, driving that beat-up Chevy. The love you show for me in your eyes and even in your touch. I'm not sure I really knew there was a God until I met you."

"George, do you mean that?"

"You know that passage in the Bible you're always quoting," he softly replied. "That one about helping those who have less than we do."

"Matthew 25:35–40?" she asked. "The verses about reaching the least of these?"

"Yeah, that's it. I watch you live that every day. In fact, if it wasn't for you, I'd feel sorry for myself all the time. But you always make me realize that even though we don't have much, we are somehow rich in so many ways."

He smiled as he thought back to the ad he'd read last night, "Now, we don't have a Packard. That's what you really deserve."

"No, I don't." She laughed. Then, shaking her head, she added, "We are rich today. No doubt about that."

His words now spilling out like water over Niagara Falls, George added, "Carole, I mean it, I lived on instinct, not faith, until you came into my life. When you came to me my whole perspective changed. I stopped worrying about what I didn't have. I was just lucky to have you."

"Then the Lord did bring us together," she solemnly assured him. "And if you see all that in me, He must have given you vision problems in the process."

She grinned. Then her voice became low and took on a much more serious tone, "When I was little, Mom told me to pray that God would bring a special man into my life. Well I started when I was six praying that prayer. And He did!"

George was suddenly so overcome with emotion he'd almost forgotten why he was at the hospital. The only thing on his mind, in his heart, or in his eyes was Carole. She was the whole world. Nothing else mattered. He was leaning down to kiss her when the door swung open and a fast-talking, short, energetic nurse belted out, "Anybody here want to hold a baby?"

Twisting in the chair, George sat paralyzed as the woman quickly crossed the room and gently pushed Rose toward the completely unprepared new father. Instinctively, he opened his arms for the white-draped bundle and whispered, "I'm not sure I know how to do this."

"As long as you don't drop her," the nurse explained, "there's not really a wrong way. Just cradle your arms, and I'll place her in a spot right beside your heart. One look at your face tells me she already owns that anyway."

It was with unbridled excitement coupled with trepidation that he took the baby. He couldn't believe how tiny and perfect she was. He'd never felt so overwhelmed or so humbled. His eyes misted and his throat closed up. As Rose rested there in the cradle formed by his left arm, George gently traced his index finger along her forehead and chin.

"So what do you think?" Carole softly asked while laying her left hand on his shoulder.

Never taking his eyes from the tiny life they had created together, he said, "Can we really do this?"

"I think you already have," the nurse joked.

He forced a grin, but in truth he was suddenly deeply troubled. What kind of father would he be? Could he really keep this little girl safe? Could he really find the wisdom to guide her steps through life? Could he always be there when she needed him? Before this moment it seemed so easy. Now he wasn't so sure.

"Mr. Hall," the nurse said as she leaned over and took Rose, "you have the rest of your life to spoil this child. Right now she needs her mother. I'm betting you could use something to eat as well. So you march yourself out that door, and don't come back until later this afternoon."

George didn't argue. After a single nod, a quick kiss planted on Carole's forehead, and one final look at his new baby, he did as the nurse ordered.

A minute later he was still lost in a fog of uncertainty as he pushed the door open. Standing on the hospital steps, he was rudely awakened from his contemplation with a flash of lightning and a crash of thunder. Ten steps beyond the door and a full fifty yards from where he'd parked his car, the skies let loose. By the time he threw open the old Chevy's driver's door, he was soaked to the skin. Pulling the key from his pants pocket, he inserted it and hit the starter. Nothing happened.

"Come on, baby," he pleaded as he mashed the button several more times. But the motor didn't make a sound. He pushed hard on the horn. There was no sound. A combination of frustration and anger consumed him as he stepped back out into the rain, leaned over, and yanked the bottom front seat cushion forward to study the six-volt battery. It was with unfathomable disappointment he discovered the cables were tight. Hence the old battery was dead.

"You having problems?" a voice called out from a police car.

"Yeah, my battery's shot," George hollered.

"And you're getting mighty wet, too," the cop noted. "I've got some cables. I'll be happy to give you a jump, but before I do you might want to fix that tire."

George stepped back from the door and glanced toward the back of the car. The rear, driver's side tire was so flat the rim was partially submerged in a puddle not more than an inch deep.

Maybe this was a sign. Maybe God was telling him that as a father, he was in way over his head.

Chapter 6

It took George the better part of an hour to change and fix the flat and get the old coupe running. But it wasn't running well. It limped along at twenty miles an hour the whole trip, the car wheezing like a ninety-year-old chain-smoker suffering from emphysema. It was just past eleven when the mechanical crate jerked into his drive and, with a final sputtering cough, died. As he stepped out, the back passenger-side tire, which had been fine, blew out with a bang loud enough to wake anyone within five blocks.

"Great," he sighed. "This is just what I need. Of all days for you to let me down."

Still consumed by automobile misery, he did note some good news. The rain—that had been falling in buckets ever since he left the hospital —quit. By the time he walked through the entry to the house, the sun pushed through the clouds and brought a bit of light and hope into his world. He quickly made a ham sandwich, chased it with a six-ounce bottle of 7Up, and headed to the bathroom. After drying off and changing his clothes, an exhausted George collapsed in a heap on the green divan. Though he was so tired his bones ached, he only tossed and turned for fifteen minutes without nodding off even once. Maybe it was because of the excitement of being a new father or the frustration of having a bum car, but for whatever reason, sleep evaded him. It was thirty minutes after the hour when he got up and walked back out into the front yard to take another look at the tired old Chevy.

"Hey, George," Glen Adams called out from across the street. "Heard you have a brand-new daughter. You must be one happy feller this morning!"

Glen was a good man and a great neighbor. Outgoing and warm, he was the prototype for the person whose chief worry was not about the size of his paycheck but rather which lure to use when fishing the Middle Fork River. In his fifties, the stocky bricklayer and his wife had moved past the parenting stage and into the spoiling grandkids phase. From what he'd told George, it was the best time of his life.

Waving, the new father nodded and laughed. "She's the prettiest thing in the whole world."

"That can't be," Glen said as he crossed the street.

"What?" George said, surprised by the man's retort.

"No," the neighbor announced, "my new grand-daughter already has that title. I'm guessing Rose will just have to settle for second place."

George shrugged. "Maybe we can call it a tie. What are you up to today, Glen? Now that it's clearing up, I'm guessing you'll be going fishing?"

"Be a good day for it. Rob Martin caught a six-pound catfish down by the highway bridge yesterday. But I've got other things on my mind today. In fact I'm just about to drive over to the Watling sale and auction. Old Abbi had a bedroom suite my wife has been yearning to claim for at least a decade. I don't care what it costs; I'm going to get it for her. When I do that I can finally tell her about that flat-bottom boat I bought and have hidden in the shed. She never goes in there. Once she has the four-poster bed she won't care much that I bought the boat."

George laughed. "You didn't tell her?"

"Of course not," Glen quickly replied. "She thinks the fact I already have two other boats would have made this one unnecessary. She just doesn't understand fishing. But I understand her temper and what soothes it, so I have to get the bedroom suite. If I don't, that boat is not going to do me any good at all."

"I'm thinking about going, too," George chimed in, "nothing I probably need, but I would like to see what her car goes for."

"The Packard?"

"Yeah. Be nice to have a car that runs like a watch rather than one that performs like a three-legged mule."

Glen rubbed his chin and glanced over to the well-worn Chevy. He grimly studied the beat-up car for a few seconds. "It has seen much better days." He continued to take stock of the coupe before adding, "I don't know how much ready cash you've got, but I'm thinking that Packard won't go for as much as you might expect."

"It's practically new," the younger man shot back. "A car like that will likely go for more than nine hundred."

"A car *like* that would," Glen agreed, "but that car has a strange legacy. Most of those here in Oakwood whisper when they speak of it. They think it's cursed or haunted or something. At the very least it is the bearer of bad luck. Millie told me that if I came near it she would divorce me."

"What?"

"I know it sounds crazy, but counting Abigale, three different people who have touched that yellow beast have died. I heard a joke yesterday that the car had seen more dead folks than Floyd Bacon's hearse."

"That's ridiculous," George shot back, "cars don't have souls. They don't commit premeditated murder. They're just pieces of engineering that get you from point A to point B. Now some, like that Packard, do it with a lot more style, but their function is the same. My car has gotten to the point where it only stays at point A. So I've got to do something." He leaned closer and whispered, almost as if he was scared someone might over-hear his question, "So you think it might go cheap?"

"I think so!" Glen assured. He paused, took another look at George's coupe, and added, "There's more spit and bailing wire in your old heap than there is gas. I'll admit you've got to get something, but that Packard's not for a married man with a new kid."

"Are you kidding? That car has all the room a family would need. And it is barely broken in. It would last us until Rose went to first grade without missing a beat."

"Maybe that'd be true," came the reply, "and if you were single I'd say go for it. But you have responsibilities now. You owe it to Carole and that baby to make a wise decision. And though I don't buy into ghost stories, I'm still thinking that if I were in your shoes, I'd look at something other than that car. You know folks could be right; it might be cursed somehow."

George swallowed hard to keep from laughing. Trying to keep a straight face he noted, "You've never hit me as the superstitious type. I've watched you lay bricks six stories up on a windy day. Didn't think anything scared you."

The middle-age man blushed, turning his pale green eyes to the street and pushing his hands deep into his brown pants pockets. He didn't reply either, probably because he couldn't come up with the words to justify his worries. Instead he started humming "When the Blue of the Night."

"Tell me this, Glen," George asked, ignoring

his neighbor's feeble attempts at crooning, "would you buy a car that had been owned and driven by, say, John Dillinger?"

Turning to meet George's eyes, Adams answered, "If it hadn't been shot up, and it ran well, sure, why not?"

"Well that car would have probably seen a few deaths in its time as well."

The older man shook his head. "You're not getting me to fall into that trap. That imaginary Dillinger car you just dreamed up didn't do the killings. He and his gang were the ones murdering people, not the car! This Packard killed two men." He paused and licked his lips before clarifying his remarks, "Or at least it was the cause of their deaths. Now, I don't know this for a fact, but I heard someone say yesterday that a man who worked on the assembly line died because of the car, too. I don't really believe in demonic possession, especially of something mechanical, but in this case I might make an exception."

George grinned. "Suit yourself, but I'm not buying it. At least I'm not buying your fears. But I might just go over to the sale. If no one else bids on it, I might be buying the Packard. No use turning down a bargain, no matter its history. Besides, I was taught a long time ago at Sunday school that superstitions like that aren't of God."

Glen shrugged, his eyes catching the noonday

sun, and his furrowed brow displaying genuine concern. "I wouldn't do it, George. Maybe I'm being silly, maybe the whole town is, but I just get the sense that for all its beauty and power, there's something evil lurking in that auto. I sure don't want to see you bring anything into your life that might end up hurting your family."

The new father smiled. "Don't worry about me. I'll see you at the sale."

As Glen wandered back across the street, George took another look at his old Chevy. Keeping it was simply out of the question. This pile of junk was so far gone, a farmer wouldn't even want it to turn into a doodlebug tractor. He had to have something dependable in order to get to work each day as well as take his family to all the places they would need to be going. But what were his options?

Until he visited with Glen, George figured he'd have to haunt the want ads or the used car lots to find something he could buy that would serve the family for at least a couple of years. But now, after hearing the story of the silly curse attached to Abigale Watling's Packard, he sensed that the few hundred he had in savings might just buy the ride of his life. At the very least it would be worth going to the auction to find out.

Chapter 7

Janie's Auction Barn was just as advertised. Years ago it had been a general purpose, clapboard-sided building on the old Seymour farm. During its early days it had spent most of its life housing farm equipment, tools, animals, and hay. As Oakwood grew east along Muncie Road the farm had slowly been enveloped by clusters of small homes. During the period of growth, John Seymour sold bits and pieces of his farm to builders before finally letting go of the old barn and family home. With that sale completed, he retired and moved to a large brick home in Danville. While his modest home was torn down to make room for Clyde Jennings's sprawling two-story stone house, the red barn was spared. Then Janie Timmons purchased and converted the fifty-year-old structure into her place of business. Because the building was laid out so well for sales, the woman always moved her large estate sales, like this one, to the barn.

By the time George stepped into the structure, scores of men and women were wandering the barn's main room, inspecting the lots of goods Janie had brought over from the Watling place. Most of the crowd's attention was focused on the aisles of antique furniture. In among the columns of finely crafted pieces of wood, Glen Adams, his normally kind face now sporting a firm, almost menacing scowl, was standing in front of the tiger oak bedroom suite his wife wanted. Like a mama lion protecting her cubs, he paced back and forth in front of the pieces he was bound and determined to claim as his own. George couldn't help but laugh as his neighbor literally barked at anyone who dared pause in front of the bed, dresser, and chest; and if they lingered more than a few seconds, Glen pointed out scores of flaws, some real, most imagined, in order to dissuade them from making an offer. Looking past Glen and a few dozen other anxious bargain hunters toward the far back corner of the building, George spotted the Packard. The car had been pulled in through the back door just far enough to get the sliding entry closed, thus it was sitting more than thirty feet from any other sale item. Surprisingly, not only was no one hovering to examine it; few were even casting a glance its direction. For that reason nothing blocked George's field of vision as he took in the magnificence of the mechanized marvel.

Even from fifty feet away, it was impressive. With its vertical chrome grill bars, large twin headlights, optional Tripp lights, wide, whitewall tires, and custom radio antenna, it was something to behold. The fancy car looked out of place in a barn that tractors and horses had once called home. It should have been in a carriage house or parked next to a large, imposing mansion. Yet like a lonely orphan it sat among leftover sale items from past auctions seemingly crying for someone—anyone—to come look it over and take it home. Even though there was a lot to see, no one seemed interested in what had to be the brightest and possibly the best luxury sedan in the small community.

To check out the one item his heart desired, George had to dodge elbows and purses and push through a sea of excited prospective buyers of everything from furniture to clothing. The frenzied scene reminded him of a bargain basement post-Christmas sale where everything was at least 80 percent off. And as the clock ticked closer to the actual time for the auction, the proceedings seemed to be taking on the aura of war. It was man-against-man, woman-against-woman, and sometimes even woman-against-man as prospective bidders locked in a battle of wills to claim at least one piece of Watling's estate as their own. Yet after he made his way through the maze of items plucked from the Victorian mansion and passed those fighting to own them, he suddenly found himself all but alone at the back of the drafty building. For the moment he was the only person interested in the car.

He had taken the time to look at scores of quality vehicles in his life, but this yellow piece of Detroit iron had a quality and style like nothing he'd ever beheld. The stately auto seemed almost alive, and George could swear it was calling out to him. He drew closer. It was immediately obvious that someone had spent some time with it over the past few days. The finish had been freshly waxed so it reflected the images of the scores of shoppers looking at Abbi's treasures. The chrome had been polished so well he could have used the hubcaps for shaving mirrors. To top it all off, the tires' wide whitewalls were as clean as a preacher's Sunday shirt.

"Quite a machine!"

Shocked to no longer have the back of the barn to himself, George twirled on his heels and found himself face-to-face with a middle-aged woman. Her deep red hair set off her yellow print dress. Her eyes were almost the same shade of blue as the pattern in the blue willow plate she carried in her right hand. Yet what defined her was her smile. It was anything but forced, displaying a perfect set of white teeth framed by plump red lips. Three decades earlier she probably drew admirers from five counties away, and she was still attractive enough to have eyes follow her every move.

"I'm Janie Timmons," she announced as she closed the last few feet between them. "I don't think I know you."

"George Hall."

"Nice to have you at the sale and auction," she

quickly replied. "What brings you out today? Anything special you're looking for?"

"I read about it and decided to come over and see what you had." A tinge of guilt swept through him as he realized he'd just told a lie. What had kept him from admitting that he was here for the Packard?

"Well," Timmons explained, "Miss Watling collected a great number of really unique treasures. There is some amazing stuff here, and the best part is that the proceeds of this sale are all going to charity. Her European antiques are being auctioned in a few minutes. Other things, like this car, will just be sold for the best offer we can get by the time that auction is over. I wanted to auction the car, but her final will, drawn up just days before she died, said the Packard had to be sold, not auctioned. I have no idea why. Anyway, when it comes to things like this sedan or that lawn mower over there, I can assure you, every offer will be considered. By the way, if you've got cash, later on tonight we're going to auction off her jewelry and art. There will be some really rare things that will come up then."

George turned his head back toward the Packard. On the passenger side of the windshield was a piece of paper with the price in block letters. He was so disappointed by the figure, he didn't even turn back toward Timmons as he noted, "So you're asking nine hundred for the car?"

Timmons nodded. "It is really worth that. It only has about six thousand miles and runs like new. You check it out, crawl underneath it, sit in the driver's seat, pop the hood, and after you've done all that, then make your offer. There's no minimum. At the end of the day it might just stand up." She smiled, turned, and walked back toward the main part of the barn.

George nodded as he gently ran his hand up the Packard's long hood. It was certainly worth the asking price, but sadly that was a lot steeper than he could afford. So for the moment he could admire this piece of rolling art and dream of a day when he could own something like it.

Strolling to the driver's door, he opened it and slid in. Resting his hands on the brown banjo-style steering wheel, he studied the gray horn button and its green-and-red Packard emblem. Then he noted the round speedometer that went all the way up to one hundred and twenty miles per hour. His Chevy was lucky to hit forty. The Packard's four gauges, indicating engine temperature, generator charging, gas level, and oil pressure, were set in two round dials on each side of the speedometer. To the far right, built into the glove box, was a clock. The choke, throttle, and light switches were in the center of the car's chocolate-colored dash. The radio was between them. He noted the added switches for the Tripp lights and optional heater.

He smiled as he placed his hand on the floor-mounted shifter. The round Bakelite knob perfectly fit in his palm. He pushed the clutch and shifted the car's gearbox into reverse, down to first, up and over to second and down to third. He then ran his fingers over the gray cloth that covered the seat and door panels. The material felt like rich velvet.

"It drives as good as it looks."

Once more startled by someone interrupting his solitary moments with the car, George glanced across the front seat to the open passenger window. Leaning in was a man in a pinstriped suit about the same color as the Packard's upholstery.

"My name's Samuel Johns. I was Mrs. Watling's attorney. She was sure proud of this car."

"There's a lot to be proud of," George agreed. "Don't see many like this in Oakwood or even Danville. I guess you'd have to go to Springfield or Chicago to find more than a half dozen. And I doubt there is another in the state this color."

"No, the color was a special order," the attorney explained. "And you're right, most folks are a bit too practical to drive something like this in this town."

"Or too poor," George added.

"Well there is that, too," Johns agreed. "You thinking about making an offer?"

George shook his head, "No, just dreaming. We just had a baby this morning, so dreaming is all I can afford to do."

Patting the steering wheel a final time, George eased out of the car. As he closed the door, an elderly man approached.

"I wouldn't buy that automobile if it were the last vehicle on this planet," he loudly announced to no one in particular. Then looking at George, the stranger added, "I knew Abbi pretty much all her life. I'll tell you this, it wasn't her heart that killed her; it was this car. She'd still be with us if she hadn't bought that Packard."

"Frank," a man in a blue suit, white shirt, and black tie laughed as he joined them, "you don't really believe that. You're in my congregation every Sunday morning. You've got to have more faith than to believe owning a car can kill you."

As if buying time to organize his thoughts, the old man ran his bony hand over his balding head before replying, "When it comes to this Packard, I think it's cursed. That man at the dealership who got killed when this vehicle fell on him was my nephew. Good young man, too! He and his wife had a baby. That lift had never failed before, and it hasn't failed since. How do you explain that, Reverend Morris?"

"I don't explain it," he replied, his voice soft and reassuring, "but I'm guessing that your nephew might have done something that caused the lift to fall, maybe he didn't set the locking mechanism. I do know this: that car didn't have anything to do with it."

"Believe what you want," Frank muttered just before stomping back to the main part of the barn.

No one spoke until the little man was well out of earshot. It was the attorney who finally broke the silence. "Preacher, you thinking about buying the car?"

"I'd love to own it," the middle-aged clergyman replied, "I've wanted a Packard since I was a kid. My Grandpa once owned one of the Packard twin-six models. That was about the time of the war. But I'm going to pass on this one. Just don't have the money right now."

The preacher forced a grin, shoved his hands into his pockets, and turned his head toward George. "I found out a few minutes ago that you've got a daughter. I figure that gives you an excuse to miss church tomorrow morning, but we are looking forward to having you and Carole bring that little one real soon. Congratulations!"

"Thank you, sir. I'm looking forward to showing our Rose off. She is a pretty one!"

Patting the new father on the shoulders, the preacher added, "I'm sure she is. You take care. I need to get back over and grab a seat for the auction. Molly wants me to buy a sideboard for her."

Morris ambled back toward the front of the building, once more leaving George alone with Johns. Both stared at the vehicle for some time before George broke the silence. "So I take it you don't believe that the car's cursed?"

"What's your name, son?"

"George Hall."

Johns propped his foot on the front bumper and leaned over until his elbows rested on the top of the driver's side fender. "George, I'm fifty-two years old. I've been around long enough to remember when there were no cars. I went to college by train. I didn't buy my first automobile until I was twenty-five. It was a used Buick. Since then I've owned more than a dozen different makes and models, some have been good and some have been bad, but none of them have been possessed by evil spirits."

Tapping the Packard's hood, he added, "In my profession you learn that at least half of what you hear is nothing more than rumors. I've found that gossip fuels more court cases than real facts. Yes, a couple of men did die after this car came to town. But what killed them was their own carelessness, not the Packard. And I'd bet dollars to doughnuts that this car had absolutely nothing to do with Abigale Watling's death. If you and I were to listen to the conversations of others in this barn, I figure some of them are giving Abbi's Packard credit for every soldier's death in the Great War. They might even be blaming it for our current dismal economic times."

George grinned. "People are strange."

"Sure are," Johns agreed. "When you get them together in one place they spook easier than wild horses. But I'll assure you of this, if someone doesn't buy this car, I will. I'm not going to let a good deal or a great car pass me by."

"You're serious? You aren't worried?"

"George, I'm worried about a lot of things, but none of them concern this car." Johns pushed off the sedan and walked over to where the young man was standing. "I sense you're not buying into the gossip either."

"No, but even though my car is busted so bad it will never run again, and even though I love this Packard, with its canary yellow paint, I've got four hundred I can spare. That's all. So I'm going to have to sacrifice my dreams and be satisfied with something like a used Ford or Plymouth. Nothing wrong with that."

"You mind taking a bit of advice from an older guy?"

"No, not at all."

"Everybody in this town is scared of this car. There's an hour until the sale part of this event is over. Make Janie an offer. Who knows? You might be the only one with enough courage—no, not courage, *sense*—to bid on Abbi's favorite ride."

George considered the words as he turned and looked back at the sedan's long nose. "Are you serious?"

"What do you have to lose?"

Chapter 8

Even as he heard the auction heating up behind him, Timmons's voice on the loudspeaker, and the shouts of members of the audience as the most impressive pieces of furniture crossed the block, George could not pull his eyes from the Packard, much less allow his body to stray more than a few feet from where it sat. Like a kid with a new bike, he was constantly touching the car, studying every angle, and dreaming of all the places it could take him. Yet even as his hopes deepened, his faith eroded like a beach taking on a hurricane. So as the seconds became minutes and the minutes became a half hour and then an hour, he grew more and more skeptical. No matter what Carole believed, he just knew miracles didn't happen to people like them. The Depression had made that plainly clear. For those without wads of cash, there were no surprises. Life was all about getting what he paid for, and the fact was that those without money couldn't pay for much of anything. So why was he hanging around? Why was he holding on to the hope that somehow he could buy this car for less than fifty cents on the dollar? He might as well hope to win the Irish Sweepstakes.

Yet as much as he didn't want to admit it, he

was still here because of his faith. It was faith alone that was holding him in the barn. Maybe the imagined curse was even the Lord's way of making sure he was the only one who would make an offer on it. Yet, even as he clung to hope, it seemed as silly as believing the Easter bunny left chocolate eggs. A few might hold stock in bizarre curses, but most logical people saw them for what they were, just twists of fate. And rich folks, the kind with the money to buy a car like this, surely wouldn't back off because of a couple of accidents. Or would they?

As the image of Rose flooded his senses, he once more pictured her in his arms, realizing how messed up his priorities were. He was wasting time hoping for something that couldn't happen rather than celebrating something that already had. But as the old Chevy wouldn't even start, leaving to visit his wife and child wasn't much of an option either. So even if he walked back home, he'd be stuck at the house until he could find someone to give him a lift to Danville. That reality sunk his spirits to an even lower level. Suddenly all the faith he had in himself evaporated like the dew on a hot August morning. Just like the St. Louis Browns, he was a loser. Always had been, probably always would be, too. And like millions of others he was completely at the mercy of things out of his control. How many people in this world had a new daughter and no way to even go see her? Yet as bad as that thought was, there was something even worse.

If he didn't have a car to visit Carole and Rose in the hospital, then he also didn't have a way to bring them home in two days. And even if someone loaned a vehicle to him for that trip, how could he get to work? Maybe instead of hanging around the sale, he needed to be searching the newspapers for a place to live in Danville. If they lived in the city, he could ride the bus to work and wouldn't need a car at all. That would be a crushing blow to his ego, but maybe it was the smart thing to do. It would save money, and with a new mouth to feed and all the things Rose was going to need over the next few months and years, he really needed to hang on to what little savings they had.

Thoughts of the great responsibilities of being a father tore at him like a winter snowstorm, leaving him spiritually battered and cold. Though he tried to keep them at bay, question after question pushed into his mind, and he had answers for none of them. Overcome by thoughts of his own inadequacy, he was suddenly filled with nervous energy that drove him to start walking. But a mind that wouldn't stop worrying only took him on a trip that lasted no more than a few steps.

Overwhelmed, George looked back toward the

car. A few minutes ago it was all he thought he needed to make his life perfect. Now he realized he needed so much more. The Packard had style, but style couldn't put food on the table or help him raise his kid. So this was a pipe dream he had no business dreaming. It was time to get back to reality. Yet even as logic urged him to leave the barn and go back to his house, to pick up the afternoon paper and study the want ads for homes or apartments in the city, the car still begged him to embrace it. It called out to him, demanding his attention. In a very real sense, it had gotten so far inside him that he couldn't walk away from it. Samson had his Delilah and George had this Packard, and that drove him to shove his hands into his pockets and start walking back and forth again.

After thirty minutes of pacing, his exhausted legs overruled his soles, demanding he find a place to park his body. With no chairs in the vicinity, George opted to once again sit behind the Packard's big steering wheel. Perhaps it was fatigue, the weight of his worries, or maybe it was the fact that he hadn't bothered to eat lunch, but for whatever reason, the plush bench seat had a profound effect on the new father. Within seconds of closing the yellow car's heavy door, he fell asleep.

Because all the action was at the auction podium, it was likely no one would have ever noticed George's unplanned nap if he had just remained in an upright position, which he did for fifteen minutes. Yet, as is human nature, when the mind is asleep, bodies demand comfort. In this case it was the man's fifteen-inch neck that set in motion what would become one of the most embarrassing moments of his life.

When he had initially succumbed to his need for sleep, George's head rolled over on the top of the car's front seat. This angle was anything but ideal. Thus, after a few minutes, he unconsciously lifted his head so his chin rested on his chest. Gravity took over from there. Inch by inch, George's face fell farther and farther forward. It would be that end of that gradual movement that would take the spotlight off the auction and make the Packard's perspective buyer the center of everyone's attention.

George's nose hit the horn button first, followed a second later by his forehead pressing onto the outer horn ring. With the weight of his body now pushing on the horn, the Packard's twin trumpets echoed off every corner of the building's walls and ceiling. The constant sound blast could have likely awakened the dead and was so loud it caused many adults to bring their hands up over their ears and children to run for the exits. Yet numbed by exhaustion, George didn't react. He heard the noise, but to him it was nothing more than a part of his dream. It was only the muffled shouts of agitated auction patrons that finally jerked him back to reality.

As his eyes opened, the car's round speedometer completely filled his field of vision. Still not fully aware of where he was or what he was doing, George ignored the horn and the shouts, all the while trying to figure why the speedometer was so large. It was only when he realized his nose was as flat as a new dime that he began to grasp what was happening. Finally, the screaming crowd and blasting horns jerked him back to the present. Grabbing the wheel with both hands, he pushed himself upright. As soon as his forehead lost contact with the horn ring, the drone of the steel trumpets stopped, and the barn was immersed in a deep, hushed silence.

Looking out the window, George noted scores of angry eyes and twisted faces. Everyone's attention was focused squarely on him. Embarrassed, he grabbed the door handle in his left hand and pushed down. As the door sprang open, he stepped out. All eyes were still on the man as the heel of his size-ten, wing-tip, left shoe caught the Packard's wide, rubber-ribbed running board. Though he made an effort to grab the top of the door with his right hand, he missed it by more than a foot, falling face first onto the barn's dusty, wood-planked floor.

Pain shot through his cheeks and down his neck, as a stunned George found the ground as uncomfortable as the Packard's seat had been inviting. He remained motionless, and an even more dramatic hush fell over the crowd. Finally, just before he regained his senses enough to push himself upright, a woman screamed, "My God, the Packard's killed another one!"

In a different time or place, people might have laughed at the frantic woman's observation, but even as George rolled over, using the car's running board to lift himself from the ground, no one laughed. In fact no one said anything. The barn remained eerily silent with all eyes locked on to the man struggling to find his balance.

"Mr. Hall!" Janie Timmons's voice was dramatically increased in volume by the public address system. "Are you all right?"

"Yes," he meekly assured her. But with blood now flowing from both nostrils he looked anything but the picture of health.

"I'll check him out," Johns called out from the last row of chairs, "you all just keep the bidding going. And remember, every dollar goes to orphans, so don't be misers."

By the time the lawyer got to the car, George had pulled a handkerchief from his pocket and was applying pressure to his nose. Meanwhile, Timmons refocused the crowd and was asking for more bids on a rolltop desk.

"You took quite a fall there, son," the lawyer said with a smile. "You look like you've been through a fight with Jack Dempsey, and judging by your nose, I don't think you lasted the first round."

George felt too stupid to acknowledge the joke, but his shame did provoke a need to explain why it happened. "I just nodded off. I haven't had much sleep, and the car's seats are so comfortable. . . ."

"No reason to go into that," Johns cut in. "For the moment, why don't you just sit on the running board and lay your head back until the bleeding stops."

Sensing that was his only recourse, George eased down on the very thing that had caused his injury. "Maybe it is cursed," he muttered bringing the white cloth up to his nose.

Johns shrugged. "I still doubt it, but I'm not the one with the battered face."

The bleeding stopped about the same time the last piece of auctioned furniture found a new home. The new father had just risen to his feet when Janie Timmons arrived for a closer inspection.

"You sure you're okay?"

"Yes. I'm just a little clumsy at times."

"Well that's good." Grinning, the woman added, "I mean that you're all right is good, not that you're clumsy." Turning toward Johns, she grabbed his right hand and announced, "Well about the Packard, I guess it belongs to—"

The lawyer cut her off, "Yep, you're right, it belongs to Mr. Hall here. He can bring that new daughter home from the hospital in style. I can witness the paperwork. Let's get this deal made so he can be on his way to see his little girl and wife."

A mystified Timmons dropped her hand along with her jaw, looking first to the lawyer and then over to George as if to ask, "What just happened?"

Chapter 9

The car's new owner had backed the Packard out of the barn and was a half a mile down the road before Timmons finally looked toward the attorney. Her expression was a mixture of confusion and frustration.

"You outbid that young man by two hundred dollars. Did you suddenly get cold feet? Are you now believing the sedan is cursed?"

"No," he quickly assured her. "Not even his tumble got me to believe any such thing."

"Give me a hand closing these doors," she moaned, her displeasure evident in her tone.

After the pair had pulled the large wooden doors shut and latched them, she poked a finger into Johns's stomach. "You and your urging bidders to be generous! You cost that children's home some money today, and I doubt Abigale would have liked that. She told me two weeks ago that when it came the time for me to sell her estate I was to squeeze every nickel out of each sale. There are a lot of nickels in that two hundred dollars you just cost me!"

He smiled, pushed her finger back from his gut, reached into his coat pocket and retrieved a money clip. As she looked on, Johns peeled off eleven twenties from the roll and handed it to the woman.

"You gave me one too many," she noted.

"Consider it a donation to the cause. I wouldn't want you to think I'm either superstitious or cheap."

After stuffing the cash into her front dress pocket, she said, "I don't understand. You wanted that car."

"Yeah, I wanted it, but I didn't need it. The young man did. Sometimes needs are a lot more important than wants."

"Sam, you sound like your wife has been dragging you to church again. But I'm sure I haven't seen you there. I can't even remember the last time you darkened those doors."

"No," he laughed, "and I figure the next time I'll see the inside of a church will be at my funeral. But that doesn't mean I don't read the Bible."

"Well, Mr. Johns, that might surprise me even more than your paying for that young man to win the auction."

"It is what Abbi would have wanted," he modestly replied. "Most days I look in that mirror, I don't like what I see. I let Abbi down. But today I feel a little better about who I am."

She ran her right hand through her red hair. "Now I'm really lost."

"So am I," Janet Carson said, walking up to join the conversation.

"That red skirt looks great on you," Timmons noted. "And that green blouse, wow, I wish I was still young enough to fit into something that small."

Johns shook his head in agreement. "Janet, you always look nice."

"Thank you both. I try not to look like the old maid teacher I am!"

"You aren't anywhere old enough to be considered that," the man shot back.

"But the clock is ticking." The younger woman laughed. "Now what's this about a mirror?"

"We made a lot of money for the children's home today," Timmons said. "And there will be more to come with the auction of the jewelry and art."

"I've noted that," the schoolteacher assured her, "but it was your comment that has me a bit confused." She looked at Johns.

Both women studied the lawyer as he stuck his hands deep into his pants pocket and shrugged. "Here's the deal. Whenever I read the parables I always feel like Christ is talking directly to me. It's like I'm looking at my own life through His words. Today I felt like the man who had everything, and I was looking at another man who needed what I had. Without reading the Bible, I don't think I would have made the decision I made. It is like seeing yourself in the mirror and having that image remind you that you need to change something about yourself. Now let's cut this Sunday school talk off before I regret not buying that car."

"I've got the money for the Packard," Timmons said, shaking her head. "It is young Mr. Hall's car now, heaven help him. I should get back to work anyway. If you want me, I'll be in my office making sure I have all I need for the next part of the auction. And, Sam!"

"Yes, Janie."

"There is a mirror that hasn't sold yet that you might want to buy."

After the chuckling businesswoman had made her way to the far side of the barn, Janet lowered her voice and whispered, "So have you and Sheriff Atkins found out anything?"

"No," he said, disappointment in his gloomy tone. "No big spending going on. At least not yet. I promise you this; we'll solve this thing. It might take years, but somehow justice will be served."

"Thanks. I have faith in you. My bus takes off in

about an hour. But I couldn't leave without saying thanks for all you did for my aunt."

"I was paid well for my trouble," he assured her, "but I'd have done it for nothing. And from here on in, everything is off the books."

"She trusted you," Janet assured him, "and I think she knows you're still taking care of things the way she'd wanted."

"I hope so." He grimly sighed.

Janet turned back toward the barn's main room. Excited patrons were carrying the treasures they'd won out to their cars and trucks.

"Kind of sad to see her stuff spread out in a hundred different directions," Johns said. "It took her a lifetime to bring it all together."

Janet shook her head. "I kind of think she'd be happy that so many were blessed with things they'd always dreamed of having. It's like a little piece of her will now be in half the homes in the area."

"With as many people as she helped," Johns corrected the young woman, "a big part of her was there long before anyone purchased a piece of her furniture."

The schoolteacher turned to face him, her right eyebrow arched. "Guess helping others was her legacy. That's something to shoot for in my own life."

Johns nodded. Abbi's touch was all over the area. She had given away not just her money;

time and time again she had given her heart. Everyone in the town was better for having known her. That was what made his suspicions about her death even more difficult to swallow. This wonderful, caring woman, as eccentric as she was, deserved a better final chapter than the one now written for her. He only prayed he could be a part of making sure when the life's book was finally completed the biggest mystery would somehow be solved, but for the moment he had nothing new to hang those hopes on.

Chapter 10

Carole Hall had been delivered to the hospital's front door in the customary wheelchair and now stood on the hospital steps, her baby in her arms, and her husband beside her. She glanced out toward the parking lot for the family's Chevy coupe. But even in the bright morning sunlight of a perfect summer day, she couldn't spot it. As their car was always the most beat-up jalopy in any lot, she was more than a bit mystified.

"Did you borrow someone's car?"

George grinned. "No, I brought ours. You don't think I wanted my daughter's first ride to be a charity case. She's just going to have to get used to our car."

Carole surveyed the street and parking lot

again. The familiar Chevy wasn't there. She was sure of it. "Did you park around back?"

"No, sweetheart. I parked on the street. Didn't want you walking too far. After all, you just had a baby, and that is a pretty traumatic event."

The new mother once again scanned the landscape. There were lots of cars around the hospital. They were old and new. Most were Fords or Chevrolets, but there was a fair number of Dodges, Plymouths, Hudsons, and even a long-nosed Lincoln and a sporty Auburn, but their coupe was not one of those. She glanced back to her husband. As she did, his grin was larger than the cat that swallowed the canary.

"That yellow one, parked right behind the Auburn." He was pointing. "That's ours."

Carole's gaze first darted to the red-and-blue speedster and then to the bright Packard. As the incredible sedan filled her eyes, she whispered, "It's ours? How?"

"I bought it at an auction today," he explained.

She whirled to face her husband, a half-crazed look in her eye. Holding Rose tightly in her arms she asked, "Have you lost your mind? We can't afford to make payments on a car like that. George, what were you thinking?"

"I stole it," he calmly replied.

"Did you rob a bank, too?"

"No." He laughed. "I paid cash for it. No one made an offer on it. I got it for four hundred."

Carole's eyes went back to the car, desperately searching for flaws. "Four hundred? What's wrong with it?"

"Nothing," he assured her. "It is like a brand-new car, though it is cursed."

"Cursed?"

"I'll explain later. It's just local gossip anyway. But for the moment I want to get you and Rose into our Packard and drive you two beautiful women home."

Sliding his hand under Carole's elbow, George ushered her down the steps to the car. As he opened the front passenger door, she couldn't help but smile.

"It is beautiful," she noted as she slid, with her baby in her arms, into the seat.

George nodded, closed the door, sprinted around the Packard's nose, and jumped in the driver's side. After gently touching his daughter's head, he flipped the key and hit the starter. A second later the eight cylinder motor quietly came to life.

"It's really ours?" Carole asked as he pulled out into the street, turned a corner, and headed east toward Oakwood. "I mean this isn't some kind of joke?"

"No," he assured her, "it is ours. I have the ownership documents in the glove box."

As her eyes scanned the ornate instrument panel, she grinned, "This is amazing. It's like we are somebody. I feel like a queen."

"In my eyes you are, and that little girl is a princess," he boomed, his voice filling every corner of the car's massive interior. "So you should ride in a car befitting royalty."

"George, you're so crazy."

"No," he replied, "just in love. I'm crazy in love with you, Rose, and life in general. And that faith you are always talking about. The faith to say a prayer and expect results . . ."

"Yes," she answered.

"Well, I said a prayer that this car could be ours. And I think God convinced everyone else that it was cursed so that we could afford it. He knew we had to have a good vehicle, and He arranged for us to get this one."

She shook her head. "I'm not sure that's how it works."

"Are you sure it's not?"

"No," she admitted. "It just doesn't sound right to me."

As George pulled off of Main Street and onto Highway 150, he shrugged. "All I know is that we should never look a gift horse or a gift of horsepower in the mouth. Take my word for it," he added as he patted the steering wheel, "this yellow Packard is going to be the best thing that ever happened to us."

"Don't know about that, George," Carole replied. "I think I might put Rose a bit ahead of the car. But I will agree that it is the brightest-colored thing in our lives. There can be no doubt about that!"

As the car roared down the highway, the new mother looked down at her baby. And just then the little one smiled. She must've liked the car, too.

Chapter II

August 8, 1937

It was a warm, muggy Sunday morning, a day surely made for being lazy and resting. But at least one person in Oakwood had not slept in. Even though it barely had a hint of dust on the hood, George had gotten up early to wash and wax the Packard. He wanted it clean enough to eat off of before driving it to church. Rose was being christened today, and he had to make sure her six-block ride to the Methodist Church was in a fully polished sedan worthy of a president or king.

Now, three hours later, outfitted in his best suit, a navy blue, double-breasted pinstriped model, a white shirt, and red-striped tie, he looked every bit the magazine image of a proud father. And in the three weeks since his baby had come home he had learned a great deal. He could warm up milk, fill a bottle, burp Rose, and even change her diaper. Just last night Carole had let him bathe

Rose for the first time. So he felt a bit more confident about being able to fulfill the scary and often over-whelming role of being a father. It had not been nearly as hard as he imagined in those moments before Rose came into this world.

He stood on the porch admiring his work as Carole came out onto the porch with the baby in her arms.

"It looks brand-new," she noted, taking a place beside him. "And, Mr. Hall, why do you have such a large grin on your face?"

"Probably better than new," he corrected her. After turning and wiggling his finger in his daughter's face, he added, "Nothing's too good for my little girl. And the answer to Mommy's question is that I'm grinning because being a father is just about the best thing in the whole wide world."

"Being a mother's not bad either," she chimed in. "But I've been wondering something."

"What's that?" he asked.

"George, how much is that car really worth? I mean, if it were on the market somewhere other than Oakwood where people are scared of it."

As he moved his gaze from his child to his wife's face, his expression changed from that of a proud papa to one of a hurt child. "Why do you want to know something like that?" he demanded.

"It just seems to me that it might be smart if we sold the Packard in Chicago or Indianapolis and then used that money to buy a cheaper car. Then we'd have some savings in the bank again. Might need it for a rainy day."

"Are you kidding?" he shot back. "Give up the Packard? You don't turn your back on a deal like this. You drove it to the market yesterday. How did it drive and ride?"

"It was incredible," she admitted.

"And this baby will last us years longer than a used car. It will be no trouble at all. You know the company saying, 'Ask the man who owns one!' Well now that I've owned one, I know what they are talking about. Packards are not just good on the highway; they don't break down. Imagine the money we'd put into keeping an older model running. You know what they say about Fords? The letters stand for 'Found On the Road Dead.' And Chevys aren't any better. We know that from experience. This car will never give us a moment's grief."

"I know it's a fine car," she sighed, "and I know we couldn't replace it with the little money we have in it, but, George, the way people look at it unnerves me. The boy at the market wouldn't even carry my groceries out yesterday. He was that scared of the car. And you should have seen the looks I got as I drove it. It's like we're lepers!"

George shrugged as he turned back toward the Packard. "So what? You don't believe it, do you?

You've got more faith than to believe a thing can be cursed!"

"No, of course not, but it seems everyone else does, and that changes the way they treat us. Haven't you noticed that none of the neighbors have come calling since we bought the car?"

He'd noticed and, though he'd come up with a dozen different rationalizations for the lack of visitors, he knew the treatment they'd received had to be about the car. He figured that after a few days that would change, but it hadn't. Even Glen Adams didn't cross the street to talk anymore. Even at work, in Danville, the other employees whispered.

"George, they're treating us like lepers," she noted. "I know you have felt it, too."

"Yeah," he admitted, his focus remaining on the car, "but that will change in time."

Carole moved between her husband and the Packard. "But what if it doesn't? What if a month from now people are still shunning us? What if no one wants to hold Rose or even talk to me?"

George reached out and took Rose from his wife's arms. No longer scared that he was going to break her, he cradled her against his chest and grimly smiled. As he studied her tiny face in the morning sunlight, it seemed she smiled back.

"Carole, she is so beautiful."

"Yes, she is," the woman replied. "I know that

nothing is more important than Rose. And you know that, too, right?"

He nodded, "And I don't want anyone missing the chance to get to know this little gal."

"So," Carole cut in, her tone hopeful, "does that mean you'll sell the car?"

He sighed as he handed the baby back to his wife. "If by Labor Day nothing has changed, then we'll see what we can get for it in Indy."

"That's a promise?"

"I wouldn't lie to you, Carole. But I think that in the next thirty days folks will come to see that car as the bargain they missed. Now it's time to get to church!"

"It's a pretty day," she sang out. "Let's walk."

George shot his wife a look that would have stopped an angry rhino in its tracks, "My golly, as much time as I spent cleaning it up, we're taking the Packard. At least give me that bit of pleasure."

Chapter 12

The service went well. Rose didn't cry, not even when the preacher held her in his arms to show her off to the church. It was also appropriate that Reverend Morris's message was based on Carole's favorite scripture, Matthew 25:35–40. The words seemed to open a door for those in the church to at least approach the family to fuss a bit over

Rose. Yet once the new parents left the sanctity of the church building and walked toward the Packard, even the August heat couldn't shield the Halls from the icy winds of fear and dread from the other parishioners.

Each Sunday morning the parking places along Elm Street were completely filled for the services. People drove to church early just to grab one of them. Yet even though it meant walking a half a block or more, the two places on each side of the Packard were open. Placing his arm around Carole, George escorted her to their car. As he did, everyone behind them stopped talking. A hundred sets of eyes followed the man, woman, and child as they made their way to the sedan. George opened the passenger door for his wife, and after she and Rose slid in, he closed the door and slowly made his way around to the driver's side. Only after he'd shut his door did Carole break the silence.

"Do you see what I mean? It's like we have a disease."

"I can't believe how stupid people are. It's just a car, for heaven's sake."

"Let's get out of here," Carole demanded.

Sliding the key into the ignition, George flipped it over and hit the starter. The straight eight quietly came to life. As he slid the transmission into reverse, Carole looked back at those silently staring at them. She forced a smile and nodded.

After George backed out into the street, shifted into first, and headed the car south down Elm, she took a deep breath. It was good to get away from the church and congregation.

"This isn't the way home," Carole noted as they passed the Green Street intersection.

"Nope," he replied, "I'm talking my girls out to eat at the Colonial Parkway."

"All the way in Danville? Isn't that kind of expensive?"

"This is a special day," the determined man answered. "Rose will never be christened again. I want to do this day right. Besides, you look stunning in that dress, and I want everyone to know just how lucky I am."

Carole shook her head. "There you go again."

"Get used to it," he replied as he pulled the car onto Route 150. "I'm going to spend the rest of my life showing you just how beautiful you really are."

"George, do you think people will ever get over the deaths associated with it? I know it's silly, but I get the idea they are scared of the car."

He shook his head, "Who knows? Remember when the Bosh family was killed by leaking gas in their home and then the next couple that moved in—what was their name? Yeah, the Panes. They died just a few weeks after moving in due to some kind of illness. And no one ever bought the home after that. They eventually tore it down.

Even normal people can buy into stupid legends."

As George concluded his story, the Packard reached fifty, and it left the misguided souls at church far behind. The family's mood lightened. After all, other than the heat, it was a beautiful day!

"Turn on the radio," George all but sang out. "Let's find a song to sing along with. I love that new one by Tommy Dorsey. What's it called?"

"You mean 'Satan Takes a Holiday'?" Carole laughed as she adjusted the dial. "Not sure that's a song for Sunday."

He shook his head. "Well, maybe that's not the one I meant."

"I think it is," she shot back. As the radio came to life, a new Bing Crosby tune filled the car.

"That's nice," George said. "Do you know the name?"

"Whispers in the Dark."

He shook his head. "It seems like all the titles are speaking to us today."

She nodded, traced her finger along Rose's cheek, and then looked up. What she saw caused her to momentarily freeze. Finally gaining her voice, she screamed, "George, look out!"

A three-ton gravel truck was barreling down Mill Road where it intersected the highway. The driver seemed completely unaware of the stop sign that was looming ahead and, even if he did see it, there was no way he'd be able to stop six-thousand pounds of rock before coming onto the highway.

George craned his head to the left and then the right. Carole knew there was no place to go. The ditches were too deep. If the rig pushed the Packard into them they would surely roll over. Taking on the truck was an even worse option. When that huge Diamond T rig slammed into them it would tear the car to pieces.

George grabbed the steering wheel in a viselike grip and pushed the brakes to the floor. As they braced for the impact they both knew would be coming, he glanced over to his wife.

Carole, frozen in panic and fear, was still cradling Rose in her arms. As the truck filled her view, she began mumbling a prayer.

What good was a prayer, Carole thought. Had they tempted the devil with this purchase? The song was wrong; Satan never took a holiday!

Turning her eyes back to the highway, she grimly noted that the truck driver had finally seen them. Sadly it was too late, even as the truck driver stomped on his brakes, the inevitable and fatal collision was just seconds away. As the truck's brakes squealed, Carole closed her eyes and grimly counted down her last seconds of life.

Chapter 13

The crash didn't come. There were no sounds of metal hitting metal, of fenders denting or glass breaking. When the car came to a stop, the only thing filling the air was Bing Crosby's voice coming from the Packard's radio speaker.

Opening his eyes, George Hall stared out the windshield. The gravel truck was directly in front of him; he was staring at the large dual axle's twin wheels just under the truck's dump bucket, but those wheels weren't turning. Somehow the driver had gotten the truck and its thousands of pounds of cargo to stop. George's car had stopped as well. It was sitting in the middle of Highway 150, its motor idling and its chrome bumper just inches from the truck's now stationary load. This was impossible! George had been driving long enough to know that cars couldn't go from fifty to zero in that short a distance. It just couldn't happen. And yet it had.

After sliding the transmission into neutral, George looked toward his wife and child. Carole was still praying, and Rose was still sleeping. Yet they were fine. Except for Carole's purse sliding off the seat and onto the floorboard, everything was just as it had been a few moments before.

After setting the parking brake, he reached over and placed his hand on his wife's arm. "You okay?"

"Yes," she whispered. "George, I thought we were going to die for sure."

"So did I," he replied. "And she just slept through the whole thing." Bathed in an overwhelming sense of relief, he gently rubbed Rose's forehead. As he did, her eyes popped open and she grinned.

"You all right?" someone yelled.

The truck driver's voice pulled George back to the situation at hand. Grabbing the driver's door handle, he pushed it down and stepped out. As he straightened his six-foot form, the other man leaped from his cab and hurried over to the car.

"I thought I'd killed you," he blurted out. "My mind was wandering, and I forgot where I was. And I am so sorry!"

"We're fine," George assured him. He glanced behind their car to the highway. From the skid marks, he could tell the exact spot he stepped on the brakes. Turning back to the driver, he quipped, "Except for leaving some rubber on the concrete, it seems our car is all right, too."

"You're lucky you have such a fine car," the truck driver breathlessly noted. "If you'd been driving something else, something that didn't have those big brakes, you'd've plowed right into me. I'd have been carrying that guilt for the rest of my life, too."

The man walked over to the yellow car and lightly tapped on the hood. "Some piece of engineering." After running his hand along the fender, he said, "I'm Ben Larson. Kind of figured you might want to know the name of the guy who almost killed you."

His knees still a bit rubbery, George stuck out his hand. "George Hall. And the important thing, Mr. Larson, is that you didn't kill me or my wife or our baby. We're all fine. Just one of those lucky things we got stopped in time."

"Mr. Hall, you can call it lucky if you want," the man shot back, "but luck didn't have a thing to do with it. It was your Packard's brakes."

A honking horn from an approaching motorist caused both men to whirl and look to the east. The almost-wreck was blocking the U.S. highway, and it seemed the oncoming motorist was not in a patient mood.

"Looks like we have the whole road blocked," Larson noted. "Guess we need to get moving."

"Guess we do," George agreed.

"Sorry about this," the truck driver said.

"No problem," George assured him as he slid back into the car.

As they waited for Larson to move his truck, Carole leaned closer and patted her husband's arm. "I overheard what he said. We wouldn't have had a chance in our old Chevy, would we?"

"No, honey, we'd have slammed right into the

side of his truck. Probably would have taken our heads off."

"So," she sighed, "in this case there are now three people whose lives were saved by the Packard. As I see it, that kind of evens things up."

"So," he asked, "does this mean we keep the car?"

"I'm not giving away anything that saved my daughter's life," she assured him. "I don't care if people are scared of this old car. I know better."

As the truck moved forward, George eased the Packard back into first and continued his trip toward Danville. He'd make sure the story of what happened was told all around town. He would make sure that everyone knew the curse had been broken.

Chapter 14

After returning from their celebratory lunch, George made a call to John Osgood, an old high school friend. Osgood was the feature writer for the *Danville Commercial News*. After an exchange of pleasantries, George guided the conversation in a direction he hoped would land him in the pages of the local newspaper.

"So," Osgood said, "you're telling me it was the *supposedly* cursed Packard that saved your life?"

"No doubt about it," George assured him. "If

you don't believe me, you can ask the truck driver. He'll swear to it as well. In fact he was the one who pointed it out to me."

"But," Osgood argued, "why is this so important that you need to tell me about it? I mean, not getting killed in a car crash is hardly news when the crash doesn't happen."

"Yeah," George explained, "but it becomes news when that yellow Packard is involved. This is the very car you wrote about a few months ago, killing that guy at the railroad yard and at the dealership. I own the car that everyone thinks is possessed, and it is the same car that kept my daughter, wife, and me from being killed. You see where I'm going with this. It would be a great human interest feature, and that sells papers."

"Oh, I see where you're going," the reporter assured him. "It is kind of an exorcism feature. Might be good, at that. Can I get a picture of you and the car?"

"You can come over this afternoon and get a photo with the whole family."

"Okay," Osgood replied, "I'll do it. But what's your angle? This kind of publicity isn't going to make you any money. It won't get you a raise."

"But it might just change folks' view," George quickly replied. "We're being shunned right now. If the car's reputation changes, then maybe folks will start thinking it's a good luck charm."

"Sounds good." Osgood laughed. "Though keep

in mind this whole thing is so silly. How about I get to your place around four?"

"We'll be ready."

Hanging up the phone, George wandered back through the house onto the porch. The afternoon heat was stifling. With no breeze it felt like an oven. Yet he didn't care. He'd been right to ignore the gossip and buy the car. That had been proven today. And when that story ran in tomorrow's paper, others would see it, too.

Chapter 15

For two years George had been trying to impress his boss. He'd gotten a few pats on the back and even two small raises, but twice he'd watched others be awarded the assignments that paved the way for them to move on to larger companies while he had been left behind. It seemed his work was adequate but never great. More than once he'd been told that he was a skilled draftsman but that he just didn't have the imagination to do anything beyond normal expectations. How in the world could he find the gift of imagination? They hadn't taught it at school, and it sure wasn't hiding somewhere in his desk. It seemed he would be doomed to be just another cog in the company machine forever, and that was so frustrating.

It was four in the afternoon when an unexpected

thunderstorm brought a hint of coolness to the air. As George sat at his desk working on a drawing of a new piece of equipment needed by Johnson Drafting and Design, Felix Mondell walked through his open office door.

"George, isn't this rain a relief?"

As George glanced up from his work, Mondell tossed the afternoon edition of *Commercial News* on the desk in front of him. "By the way, that's a good story on you. Good for business, too. Folks in the industry like to see a man who knows a good deal and seizes on it. I've already had one of our clients call in asking about you."

Though he had already read the piece, George pretended surprise. "Thank you, sir. I'm glad the paper ran the story. I wanted to dispel that nonsense about a curse."

The short, slightly built Mondell traced his pencil-thin mustache with his index finger and laughed. "You did more than just dispel it; you derailed it! Folks are probably talking about this all over the state. In fact, the president of Packard called about an hour ago wanting to speak with you. As you were out of the office, I took the call."

"Wow," George bubbled, this time genuinely surprised. "Alvan Macauley called here looking for me? I had no idea. I wonder what he wanted."

"George, this is big!" Mondell shot back. "Because of that story, Packard is going to give us a bit of drafting work. Can you believe that? I'm going to meet with some of their engineers at the company's Detroit offices next week. Imagine us working for one of the big auto companies! And it is all because you had the courage to buy that car!"

"That is good news, sir," George chimed in.

"And, George, they want to use your story and your family in an ad. They are going to pay you for it, too. You will kind of be like a spokesperson for them. That's what Macauley called about."

Mondell reached into his vest pocket and yanked out a slip of paper. After tossing it on the desk, he added, "Here is the name and number of their guy in promotion who wants to talk to you about making the deal. In a couple of months your face will be in *Life* magazine. Imagine that!"

George was too overwhelmed to speak. Leaning back in his desk chair, he considered what this would mean not just to Johnson Drafting and Design but also to him and Carole. This could be life changing. He glanced back up to his boss, "How much do you think they will pay me?"

"They said something on the phone about a thousand."

It was more than George made in a year. "Wow, if that's true we could move to a nicer house. I might even be able to buy one."

"You'll be able to move." Mondell laughed, his eyes twinkling. "And that has nothing to do with the Packard. George, you have always been dependable. No one can doubt that, but I've been waiting to see your spark, that fire in your belly, that creative stroke that sets you apart from others, and today I saw it. I want to keep you with us. Don't want anyone stealing you now that you've found that special imaginative element that sets you apart from others, so I'm giving you a twenty-dollar-a-week raise starting right at this moment. Reading that story and thinking about how close I came to losing my best man made me realize just how much you mean to this company." The short man grinned and added, "Put it there!"

Standing up, George reached his hand across the desk. After they shook, Mondell smiled even bigger. He was obviously thrilled. He actually believed this story was going to put Johnson Drafting and Design on the map. And who knows? Maybe he was right.

"George, make the call, work out the details, and then take the rest of the day off. In fact, take tomorrow off, too. Breathe in the air; take your family on a picnic; look for that new house! Do whatever you want! On Wednesday we'll start working together on that deal Packard is making with our company."

Chapter 16

It was just past five when George flew through the front door of their small, drafty, rented house and raced back to the kitchen. He found Carole at the stove working on supper. Sweeping her into his arm, he dipped her down and presented her with a huge, sloppy kiss. After pulling her up and twirling her across the wooden floor, he all but yelled, "You're not going to believe what happened to me today!"

"Shhh, the baby's asleep. You'll wake her."

"Sorry," he whispered, his face still framed by a grin the size of a breakfast saucer, "but this has been the greatest day of my life!"

"It's been pretty good here, too." Carole laughed. "Ever since that story came out, the phone hasn't quit ringing and a dozen different people have come by to visit."

"That's nothing," George said, his voice once again approaching a shout.

"Hold it down," she begged him.

"I got a raise," he whispered, "and the Packard Company is going to pay us two thousand dollars to be in an ad and use our story. At first they were talking about half that, but then they added a radio pitch and doubled their offer. Honey, we can move out of this dump and into a nicer place.

We might even be able to buy the Casons' place. It's been for sale for a while, and it has the huge backyard and a nice garage, too."

"We're going to be in an ad?" she blurted out, disbelief showing in her tone. "You mean a local ad in the paper?"

"No," George crowed, "in magazines like *Life* and *Time*. And on national radio, too!"

"And it's all because of the Packard!" She laughed.

"Sure is," he assured her.

"And just think, George, I wanted you to sell that car. I'd have been giving away a gold mine. Sure glad you're the brains in this family."

"I doubt that I'm the brains. Felix gave me the next couple of days off. Let's use them to look at the Cason place and make an offer."

"Okay," she sang out, "but isn't there something else we need to do first?"

"You mean eat? Celebrate?"

"I was thinking about maybe offering a prayer of thanksgiving. It seems God has been smiling on us."

George hadn't stopped to consider his faith in a long time. Maybe he'd thought God had forgotten him. Besides, was this God's doing, or was it merely a run of good luck? Getting the deal on the car right when his broke down . . . The fact that he was able to purchase it for the money he had on hand . . . The car's brakes saving their lives. Did God really set up false curses so that people like him could be blessed?

"George, what are you thinking about?"

"Nothing," he lied. If the Lord was behind all this good fortune, then was He also behind the death of the two men associated with the Packard? Was there a way to separate the good from the bad and only give God credit for the half that blessed them?

The ring of the phone drew Carole from his side.

"Hello . . . Oh, Mary, yes it was a blessing we weren't killed."

George took his thoughts with him to the front porch. As he eased down into a metal lawn chair, he glanced back at the car that had suddenly brought so much fortune into their lives. Was there something more than just the car at work here?

Chapter 17

March 15, 1940

Tax day! Could there be a worse twenty-four-hour period in the history of the world? Especially this year!

Life had been too good since Rose had come. It was almost impossible for him to believe it had been two-and-a-half years. Where had the time gone? But how great those years had been. The continuing deal with Packard, the money that came from the generous raise at his new position with Johnson Drafting and Design, and even a small inheritance from his uncle Jim Henley's estate had moved George into a higher tax bracket. He'd been in shock since the night before when he figured his income tax. Just paying Uncle Sam was pretty much going to wipe out all their savings. It didn't seem fair, and it couldn't have happened at a worse time. Rose needed new clothes. He'd spent a bundle on tires and a new battery for the car, and Carole had been offered a chance to buy her cousin's flower shop. It was something she really wanted to do, and he'd been happy to approve the deal a few days ago. But that was before he discovered the government had different plans for his modest savings.

He had just written the check to the United States Treasury Department and sealed the envelope when Carole walked into the kitchen. She had a huge grin on her face. "Do I need to go to the bank to get the thousand for the down payment on the shop?"

"Carole," he quietly answered.

For the first time in years she didn't seem to notice the worry etched on his face or dripping from his tone. With hardly time for a breath she rattled on, "George, you have no idea how long I have wanted to own that shop. As a kid I would walk in there, and just smelling those flowers lifted me into the air. I felt like the luckiest girl in the world when I worked there in high school. And now that place will be mine. It won't be Betty's Flower Shop anymore; it will be Carole's. And I can use the Packard to deliver flowers. And the best part is that Rose can stay with me at the shop."

He nodded. How was he going to break the news to her? Betty had to have the money. She and her husband were moving to the West Coast. That thousand dollars would pay Betty's rent for months until they could get on their feet. He wouldn't just be shattering his wife's dream; he'd be derailing Betty and Frank's plans, too. But what could he do? They didn't have the money, and even if they cut way back, they wouldn't have the money for several months now.

"Listen, Carole."

Their toddler strolling into the house inter- rupted the speech George dreaded giving. "Hello, Daddy!"

"Hey, Rosie," he said, pulling the little girl up into his lap. "Where have you been?"

"Playing out by the car."

George smiled. "You playing with your dolls in the garage?"

"Yeah." Rose laughed. "And playing with money, too."

Crawling down from his lap, Rose laid a doll and some crumbled paper on the table and moved off toward her room.

"What an imagination!" He chuckled. "Wonder what she thought was money."

"Probably some play money from one of the board games you bought at that estate sale last year," Carole said. "The one called *The Landlord's Game* was filled with fake bills. Now, speaking of money, do I write a check to Aunt Betty, or do I get the money from the bank? Or do you want to do that?"

George felt as if Joe Louis had punched him in the gut. This was going to be one of the toughest moments of his life. "Carole, about the money. I've been figuring our taxes, and . . ."

"George, I'm sure you did a great job with that, too. You were always so good with numbers, but quit stalling around. I need to get going. Are you going to make me get down on my knees and beg, or are you just looking for a big old kiss?"

"Carole . . ." His words failed him.

"Oh, George," she said, pushing by him to the spot where Rose had placed her doll. Moving the toy to one side, she picked up ten real one-hundred-dollar bills from a stack of yellow and blue play money. "Silly, why didn't you tell me you already got the cash?" She glanced at her watch. "Aunt Betty's waiting. I've got to run." She pushed the bills into her purse and leaned over to kiss George on the cheek. "You play such games with me. I sure wish you'd have put these bills in your wallet rather than crumpling them in your pocket." A few seconds later, before he could even question what had just happened, Carole was gone, the door slamming behind her as she rushed off to complete the most important transaction of her life.

A stunned George looked across the table to the play money. Picking it up, he studied each bill. All of them had Parker Brothers written on them. Yet the money Carole picked out of this batch was real. He hadn't put them there, so who had? Rose? He was sure of one thing. The money hadn't been on the table when he did the taxes. Rose must have brought it in. Rushing out of the kitchen to his child's room, he found her in the middle of her bed playing with a stuffed lion.

"Rose, where did you find that money you brought into the kitchen?"

"From the game."

George dropped the play money he clutched in his hand onto the bed. "Not this money, the money that looked like this." Reaching into his pocket he pulled out a five-dollar bill. "There was some money you had that looked like this mixed in with the play money. Where did you get it?"

The little girl studied it for a few seconds and shrugged.

Sitting down beside her, George took the lion

from her lap and tossed it into a chair. Holding the five in front of her face, he softly begged, "Honey, this is very important. I need to know where you found the green money. It looks kind of like what I'm holding here."

She said nothing. Instead she jumped from the bed and walked toward the back door. George followed her through her room, across the kitchen, and outside. It seemed spring had come early. The temperature was in the fifties, and after a long, cold winter it felt like spring was just around the corner. Thus neither he nor his daughter bothered with a coat as she led him to a place beside the garage. There, next to an old ash can, she pointed to a spot where the shade from the garage's overhang had protected a patch of snow from the sun's direct light.

"You found it here?" George asked, bending over to examine the area.

She nodded.

"Was there any more?" he asked. "Or did you bring it all in?"

"Just that. One, two, three, four, five, six, seven, eight, nine, and ten."

"Wonder how it got here?" he whispered. Pushing the ash can to the side, he scanned the rest of the ground. Nothing! Peering into the trash bin, he saw nothing as well. But Rose had found this money, and it had to have come from somewhere.

As he stood erect he noted the wind was

blowing about ten miles an hour out of the south. Maybe the bills had blown in. Maybe someone had dropped it out of a purse or a pocket, and the wind had caught it. Maybe that was it. But ten of them? That part was hard to explain. If someone lost it, that person was going to be awfully upset. He had to find out. As much as he didn't want to, he had to know the truth.

"Rose, let's go back inside and put on our coats. You and I are going to take a walk and knock on a few doors. We need to find out if someone lost any money today."

What he figured would be easy wasn't. An hour and a half later they had knocked on every door within five blocks without discovering anyone who was missing any money.

"Rose," George said as he rapped on a final door, "if no one here is missing any money, then I guess we'll just have to figure it fell from heaven."

"Or was dropped by a bird," she added.

George hadn't considered that. Crows were notorious for stealing things.

As he turned to head back toward home, George noted a scruffy man approaching. He hardly looked like someone who had ever seen a hundred-dollar bill, much less lost one, but he decided to ask nonetheless.

"Excuse me, sir," George said, his words stopping the man in his tracks. "I'm George Hall and this is my daughter Rose. Did you lose some money?"

The stranger was older than George, ill-kempt, and smelling of a mixture of alcohol and tobacco. His dark eyes were menacing, and as he opened his mouth to speak, George could see that his teeth were stained.

"How much?" the man growled.

George pulled Rose closer to his side, trying to shield her from the man's glare, before answering. "We found a few hundred-dollar bills."

There was an awkward silence for a few moments before the man grinned. "If it was anything more than a quarter, I ain't lost it. Never had much in my whole life. Just haven't been lucky."

"I see," a relieved George replied. "We'll be on our way, then. And thank you."

"Sure," he replied with sly smile. "I know your face. You're the guy with that yellow Packard? I've seen the ads in the magazines."

"Yes, that's our car and I'm that guy."

"That's a mighty fine ride." The man laughed. "Mighty fine indeed."

"Well, good luck," George replied. "We need to be on our way. My wife will be home soon."

George was in such a hurry to put the stranger behind him he all but dragged Rose down the walk. Though he didn't look back, he felt the man's eyes on him well after they'd turned the corner.

He'd seen lots of hoboes during the past few years. Scores of strangers walked the highways or hopped on trains. But there was something about this man's eyes. They looked evil. And his voice had an edge to it that reminded him of the villains in horror films.

Later that night, after everyone had gone to bed, a strange, unsettling feeling kept George awake and finally pulled him out of bed. He wandered out to the garage and made sure the doors were locked and then walked through the house, checking the locks on each door and window. After finishing his mission, he glanced out through the front door and thought he spotted someone across the street standing by a tree. Stepping away from the window, George flipped off the lamp. When the room was completely dark he glanced out again. There was no one there.

Chapter 18

He'd dug through drawers and in chair cushions in his dilapidated three-room house and still couldn't find very much money. He doubted the meager amount he'd uncovered would buy him the time he needed to fully explain the situation. Yet the information was too important not to make the call. Even though he wasn't sure he had the coins he needed, he headed out into the night air and walked the five blocks out to the highway.

There were three pay phones he could use at this time of the night in Oakwood. One was in an all-night gas station. That place was always too crowded for privacy. Another was in the lobby of a travel court, but the owner was the town's biggest gossip. So that was out. Thus, though it required the longest walk, he had to go to the garage out on the highway. He figured no one would be there, and they had a phone booth beside the station. That would work.

He was lucky. Dylon's Garage was bathed in complete darkness. Except for a cat hiding under a bench in front of the office, not a living thing was visible. After taking a final look over his shoulder, the man stepped into the booth and slid the door closed. Pulling out his billfold, he found a slip of paper and set it on the tray under the phone. He studied the number for a moment before lighting a match so he had enough light to see and dropping a nickel into the machine and dialing a zero. After a woman picked up, he spat out a number and, before she could reply, growled, "I need to reverse these charges."

"So this is a collect call?" the operator asked.

"That's what I said."

"And your name is?"

"Just give the party on the other end the initials—G. T."

"That is 'G' like in *general* and 'T' like in *truck*."

"Yep."

"Just a moment please."

"And who is it you want to speak with?"

"The guy who answers."

"His name?"

"It doesn't matter," he barked. "The guy I want will be on the other end. Just make the call. A front's moving in, and it's cold in this booth."

"Yes, sir."

The temperature had dropped twenty degrees since sunset, making it painfully obvious that winter wasn't finished with Illinois just yet. As the shabbily dressed man shivered in the tiny booth, he glanced out toward the highway. Except for an occasional truck, the world had gone to sleep. That suited him just fine. He had little use for people any time of the day or night.

"Hello," a sleepy voice grumbled into the phone.

"This is the operator. I have a collect call from a Mr. G. T."

"What?"

"I said I have a collect call from a Mr. G. T."

"Is this some kind of joke?" he barked.

"No sir, this is the operator, and I was instructed to place this call. Will you accept the charges?"

"No one would call me at this time of night. You must have the wrong number. So you call tell the caller to go to—"

119

"Operator, tell him the G. T. stands for Go To," the man in the booth cut in.

"Sir, the party says that the G. T. stands for—"

"I heard him. Yeah, I'll accept the charges." The man waited until he heard the operator hang up before he snapped, "Thought I'd heard the last of you. You can't pinch any more from me. I've given you the last dime you're going to get. This well is dry!"

"I doubt that."

"You're even more stupid than I thought then," he hissed. "I can't believe I accepted these charges!"

The man in the booth allowed those words to grow as cold as the night wind before saying, "It seems some of the money might have turned up today."

"What?"

"You heard me."

"How much?"

"From what I can gather, a few hundred, maybe a bit more."

"Where?"

"Beside a garage on Elm Street."

Suddenly interested, the man on the far end of the call asked, "How?"

"I don't know that yet, but I've got a theory. A good one, too! I'm not going to let you in on it right now. That will only come when we speak face-to-face."

"I've got enough dirt on you to send you up for a long time," the man warned.

"Shut up. I've got just as much on you, and you've got a lot more to lose."

"So you actually know where it is?"

"It's been right in front of us all the time. Yet I don't think I can get my hands on it without a big diversion. You will have to help me carry off the plan. We need to meet very soon."

"When and where?"

"I've got no wheels," the man in the booth explained. "So you have to come here."

"At your place?"

"No, in Danville. There's a bar on State Street. It's called the Lamplighter Tavern. Be there at three in the afternoon tomorrow. Not many folks there at that time."

"This better be on the level."

"It is."

"So you going to be there?"

"I'm making it."

"If you don't, you'll pay for it dearly!"

G. T. didn't wait for a reply. Dropping the receiver back onto the hook, he slid the door open and stepped out into the harsh wind. The first few flakes of a March blizzard were swirling around his uncovered head. Shoving his hands deep into his pockets, he hunched his shoulders and retraced his steps back to the drafty rented house he called home. With any luck, his mailing address would soon be changing to a warmer climate. That day couldn't come too soon.

Chapter 19

March 27, 1940

Carole's first week at the store had been incredible. She'd been signed to do two weddings and was the designated flower shop for one of the largest funerals the community had seen in decades. Milt Bauer had been the state's wealthiest farmer and one of the county's most influential citizens. Everyone owed him. Thus almost all the families in the region called in and ordered flowers. It seemed each caller wanted to have the most expensive spray there, and thus each new order made more than the previous one. The fact that a heavy snow had prevented many of the locals from being able to drive to Danville to pick arrangements had created even more sales for the little Oakwood business. Thus Carole, Rose, and the yellow Packard made scores of trips down the snowy streets from the flower shop to the Bacon Funeral Home.

On Monday morning at ten, things had finally slowed down. Carole and Rose had the store to themselves. Rose was playing with her dolls in a corner of the office that had been converted into a child's activity center. There was a dollhouse, a half-dozen picture books, and some wooden building blocks all designed to keep the little girl occupied. Against the back wall was a small bed for afternoon naps, though so far the store had been far too busy with deliveries for Rose to be able to sleep. Most of the child's naps had been in the backseat of the car.

As Rose played dress up with her Shirley Temple doll, Carole switched on the radio. After the local forecast, which called for clearing skies and above-freezing temperatures, the disc jockey announced, " 'When You Wish Upon A Star' by the Glen Miller Orchestra."

"That's going to be a big hit, Rose," Carole told her daughter as the song's first few lines burst through the speaker. "Got a good message there, too. But you just remember, it's not wishing, it is praying that works miracles."

She looked at her daughter and smiled as Rose sang along with the tune. What a wonderful child she was. She was no trouble at all. She could pick up and go on a moment's notice or play for hours without complaining while Carole worked. And she was so smart. She was already reading from first-grade primers. She was artistic, too. Her drawings looked like cats and dogs; they weren't just scribbled lines. And on Saturday she had even helped Carole arrange flowers in the display case. The results were so impressive she'd left a few of Rose's creations in place. Even if she and George never had another child, this one would be more than enough. She was simply so perfect Carole couldn't imagine life without her.

A ringing phone pulled the woman from an order she was filling out and over to her desk.

"Carole's Flowers."

"Honey, it's me."

"George, I thought you had the day off and were going over to the park with Glen."

"I did," he assured her, "but I'm back now. Do you need any help? Want me to watch Rose for you?"

"No, you just rest. This is my first slow day. And believe it or not, I'm grateful for that. I can handle things here, and I think Rose likes playing in the shop. Guess it's a case of like mother, like daughter. Besides, I just got her pigtails fixed. They look so cute and she's so pretty, I want to show her off a bit."

"Just like her mom," George shot back. "Okay, I won't bail you out. I've got a book I want to read anyway. If you need anything, just pick up the phone and let me know." Just then the bell over the front door jangled.

"I will," she shot back. "Got to go, someone just walked in. See you later."

Carole put the phone down and glanced over to her daughter. "You just stay right there and play. Mommy will be back when I'm finished with this customer."

Sweeping through the door that separated the

office from the main part of the small store, she noted a heavyset man in a dark suit looking at a display of plastic yellow roses. His skin was clammy and in spite of the cool weather, there was a bit of sweat beading on his brow.

"May I help you?"

"Perhaps," came his carefully measured reply. "That's a great song you got playing on your radio."

"I can turn it down if it is too loud. My daughter and I love it."

"No, I like it, too," he assured her, "but I didn't come in about the music. I spotted something through the window that kind of interested me."

"A flower?"

"No, a piece of furniture."

"We don't sell furniture," Carole apologized, "just flowers."

"But that rolltop desk over in the corner of the room. The one you have the card displays setting on. That is a nice piece."

Carole's eyes darted to the oak desk. "The former owner of this store got that at a sale a few years back. She is just storing it here until it can be shipped out to California. That's where she lives now. I can't sell it, but if the price was right she might. Going to be a lot of trouble to move a few thousand miles. I could write her a letter if you want to offer a price."

"Yes," he said, his gloved hand tracing the upper

of his three chins. Walking over to the desk, he lightly rapped on the top. "It's solid. The finish is in good shape, too! Does the rolltop work?"

"I don't know," she admitted. "We can see." Reaching the handle, she slowly pulled it down. Stubbornly at first, the top moved. A second, harder pull moved it through the carved channels and down to the top of the desk's work area.

"It's noisy, but it works."

"You're right about that noisy part," he quipped. "I couldn't even hear the radio playing when you pulled it down. Let me try it." He pushed it up, and as soon as it got to the top he yanked it down. He continued the up-and-down exercise a half-dozen more times until Carole reached down and put her hand on his to stop him.

"Please, if you keep doing that you're going to give me a powerful headache, and I didn't bring any powders to work with me today."

He glanced past her to the front window and smiled. "The desk isn't really as large as I thought anyway. But I would like to buy some of those red carnations that you have in the window. Could I purchase a half a dozen?"

"Sure. Do you want them in a vase?"

"No, a box will be fine."

"I'll get them for you."

As Carole retrieved and counted the carnations, her customer stood beside the counter and observed the quiet, unhurried traffic passing by the shop. As much to make time pass as to create conversation, she called out, "Not much happening this time of the day in our small town. Where are you from?"

"Chicago."

"You here on business?"

"Just passing through," he explained.

Carole pushed the lid down onto the box and tied a piece of twine to secure it. She pushed it across the counter as she announced, "That will be two twenty-five."

The visitor reached into his pocket and produced two ones, setting them beside the box, before separating three nickels and a dime from his change with his gloved hand. Placing the coins in her hand, he thanked her, picked up the box, and headed toward the door. As he stopped outside, Tommy Dorsey's "All the Things You Are" came on the radio.

"The station's playing some great music today, aren't they, Rose?"

The little girl didn't answer. *Must have fallen asleep,* Carole thought. *Probably completely worn out from last week.* Moving quietly back through the door to the office, she peeked around toward the play area. Rose wasn't there. She wasn't in bed either. In fact, she was nowhere in the room.

"Rose," she called out frantically. "Rose, where are you?"

There was no answer.

She raced over to the back door. Though they rarely used it, maybe her daughter had decided to go out into the backyard area to play. The fact that it was slightly ajar gave Carole a measure of hope. Yanking it open, she glanced out into the snow-covered yard. There were no small footprints, but there was a set of large ones both coming and going, and the back gate, which was never used, was open. Carole's heart began to race. Where was she?

Maybe George came and got her, she reasoned. Racing back into the office, she hurriedly called home. One ring, two, three, and finally a fourth!

"Hello."

"Honey, it's me, did you come and get Rose?"

"No," came the groggy reply. "I tried to read some, but I must have fallen asleep on the couch."

"Nooooo!" She cried. "Oh, Lord, no!"

"What's wrong?"

"George, she's gone."

"What?" He now sounded fully awake.

That's when she saw it—the note sitting in the middle of her desk. It looked like a child's art project. Letters had been cut out and glued to a white piece of paper. The message was clear.

"She's been kidnapped," Carole whispered into the receiver.

"What?" George shouted. "How can you be sure?"

"I've got the note in my hands. It says, 'I have

your kid. Don't call the cops or she dies. Get $5,000 in small bills. Will call with instructions.' George, what are we going to do?"

"Don't move. I'll be right there."

Chapter 20

George sprinted the eight blocks from their home to the flower shop. He rushed through the front door, leaving it wide open. A quick survey assured him Carole was in the back. Five quick steps took him to the office. She was standing over her daughter's dollhouse, her chest heaving, tears rolling down her cheeks and dropping to the floor.

"Carole!"

She slowly turned to face her husband. Her eyes were already red, her face drawn, and her mouth quivering. She tried to form words, but her lips only made it through a single syllable, "Why?"

George had no answer. And as much as he felt called to throw his arms around Carole and try to soothe her fears, a greater calling demanded his attention. Rose was gone, and it was his job as a father to bring her back.

"Where's the note?"

Carole pointed to the desk. Spotting it, George quickly read through the very simple message. They were going to have to wait to get further instructions. But when would they come?

"We need to call the police," she whispered, moving toward the phone.

"No!" he shouted while catching her hand and gripping it tightly enough that she flinched in pain. "I'm sorry," he said, in a much lower tone as he released his grip. "But we can't. If we do they might kill her."

"But how would the people who took her know?" she demanded between sobs. "The police always tell you to call them. That's what they say on the radio. They've preached that since the Lindbergh baby was taken in '32."

"Well, the people who say that on the radio don't have kids who have been taken," he shot back. "And the Lindbergh baby was killed, so you can't go by that. Now, let's figure this out. Go lock the front door, and put the CLOSED sign on the door. Then come back here and we'll talk this through."

Wiping her eyes, Carole walked through the door and into the shop's main room. When he heard her snap the lock, George stepped over to the back door. He slowly opened it and peered out at the lawn. There were fresh footprints in the snow. Stepping out, he made an impression beside one of them. Whoever had taken Rose looked as though they wore a size or two smaller than his tens, but it was definitely a man's shoe.

"You found the tracks," Carole whispered as she came up beside him.

"But they don't tell us much," he sadly explained. "George, what are we going to do?" Her voice was filled with such great pain he wanted to cry. Yet he couldn't let himself break down. Not now! He didn't have an answer, at least not one that would comfort his wife, so he bit his tongue, shook his head, and stayed silent. Closing the door, he glanced back to the note as another dilemma hit him.

Five thousand dollars! Where was he going to get that kind of money? He only had a few hundred in the bank.

"Why Rose?" Carole asked in a pleading tone that forced his eyes back to hers. "We aren't rich. We don't have anything that is worth anything. I thought people kidnapped rich people's children. You know, like Lindbergh's baby."

He'd already wondered the same thing. It simply made no sense. Did the man who took Rose have him confused with someone else? His eyes wandered to a framed advertisement from *Life* hanging on the wall. That image showed him leaning against their yellow Packard with Rose sitting on the car's long hood. That just might be it. The fact that they had done a few national ads and had some spots on Packard-sponsored radio programs might have led someone to believe they had money. That was the only reason that made logical sense.

The phone's ringing literally caused both of

them to jump into each other's arms. Their eyes locked onto the black, Western Electric desk model as it rang a second time.

"Answer it," he urged her. "And don't let your fear show in your voice."

He allowed his arms to fall and pushed her toward the desk. She took two hesitant steps forward and reached for the receiver. After a final look back toward her husband, she picked it up.

"Carole's Flowers." She all but choked on the words.

"Is this Mrs. Hall?" The voice was so loud and strong that George could understand every word from where he stood.

"Yes," she quietly answered.

"I have your daughter." George didn't miss Carole's quick intake of breath. Instinct demanded he hold his breath as he waited for her speak.

"Is she all right?" Carole's question was tinged with both fear and hope.

George closed the distance to the desk and put his head next to his wife's. He listened carefully to the caller's measured words.

"She is fine, and she'll stay that way as long as you follow my directions."

"I'll do whatever you want," she assured him. "I just want my baby back."

"Have you called the cops?" His tone was demanding.

"No."

"Good. Don't even think about it. Now, about the money."

George grabbed the phone from his wife. "We don't have that kind of money."

"You bought that flower shop," the man calmly replied. "Folks who can do that have a lot more than what I'm asking for. So you can get it. And if you don't, then you'll need to come up with money for the kid's funeral. Do you understand?"

"If you hurt our daughter!" George barked.

"You'll do what?" The man on the phone chuckled. "You don't know who I am, and you don't know where I am. I could walk past you in five minutes, and you wouldn't have a clue that I'm holding your kid. I'm the only one who can make a threat here. Get used to that fact or suffer the consequences. You got it?"

George didn't answer. He didn't have to. He didn't have the cards and he knew it.

"I'll give you two days to get the money. Sometime on Wednesday afternoon I'll call this number. You'll be told where you need to make the drop and when you can pick up the kid. Up until then you just keep living your life like you always do. You go to work, you have your wife keep the shop open, and you don't let anyone know that your kid's gone. You understand?"

"Yes," George quietly answered.

"And you, Mrs. Hall?"

"Yes?" she said.

"If you don't get the money and follow these instructions to the letter, if you slip up anywhere, the kid dies."

The line went dead. George looked to Carole. What in the world could they do?

As Carole sobbed, he collapsed in the desk chair and thought back to the night Rose had been born. It seemed like just yesterday he'd wondered if he was up to the job of being able to protect her and keep her safe. It hadn't even been three years, and the answer was now painfully obvious.

He had failed!

Chapter 21

"It's my fault," Carole wailed as George turned and shot her a helpless look.

"Could you hear enough to know what he said?" George asked.

"I heard it. If only I hadn't insisted she stay with me today. If only I'd let you take her."

"If they wanted her," George softly declared, "they would have waited until tomorrow or the next day. It's not your fault. Neither of us could have anticipated this."

"But why us?"

Her question lingered in the air for thirty seconds. He didn't want to admit what he sensed, but as she stared at him with that helpless, forlorn, and hurting expression, he had no choice. "This guy probably thinks that because we did those Packard ads we are celebrities. After all, we both signed a few autographs."

"But that only paid two thousand dollars," she argued. "That went to buy our house. Then all we got was a thousand a year to keep endorsing them. They are asking for more than that!"

"You and I know that," George explained, "some of our friends do, too, but this guy probably doesn't."

He held out his arms to her, but like a wounded animal, she backed off, fear and mistrust in her eyes.

"The car? It's that car I asked you to sell so long ago. The one you just had to have. That's why Rose is gone?"

He shook his head. He didn't blame her for lashing out. He deserved it. In fact, he wished she'd scream at him or maybe just beat him senseless. But there may be more, and she'd had to know it all.

"Carole," George softly said, "there is something I don't understand. He said something about us buying the flower shop."

"So it might be my fault for buying the shop?" she asked, her face twisting, suggesting a pain too great to endure.

"Have you told anyone about the cash we found?" He softly asked as his eyes moved from the ransom note to her tear-stained face and back to the note.

"A few people," she cried. "Was that wrong? Did I open the door for this?"

"I don't think so," he assured her. "I mean, I told a few folks at the office, too. It could have been me." He sighed. "Maybe it was both of us combined. Maybe that made us appear rich."

"George, how much do we have in the bank?"

"A couple hundred," he moaned. "A lousy couple of hundred."

"What are we going to do?" It was as if her own words knocked her against the wall. She leaned on it for a moment before adding, "What are we going to do?"

He shook his head. "Don't have enough time to sell anything. We're going to have to come up with another way to get the cash."

Yanking his wallet from his pants, he emptied the contents onto the desk. He quickly leafed through a host of slips until he found a yellow piece of paper with a name and number scrawled on it. Grabbing the phone, he dialed the operator and asked for long distance. As he did, his wife fell to her knees and began to pray.

Chapter 22

"Thanks," George said as set the receiver down. He looked over to his wife and nodded. "We've got the cash."

"How? Who was that? I don't understand how you could make one call and get five thousand dollars."

"If the car got us into this," he told her, "it might also get us out of it. The man I called was Gerald Shortsleeve. He's with the marketing department of the Packard Company. He's going to get the money we need out of company funds tomorrow morning and then drive down here from Detroit in the afternoon. He'll meet me at the office."

"Is it a loan?" she asked.

"Only if we get it back," George replied. "Otherwise it is a gift."

"He gave it to us just like that?" Carole marveled. "Why?"

"Our ads have sold a lot of cars for the company. He said that if it was the ads that created the problem, Packard wants to make it right. But I did have to agree to one thing."

"What's that?" she asked as she pushed herself off the wall and on unsteady legs moved back toward her husband.

George leaned against the desk. "After we get

Rose back safe and sound, he wants us to tell the police what's going on so they can track down those responsible."

"Oh, George," she said, a hint of hope evident in her tone. "Will this work?"

"It has to," he said. "It just has to."

He glanced toward the front of the store. "We've got to get the shop open. That's one of the rules. If that guy finds out this place is closed, he might do something to Rose."

"George," Carole whispered, "I can't. I'm not strong enough. Anyone who sees me will know something is wrong."

Placing his right hand on her chin, he lifted her face until their eyes met. "You have to be strong for Rose. You just have to be. Everything we do over the next two days has to look perfectly normal. No one can guess anything."

"But people know she stays here with me," she argued. "If she's not here . . ."

"You tell people that she's staying for a few days with my aunt in Indiana."

"But you don't have an aunt in Indiana," she argued.

"No one knows that but you," he explained. "Make up a name, something you can remember, and if anyone asks, just tell them."

"Ruth," she suggested. "She was a strong woman in the Bible. Just saying her name will remind me that I have to be strong as well."

George nodded. "You know that verse you're always quoting, about being strong and of good courage? Well you have to live it now. We both do. Everything we say, every move we make, everything we do is for her. Now we're going into that showroom and get this store open."

With George following her from the office to the door that separated the two rooms, she grabbed the knob, twisted it, and in short, measured steps made her way back to the front door. After taking a deep breath she flipped the lock. A few seconds later she turned the sign around to OPEN and looked back toward a display she'd been working on earlier in the day.

George observed her as she made her way to the flower-arranging table and began to work on an order. Carole would somehow do what she had to do. He was sure of it. But could he keep up the front so well that no one guessed that his whole life was upside down? It would be the biggest test of his life. Glancing out the front window, he noted their Packard parked in front of the shop. Had the car ads set this in motion? He had no idea, but for the moment he wished he'd never seen that car.

Chapter 23

The next two days were the toughest days of their lives. Neither of them slept more than an hour or two, and food offered no appeal. They lived on soft drinks and coffee. One of the few encouraging moments was with the Packard Company's representative, Shortsleeve. He dropped the money off in a blue duffel bag, assuring George that the company had not called the police, as he had requested. Even after George showed him the note and explained the phone message, the visitor still questioned if this was the way to play the game. Even though he felt uneasy about George's choice, the Packard representative left, promising to keep his pledge. Once he was alone, George opened the bag and made sure it contained assorted bills in small denominations. He counted it to make sure it was all there.

Business was light at the flower shop, for which George was grateful. Several people called wanting flowers delivered, but only a handful of patrons visited the store in person. Of them, only Maud Jenkins, who always seemed to lack tact, asked about Carole's red eyes and puffy face. Thankfully she accepted the explanation of allergies without question.

Both George and Carol sensed that someone

was watching them, but if there was someone following their every move, they never spotted him. That fact unnerved them more than being able to see someone watching their every move.

Beyond missing Rose, time was their worst enemy. The hand of the clock seemed to never move. A minute was like an hour, an hour like a day, and day was like a month. And during that span they aged years. It showed on their faces, in the way they moved, and even in their reactions to normal daily events. They were wound so tightly that each of them pounced on even the slightest offense. They barked at each other for everything from looking out the window too much to pouring but not drinking countless cups of coffee. As the hours ticked closer to the time they expected the call, they all but quit talking to each other. At the shop and at home they spent as much time as possible in separate rooms.

At noon on Wednesday, George announced that he wasn't feeling well and left the office. The fact that he had deep, dark circles under his eyes helped him sell that he was sick. In fact he looked so bad his boss ordered him to rest up for the remainder of the week. George accepted the offer without argument. Having that time off would allow him to take care of the money drop no matter where or when it happened.

He got to the flower shop just after twelve thirty and took a seat next to the office phone.

When she wasn't with a customer, Carole sat next to him. Each time the phone rang, their eyes met. Only after he had nodded his assurance did she pick up the receiver. Six calls came in between one and four that afternoon, four of them were flower orders, one was a wrong number, and the final one was a man trying to sell business insurance.

"Maybe he's not going to call," she sighed as she set the receiver in the cradle for the sixth time. A horror-stricken look on her face, she added, "George, maybe we did something wrong. Maybe he saw something I did—he panicked and killed her." The final word sent a gush of tears from her red eyes. Covering her face with her hands she allowed her head to fall to the desktop.

She just couldn't hold it together anymore. George couldn't blame her. If he hadn't been so tired he would have lain down and given up, too.

Unable to cope, George pulled himself upright and walked wearily into the shop. Surely it was close enough to closing time that no one would question them locking the doors now. He snapped the lock, flipped the light switch off, and reversed the OPEN/CLOSED sign. Looking past their Packard, he studied the street. The grocery store parking lot was about half full, two cars sat outside Tom's Hardware, and the café looked as

142

though it was empty. The bank, which had closed two hours before, also showed no signs of activity. It was a typical Wednesday—typical everywhere except in the lives of him and his wife. It appeared nothing would ever be typical for them again.

Carole lifted her head from the desktop when he returned to the office. She dabbed her eyes with a handkerchief as he took a seat. Glancing his way, she offered, "I must look a fright."

He nodded. "We both do."

"Did we make a mistake not calling the police?" she asked.

"I don't know." He sighed. "I just don't know. He still has some time. Don't give up hope yet."

"Do you think she's scared?" Carole's words hung in the air like an unwanted summer fog. Try as he might, George simply couldn't think of a comforting answer that would bring any hope to his shattered wife. After all, he'd wondered the same thing a thousand times over the past few days. All his questions did was prove that he had not done his job as a father.

"Carole," he began, but the phone's ring cut his words short.

She glanced at him and he nodded once more. Just as she had earlier, she reached for the receiver, lifted it from its cradle, and said, "Carole's Flowers."

He looked at her for any sign that this was the

call they had been waiting for. The answer came when she lifted her eyes to his and nodded.

"Is our daughter all right?" she asked the caller.

George put his ear next to hers so he could hear, too.

"She's fine. She'll stay that way if you do just as I ask."

"We will," Carole assured him. "We just want her back."

"Do you have the money?"

"Yes." She then added, "And we haven't called the police."

"Smart girl," he said. "Grab a pencil and write this down. You must follow these instructions to the letter, or the girl dies. Do you understand?"

"Yes," Carole assured him. "I understand. I have a pencil and a piece of paper, just tell me what we need to do."

"South of Terre Haute, Indiana, there is a place called Prairie Center. It is a wide spot in the road on Highway 63. You got that?"

She hurriedly scribbled the information. "Highway 63, Prairie Center."

"Drive two point five miles south of Prairie Center. On the right will be a little picnic area with a table, trash can, and small pull-off area. You can't miss it. There are three large elm trees, and the table is in the middle of that stand of trees."

As George listened and watched, Carole wrote

and talked, "The rest area is two and a half miles outside of town."

The droning instructions immediately picked up. "At ten tomorrow morning, park that yellow car at the picnic area, leave the cash on the back floorboard, and then start walking south toward the town of Fairbanks. Walk that direction for thirty minutes at a steady pace. You will be watched. At ten thirty, turn around and walk at that same pace back to the picnic grounds. Don't get there before eleven. Have you got that?"

"Walk south for thirty minutes, then turn around and walk back. And we aren't supposed to get back to the drop point before eleven."

"Not *we*," the voice corrected her, *"you."*

Grabbing the phone, a suddenly livid George protested, "She's not going to do this on her own. I have to be there, too!"

The words had no more cleared his lips when the line went dead. Carole looked to her husband, panic written on her brow and hopeless rage boiling in her gut. "What have you done?" she screamed. "You just killed our little girl."

"But he was going to make you drive there all alone," George shot back.

"And you think I couldn't handle it?" she yelled. "You made him mad, George. He might be killing our little girl right now. How could you be so stupid?"

Sinking into the chair, George buried his face in

his hands. He'd been warned about playing by the rules. The kidnapper had demanded it.

One emotional outburst may have sunk the whole ship.

The phone's ring caused him to bolt upright. Carole glared at him as she hurriedly answered, "Hello." She nodded toward her husband before adding, "Yes, he understands. Okay, he can ride as far as Prairie Center, and I can drop him off to wait until I come back." She nodded again. "I'll tell him he will be watched, so he better not talk to anyone. What else do I need to know?"

With George watching, she listened intently but wrote nothing down. A minute later, she set the phone back down.

"So you heard," she asked, her voice amazingly steady, "that you get to go with me up until I leave for the rest area?"

He nodded and asked, "What else did you find out?"

"When I get back to the picnic grounds, the money will be gone, and Rose will be in the backseat of the car. He said she'd be fine, but they would tie her up so she couldn't get out and walk away. When I get there and untie her, I can drive back and pick you up and go home."

"That's it?" he asked.

"Well," she added, "he told me that we had to drive the Packard. He explained it would be the

146

easiest car for him to spot. If we take anything else, Rose dies."

"And nothing else?" he asked. "We leave them the money and that's it."

"That's everything. And we have to do it their way. No slipups! You do understand that, don't you?"

The man behind this scheme had all his bases covered. He had this thing planned so there would be no chance of his being caught. There would be no adults to identify him, no finger-prints, no way to trace the loot. His five-thousand-dollar payday looked like a sure bet. And with no man at the drop site to attempt to overpower him, the chances improved even more.

"I think we need to go home, George," Carole suggested. "Let's at least try to sleep a little. And we also need to plan out the route to this place so we get there in plenty of time. We can't afford to be late."

"I've got an Illinois and Indiana map," he assured her. "I know the area pretty well, too."

Moving toward her husband, she tugged his arms open and leaned into his chest. As she did, his arms tightly encircled her. "We'll get our baby back tomorrow," she sighed.

Mutely, he patted her back. Maybe the night-mare was about over. All they had to do now was make it through one more long night.

Chapter 24

They arrived at the tiny hamlet of Prairie Center just before eight. Though hope of a reunion with their little girl buoyed their spirits, neither had spoken during the three-hour trip. Once again, time seemed to barely move as the seconds dragged by. Parking their car off a side road, the couple silently watched the Packard's clock slowly edge closer to the appointed hour. Finally, at just after nine thirty, George spoke. His words meant nothing to him or his wife, but at least they broke the horrid silence.

"It's not much of a town."

"I think I can leave you at that garage," Carole said, pointing to a tiny, frame structure to their right about a half block up the street.

"It is either that or the church," he solemnly replied. "At least the temperature's in the forties. It could be a lot worse. Still I wish I could go with you. Maybe if I hid in the backseat . . ."

"We have to do it their way," she forcefully interjected. "Whoever has her is probably watching us right now. We have no choice. It's not that I don't want you there, but I can do this by myself, George. I have to."

He patted her gloved hand with his own. "I

know you can. But staying here and waiting is going to be so hard."

"Keep your eye on the end result," she urged him. "And please keep praying."

Praying was the last thing on his mind. For the past two days, as he had looked back over the events since Rose's birth, he'd come to the conclusion that prayer had little to do with their good fortune or bad. It was just fate. Fate had brought them the chance to buy the Packard. Fate had put the gravel truck there, and fate had given them the chance to make a bit of money off it. Fate had even dropped the thousand in needed cash for the down payment on the flower shop. Now fate would decide this as well.

Was blaming fate a cop-out? Perhaps, but it made accepting the final results so much easier. There would be no one to blame; it would be fate's fault. It was much harder to get mad at fate than at God. If God was behind this, George couldn't forgive Him at all.

He glanced to the passenger seat at his wife. She was so much different than he was. He could see that she was praying. She was probably asking God to grant her the strength to do what was asked of her. Yes, her faith had been shaken in the past two days, but unlike his, it hadn't completely fallen apart. And when she held Rose in her arms again, that faith would be justified. But he simply couldn't get there. Not yet.

She opened her eyes and looked into his. "What are you thinking about?"

"The *ifs,*" he grimly replied. "What if we hadn't gotten the Packard? What if I hadn't signed us up to the do the ads? What if I'd come and gotten Rose that day rather than taking a nap? They just go on and on."

"And they never stop," she replied. "Life is full of *ifs.* We call them decisions. We make choices and they affect us forever. But in this case we don't know if any of those decisions created this situation. The only thing we can really be sure of is that having this car and doing the ads opened the door to get the money to pay the ransom."

He nodded. She was right again. So maybe it wasn't just faith or fate. Maybe there was more to it. And maybe someday, long after this nightmare was over and he could put the *ifs* in order in such a way to fully understand why everything happened as it had, he'd come to understand her perspective, too.

"I think it's time," she noted, tapping the clock on the dash in front of her. "Do you want me to drop you off at the garage or just leave you here?"

"Here is fine." He sighed. "I'll just walk around town for a while. Couldn't sit still if I wanted to, and I certainly don't want to talk to anyone."

As he opened the driver's door, Carole moved her purse and slid behind the wheel. Holding the door open, he watched as she started the car. With tears in his eyes, he whispered, "You be careful."

She glanced his way, forced a smile, and softly vowed, "I'll bring her back with me."

There was no reason to say any more. George pushed the door shut, took a step back, and watched the sedan move slowly down Highway 63. His eyes stayed glued to the Packard until it finally drifted around a curve and was out of sight. Turning the collar of his overcoat up to protect him from the breeze, he glanced to his right at a gravel road that led past an old farmhouse. That seemed as good a direction as any to kill what would likely be the longest hour of his life.

Chapter 25

Two and a half miles could be a very long trip, especially when your daughter's life hung in the balance. In the bright morning sunlight, traveling a road few ever used, Carole Hall was a woman intent on carefully measuring each tenth of a mile on the odometer. She was also just as careful about the time. And even though her heart demanded she get to the drop point as quickly as possible, her mind, focusing on the instructions she'd been given, forced her to slow the car to fifteen miles-per-hour in order to not arrive at the roadside park before the assigned moment.

For Carole the next few moments were an

eternity. It was as if time had stopped. Thus every sound of a car rolling down the gravel road was magnified. Each movement of a rabbit or bird along the ditch line startled her. Even the sun bouncing off the yellow hood was numbing. She felt eyes on her every movement, but she saw no one. And it felt as though her racing heart was going to tear through her chest and fall in her lap. Foot by foot, as she grew closer to the place where her daughter would soon be dropped, her silent passenger—apprehension—seemed to squeeze her so tightly she could no longer breathe.

The dash clock said precisely eleven when she spotted the three tall trees. But just to make sure of the time she also checked her watch and turned on the radio. She searched the dial until she found a station with the news. Only then did she feel confident it was ten.

She spotted the lone picnic table under the large trio of elms. Just as she expected, there was no one there. She slowly guided the Packard to a parking spot between the table and the trash can and eased to a stop. Once in place, she set the brake and turned off the key. The only sound was the breeze. Reaching into the passenger floorboard, she picked up the duffel bag, unzipped it to take a final look at the cash, then rezipped it and tossed it into the backseat. Pushing the door handle down, she stepped out into the morning air.

Before facing south, Carole took a few moments

to button her overcoat and slip on her gloves. After saying a quick prayer, she set her jaw and began walking down the road. Step-by-step she moved farther from the car, the money, and the place where she would be reunited with her daughter in just under an hour. That thought kept her stepping quickly down the road, and the fear of doing something to mess up that reunion kept her eyes focused on what was ahead rather than turning around to see if there was any activity in the park.

The world around her was pure pastoral America. There were a few farmhouses, barns, and fields. In between those were stands of woods, their trees stripped and naked of leaves. The smell of woodsmoke filled her senses, and the sounds of lowing farm animals reminded her of her own youth spent in the country just outside Oakwood. In a very strange way it was all incredibly beautiful, but on this occasion, with so much hanging in the balance, there was nothing comforting about it.

The quietness of the rural world was invaded by the sound of a vehicle on the road behind her. Suddenly she was frightened. Who was it, and where were they going? As the rubber tires made crunching noises on the gravel, she was tempted to glance back. But she knew she shouldn't. Even when the vehicle was just a few feet behind her, she kept walking, her face forward, one foot following another. It was only when the pick-up truck pulled up beside her that her curiosity overcame her fear, and she turned her head ever so slightly to the left.

"Hello, miss," a man in a flannel shirt and bib overalls yelled out over the engine's noise. "I noted the car back at Mulligan's Rest Stop. Was that yours? Are you having some trouble?"

The lanky man's smile and friendly tone spelled out his genuine concern. At any other time she would have welcomed it. But not today! She didn't need a friend; she needed solitude. Thus she had to get him to move on as quickly as possible.

"No, I'm fine and so is my car," she assured him as she continued to move toward the south. "I just wanted to take a walk and loosen up a bit. I've been in the car for a while. I needed to stretch."

"I'd be happy to give you a ride if you need one," he called back. "If you're having some kind of trouble there's no harm in admitting it. No one is going to hurt you."

"No," she answered, forcing a smile. "I just come from a long line of walkers. My family always said a walk puts things in proper perspective. So no matter where I am, I try to get a little exercise in every day. This looked like a real safe spot to me."

He nodded. "No doubt about the safe part. Everyone around here is real friendly. Well, if you're sure you aren't having any trouble, I'll move along. Enjoy the fine day."

"Thanks," Carole replied. She gave a slight wave as the man picked up speed. It was only when he was fully past her that she noted the milk cans in the back of his trunk. He must have been on his way to town to deliver a load. For him it was just another day. How she longed for the time when she'd have just another day again.

After the truck topped a hill, she looked down and pulled her coat sleeve back from her arm to check her watch. She'd dropped the car off ten minutes before. She still had twenty minutes of walking south before she turned around and headed back. She was sure those fifty minutes would likely be the longest of her life.

She was pretty much prayed out, so she opted to sing as she walked. As her short legs pushed forward, she thought of a hymn they often sang in church—"Farther Along." The song's message, which questioned why bad things happened to good people, resonated in her soul. While the fact that there might not be any earthly answers to that age-old question offered no comfort at all, the melody spoke to her at the moment, as did the chorus, "Cheer up, my brother, walk in the sunshine, we'll understand it all by and by." She needed to understand, and she hoped someday in the not-so-distant future, she would.

It was "Farther Along," "Amazing Grace," and a

few other gospel standards that kept her company as the minutes passed. She was singing "Nearer My God to Thee" when she hit the half hour mark and turned around. At the forty-minute point she was embracing the strains of "Just a Little Talk with Jesus," and ten minutes later she was humming "The Great Speckled Bird." She kept singing until 10:58, when she rounded a bend and the rest stop came into view.

"No," she whispered. Straining, she studied the scene again. The Packard wasn't there. There was nothing there except for the trees, the table, and the trash can.

Pushed by terror, she broke out into a sprint. Racing across the road to the table, she craned her head in every direction. There was no car and there was no Rose. What had happened? What had gone wrong?

Panic gripped her, squeezing her heart with viselike power that brought her down to her knees. "No," she yelled at the top of her lungs, "no, no, no!"

Pushing off the ground she looked in every direction as she screamed, "Rose! Are you here, Rose? Rose, answer me! It's your mother! Rose!"

She screamed until she was hoarse and on the verge of collapse, and still there was no answer. No one called back. She was totally alone, two and a half miles from George, with no car and no hope. Not knowing what else to do, she staggered back onto the road and headed north. So tired she could barely stand, she forced one foot in front of the other, swaying like a drunk as she fought to keep moving. She was less than a mile from Prairie Center when she reached the breaking point and collapsed in a heap on the side of the road. Exhausted and defeated, she didn't even attempt to rise. It was over—she knew that—and now nothing mattered anymore.

Chapter 26

"Sir!"

George Hall was leaning against a tree just down from the garage in Prairie Center when he heard a man in grease-covered pants calling out to him. What would he want with him? Unless the man had decided that George was a suspicious stranger who was up to no good . . . How would he talk his way out of that? Explaining that his wife had dropped him to wander around the tiny hamlet was not going to be easy. He couldn't tell the truth, and there were no lies that would even begin to make any sense. Still he couldn't just ignore the man. Unfolding his arms from over his chest he pushed off the tree and waved. "Yes."

"This might sound strange," he said as he came closer, "but do you know a woman that was walking down the road? This lady is kind of small, blond, and is wearing gray slacks and a tweed coat."

"That's my wife," George answered, moving quickly forward to meet the smaller, wiry stranger. Why was she walking? Did she have car problems?

"Well, Slim O'Conner," the stranger explained, "a farmer who lives down the road a bit, just found her. She'd collapsed or something. He wasn't surc. Slim took her over to the preacher's place. Reverend Willis's wife, Jenny, has some nurse's training. You want me to take you over there?"

"Please," George frantically replied.

"My old jalopy is beside the garage. It doesn't look like much, but it runs just fine. The parsonage is just about half a mile south of here."

The men hurried over to the ancient Dodge coupe and jumped in. As promised, the car fired right up, and the man pushed the rusting vehicle south down the dusty road. A few minutes later he pulled into the drive of a white house located about a quarter mile from a community church.

"They took her in the house," he explained. "Just let yourself in. No reason to knock."

A frantic George leaped from the car and bounded up the four steps to the porch. Pushing the door open, he found himself in a small living room. And there, lying on a large brown couch against the far wall was Carole.

"I'm her husband," he explained to the startled looking woman as he moved to Carole's side. "What's wrong?"

"I think she's just plain tuckered out," the heavyset, middle-aged woman answered. "I can't find anything else bothering her. Does she have a weak heart or anything?"

What had they done to her? Had she been assaulted? George studied his wife carefully. Her breathing was regular, but she was so pale. There were no bruises or obvious signs of violence. It was just as if she was asleep. Had they drugged her? Maybe that was it! Glancing back to the woman who'd been caring for Carole, he shook his head. "She's never had any health problems at all," he choked out. "What did they do to her?"

The kindly woman with deep blue eyes and salt and pepper hair smiled, "Well, it looked like she had walked a long way down the road. Maybe she's just wore out. Has she had anything to eat today?"

"No," George answered, his eyes going back to his wife. "Neither of us has eaten much this week." He ran his hand over Carole's cheek. Maybe Rose could tell him. He needed to see his little girl, give her a hug, and ask what happened to her mommy. Looking back toward a man in overalls standing in the archway between the living room and kitchen, he asked, "Where's my child? The little girl about three who was with my wife?"

The man slowly shook his head. "I only saw the woman."

"What?" George asked, his voice rising.

The man again shook his head.

What had happened? Why hadn't she gotten Rose? Glancing back to Carole, tears now filling his eyes and panic squeezing his heart, he pleaded, "What happened? Where is she? You have to wake up!"

Looking back toward the farmer the now unhinged husband cried, "What about a car, a yellow Packard sedan?"

"I saw it at the picnic grounds earlier this morning," the man assured him. "That was the first time I saw your wife. She was walking south. I tried to give her a ride, but she refused. Said she needed the exercise. The car was there then, but not when I returned. And it wasn't on the side of the road between there and here either. Did you two have some kind of fight?"

"No," George answered, "we had something much worse."

The room was silent for a few moments. Finally, Carole opened her eyes and weakly whispered, "She wasn't there."

George nodded. He didn't have to hear any-more, he knew what she meant.

Jenny Willis leaned closer and asked, "Who wasn't there?"

"Our daughter," he softly replied, tears clouding

his eyes. "Somebody took her. They were supposed to give her back if we gave them five thousand dollars. It seems they took the money and our car but didn't bring us our Rose."

"We should call the sheriff," the farmer matter-of-factly said.

"Use our phone," the woman suggested. "Better call Dr. Russell, too."

"They didn't leave her," Carole moaned. "George, what did we do wrong? I tried to follow their directions. I really did. What did I do wrong?"

"I don't know, sweetheart," he replied. "Did they take the money? What about the car?"

"Oh, George," she whimpered, "I messed up. They took it or at least someone took it. And they still have Rose. What does it mean?"

He patted her hand and shook his head. Yet as he stared into her round face he saw nothing. The nightmare he thought would soon be over had just begun. This nightmare might never end.

Chapter 27

Henry Reese was thirty-five. With a rock-solid jaw and his blocky build, he would have been at home playing for the Bears. While he did play football when getting his degree from Iowa, his focus had always been the law. After passing the bar, the six-foot-two-inch, black-haired man worked for the Windy City's district attorney for six years before joining the FBI. His singular determination and clear view of right and wrong made him perfect for the bureau.

While Reese, with his good looks and dark brown eyes, was the Hollywood mold for a G-man, the other investigator was just the opposite. Helen Meeker could have been a model. With her piercing blue eyes, auburn hair, and willowy frame, she would have turned heads in showrooms in New York or Paris. But her father had been a skilled prosecutor and her grandfather a homicide detective, so Helen naturally followed in their footsteps. She graduated at the top of her class from New York University at just eighteen and received her law degree from Columbia when she was twenty. As the FBI only took single men as agents, Helen had to use her father's impressive contacts to knock down the bureau's door.

J. Edgar Hoover was opposed to her working in any capacity with the bureau, but Meeker didn't let that fact stop her from getting to where she wanted to be. When Hoover turned her down on the grounds that women would not be a part of his organization, she went to work for the Secret Service. Within a year she was assigned to the White House and renewed a family friendship with Eleanor Roosevelt. On a lunch date with the First Lady, she explained her dream of working as an FBI agent. Eleanor took her pleas to her husband. As Franklin was already impressed with Meeker's work as a part of his staff, he didn't put up much of a fight before calling Hoover and ordering him to participate in what Eleanor called "The Grand Experiment." Thus Meeker, though technically still employed by the Secret Service and under the supervision of the President, was on loan to the FBI, where she essentially had all the powers of any other agent. When this case, involving the kidnapping of a little girl, fell into the FBI's lap, she called Eleanor again, and that led to Meeker and her partner being assigned as the lead investigators. The determined twenty-eight-year-old woman was on a plane to Chicago within two hours of getting the assignment. Now she stood at the picnic area with Henry Reese.

"They were so stupid," Reese barked. "If they'd called us in the minute she was taken, we might have the kid back now."

As Meeker watched the rest of the FBI team search the site for evidence, she nodded. He was right, but she also understood why many folks wouldn't make that call. Fear often overcame logic even in smart people when their child was involved. She'd seen it happen on at least one other occasion. Besides there was no time to blame the parents—a child's life was at stake. Clues had to be found, and the puzzle of who took the girl, why it happened, and where she was now had to be put together. The clock was ticking.

Meeker marched through knee-high grass to a place on the far side of the car. An Indiana state trooper was on his hands and knees studying the ground. She allowed him to work for a few more seconds before asking, "Any blood or signs of violence?"

He shook his head. Strolling back over to Reese, she looked down the road in both directions before mumbling, "What would they need with the car?"

"What?" he shot back.

"The car. It makes no sense." Turning to where their eyes met, she added, "The only thing I can think of is the fear of fingerprints or other evidence that they might have left when picking up the money. Did they hot-wire it, or did the mother leave the keys?"

Reese shrugged. "They likely hot-wired it, though in questioning the victim's father I found out there was an extra set of keys hidden under the mat. So they might have found those and used them."

Meeker's blue eyes shot back to the road. "Have they searched the ditches and fields between here and the next towns?"

"They have, and they found nothing."

She crossed her arms over her dark blue coat; something wasn't right. The case didn't fit the norm. No one kidnapped a girl from a middle-class family. After all, money was the motive in crimes like this, and risking the death house over five thousand was simply not logical. She marched back to where a dozen agents were carefully studying the spot where the car had been parked.

"What about the car?" she barked. "What do we know about it?"

Reese walked up beside her and shoved a piece of paper into her hand, "Here is the license number. It was a 1936 Packard four-door sedan in very good condition. There was no body damage. The family tells me it looked almost new. It was an eight cylinder model."

"That limits our search to tens of thousands of vehicles," the woman complained. "I know that fact from having walked through the Packard plant back in 1936. It was their most popular model. The license plate will surely be switched, so not much to go on."

"There is one unique thing about the vehicle," Reese cut in. "It's bright yellow."

Meeker turned as if to study her partner, but she didn't see him. Her eyes were focused on something that happened almost four years before. Could this yellow Packard be the same one that had stopped the assembly line the day of her visit?

"You said bright yellow?" she almost whispered.

"It is supposedly a one-of-a-kind yellow," Reese

explained. "The owners never saw another one like it."

Meeker walked back toward Reese's Ford sedan. As she leaned against the fender, she once more studied the spot where the Halls' car had been taken. Could this Packard be the same one she'd encountered at the plant? Could this same car have now been involved in two tragedies? What were the odds?

"We need to talk to the parents. Maybe they can offer us something."

"The father was taken to Chicago this morning," he explained. "We can interview him at the FBI headquarters there."

Opening the passenger-side door, Meeker slid into the seat. As her partner ran around the front of the Ford, she took one final look at the crime scene. She prayed that the missing girl was alive, but in her heart she doubted that to be true, and she wondered how the parents would ever cope if that was the case.

Chapter 28

Meeker knew the type well. She figured George Hall for a small-town boy who had no real interest in the big city, unless it was a day trip to watch the Cubs. On top of losing his daughter and dealing with a wife who might well be suffering a complete breakdown and was under doctors' care and on sedatives, he found himself in FBI headquarters in an office with four other people. Two he at least knew. On the suggestion of the FBI, Samuel Johns and Jed Atkins, the local sheriff, had driven up from Oakwood to sit in on the meeting. The other two in the small office on the seventh floor of the Illinois headquarters of the FBI were complete strangers. Now, as the quintet sat down at a conference table, it was time to see if Hall knew anything he hadn't shared with the field agents.

"Mr. Hall," Meeker began, "we have no time for formalities. Our people on the scene have given me the little information they could piece together. We visited the scene as well, and I have read your and your wife's statements. I'm hoping, as is Agent Reese, that we can come up with something the others might have missed in earlier interviews. My first question is very simple." She paused and licked her lips. "Why didn't you contact us when your daughter was taken?"

George looked down at the oak table and shook his head. He didn't look up when he mumbled his explanation, "The note said not to. I was just doing what I was told." He finally turned his gaze toward the FBI agent, tears in his eyes, and sobbed. "If I called the authorities they told me they would kill Rose."

Reese, his voice firm and unapologetic, stepped

into the dialogue. "And that is what they always say. Did you ever hear you daughter on the phone calls, or were you given any proof that she was alive?"

"No," George admitted.

Meeker jumped back in, "From your earlier interview, you seem to believe that the kidnappers thought you had money because of the advertisements you did for the Packard Company. Is that right?"

"What else could it be?" George replied. "Neither Carole's nor my family have any money. This was all just a big mistake."

Meeker nodded, glanced over to her partner, and signaled for him to follow her to the window. The two got up and moved across the room. They turned their backs to the others and spoke in hushed tones so that their visitors couldn't hear.

"Any word on the car?" she asked.

"No," he replied. "It's as if it disappeared into thin air."

"Kind of hard to hide a bright yellow Packard," she observed.

"But there're a lot of barns in Indiana, and we have no probable cause to search any of them."

Meeker stared out the seventh floor window at the Chicago skyline, but she saw none of it. The only thing she saw was a frightened little girl desperately wanting her parents. The image was so sharp and defined she could almost hear her cries. But too much time had passed since the girl had been taken. The delay in calling them in on the case not only put them in a deep hole but also likely meant the young girl was dead. What a senseless tragedy. Something that might have been avoided if the flower shop's phone line had just been tapped when the kidnapper called.

"Any leads on where the ransom calls came from?" Meeker asked.

"There are no records that we've found that indicate they were long distance."

She nodded. That wasn't unusual—most kidnapping victims were known by those who kidnapped them. In fact, the child's body, if she was dead, was likely very close to the family's home.

"Henry," Meeker whispered, "something really bothers me here. Hall thinks this is tied to the mistaken impression that he had money. Yet if someone local pulled the job, they would have been aware the family didn't have five thousand dollars to their names. There is something we are missing here. There has to be another reason for setting this whole thing up."

"Are you thinking," Reese grimly whispered, glancing over her shoulder to make sure those sitting at the table couldn't hear them, "that we're dealing with a sicko who likes little girls?"

"Could be." She cringed as the words came out of her mouth. "We need to check and see if there are any ex-cons with that kind of record living in the area who might have spotted Rose and pegged her to grab."

"If that is the case," Reese soberly added, "then the money would have been a ruse."

"Could be," she agreed, "or the icing on the cake. They get what they want, and the cash as a bonus. Five thousand seems like such a small amount when being caught buys the person a ticket to the electric chair. Logic tells me they would have gone after someone with a lot more ready cash if it were just kidnapping."

Turning and striding back to the table, Meeker opened the file and studied Hall's statement one more time. Taking a seat, she drummed her fingers for a few seconds, her nails clicking like the keys of a typewriter, before looking back to the distraught man.

"Mr. Hall, you said in your previous interview you found ten one-hundred-dollar bills you needed to make the down payment on the flower shop. Is that correct?"

"Yes," he replied. "Well, actually Rose found them beside the garage door."

She quickly looked to the sheriff. "Anyone report a robbery or losing any C-notes?"

The sheriff shook his head. "Nothing that we know of. Since we got word of the kidnapping I've made a lot of calls, and no one reported any money missing. It seemed the cash literally fell out of midair."

"And no more was found?" she asked.

Atkins and Hall shook their heads.

"Henry, why don't you get a team down there to really look over that garage. See if you can find any more cash. Look under the floor, in the rafters, everywhere."

"You thinking," the other agent chimed in, "there could be a connection to a larger chunk of cash?"

"I don't know," she admitted. "I'm grasping at straws. I mean, why kidnap the kid rather than just grab the loot from where it was hidden?" She drummed her fingers for a few more moments and added, "Unless they didn't know where it was hidden."

"I'm following you," Atkins said. "An old bank job or a robbery where the loot was never recovered. Maybe part of the gang that pulled the job got double-crossed somehow and came back looking for it. So when those bills showed up, they assumed George found the cash."

George's eyes widened at the comment. "So, what are you saying?"

"Then," Reese added, ignoring Hall, "we need to go through local and state records, as well as those of the Treasury Department and the FBI, and try to find a robbery where five thousand dollars was taken."

"No," Meeker corrected him, "more than that. The kidnapper knew that a thousand had been spent on the down payment. They couldn't get that back, so they opted for what was left."

"A kidnapping as a cover for the recovering of stolen loot," Reese noted, "that's a new one on me."

"It makes perfect sense," Meeker explained. "In fact it makes a lot more sense than this kidnapping than if they had just demanded the five thousand out of Mr. Hall; he'd have gone straight to the police. But if you steal the kid, make it look like a kidnapping, then the family is much more likely to produce the cash and not involve us. And when you think about it, it worked perfectly."

The room grew suddenly silent as each of the five considered the theory. It was George who finally posed the haunting question that demanded an answer. His voice shaky and tired, he asked, "So this had nothing to do with anything Carole and I did?"

Meeker's businesslike tone grew soft and compassionate. "Probably not. How long have you lived in your home?"

"A couple of years."

She looked toward Johns and Atkins. "Did either of your know the people who lived there before the Halls?"

Johns nodded. "The Casons were there for about ten years or so. They built the house."

"What kind of people were they?" Meeker asked.

"Good folks," Johns replied. "Went to church,

172

helped in the community. Ben was a car salesman at the Ford house. They had three kids, all of them graduated from high school."

"You're almost right about them being a good family," Atkins noted, "but you forgot about Milt. He got into a couple of scrapes when he was in his late teens. Ran around with a rough crowd in Danville. Spent a few months in the county jail before joining the military."

"Is he still in the service?" Meeker asked.

"Yes, the Navy."

Meeker's eyes caught the sheriff's. "What kind of scrapes, as you called them, was he in?"

"A couple of robberies, car theft."

"There you go," Meeker solemnly noted. "Let's find him and grill him. If he fesses up to hiding any money there, maybe it will give us leads on who was trying to get it. That will take us one step closer to finding those responsible for taking Rose."

"I'll get someone on it this afternoon," Reese chimed in. "And I'll start looking for unsolved robberies in the area dating back to before the Halls bought the home."

"That pretty much covers things for the moment," Meeker noted. "Anyone else have anything to add?"

Almost apologetically George lifted his hand and looked toward the woman. "Could I ask a question?"

"Of course you can, Mr. Hall."

His voice cracking, the father whispered, "If you find those men, the ones who might have been in a robbery with Mr. Cason, will you find my girl?"

"We hope so," Meeker assured him. "We certainly hope so. Thank you for your time, and if you think of anything else please let us know immediately."

Meeker remained seated while Reese escorted Johns, Atkins, and Hall from the room. Only when the door had closed did she get up and once more move to the window.

"Case seems to mean a lot to you," Reese noted as he moved beside her.

"They all do," she replied. "Remember you volunteered to be a part of 'The Grand Experiment' as well. If we fail, then the FBI will stay a men's club for a very long time."

"Helen, how long have we been working together?"

She shrugged. "Maybe too long."

"It's been six months. During that time we have worked all kinds of cases—three murders, several drug cases, some robberies, and even income tax evasion. And you were coolly professional on all of them. Yet, when you were trying to be tough with Hall, I saw a tear in your eye. The iron maiden almost cracked."

"I've been having problems with my eyes the

past week," she snapped. "Just had something in them. That's all."

"No, it's more than that," Reese replied, not giving the woman any wiggle room. "This case means something . . . something personal. I can't figure what it is. You don't know the family, you've never been to the town, so there doesn't seem to be any kind of tie, but there is. I know you well enough to know there's something special here. Level with me."

Turning from the window, Meeker looked directly into her partner's eyes. "It's a case. That's what it is. And what are the odds of solving it? From our experience, you with the FBI and me with the Secret Service, both of us know those odds aren't good. What are the chances that girl is still alive? Almost zero! That's especially true if the real reason involved was getting back loot from a robbery. The kid was just a pawn. Odds are we won't even find her body. Imagine being a parent and having a kid taken. Then never even being able to have a funeral. Never saying good-bye."

"Yeah," Reese replied, "would be tough."

"More than tough," she shot back. "It will likely destroy that family. That Hall guy we just met, he'll carry guilt the rest of his life. He'll beat himself up. Maybe even become suicidal."

"How can you know that?" Reese demanded.

"I've done my homework," she sadly replied.

"I've made studying kidnapping cases my hobby since I was in college. There are no sadder cases."

Meeker turned back to the window and studied the streets of Chicago. Thousands of people were strolling down the sidewalks, cars were bumper to bumper on every street, and the elevated train was carrying hundreds more to jobs or adventures. Among those thousands of people, one of them might have the clue that would solve this case. But which one?

"I'm going to get started on my homework," Reese said.

"I'll join you in a minute," she assured him.

When the door closed and she was alone, a single tear ran down the agent's face and fell onto the windowsill.

Chapter 29

April 23, 1940

It hadn't been a good day for Bill Landers. He was sitting at the counter in a diner, twenty miles south of St. Louis. His six-year-old Studebaker had once more let him down. It was the third time this month. And on each occasion the sedan had died by the side of the road it had cost the salesman another chance to close a deal. At this rate he'd be broke and jobless by the end of the month.

Landers lived by himself in a tiny house in Bryant, Arkansas. The small community just south of Little Rock was known by some as the "Bauxite Capital of America." About half the jobs in the community revolved around aluminum. And with the war cranking up in Europe, there were lots of plants using the metal in the "lend-lease program" that the President had established with the countries fighting Germany and Italy. So there was money to be made in aluminum, but Landers was not one of those making it, and his boss at Bynum Aluminum was tired of his sales-man failing him. The clock was therefore ticking.

Today, Landers had been scheduled to meet with three different companies. Yet he couldn't secure those deals on the phone—he had to do it in person. And that meant more than just meeting with the company owners; it meant taking them out to eat and showing them a good time. And he couldn't do that without a good car!

The mechanic at the shop that had towed him in gave him the bad news. The block had cracked. There was no way to fix it short of putting in a new motor. But with the bad brakes and worn interior, not to mention a transmission that slipped like a dog on ice, investing any more money in the car was simply not an option. Yet buying a new one was also impossible. Thanks to a failed marriage and losing his last job, his credit was lousy and the cash he had wouldn't purchase anything much better than the Studebaker.

Landers looked across the counter and into the mirror. For a man in his early forties, he didn't look too bad. His hair was still dark brown, his jaw firm, and his skin pretty much wrinkle free. But the eyes told another story. They were sunken, dark, and lifeless. Anyone who looked into those eyes would read him like a book, and the ending wouldn't be a happy one.

"What can I get you, Mack?" the skinny college-aged kid working the counter asked.

"A new car," Landers cracked.

"Tell me about it," the kid replied. "Mine busted last night. Dropped an axle. I'll be on foot for at least a week until I can scratch up the dough to fix it."

"I may be walking the rest of my life." Landers sighed. "And if I don't get to Indy by tomorrow morning at ten, I'll lose my job as well. This trip was my last chance. I was pretty much told that if I didn't land a big contract not to come back. With my car officially dead, guess I'm a man without a country."

"Without a country?" The kid looked confused.

"Just a saying." He shrugged. "Why don't you give me a ham sandwich on rye and a Coke. I still have enough for that."

"You want it grilled?"

"Sure, why not. I might as well live it up!"

The skinny kid mixed a fountain drink, dumped

some ice in the glass, and set it on the counter. As he left, Landers reached for a straw. Before he could grab the dispenser, a gruff-looking man handed him a wrapped straw.

"Thanks," Landers said.

"No problem," came the quick reply. "I didn't mean to eavesdrop, but I heard you were having issues with your car."

"You heard right." The salesman tore off the paper wrapping, stuck the straw into his glass, and took a long sip.

"I may be able to solve your problem," the man announced with a grin. "I've got a pretty nice car that belonged to my uncle. When he died, my aunt gave it to me. I don't need it as I've got a new Mercury."

"What kind is it?" Landers asked offhandedly. "I mean what kind is your uncle's car?"

"A Packard sedan. It has an eight, not one of those cheap models with the six. Good shape, smooth riding, and lots of power. Tires are in great shape, too. I'd be driving it myself, but like I told you I got this new Mercury."

"So you said," Landers replied. "What year?"

"It's a '36, but it's low mileage, and my uncle really took good care of it. New blue paint job, too."

"Here's your sandwich," the kid said as he set a plate in front of the salesman. "You need anything else?"

"No," Landers replied. "What do I owe you?"

"Thirty-five cents."

Landers pulled two quarters from his pocket and set them on the counter. "Keep the change."

"Thanks," came the enthusiastic reply.

Before biting into his supper, the salesman casually studied the man seated to his right. The guy had a seedy look about him. He dressed pretty nicely; his clothes looked new, but he didn't appear comfortable in them. He was also about two weeks overdue for a haircut and three days past due for a shave. He was simply not someone that Landers felt he could trust, and normally he would have politely dismissed him, but there was that old saying about looking a gift horse in the mouth. . . . And if the Packard could be bought for the money Landers had in his pocket, and it was as good as this guy claimed it was, then this unseemly character might well be the key to his holding on to his job.

"So where's the car?" Lander asked between bites.

"It's a couple of blocks away," the man answered in hushed tones. "In a garage a friend of mine owns. I can run down and get it if you want to drive it."

"Don't get the cart in front of the horse." Landers laughed. "Or in this case, the Packard."

"What do you mean?" the man asked.

"Nothing worth noting," Landers explained. "I

just need to know what you're asking for it. No reason for you to go to all that trouble if I don't have the cash with me to buy it."

"I'm asking a hundred and a half."

The salesman shook his head, "Sounds pretty cheap for a car that is as solid as you claim. Especially a Packard!"

"I just need to move it," he replied. "I'm leaving for the West Coast in a few weeks and can't take it with me. I got nothing in it anyway. So for me turning it fast is more important than making big dough."

"Okay," came the salesman's reluctant reply. "I doubt if it is that good, but I'd be a fool not to at least take a look. You go get it while I finish my meal. I'll meet you out front."

The sandwich was the best thing Landers had eaten in days. He was tempted to order a second one, but there was a deal he needed to make or pass on. He figured it would be the latter. So, he pushed his one-hundred-sixty pounds off the stool and out the door. Just as he stepped out into the lot, the Packard rumbled up.

The owner left it idling as he stepped out. "Runs real smooth."

Landers nodded. The body was razor straight, the dark blue paint shiny, the chrome good, the tires had lots of tread, and the interior was only stained in a couple of places.

"Want to take her for a drive?"

"Sure," Landers answered, opening the door and sliding behind the wheel.

"Want a smoke?" the man asked.

"No," the salesman replied, "don't use them."

"Suit yourself." The man pulled out a pack of Lucky Strikes, used his index finger on his left hand to tap out a cigarette, placed it between his lips, grabbed the Packard's lighter, took a long draw, and pulled the cigarette out of his mouth. As the smoke hovered in the air, Landers twisted the key and hit the starter.

With the owner in the passenger seat smoking, the salesman put the car through the paces. He pushed it up to seventy, slammed on the brakes, went through the range of gears several times, and attacked a series of bumps and potholes. In each case the Packard performed and handled like a new car.

"Your uncle did take good care of it," Landers said as they pulled back into the diner's parking lot. Stepping out of the car, he carefully looked it over again. "Tell you what. Let me step back into the diner for a minute. I'll come back out, and we'll see if we can make a deal."

With the car's owner standing hopefully by the sedan, Landers went back into the diner and over to the counter. Catching the kid's attention, he leaned forward and posed a simple and direct question, "What do you know about the guy who's trying to sell me the car?"

The kid looked up and smiled. "He's been in here every day for the past couple of weeks. He lives with the Hooks family down the street. They're pretty good folks. Other than that, I don't know much. Why?"

"I'm just wondering," Landers mused, "if the car could be hot. I mean this is serious business, and I can't afford to play footsie with the law."

"Well, a lot of cops eat in here," the kid shot back. "If that was the case, I figure that guy would be hanging out somewhere else. And he's driven it up here a few times."

"Thanks, kid. That's what I need to know. Here's a buck toward your car repairs."

The kid was still grinning when Landers strolled back outside. After waving at the man he asked, "Will you take a C-note?"

The man grinned. "How about a hundred and a quarter?"

The salesman nodded.

"I'll give you a bill of sale," the man replied. "The title is with my uncle's things at the bank. Give me your address, and I'll mail it to you next week when the will is read and the property distributed."

"You sure you own this car?" Landers anxiously asked.

"Yep, but in a few minutes you will."

If his job hadn't been on the line, Landers would have walked away. After all, that was what his gut told him to do. But it was either this car or the unemployment line, and that appealed to him even less than the risk of getting into trouble with the law. Besides, if he was picked up and the police told him the car was hot, he could just explain the situation. After all, he was getting a bill of sale, and that had the seller's name on it. So he had his bases covered. Now all he had to do was get his stuff out of the Studebaker and head for Indiana.

Chapter 30

"You just tell your company they'd better reserve lots of boxcars to get aluminum to us. We will quickly become your biggest customer! These Brits need a lot of planes right now."

"Thank you, sir," Landers said while reaching for Paul Bowan's hand. "I'll make sure the trains are ready and the materials are here in time."

"Landers," Bowan's booming voice caught the salesman right before he stepped out the Airflow Company's president's door.

Turning on his heels, the salesman quickly answered, "Yes, sir?"

"Landers," Bowman repeated his name, "see my secretary on the way out. Have her give you the contact information for Lester Franks. He heads up Franklin Aircraft. They are looking for good sources for aluminum as well. I think he'd be a good customer for you, too. You could circle by his office in Lexington on your way back to Arkansas."

"I sure could!" Landers assured him. "Thanks again, sir."

He couldn't believe it! After months of not being able to even get in to talk to the president of any company, he just made the biggest sale in the history of Bynum Aluminum. Not only had he saved his job, he had likely earned a huge bonus. What a difference a day could make!

As he slid into the Packard, Bill Landers had a smile on his lips and a song in his heart. For the first time in his life he felt lucky. What had happened? Why suddenly had everything gone right?

Patting the Packard's dash, he said, "Old Blue, you and I are going to have a beautiful friendship."

It was almost noon, and hunger had set in with the force of a winter wind. Landers knew very little about Indiana and had no idea where to grab a bite. Thus he stopped at the first place he saw—Plunky's Café.

There was no counter, so Landers slid into a booth. Judging by the crowd, he figured the food must be great. He spied a man to his right who was carving up a large steak and savoring every bite. Licking his lips, Landers anxiously glanced around for someone who could set him up with a piece of that choice beef. As he waited to be served, he looked around the building. From the cowhide cushions in the booth to cowbells lining the walls to the huge photos of prize-winning steers hanging on the wall, everywhere he looked there was a cattle theme. So he halfway expected the waitress to moo when she came to take his order. And he didn't care as long as she got to him soon. Yet the place was so busy it took another ten minutes before a cheery looking heavyset girl in her twenties headed his way.

"What's up, big boy?" she asked.

He grinned. "Looks like you're busy. You have a special or something?"

Her eyes swept the room and fell back on him. "It's always this way. You got here just in time. By twelve thirty there will be an hour's wait just to grab a spot to rest your behind."

"I've been lucky all day today," Landers announced, "and it seems my choice of places to eat just continues that run. By the way, what's the story on this place?"

"I have the speech memorized." She laughed. "Every outsider who comes in here wants to know. So here it goes. Alexander Plunky, the owner, had a farm about twenty miles east of Indianapolis. His wife, Gladys, had long been known as the best cook in the area. In 1934, the husband and wife combined what they did well and opened

Plunky's in this empty barn on the outskirts of town. The result was a steak place that has earned a stellar reputation all over the Midwest."

Landers shook his head and grinned. "Well done, if you will pardon my pun. Now what do you think is the best thing on the menu?"

"Well, it's kind of pricey," she explained, "but I'd say the T-bone with the baked potato. But you might not want to spend the two-fifty it costs, so perhaps you'd want to go with the sirloin. It's tender and tasty and costs half that."

"Bring me the T-bone and make it medium."

"You must be in the chips."

"I'm getting there." He laughed. "Or as we say in the south, I'm walking in high cotton!"

"What do you do?" she asked as she scribbled down the order.

"I sell aluminum to the manufacturing industry."

"Really?" she quipped, her eyebrows lifting halfway up her forehead. "You're not going to believe this, but there's a guy a couple of tables over who comes in every day. His company builds farm equipment, and he uses a lot of the stuff. He's always talking about how difficult it is for him to get enough to keep his plant running. Maybe you should talk to him."

Landers grinned. "Where is he and what is his name?"

"The name is Biggilo . . . Mick Biggilo," she explained as she pointed over her shoulder. "You see that huge hunk of a man wearing the gray suit in the corner booth? Well that's Big Mick."

Big Mick had earned his moniker. Even sitting down he looked tall. His hands were twice the size of a normal man's, and he used them as his spoke. At this moment the man with him was getting more than an earful as Mick's mitts were flying in all directions to emphasize his every word.

Beyond his hands, Mick's shoulders were wide as a yardstick and his neck would have dwarfed the trunk of a ten-year-old oak tree. Clean-shaven with a thick and unruly crop of blond straw on his head, the man's green eyes sparkled like a lake on a summer day.

Landers shook his head and noted, "The guy's grandfather must have been Paul Bunyan."

"Yep." She giggled. "You're not the first person to say that. But he's really a teddy bear. He tips great, too. Do you have a business card? I'll take it over to him."

Landers fished in his coat pocket and pulled out a card. As he handed it to the woman, he glanced back toward Big Mick's table. The factory owner was still involved in some heavy conversation with the smaller, thin man. Whatever they were visiting about seemed pretty serious, too, as neither was smiling.

Bill's eyes followed the waitress as she pushed through the crowd to Mick's table. Once there she leaned over, handed the large man the card, and pointed to where Landers was sitting. Mick nodded, gently slapped the woman on the shoulder with his big right hand, and pulled himself from the booth. Five steps later he was peering down at the Arkansan.

"Says here your name is William Landers." His deep, booming voice matched his size.

"I am, but most folks call me Bill."

A ham-sized hand came forward, and a second later Landers was experiencing a grip firmer than any he'd ever known. He half expected to have to see a doctor when the big man finished the greeting. Finally, Big Mick dropped his massive frame into the seat opposite Landers. He wasted no time spelling out what he wanted.

"This tells me that your company can fill anyone's needs for aluminum. Is that right?"

"I believe we can," Landers assured him, "and our price is right, too."

"Price is important, but not as important as volume. I can't make enough of a newfangled hog feeder I designed. Everyone wants to buy them. And now I've developed cattle feeders as well. May not sound like much when compared to the aircraft industry, but I can assure you there are a lot of pigs and cattle in this world that have to eat, and farmers want feeders that will stand up in the weather. So I need a lot of aluminum. You see where I'm headed here?"

Smiling even though his right hand was still stinging, Landers nodded.

"Bill, I'm going to write a figure here on this napkin. You take a look at it and tell me if you can deliver anywhere near that much to my Muncie plant each month."

The big man took out a pencil and scribbled a number on the white paper. He then pushed it across the table toward the salesman. Landers could feel Big Mick's stare as he studied a number that was ten times what he expected.

"Mr. Biggilo."

"Call me Big Mick."

"Big Mick, would you give me time to make a call to our office? I want to guarantee how much we can deliver before I commit."

"There's a phone in the back." He pointed to a door that had OFFICE written in six-inch blue letters. "Tell Plunky that Big Mick will pick up the long-distance charges."

Landers hurried across the crowded restaurant to the office. He knocked and waited for a voice on the other side.

"Come in."

"Big Mick sent me back here to make a long-distance call," Landers explained. "He said he'd pick up the charges."

The tall, dark headed, beady-eyed Plunky grunted, pointed to the phone, and got up and left. Two minutes later Calvin Bynum was on the line.

"So, Bill, you're telling me that this guy is looking to buy this much every month?"

"He says he can't make them fast enough," Landers assured him.

"And you got the Airflow contract, too? And neither balked at our price?"

"Well Airflow didn't, and Big Mick assured me he was more concerned about getting the material than what it cost. So, Mr. Bynum, can I can cut this deal?"

"Okay, Bill. We might have to add another shift, but if you close on this, both you and I are going to make a lot of money. In fact, you can get rid of that old Studebaker and buy a Packard or a Lincoln with the bonus you'll be earning."

Landers laughed. "Already got a Packard, but I'll find a way to spend it. Don't worry about that. I'll call you later when we get everything signed."

Setting the phone down, the salesman got up from the desk and walked over to a mirror. He straightened his tie and grinned. He had gone from the bottom of the barrel to the top of the mountain in less than a day, and he'd ridden there in a Packard. Not a bad way to go at all!

Chapter 31

"We might have something, Helen," Reese announced as Meeker walked into the room that had become their Chicago office.

The woman didn't have to ask if what he had was good news. His face told her that the story was discouraging. Nine would get you ten that this was the news she had anticipated but hadn't allowed herself to even think about. Setting the six-ounce bottle of Coke on her desk, she perched on the corner of the worktable and nodded.

"They found the body of a little girl along the Wabash River last night," he explained, his tone as ominous as the subject was horrifying. "It was discovered about fifteen miles from where the Halls dropped the cash."

Meeker pushed off the table and, with her arms folded across her chest, slowly walked over to the window. The news was hardly unexpected. History proved it was far easier to kill the victims in a kidnapping than leave them alive so they might be able to identify the person or persons responsible. Yet for the past three weeks she'd been hoping that this case would be different. As she'd studied the photos of Rose Hall, as she found out more about her personality and her likes and dislikes, as she'd come to know her favorite color and foods, the little girl had become very real to Meeker. She could almost hear the little girl singing along with Glen Miller on the radio. Now Helen wished Carole Hall had never shared that story with her. This was not just a case number with an objective, this was an almost three-year-old child whose parents loved her dearly. So the news was hard to stomach. She didn't want to hear it. She didn't want to face it. She didn't want to know that she hadn't saved Rose Hall.

"You want to know the rest?" Reese asked from his desk.

She didn't turn around as she spoke. "Go ahead."

"A fisherman found the body along the bank where a creek feeds into the Wabash. The girl was blond, had shoulder-length hair, small features, and fair skin. The shoe size and height match Rose Hall. She'd been in the water too long for a facial identification."

"Where is she?" Meeker's tone was stoic.

"Indy," he replied. "They are doing an autopsy right now."

"Do they have our records?" she asked, still looking out the window. "Have they seen our files?"

"Yeah," he assured her.

Meeker turned back to her partner. As she spoke, her arms remained folded. "This officially adds another charge to our case. Murder rides along with all the other occupants that Packard has been carrying. That means we might be able to get a few more G-men on the case."

"Not the way I wanted to secure more resources," he answered. "Who is going to tell the Halls?"

"I'll do it." She sighed. "It might be easier coming from a woman. And even if we don't have an official confirmation, they need to be told we have found a body that could be the girl's. Odds are that news is already on the radio in Indiana. It won't take long to get here."

She walked resolutely back to her desk, sat in her chair, and picked up the phone. Before dialing, she looked again at the photo of Rose Hall that she had sitting on the corner of her desk. What a beautiful child she had been.

"How do you think they'll take it?" Reese asked.

She glanced across the room. From the despair in his eyes, someone who didn't know the situation would have guessed the rugged agent to be the mourning father.

"You're not as tough as Hoover thinks," she noted.

"No," he admitted.

"Henry," she said, "it will crush them. But it is better to know your daughter is dead, to have the actual proof, than go through life without that knowledge. As cold as it sounds something good might come out of this. They'll have a funeral. They will be able to mourn. There will be an ending."

"And that's good?" he asked.

"It's better than never knowing," she offered.

She once more looked at the phone before setting the receiver back in the cradle. She glanced across to the man and shrugged. "Does the press know about the body being found?"

"I can ask for a press blackout," he replied. "Last I heard the newspaper doesn't know about it."

"Make the call and keep it quiet," she quickly shot back. "Then I won't have to make that call until we ID the body."

"It might be a while," he told her.

"The news needs to be concrete," she said. Meeker picked up the newspaper she'd bought that morning but had not yet read. After taking a long draw of her Coke, she turned to the funny pages. Though she needed a laugh, she doubted the *Tribune* could make that delivery after her morning.

An hour later, after reading everything including the want ads twice, she set the paper down and watched as her partner answered the ringing phone. After his hello, he nodded in her direction. She knew this would be the confirmation they needed.

"I see," Reese said. "And what else do you have?"

He waited for another sixty seconds. As he did Meeker opened her case file and pulled out the number to Carole's Flower Shop.

"Got it," the man said from his desk on the other side of the twenty-by-fifteen-foot room. "Thanks."

Setting the phone down, he looked over at Meeker and grimly smiled. "It's not her." He paused as the full realization of what it meant set in. "It was a four-year-old girl from Newport. She and her father had not been seen since earlier in the month. He was out of work and his wife had left them, so locals just thought they'd moved away. Guess they hadn't. They found his body about an hour ago not far from the spot where they found hers."

Meeker shook her head. "You mean he was so overwhelmed that he killed his daughter and took his own life?" The thought was simply too much for her to comprehend.

"No," Reese assured her, "seems it was just a tragic accident. They were out fishing. . . ."

Chapter 32

May 1, 1940

"So you still don't know a blasted thing?" George shouted while pounding his fist into the counter as rage and frustration shaded his face crimson.

Helen Meeker stood in Carole's Flower Shop, as the father's words tore through her like a sharp knife. For a month she had worked every angle on the case, and she had nothing to show for it. During that time she had avoided admitting that fact or the lack of new evidence to Rose Hall's parents. But the time had come to level with them that the FBI, with all its investigators and resources, had hit a dead end. The parents had a right to know that.

"I'm sorry," Meeker replied, her carefully measured tone indicating the sincerity of her message. "I want you to know this is the most important case in the world to me. I really mean that."

"But it must not be too important for the FBI," George shot back.

Carole, who'd been listlessly working on a flower display, cut her husband off, "George, bite your tongue."

"I'm tired of staying quiet," he screamed.

"These people are supposed to find our baby, and what have they done? Nothing!" Rushing from behind the counter to where the agent stood, he wagged an accusing finger in the visitor's face and went on, "If the FBI really cared, they wouldn't have assigned a woman to the case. The fact that we got you rather than a man pretty much proves Rose didn't matter to them!"

The words stung, but she'd gotten that reaction on many of the cases she'd been assigned. She had grown very used to the comment. "We must not be important because a woman is on the job."

"George didn't mean it," Carole said, as she crossed the room to where the man and agent stood nose to nose. "It's just the pressure. It's just that you can't tell us anything. We need some answers. We need some hope."

Stepping back from the man's accusing finger, Meeker walked over and put her hand on the hurting mother's shoulder. "You need a lot more than answers, you need to have your little girl back. Bringing her back to you has filled my every waking hour and my sleepless nights."

Moving back eye-to-eye with Rose's father, she added, "And you're right, there is a woman on this case. I'm here for a reason, and it's not because the FBI doesn't care. Mr. Hoover checks with me several times a week on this specific matter. He knows your daughter's name and asks about her each time he calls. Right now we have a dozen agents all across the country following even the most obscure leads. I can't begin to tell you the money and man-hours that have been expended on this case. And the reason it remains open and the reason we are working so hard is that there is a woman assigned to it. I won't let them give up. I won't let them turn their back on your little girl."

George's eyes dropped to the floor, and his hands pushed into his pants pockets. He was a defeated soul.

"Listen, Mr. Hall," she solemnly said, "I have studied kidnapping cases more than anyone else at the FBI. I know them inside out. I know the reason kids are taken, and I know the odds of solving these cases. I know what has worked to nab suspects and put them behind bars. I know the proven steps needed to get a child back alive. I know more about that than Hoover himself. This is my life's work, so you have the best person for this case in front of you right now!"

Meeker's eyes darted from George to Carole and then to the front glass. She took in the placid street scene for a second before shrugging her shoulders and walking over to the counter to pick up her purse and resolutely moving toward the door. As she grabbed the knob, she looked back at the Halls. "I wouldn't blame you if you didn't believe it, and I understand that you're angry and frustrated, but having a woman on this case is not the problem. If there is any way in the world to bring Rose home to you, I will or I will die trying."

The Halls might have said something, but if they did, the agent didn't hear it because she was already out the door. Sliding into her car, she hit the starter and pointed the Ford's hood toward Chicago.

Chapter 33

Meeker pushed her hair off her forehead and leaned against the desk she was using at FBI's Chicago office. As her legs pushed into the piece of furniture, she glanced across the room where her gaze fell on Henry Reese. As she was hitting nothing but dead ends, she hoped he was doing better. "What about Mr. Cason? Did you find him?"

"Yes and no," her partner explained. "I know where he is, but I can't get to him. He's on a ship bound for the Philippines. He won't be back in the States for six months."

"You're not giving me the news I want to hear, Henry. How about the car? Any leads on finding it?"

"We've got the cops in Indiana, Missouri, Kentucky, and Illinois looking for it, but nothing has turned up. For the last month we've had local radio stations all over the area putting out bulletins asking people for help, and there's hasn't been a single call. The car has simply disappeared."

She rubbed her forehead as she asked, "Do you think it's in a river someplace?"

"Maybe." He sighed. "Or perhaps chopped up for parts." He shook his head. "You've been out of the office. What have you been up to? You find anything?"

"I was with the parents yesterday," Meeker explained. "They're in bad shape. George has lost at least twenty pounds, and Carole looks like the walking dead. They aren't handling this well at all. But what can you expect? We have to give them something to hold on to. We have to give them some kind of hope!"

"Yeah," he said, "but we can't make up lies. That would be even worse than telling them nothing. And you know as well as I do what has likely happened."

She knew. Most kidnapped children were killed within three days of their abduction. A few survived as long as a week, and it'd been a month.

"So," he asked, "did you level with the Halls about the odds of us ever finding their child alive?"

She glanced over to her partner and shook her head. "Would you have?"

"No, but the fact is we aren't going to find that

201

kid. At some point they're going to have to face that fact."

"They won't have to be told," Meeker explained, "it will hit them like a ton of bricks when Rose's birthday rolls around. And at Christmas, they'll realize it then, too. For them, there won't be any light days or easy laughs, not for a long time. Maybe never."

Her words hung in the air like the smell coming from the stockyards. Neither of the agents could escape it. It filled their senses making them feel helpless and sick.

"You need to get away from this case," Reese suggested.

Pulling herself off her chair, she walked over to the window. Below her, just like it had been every day for the past month, was Chicago. Maybe Rose was down there.

"What are we missing?" Meeker asked.

"I can't think of anything," Reese answered.

"Do you think this was pulled off by just one person?" she asked, folding her arms over her blue suit as she turned back to face her partner.

"My gut feeling?" he asked as he raised his eyebrows.

"Yeah, what does your gut say?"

"No," the man answered. "It would have to be two people to make it work this smoothly. One to get the girl and hold her, the other to watch the family."

"And to know about those ten one-hundred-dollar bills," Meeker added, "at least one of those involved has to be from Oakwood."

Moving quickly to her desk, she picked up the phone and dialed seven numbers.

"Meeker here! Get me a list of all those who bought flowers or anything else from the family's flower shop the week before Rose Hall was kidnapped. Interview Mrs. Hall and try to get her to recall every person who came into her shop. And get a complete list of anyone who might have known where the family got the money for the down payment. I want to grill that list like they're associates of Al Capone."

"We've already done that a couple of times," her partner noted.

She put the phone down and looked back at Reese. "And we need to do it again. And, Henry, we have to find that car!"

Chapter 34

At Bynum Aluminum, Bill Landers had gone from goat to king in a matter of a week. The company plant and offices were alive with activity thanks to three new large accounts the salesman had landed. With a huge bonus in the bank and a raise in salary, Landers was awash in cash for the first time in his life. He was also off the road for a while, too. Until the company could hire another full shift of workers, Bynum couldn't handle any other new contracts.

It was almost six on a busy Friday night when Landers walked into Doris's Café. The staff knew him well. At least three times a week he grabbed a meal at the counter. To honor their most loyal customer, Doris Sinks had even had his name painted on one of the counter's stools.

Easing down in his centrally located spot, Landers looked across the counter to a new face. She wasn't movie-star beautiful, but there was a kind of fresh cuteness about the dark-eyed brunette that he rarely saw in a woman approaching forty. She had a few wrinkles around her eyes and a softness at her chin, but it just served to add to her wholesome mystique.

"You must be Bill," she announced as she approached him. "Doris has told me all about you."

He'd never been good around women. He'd always stumbled on his words when trying to talk to them. His mother said he'd grow out of his shyness, but he never did. The woman he married, Betty Scroggins, had trapped him. She was pushy, six feet tall, and had the arms of a lumberjack. She'd asked him out on his twenty-first birthday, from their first date she had controlled everything and, simply because she'd told him, they'd married two months later. It lasted a year until she found someone older who could provide her with a lot more than Landers could. So at twenty-two he found himself divorced. Since that time he could count on one hand the number of women he'd taken out.

So rather than say anything to the new waitress, he did what he always did when attractive women talked to him—he just nodded.

"I understand you are quite the salesman," the woman continued with a tone as sweet and warm as heated maple syrup.

"Well," he replied, "I've done pretty well recently."

"Congrats," she sang out. "Then you have reasons to celebrate. My name is Coco Cakes. And please don't make fun of it."

"I haven't heard of a name like that before," he said, "but it would seem to be a good handle for someone who waits tables in this place. Doris is famous for her chocolate cake."

"So I've learned."

"Why did your folks name you Coco?" he asked. Realizing he might be treading into an area he shouldn't, he quickly added, "If you don't mind me asking."

"My dad thought it went well with Kalen." She smiled.

"Kalen? But I thought you said your name was Cakes."

"Traded in Kalen for Cakes when I got married," she explained.

The news took the air out of the imaginary balloon Landers had just launched. So much for anything more than small talk over the counter.

"John was a good man, too," she continued. "We had a couple of great kids together. He made a good living as a foreman in a coal mine back in West Virginia. But a cave-in a couple of years back took him from me. The girls are on their own now. I needed a job and landed here."

Landers felt a tinge of guilt in silently celebrating another man's death, but that quickly passed as he looked into the woman's face. "How did you get here from West Virginia?"

"Got a sister who lives in Benton," she explained. "She urged me to move out here and get a fresh start. I came in March. Got settled in and landed this job. Been hearing about you ever since, but today was the first time my shift came during one of your visits."

"I'm glad it did," he said.

"What would you like to order?" Her smile was wider than before.

"How about a turkey sandwich, some fried potatoes, and a cup of coffee?"

"I can arrange that," she assured him.

As she turned and sauntered back to toward the kitchen, his eyes followed her every move. She might have been carrying a few extra pounds, but at this very moment Landers would have rather spent his night talking to Coco than Ginger Rogers.

Chapter 35

"I can't do it anymore, Carole."

Carole glanced up from the kitchen table and looked across to her husband. The dark circles under his eyes now dipped below his cheekbones. He was drawn; streaks of gray were showing up in his hair; and he had the hangdog look of a man at death's door.

"George, you just have to keep the faith."

"I can't," he said. "And I don't want to either. It's been six weeks, and she's not coming back. She's gone and I have to admit that. It's easier to think of her as dead than alone, frightened, maybe abused."

"George . . ."

"No, Carole, don't try to find any words to lift my spirits. I don't want them lifted. I want to face the facts. I failed as a father. I failed as a husband because I didn't protect her for you. I've let everyone down. The world would be better off if I'd never been born."

She pushed her chair back from the table and walked over to a spot behind the man. Placing her hands on his shoulders she whispered, "I need you, George. I couldn't go on without you here. And you didn't let Rose down. What happened was beyond your control. If anyone should be feeling guilty, it's me. She was with me when she was taken. I was the one who didn't protect her."

She'd thought those thoughts a hundred times, but she'd never said them out loud before now. And facts were facts. She was the person Rose had depended on that day to make everything all right, and she was the one who let her daughter down in the worst way a parent could.

"Maybe we need to call Reverend Morris," she suggested.

Jerking to his feet and pushing her hands off him, George roared, "I don't need a preacher! I don't want to hear about this being God's plan. If there is a God, I hate Him for letting this happen!"

"George . . ."

"Don't go there, Carole! I mean what I said, and I'm tired of pretending I don't."

Through horrified eyes she watched him stomp out of the kitchen, through the living room, and out the front door. A few seconds later, she heard the old Dodge they'd bought a few weeks before start up. She knew where he was going, but she tried to pretend that she didn't. She couldn't stand the thought of him drowning his anger and frustration at a tavern. Yet the fact was, he spent more time there now than he did at home. And perhaps, in a strange way, that place offered him something she couldn't—the ability to forget.

She dragged herself into Rose's room. It was

just as it had been the day she'd been taken. Her pajamas were still lying on the foot of the bed, and the stuffed lion she so loved was still in the rocking chair. As she inventoried the room, her eyes filled with tears. George was right. Rose wasn't coming back. Yet, unlike her husband, Carole did not hope Rose was dead. In fact, the only prayer on her heart was that somewhere Rose was with a woman who would love her and give her all the things that Carole had planned to give her.

Picking up the yellow lion from the chair, she adjusted the ribbon collar and then hugged it. If only there were a way that she could somehow hold her daughter the very same way. But George was right; it was time to admit the obvious. It was time to let go, even if she couldn't pick up the pieces and start all over. And to do that, she was going to have to do something she dreaded doing.

Dropping the stuffed lion onto the bed, she walked out to the garage. There were three empty cardboard boxes at the back. She retrieved them and retraced her steps back to Rose's room. Opening the top drawer of a chest, she began to pull each tiny outfit out one at a time. She quickly studied them, tracing a button or a stitch, before dropping them into the box. This trip down memory lane was the most painful journey in her life. There was a story behind each piece of clothing, each shoe, each toy, and each book. And putting those stories into boxes was like sticking a coffin into the ground and covering it with six feet of dirt. She was burying her daughter one item at a time.

When the last thing was packed and the bed had been stripped, she carried the boxes back to the garage and placed them in the corner. Stepping back, she studied her forty-five minutes of work. In the harsh light of a single one-hundred-watt bulb was the sum total of Rose's life. It seemed to be little to show for a child who'd brought her so much love.

Glancing down, she noted another empty box sitting against a far wall. Tears began to stream down her face as she studied it. That box held the memories that would never be made and the dreams that could never be realized. That empty box, much more than the full ones, represented what she'd lost.

Falling to her knees, Carole began to sob. "I'm so sorry, baby. I'm so sorry."

Chapter 36

August 2, 1940

What a day it had been! Without ever leaving the office or putting a single mile on his Packard, Bill Landers had closed two additional deals. Even before this pair of new contracts, the deals he'd landed in the past two months had turned Bynum Aluminum upside down. In the four months since he had landed that first deal, the company was running three shifts seven days a week just to keep up with demand. And yet the success he was having as salesman paled when compared to his personal life. Landers was in love, and the feeling was like nothing he'd ever experienced.

As he pulled the Packard up to Coco's small duplex, he couldn't help but laugh. Why had he suddenly been so blessed? Where had it all turned around for him? He could trace the change down to one event—the moment he bought the car. That was when everything had changed. Old Blue was his version of a good luck charm.

"How you doing, good looking?" Coco asked as she walked out her front door to his car.

Landers smiled at the woman who'd obviously been so excited about their date she'd been waiting on the porch for him to pick her up.

"I don't look that great," he corrected her. "*You* are the good looking one in this duo."

"We'll call it a draw," she said as she leaned down to kiss him through the driver's window.

After the extended kiss, Landers opened the door and stepped out so that she could slip into the car. When she was in the middle of the bench seat, he slid in beside her. "Where to?"

"I think we should try that new catfish place out on the highway," she suggested. "I hear it's great!"

"Perfect," he answered.

As Coco turned on the radio and searched for a station, George announced, "Two more big deals today. You know what that means, don't you?"

After tuning in a popular music station and smiling as the strains of Glen Miller filled the car, she glanced his way. "What does it mean, sugar?"

"That house, the yellow one just off Main Street—I can buy it with cash."

"Good for you!" She laughed. "That's a great place. I love the yard and that little fence out front."

"So do I," he agreed. After swinging the Packard around the corner, he headed down Main Street. Neither of them spoke until he pulled up in front of the home he was hoping to buy.

"Get out," he ordered as he threw open the driver's door.

"Well, aren't you being bossy?" she announced,

pretending to be put off by his assertive manner.

"Sorry," he said, softening his tone. "Would you please join me on the front porch?"

Sliding out of the car and taking his arm, she smiled. "I'd love to."

He escorted her up the walk and onto the wrap-around porch, directing her to a swing in front of a set of bay windows. "Have a seat, my lady."

She grinned and eased down. A second later, he joined her.

"I like that dress. Is it new?"

"Thank you for noticing, and yes it is."

The checked green pattern in the shirtdress and the solid belt that separated the top from the bottom displayed the best facets of her figure. As he studied her from neck to ankle and back up, she giggled. "The way you're taking inventory, I feel like a teenage girl again."

"And you look a lot better than any girl I've seen in a long time. Maybe ever."

"Bill . . ."

She looked into the nearest window and then back to the street. "Are you sure no one will mind on us sitting here? You don't own this place yet."

"No one lives here," he explained, "and the agent told me to come on by and look it over. She even gave me a key. Want to see it?"

Coco didn't have a chance to answer as Landers reached into his suit coat pocket and retrieved a small item. A hopeful grin covered his face as he held a diamond ring between the index finger and thumb of his right hand and pushed it toward her.

"That's not a key," she whispered.

"Yes it is," he assured. "This is the key to my heart, and if you don't accept it then I don't need the one to this house."

"You're asking me to marry you?" Her words dripped with sweetness.

Sliding off the swing, he got down on one knee, looked into her eyes, and said, "Coco, will you do me the honor of being my bride?"

She didn't speak, but she did nod and take the ring from his hand. Slipping it onto her finger she whispered, "It's a perfect fit."

Chapter 37

"What a night!" Coco announced as Landers escorted her out of the restaurant and to his car.

"Well"—he laughed—"I'm still not sure fried fish and Cokes are the best way to celebrate an engagement, but it is Friday."

"So it is," she said.

After they slid into the car and he slipped it into reverse, she leaned over and kissed him. As their lips met, his foot slipped off the clutch and the car lunged backward. Before Landers could hit the brake, the Packard's rear, driver's-side fender introduced itself to the front passenger side of a 1940 Ford coupe.

"Hey," a man's voice screamed out, "watch what you're doing!"

Pulling his lips away from Coco's, Landers hit the brake, slid the transmission into first, and eased forward. After he shut the motor off, he glanced over to his date.

She shrugged and giggled. "That was probably my fault."

He winked, pushed open the door, and walked back to survey the damage.

"What were you thinking?" the stranger demanded.

"I wasn't," Landers admitted. "I just got engaged and kind of had my head in the clouds. This is all my fault. I'll cover the damages."

The stranger, dressed in a black suit and white shirt, took off his dress hat and studied the two cars. "I think your car came out worse than mine. My Ford's got a scratch, but yours is creased pretty good."

Landers nodded. There was a deep foot-long dent down the side of the fender that had literally scraped the paint off.

But the salesmen was in too good a mood to worry about the fender, so he just smiled and asked, "What do you think it will cost to get your Ford fixed?"

The stranger shrugged. "It belongs to Uncle Sam. My name's Reese."

"That's great!" Landers laughed. "Of all people to hit, I pick an employee of the good ole USA! Do you think twenty would fix it?"

"Probably," Reese shot back, "but can you give me your name and number?"

"Sure," the salesman replied while reaching into his inside coat pocket and pulling out a business card. "This has my name and office number."

Reese took the card, studied it for a moment, and then stuck out his hand. As Landers took it the agent asked, "You're William Landers?"

"Yeah, but most folks call me Bill."

"You know how the government is," Reese said, "I'll need to copy your license number and the year, make, and model of your car, too."

"The number on my driver's license is 33478. And the car is a 1936 Packard sedan. Need anything else?"

"No," Reese assured him, "that's all I need."

Landers walked back toward the driver's seat, but the agent's voice stopped him just as he reached for the door handle.

"Mr. Landers. Is your car a six or an eight?"

"It's an eight. And what a ride it is! Well, good night, and don't hesitate to call if I need to get you any more money. Once again, I'm so sorry I wasn't more careful."

After sliding in the car, starting the motor, and

pulling forward, Landers looked over at his fiancée and grinned. "The night is still young; let's have some fun!"

Coco's face showed a bit of anxiety, and her tone was deeply apologetic, "Did my kiss get you in trouble?"

"No." He laughed. "But it did cost me twenty bucks. And I must admit, that kiss was worth every penny."

Chapter 38

The ringing phone pulled Helen Meeker's nose out of the file she was studying. Setting the folder on her desk, she picked up the receiver.

"Meeker."

"Helen, it's Henry."

"You still in Arkansas? Figured you'd have that case put to bed and be on your way back to the Windy City."

"One piece of the art heist was missing," he explained. "It'd been sold to a local banker. The banker had no idea it was hot. So I had to stick around an extra day to get that painting. The museum in Chicago will be happy we got it all, and none of it has been damaged."

"Well," she replied, "at least we've solved one case this summer."

"And, Helen, you aren't going to believe this. I

literally ran into something that might be a lead on the Hall kidnapping."

After leaning back in her chair and taking a slow, deep breath, she anxiously asked, "You think so?"

"Maybe," he answered. "There was a car that backed into my car last night. There wasn't much damage; in fact it did more damage to his car than the FBI's Ford, but there may have been just enough damage on his vehicle to uncover a clue."

"A fender bender gave you a clue on our case?" She was having problems making the connection.

"Yeah, this guy, William Landers, was driving a dark blue 1936 Packard sedan—"

"So?" Meeker cut in. "There are thousands of them in this country, and the one in the Hall case was bright yellow."

"It had been repainted blue," Reese explained. "And that blue paint had been added very recently. The scrape revealed that the factory color was yellow. Bright yellow!"

Meeker bolted to her feet and leaned back against the office wall as she spoke into the phone. "Are you sure it was bright yellow and not cream?"

"Yeah," he assured her. "I went by the guy's place early this morning while he was still asleep. It is the brightest yellow I've ever seen. And the only thing under that yellow is primer and metal."

"What else you got?"

"Well, I did a little digging. . . . Landers's district covers Illinois and Indiana, as well as Kentucky, Missouri, and Kansas. I tracked down the company's owner today at a diner and struck up a conversation with him. His name is Calvin Bynum. It seems Landers brought the car back from one of his sales trips to Indiana. He told his boss he got a great deal on it and paid for it in cash."

"Have you had a chance to check if he's got any kind of record?"

"Officially," Reese replied, "I haven't checked. I'll let you put the bloodhounds on that from your end. It will create a lot less suspicion. But the locals tell me he's been a model citizen his whole life."

"If his past is clean, we can't just arrest him," she shot back, her tone and machine gun delivery betraying her excitement, "but we can bring him in and question him as a possible material witness."

"You want in on it?" Reese asked.

"Yeah," she assured him, "I'll catch the first plane to Little Rock. Don't come get me. I'll have a car waiting at the airport. Don't let him know we are on to him, but keep an eye on him. And get me a room at wherever you're staying. We'll need to light a very hot fire under Mr. Landers."

"Got it."

"I'll leave a message at your hotel once I know when I'm going to get there." Meeker paused before adding, "Thanks, Henry."

She didn't wait for him to reply before setting the receiver in its cradle. There was suddenly a lot to do. First she had to get her plane reservations, and then she had to get any records she could find on William Landers of Bryant, Arkansas.

Chapter 39

Meeker observed Landers from Reese's car parked two houses down the block. In the sunlight she could even see the yellow paint on the back fender.

"There he is," Reese said, pointing to the man standing on the porch of the house.

She nodded and turned her gaze to the man's companion, "And the woman with him?"

"Her name is Coco Cakes," Reese explained. "The owner of the diner where she works says she's a widow from West Virginia. Moved here earlier this year. Here's the file on her. It is interesting reading."

Meeker opened the folder and glanced through several pages of material. Finally, she raised her eyebrows and laughed. "Interesting, to say the least!"

"Thought you'd think so." Meeker glanced at

her watch. It was almost six. "Have they eaten supper yet?"

"No," Reese replied. "I've been on his tail since noon. Coco must've gotten off of work at the diner about thirty minutes ago."

"Good," Meeker quipped. "People seem to rattle more easily when they're hungry. I want to see this through with no gunfire. Let's play it step-by-step and slowly put pressure on the couple to talk. As you are the bigger and more intimidating, I suggest you take the lead."

Reese nodded, his eyes still on the couple as he asked, "Do we run them up to Little Rock for questioning?"

"No," Meeker said. "We don't want them to have an hour to think about their stories. We'll grab them on that swing and talk to them right there at the house. They'll be a lot more nervous if they know their friends can see what's going on."

"You ready?" Reese asked.

"Let's go, Henry," Meeker said.

The agents slid out of the black Ford and with long, determined steps crossed the street and came through the gate and up the walk to the porch. They had mounted the steps and were on the porch's wooden plank floor before either Landers or the woman looked up.

"William Landers?" Reese barked.

"Hey," he said, his tone friendly but his face

registering a bit of confusion. "You're the G-man from yesterday. . . ."

"Put your hands over your head," Reese ordered. "Both of you."

"What?" Coco demanded.

"Put your hands over your head, lady," Reese explained, pulling out a service revolver to emphasize his demands.

"What's this all about?" Landers questioned in an apologetic tone. "I'm sorry I hit your car. If twenty dollars is not enough to cover the damage, I'll make good. I promise."

"This isn't about the accident," Reese assured him. "Now get your hands up, or I'll lift them for you. And if I do, your shoulders might just come out of their sockets."

Meeker took a step forward, "As Mr. Landers knows, but you, Miss Cakes, might not, this man is Henry Reese. Henry is a special investigator for the FBI. My name is Helen Meeker. I'm an investigator for a presidential task force that works with the Secret Service. I'm on loan to the FBI."

She studied their reactions. Landers was shocked —his knees were shaking and his mouth was agape. The woman was much more matter-of-fact. She showed no fear. In fact, if anything, she wore a look of contempt.

"Henry, I've got them covered," Meeker said as she pulled a gun from her purse, "why don't you check them for weapons."

"I can assure you," Landers explained, "I don't even own a gun."

"I'll search you anyway," Reese announced as he slipped his revolver back into his shoulder holster.

The agent patted them both down. They were clean. But Coco's purse was another matter.

"Well, what have we here?" Reese exclaimed, pulling a small twenty-two pistol from the bag.

A shocked Landers looked over at his fiancée. She shrugged. "A single woman has to be able to protect herself."

"Turn around and drop your hands behind your back," Meeker ordered.

A minute later, when Reese had completed cuffing them, he spun them around and pushed them down onto the swing. Putting her gun on a porch table, Meeker took a seat in a wooden deck chair. The male agent propped himself on the porch railing.

Meeker leaned close to Landers and said, "Tell us about your car."

"The Packard?"

"Do you own another car?"

"No."

"According to our records," Reese cut in, "you don't have a title."

"You're still running Missouri plates, too," Meeker added.

"That's what this is about?" Landers moaned.

"I've got a bill of sale. The man I bought it from was supposed to send me the title. I–I–I've been working so much I guess I forgot about it. But I got his name on the bill of sale. It's in the glove box. I swear to that. You can go out and get it right now. That'll clear this whole thing up."

Meeker looked to her partner and then back to the flustered salesman. "Where did you buy it?"

"Some little town south of St. Louis. At a diner."

"Yeah," Reese mocked, "that's where everyone buys their cars. I can't count how many folks I know who ordered a hot dog, some chips, and a Chevy."

"No, you have to believe me," Landers pleaded. "I bought it from a man I met at a diner. My car broke down, and he was selling his uncle's Packard."

"What did you pay?" Meeker demanded.

"A–A–A one hundred and fifty. No, I talked him down. It was one twenty-five."

"Kind of cheap for a nice car with new paint," Reese hissed.

"I couldn't believe it either," Landers explained, "but you don't look a gift horse in the mouth. At least that's what I was always told."

"So you had no idea," Meeker cut in, "that this car was used in a crime. In fact, it was stolen from a family in Illinois."

Landers shook his head. "I guess maybe that is why the guy sold it so cheap."

"Let me tell you how it was," Reese said. "You were doing a lousy job as a salesman. You lived in a crummy house and were driving a beat-up sedan that was on its last set of spark plugs. You had to have some cash, so, in your travels someone told you about a family with a kid who had some money. You grabbed the kid, demanded a ransom of five thousand. Then you stole the car when they delivered the money."

"What?" Landers said. "I don't know what you're talking about."

"Listen, buster," Meeker cut in, "we checked your schedule. You were in Illinois the week the kid was taken. The day after the money was dropped and the car and kid disappeared, you were in Terre Haute, Indiana. That's within a stone's throw of where the car was last seen. And right after that, the folks around here said you not only had this nice Packard but you were rolling in dough."

"Wait just a minute," Coco chimed in. "You're a kidnapper?"

"Don't pretend you didn't know about this," Reese said as he pointed his finger in the woman's face.

"Hey," she spat back, "I might be a lot of things, but I don't go after kids."

"What do you mean?" Landers asked, his eyes locked on hers. "You're a lot of things?"

"You didn't know?" Meeker asked.

"Know what?"

"Your girlfriend is a player," Meeker explained with a smile. "She finds lonely men who have a roll of cash. She charms them, marries them, and then they somehow end up dead. She's been arrested three times for suspicion of murder."

"They never proved it," Coco hissed.

"There are two other cases pending," Reese added. "She's had five husbands that we know about who have mysteriously died within months of marrying her."

"People get sick," Coco smirked. "Accidents happen."

"And, Landers," Meeker chimed in, "you would have been number six. She had you marked. You'd fallen hard, and you couldn't wait to make her your little wife."

"But what about her daughters?" the salesman asked.

Coco spat, "I'm not saying anything else until I get a lawyer."

The realization that he'd been played hit the salesman like a shot from an Army tank. As Reese and Meeker let the news sink in, a siren howled in the distance. The agents watched as two local cops pulled up at the house and raced up with guns drawn.

"What's going on here?" a small, fat deputy asked.

"Would you allow me to pull some identification out of my jacket pocket?" Reese asked.

"Don't do anything stupid, and move slow," the fat man nervously ordered.

"No problem." Reese smiled. With both cops nervously looking on, the agent gently inched his left hand into his coat and pulled out his FBI badge and ID.

"A G-man," the other cop announced, his tone showing both astonishment and awe.

"And my partner works for President Roosevelt."

"What are you doing with Bill here?" the fat one asked.

"He's in possession of a stolen car at best," Meeker explained, "and involved in a kidnapping and murder at worst. We haven't fully sorted that out yet."

"What about Coco?" the taller one inquired.

"Well," Meeker continued, "she's wanted in a half dozen states for everything from suspicion of murder to theft. Don't know if she's tied up with what we want him for, but the fact that she came to town about the same time of the Hall kidnap-ping makes her a person of interest for us, too. Would you mind taking her downtown and throwing her in the jail? You can find more than enough outstanding warrants to hold her for a long time. I've got her file in the car. I'll bring it down when we bring this guy down to the station."

"Okay. Come along, Coco," the tall cop ordered.

"My real name's Debbie," she corrected him as Reese unlocked her handcuffs from the swing then locked them back to her wrists as the tall officer took hold of her shoulder.

"Actually," Reese added, "it is Margaret Mason O'Toole. She's from Andover, Kansas. So book her under that name."

"Come on, Miss O'Toole."

The woman and her escorts walked crisply out to the squad car. Only when they were about a block down the street did the agents turn back to Landers.

"I had no idea," he whispered. "I thought she was as pure as the driven snow."

Reese shook his head and looked over to Meeker. She shrugged.

"Want to continue here?" Reese asked his partner.

"Let's take him downtown," she replied. "I think the neighbors have heard enough."

Chapter 40

After they'd put Landers in the backseat of the Ford and searched the Packard, Reese pointed the car toward the local jail. Glancing toward the front passenger seat, he asked his partner, "Do you want to take him to Bryant station or back to your motel room? Might be easier to work him over without the local cops watching."

Meeker studied the driver for a moment and quickly caught his drift. "Motel's fine with me. I haven't seen your short, powerful jabs since you won the FBI boxing crown last year."

She casually looked back at the salesman. His jaw had dropped to his chest, and all the color had drained from his face. As she continued to push his buttons with her cold stare, she added, "Of course the local cops have a real problem on their hands if we opt to not check in with them."

"What's that?" Reese asked.

"You have the key to the cuffs the woman is sporting, and her file is here in the car. If they have a private room at the jail, we can still work our guest over there."

"It's your call," he replied.

"Let's go to the jail," she suggested, "unless Mr. Landers wants us to just pull the car over right here and visit. He looks to be in a visiting mood. What about it?"

"I–I–I'll answer anything you want. You don't have to get rough with me."

Moving so she was sideways in the seat, Meeker studied their prisoner. He was quaking in his shoes and had tears rolling down his cheeks.

"Henry, just keep driving around town. We'll see how cooperative Mr. Landers is. If he doesn't give out with the information we want during our ride, then we can go to the room and try your method."

Meeker licked her lips before picking a piece of paper from the seat beside her. She held it in her hand as she gently posed her question. "Bill—I believe that is what your friends call you, is that right?"

He quickly nodded.

"Okay, Bill, I fished this bill of sale out of the Packard's glove box while Henry was putting you in our car. You claim this was given to you when you bought the car at the diner?"

"That's the truth," he immediately answered.

"Did anyone see you make this transaction?"

"No, I didn't know anyone there. Hold it. Wait a minute, there was a kid working behind the counter. I talked to him about it. He could back up my story."

"Do you recall his name?"

"No, but I can describe him. And he'd know me, I'm sure of that."

Meeker glanced over to Reese. "I've got a couple of samples of Bill's handwriting from stuff I found in the glove box. It's not anywhere close to what's on this piece of paper. And the date on this sales slip is about a month after the kid was taken."

"His partner likely wrote it up to give them a cover," the other agent shot back. "I'm still thinking this is the guy. When I work him over, he'll fess up."

Meeker moved her gaze back to the fidgeting,

handcuffed man in the backseat. "Okay, Bill, tell me about the guy who supposedly sold you the car."

The sweating man swallowed hard. "My throat is so dry—"

"The man who sold you the car is what we're talking about," Meeker cut him off.

Landers nervously shook his head. His lips trembled as he began, "He had on what looked like a new suit. I think it was dark, but I don't remember if it was black, blue, or brown. It might have even been gray. He was normal height and build, and his face was kind of pockmarked. I don't remember the color of his eyes, but they were kind of dark and set deep into his skull. I guess you would call them beady."

Meeker waved her hand. "Bill, you've just described every cheap hood in all the Hollywood movies. That doesn't bode well for you. Give me something that makes me believe you were actually there and that this man really exists, or I'm afraid I'll have to let Henry get this information the old-fashioned way. I don't have to tell you how much he loves that interrogation method."

Landers shook his head and sighed. "I was looking at the car more than the man. He was just a normal guy. Nothing stood out. No, wait! There was one thing—when we were driving around, he smoked a cigarette."

"Lots of folks smoke," Reese cut in from the

driver's seat. "Don't think that fact limits the field much."

"It's not that he smoked," Landers said, his voice suddenly excited, "it's how he smoked. He held his cigarette between his little and ring fingers. I'd never seen anyone do that before."

"Bill," Meeker continued, "I want you to fully understand something. A little girl was kidnapped in your car back in March. At that time the car was yellow. Five thousand dollars was also taken at the same time. That little three-year-old girl is still missing. Whoever took her is staring at a long stretch in prison if we find her alive. If we find out they killed her, they're going to fry. I've watched an execution; I've seen a man sit in Old Sparky when they throw the switch." Meeker paused, glanced out the window at a tiny row of buildings. "It isn't pretty," she finished.

Silence filled the car for a long moment while she let that sink in. She drummed her gloved fingers on the car's seat for effect before continuing, "When they threw the switch, the man's body went stiff, his hands grabbed the chair, and smoke poured off the top of his head. He shook like a rag doll for more than thirty seconds—that's an eternity. Then they cut the switch, and a doctor went to him. He took out his stethoscope and checked the guy out. You know what?"

A now very frightened Landers shook his head.

"He wasn't dead. They had to do it again. This

time he screamed. I'd never heard a scream like that. Horrible. Before he finally gave up the ghost they had literally cooked the guy."

Landers, now as pale as a sheet, swallowed hard.

"Here's the deal, Bill," Meeker explained, "we want that kid back. If you just tell us where she is, I'll make sure you get a break. And if she's dead, I can keep you out of the death chamber and make sure you just get prison. You don't want to sit in Old Sparky. So are you going to come clean, or do we just let matters roll the way they roll?"

"I only bought the car. That's all!"

"Henry," Meeker said, "pull over to the curb."

After the car had come to a stop in a quiet residential district, her eyes locked onto Landers and she spoke in slow, measured tones. "Bill, your work log puts you within a few miles of the crime on the day when the kid was snatched and the money and car were taken. The car you're driving is the car! We checked and verified the numbers last night when you were asleep. It has been painted, which any jury will believe was to keep it from being spotted. I'm a lawyer, the daughter of one of the best prosecutors in the history of the state of New York. Any jury in the world would find you guilty even without us ever producing a body. So why don't you just come clean with us? Tell us if you killed Rose Hall, and if you didn't kill her, tell us where she is."

Meeker stared directly into the man's face. The salesman had the look of a hopeless traveler who just found out his next stop was hell. His lips were dry, his eyes moist, and his skin almost gray. After three minutes, he finally sighed. "I know you don't believe me, but I don't know what you're talking about. All I did was buy a car."

Meeker glanced from their prisoner to her partner and ordered, "Bill, you stay here and don't move." She then signaled Reese to meet her outside the Ford.

After they were both out of the vehicle and had walked around to the sidewalk, she said, "He wasn't involved."

Reese nodded. "Yep, he doesn't have the stomach for it."

"He's a sucker," Meeker added.

"His involvement with that black widow pretty much proves he's desperate enough to believe what people tell him. He bought that car knowing it was too good a deal to be true. Deep in his head he likely knew it was hot. But he had to have it. So, he played the odds."

"And," Reese moaned, "where does that leave us?"

"Let's check out the woman and see if she is connected, which I doubt, and then I have to backtrack and find the guy who sold Landers the car. The kid at the diner might be able to give us a lead on him."

"Want me to call the St. Louis office," the man suggested, "and have them get to work on it?"

"No, Henry, we need to do this ourselves. And we're going to take Bill Landers with us. If the kid recognizes him, we'll know for sure his story checks. Landers and the kid might be able to work together to give us a better picture of . . . what was the name on that bill of sale?"

"John Smith," Reese quipped.

"Boy," Meeker grimly replied, "old Bill is even dumber than I thought. Let's hope he can give us a clearer picture of this John Smith."

Chapter 41

Meeker had the Packard shipped by express rail back to the FBI lab in Chicago before the trio began their trek to St. Louis. Landers had been allowed to pack a bag and inform his boss he needed to take a few days off. Whether those days turned into a long stretch in prison would be determined by what they found at the greasy spoon just outside the gateway city. The trio checked into a hotel for a few hours' sleep before driving out to St. Charles. It was just past eight when they pulled into the diner's parking lot.

"So, this is the place?" Meeker asked.

"Yeah," Landers assured her. "He brought the car to a spot right over there. I looked it over under that streetlight before taking it for a spin. We concluded the deal in the parking place where that gray Hudson is sitting right now."

"Seems things are coming back into focus," Reese noted.

"Sure are," the salesman answered, "and the guy's eyes were a really dark brown. Almost black."

"It'd be too dark in the parking lot to see that," Meeker argued.

"Yeah, but he sat beside me in the diner. I'm also remembering some kind of deep scar on the index finger of his right hand. And he didn't have a fingernail on that finger."

Reese looked over to Meeker and smiled. "You were right to bring old Bill along. Let's get inside and hope the kid is manning the counter tonight."

The trio walked in and stopped just inside the entry. As the agents studied the fifty or so patrons who had chosen this dive for their Tuesday dinner, Landers spotted the kid. With hope in his step he moved quickly to the bar. Pushing between a man in jeans and a work shirt and an older woman wearing a striped dress, he got the counter attendant's attention.

"What's your need, sir?" the kid inquired.

"Do you remember me?" Landers asked at just the moment he was joined by the agents.

The kid took a look into the man's face before asking, "Should I?"

"I was here on April 23rd and ate a ham on rye.

It cost thirty-five cents, and I gave you two quarters and told you to keep the change."

The kid shrugged. "There are a lot of folks who place that order and pay like that. Unless they come back over and over, I don't remember any of them. Besides, that was forever ago."

"You've got to remember," Landers pleaded.

"I'm sorry," the kid sincerely answered, "but I don't. That doesn't mean you weren't here; it's just that we're on the highway and we get so many people that come in and go out. I never really look at any of them. A guy I served yesterday or this afternoon could come in, and odds are I wouldn't know him."

Landers's shoulders sank as he glanced back at Meeker. The agent shrugged and moved toward the counter. She pulled her identification out of her bag and showed it to the kid.

"What's your name?"

"Danny Fisher."

"Okay, Danny, Mr. Landers needs you to help him and so does the FBI. You've got to think real hard."

"I didn't know there were lady G-men. Wow!"

Shaking her head, Meeker continued, "The night Mr. Landers came in he was having car problems. His Studebaker had died. He had to find a car so he could get to an appointment in Indianapolis the next day. He met a man here that night who offered to sell him a Packard sedan."

Fisher's face remained blank. It was obvious he had no clue.

Meeker looked over to her companions. It seemed this was going to be a dry run. They were no closer to the kidnappers than they had been a month ago. It looked like it was up to the lab boys to find something in the car.

"Danny," she said as she turned back to the boy, "here's my card. If you remember meeting Mr. Landers, call me collect."

"Sure," he said, reaching out to take it.

"Let's go," Meeker announced.

As they moved toward the door, Landers stopped dead in his tracks, turned, and rushed back to the counter. "Danny, I came back in that night, and I asked you if I could trust the guy who was selling me the car. You said he'd been in every day for a few weeks and he lived with a family down the street. Their name was . . ."

"Hooks," the kid announced. "Sure, now I remember. The guy was quiet, kind of grumpy, had a weird finger."

"That's him!" Landers gleefully announced. "Did you hear that, Miss Meeker?"

"You told me he lived with the Hooks family?"

The kid nodded. "And you gave me a buck for the information. I remember it all now!"

Meeker eased back to the counter and asked, "Has he been in here recently?"

"No," Fisher replied, "it has been a long time since I've seen him."

"What about the family?"

"The place where they were staying is for rent. It's on Balmer Street, just off of Vine. It's a gray house, two-story. The paint is faded. But like I said, they aren't there, and the last I heard they moved west back in the early summer."

"Any idea where?" Meeker demanded.

"No, I went to high school with their only kid. A girl. Got killed in a car accident last year. I never knew the old man or woman."

"Thanks, Danny," the agent replied. "You've been a big help."

As they moved out the door and got back into the car, a suddenly hopeful Landers posed a question, "So you got something you need?"

"We got something," Reese admitted, "and no matter how little that is, it's the first break we've had in the case." He turned to his partner. "Where to next, Helen?"

"Chicago to be with the lab crew when they go through that car. But I want you to stay here and see if you can track down the Hookses. If we can find them then we can get a lead on our mysterious car salesman. He's the key to this whole thing."

"Can I go back home?" Landers asked.

Meeker shook her head. "Not until you spend some time with one of our sketch artists and then spend a couple of days going through some mug shots. Your memory was jogged tonight. I want to see what an artist can give us from your descriptions and if any of the faces of known criminals fits your car salesman.

"And, Henry," she went on, "get that boy to give our portrait makers his memories as well. Let's have a team go through fingerprint files looking for someone with a badly scarred index finger."

"Got it," Reese replied.

"But first"—she grinned—"let's go to the hotel. I need to pick up my things and get to the airport."

As Reese started the Ford and a very relieved Landers relaxed in the backseat, Meeker took another long look at the diner. The devil had been here. She could still feel his presence. And feeling the cold sting of evil was better than feeling nothing at all.

Chapter 42

The office phone was ringing as Meeker walked into the room. After she set her briefcase and purse down on the desk, she answered. A familiar voice was on the other end.

"Five rings, that's a record. I've never known it to take you more than three."

"I was just returning from lunch, Henry. A girl's got to eat. What's going on in St. Louis?

You've had two full days, surely you've got something."

"A sketch that matches no one in our files," he explained, "and no fingerprint matches, either, where the index finger matches a face anything like the guy that sold Landers the car. Worse yet, I can't find the Hookses. At least I can't find the mother."

"Okay," Meeker returned, "you left that door open. So I guess I'll walk in."

"Make yourself comfortable," Reese cracked. "Here is what I know for sure. Their names were Marge and Earl. They were pretty reclusive even before their daughter died. A neighbor said the mother took it real hard when Mary was killed. And it wasn't a car accident like the kid remembered. She was shot."

"Let me guess," Meeker cut in, "no leads on who did it."

"Yep, you guessed right. She was a good student, didn't run with the wrong crowd, and never got into any kind of trouble anyway. She was found in a city park. Whoever killed her did it execution style."

"Wow. No wonder the mother went into a shell."

"It gets better," Reese continued. "Earl died a few months ago. No one really knows how. Marge called it in, and the coroner ruled it a natural death. He was buried in a pauper's grave."

"How old was he?" Meeker asked.

"Helen, he was way too young to die of old age. The death certificate lists his age at forty-one. There was no autopsy as the body showed no obvious signs of foul play. Listen to this scoop —Hooks had no job, but local crime stoolies say he was connected to a gangster I've spent some time trying to catch. This guy is a real piece of work, too—Jack McGrew."

" 'Pistolwhip' McGrew?" she shot back.

"None other. I couldn't confirm it, but it makes a certain degree of sense since the family had no income that I could find."

"I'm guessing," Meeker jumped back on the line, "that when Hooks died Marge took off?"

"She moved," Reese confirmed, "but no one knows where. I took a trip down to Farmington, where she was born and raised, but no one had seen her there. Her only brother died of scarlet fever as a kid. Her parents died about a decade ago within a year of each other. The last time she was back in that area was for her mother's funeral. No one here has heard from her since."

"And that is your dead end."

"Yeah," Reese admitted. "I have no idea what direction to go now. It's like she disappeared into thin air."

"Then why don't you come back here?" Meeker suggested. "We'll show the sketch to the Halls and see if it means anything to them."

"See you tomorrow."

#87   08-31-2015 2:14PM
Item(s) checked out to p12106732.

TITLE: Darkness before dawn
BARCODE: 3 3028 00948 0825
DUE DATE: 09 21-15

TITLE: The yellow Packard
BARCODE: 3 3028 00946 0058
DUE DATE: 09-21-15

TITLE: Go set a watchman : a novel
BARCODE: 3 3028 01043 3433
DUE DATE: 09-21-15

Mishawaka Main

Meeker had no more than placed the receiver back in its cradle when the phone rang again. This time she answered on the first ring.

"Meeker."

"Helen, it's Becca. I've gone through the Packard. I could tell you over the phone, but knowing you, I figured you'd want to see it for yourself."

"Be right there." Dropping the phone back into place, Meeker took a sip of lukewarm coffee and headed out the door and down the hall to the elevator. Two minutes later, she was in the basement where the FBI's crime lab was housed. In one corner was the Packard. Standing beside it, grease covering several different parts of her white lab coat was Rebecca Bobbs.

Bobbs was not with the FBI. She worked for the OSS, but Meeker only had to make one call to Mrs. Roosevelt to secure the young woman's trip from Washington to Chicago. An Ohio native, Bobbs was one of the first female grads of OSS's crime lab training school. She was a bright, energetic blond blessed with a pert nose, blue eyes, and a beauty-queen smile. She employed her beautiful eyes to charm men while she noted the most minute of details at crime scenes. It was for that reason Meeker begged the First Lady to get FDR to have Bobbs pulled from a case in Maryland. She had flown in last night and immediately gone to work.

"So, what do you have, Becca?"

"I have a car that is pretty much clean, as far as evidence goes. The only fingerprints I could find in the obvious places were either from Landers or the black widow he was dating."

"So you have no prints?"

"None. But the blue paint is thin. It was a quick job. Whoever did it didn't take anything off the car. They just taped it and shot. I only found a couple of runs, so they knew what they were doing and had some skill. There are a thousand shops that do that sort of thing. They take a car the night it's stolen, quickly give it new color, and then sell it. You could probably find half a dozen vehicles just like this on used car lots within a couple of miles of here right now. Yet there is one thing that set this one apart."

"That is?"

Bobbs pointed to the sedan. "I found no prints at all in the paint. Usually the painter touches at least in one place, under a fender or the hood, while it is still wet with enough pressure to leave an impression. This guy must have been very, very careful."

"I'm not surprised," Meeker said, "considering this car was involved in a kidnapping. When you're looking at death row, you tend to cover your tracks. Becca, did you find anything I can actually use?"

"Maybe," the woman said as she opened the

back passenger door. The rear seat had been taken out and turned upside down. She flipped on a flashlight and shined it at a point between the padding and a seat spring. "Do you see that?"

Meeker leaned over, grabbed the light, and studied the spot. Under a spring was a small piece of paper. From behind her, Bobbs explained, "That's a part of some paper money."

"Can you take it out?" Meeker asked.

"Sure." Grabbing her tweezers, Bobbs carefully worked the scrap free. She then moved across the room to a table. "Let me unfold what's left." She grabbed a second set of tweezers and gingerly pulled the paper flat. The technician's ruler proved it was three quarters of an inch long and a half-inch wide.

The lab tech shook her head. "Not much there."

"Enough to know it's a C-note," Meeker said. "Let's bag it and hold on to that."

"Does it mean something?"

"Has to mean something. I just don't know what."

"Anything else?"

Walking back to the car, Bobbs opened the front passenger door and flipped the bottom cushion. Meeker came up beside her and looked in. There, stuck to the metal seat frame as if hidden to retrieve later, were two toy Scotty dogs. One was black and the other white.

"I've seen these," the agent noted, "or at least some like them."

"You can buy them pretty much anywhere," Bobbs quipped. "These dogs are each set on separate magnets and when you push them toward each other they rush to the other or push away. It's kind of a science lesson all about magnetic poles. Do you think they were the little girl's?"

"Probably," Meeker answered. "When you get finished testing them, have them sent to my office. I'm going to go see her folks in a couple of days. I'll take them down and ask."

"Will do. Sorry I couldn't find more."

"Thanks for flying in, Becca. I'll take you out for dinner next time I'm in DC."

As Bobbs took the toy dogs back to the lab table, Meeker studied the car. An idea was forming in her head. It was a long shot, but at this point she really had no other options. And if nothing came out of her next trip to Oakwood then it might be time to take some long shots.

Chapter 43

On Friday, Meeker made the three-hour drive to Oakwood alone. She didn't need Reese and felt it might go better if the Halls dealt with just one person. She walked into Carole's Flowers at three thirty. The owner was helping a teenager pick out a corsage for a weekend date. As the agent listened in on the conversation, she was able to deduce it was some kind of high school dance being held at the Danville Country Club. Oh, to be young and carefree again. On days like this, adult responsibilities weren't any fun at all.

In the five additional minutes it took for Carole Hall to convince the boy which flower was best and then fix the corsage and box it for him, Meeker thumbed through the latest issue of *Good Housekeeping*. She noted a recipe for a cream pie that looked tasty. She made a mental note to pick up a copy of the magazine when she went by a newsstand on her way to work on Monday.

As the bell atop the door rang, signaling that the boy had left the shop, Carole made her way to the corner where the agent stood. Meeker looked up and smiled. Though her eyes were sad and her complexion pale, the mother seemed be stronger than she had been during their last visit. Nevertheless, Meeker asked, "How are you doing?"

"As long as I'm working," Carole explained, her voice steady and strong, "I'm fine. The nights aren't very good." She paused, bit her lip, and added, "Thanks for the card you sent on Rose's birthday. It meant a lot."

"It wasn't enough." The agent sighed. "Not nearly enough."

Carole walked over to the window and looked out at the now empty street. "When you called I got my hopes up a little. But you'd have said something on the phone if you'd found Rose. That is unless you found her and she's . . ." She obviously couldn't bring herself to finish the sentence.

"No," Meeker quickly cut in, "we haven't found her, so don't go imagining things. What I called about was that we did find your Packard."

Carole didn't speak. Rather she just turned and waited for the explanation she was sure would follow. She didn't have to wait more than a heartbeat.

"It was in Arkansas. A salesman bought it back in April in the St. Louis area. Best that we can tell, he had no way of knowing it had been a part of a crime. Someone had repainted it dark blue. Right now we are trying to track down the man who had it painted and sold it to this Bill Landers. I was hoping the car might give us some more clues, but that hasn't happened. At least not yet."

Casting her eyes to the floor, Carole nodded.

"Carole, I was hoping George would be here, too."

A pained expression washed over the woman's face as she looked at Meeker. Her bottom lip trembled as she fought to control her emotions. Finally, her voice quivered out a completely unexpected explanation, "I should have told you on the phone, but he left about a month ago. Just packed his things and took off. He said he couldn't take it anymore."

The agent reached out and took the woman's hand. "I'm sorry."

"I understand why he left," Carole continued. "What happened broke him. No matter what anyone says, he feels he's to blame. When he realized her birthday was coming up, he fell completely apart."

She turned her head back to the window and added, "You know, George never drank. Not even when the other kids were doing it back in high school. He was always the straight arrow. But in the weeks before he left, he drank himself out of a job. He was just that miserable. I couldn't pull him off it. No one could. He drank for three straight days before he left. When he sobered up, he packed and had me take him to the train station. He called me last week, told me he was in San Francisco. He assured me he loved me, just that he felt he'd let me down too much to come home."

She walked over to the counter and pulled an envelope out from a shelf under the cash register. She waved it in the air as she picked up the conservation. "He must have a job. This arrived today. He sent me money and vowed to continue to make all the house payments and any other expenses I had. So he's trying. Maybe someday, when the wounds heal, he'll be strong enough to come home."

The fact that George Hall left his wife didn't

surprise the agent. A lot of marriages failed when children died in crimes. Those couples that didn't split never really got back on with their lives. At least their lives were never the same. The wounds didn't heal. She knew firsthand—from an experience she had never and would never share with anyone—they never would.

Reaching into her pocket, Meeker pulled out the toy dogs Bobbs had discovered in the car. She squeezed them into the palm of her hand for a moment, and then after taking a deep breath, strolled resolutely across the room.

"Carole, do these mean anything to you?"

She held out her hand, opening it so the other woman would see the Scotties. She noted an immediate flash of recognition in the flower shop owner's eyes.

"Rose had a pair like this. Her dad gave them to her at Christmas. She liked to play with them when I drove around making deliveries. I think she liked the fact that she could stick them to the dashboard."

"They were in the car," Meeker explained.

"That's why I couldn't find them when I boxed up her stuff," Carole replied, her voice now breathy and unsure. "I did that, you know. I put all her things in boxes and took them out to the garage." Her eyes went from the dogs to the agent. "Do you think I should I have done that?"

"I don't know."

Meeker turned away to hide the tears that stung her own eyes. She took a deep breath and closed her fist once more around the toy dogs. From behind her, Carole continued, "I tried that for a while. I tried to go back to before it happened and pretend everything was all right. But that didn't help me sleep. So by boxing things up I figured I could just erase the fact I ever had a little girl. But that doesn't work either. The memories don't go away even when all the tangible things are out of sight."

She took a deep breath and then continued, "The fact that I boxed Rose's stuff up might have been the last straw for George. I think having the house completely void of all of her things pushed him over the edge."

There was no answer Meeker could give, no comfort she could offer. It was a sad truth and one that she silently acknowledged even if she didn't verbally admit it. She composed herself enough to turn and again open her hand. "Would you like these?"

Carole shook her head. "No. There's no one left to play with them. Just give them to the first kid you see."

Those heartbreaking words were still hanging in the air when the agent set her briefcase on the counter, opened it, and pulled out a sketch. She placed it in front of the other woman and asked, "Have you ever seen anyone who looks like this?

It doesn't have to be an exact match, just some-one who might look a bit like this drawing."

The storeowner studied it for a moment before answering, "No."

"Are you sure? Look close."

"I'm positive. You don't forget a face like that. Those hard eyes look right through you."

Picking up the sketch, Meeker slid it back into her briefcase. As she did, Carole posed a question, "Who is he?"

"The man who sold the car to the salesman from Arkansas."

"So," Carole almost choked on her words, "that could be the man who took Rose."

"We have no proof of that."

"I hope it's not," the mother said in a hushed tone. "I don't want those cold eyes to be the last thing Rose saw."

Chapter 44

The sheriff was out, so Meeker left the sketch with his secretary. Though it would be a long drive back and the time she'd spent with Carole Hall had left her mentally drained, she still wanted to get back to Chicago rather than stay on the road.

But she wanted to get back because she had an idea that might generate some press. Maybe it would be seen as nothing more than a stunt, but she needed to bring that poor woman in Oakwood some kind of peace.

That peace had eluded her own family, and she didn't want to see another family live that way. So if a wild stunt had a chance of working, Meeker was going to go for it.

A late-afternoon rain began falling around six thirty, and the wipers on the FBI-issued 1939 Mercury had a tough time keeping up with what the storm was dropping. Rather than continue to attempt to peer between the drops on her windshield, she pulled into the first juke joint she could find. A meal in her belly and a few moments spent with folks more interested in laughing than crying might be the needed tonic to pull her out of this pit of depression, frustration, and helplessness she found herself in.

To a big-city girl, St. Anne was just another wide spot in the road. Yet the town of a bit more than a thousand people did have The Blue Note. According to the neon sign, it offered the best food in town, so she stopped. After running through the parking lot in the rain, she pushed open the door into a world she had rarely visited. A dozen or so tables sat off to her left, a well-stocked bar stood in front of her, and a bandstand and dance floor filled up a large area to her right. As she shook the moisture from her hair, a heavyset woman with bleached blond hair dropped a wet rag onto the counter and stepped out from behind the bar.

"How you doing?" Her voice was as loud as her orange and purple print dress.

"A little wet," Meeker answered. "And hungry, too."

"The band won't be here for another three hours," the lady explained as she picked up a menu and led the way to one of several vacant tables.

"I don't have time to dance."

The woman proved agile for her size, whirled on her heels, and chuckled. "Everyone should make time to dance, as well as laugh and sing. Those things keep us young."

"I don't feel very young today," Meeker admitted as she sat in a chair and took the menu.

"Too bad, honey, a pretty thing like you should enjoy your youth. It passes you by quicker than a small-town's Christmas parade." She grinned before adding, "Got a girl who'll come out and take your order in a couple of minutes. She's a college student who's just working for me for the summer. That's our busy time anyway."

A crack of thunder shook the building. "My," the woman added, "that was a loud one. Hope this lets up before the band gets here. I'm looking for a big crowd tonight. I don't need the weather to ruin it. Folks around here love to listen to Shaw's Troopers. They play some swinging tunes."

"I bet they do." Meeker smiled and said, "If

254

they have half the jive in their step that you do, then they're cool cats."

"Now you're getting with the program." The woman chuckled. "My name's Thornton, Hanna Jean Thornton."

"I'm Helen."

"Nice having you here, Helen. Like I said, the little gal will be right out to take your order. And if you need them, the facilities are down the hall just past the jukebox."

As the woman headed back behind the bar, Meeker studied the menu. The cook must have once served on an ocean cruise line, as there were dishes from all over the world. Though the Hawaiian pork chops sounded good and the Italian meatballs over pasta were tempting, Meeker had a desire to play it safe. She was surveying the sandwich choices when an apron-clad waitress set a glass of water on the table and asked, "Do you know what you'd like?"

Without ever looking up, the agent posed a question the girl had probably heard a hundred times, "What kind of sandwich do you suggest?"

"BLT."

"Then let's go with that and maybe a side of creamed corn."

"Sure. And what to drink?"

Looking up for the first time, Meeker answered, "A Coke will be fine."

The young brunette smiled. It was a funny smile

causing the left side of her top lip to rise higher than her right and thus partially closing one dark eye almost like a wink. Yet what really caught the agent's attention were the woman's dimples. They were on top of her cheeks, not next to her mouth but just under her eyes.

"You looking at my weird cheeks?" The waitress grinned. "Don't worry if you are, I've gotten use to it. People always make fun of them. My friends call them dents."

"They're dimples," Meeker corrected her. "And I like them. They're cute." Extending her hand, she said, "My name's Helen."

"I'm Alison."

"You from here?"

"No," the young woman replied, "just staying with my roommate and her family this summer. After Labor Day it'll be back to the University of Chicago. I'll be a junior this fall."

"Good for you, the world needs more women with degrees."

"I guess," she shyly returned. "I'll get your order out in a few minutes. Wave if you want anything else."

As the girl disappeared, a man got up from the bar and walked over to the jukebox. He fiddled with his pocket, pulled out a handful of change, dropped a nickel into the music machine, and made a choice. A few seconds later, the strains of "Fools Rush in Where Angels Fear to Tread" was pounding from the Wurlitzer's speakers and making the jukebox's bubbling lights flash in time with Glen Miller.

The man who'd picked the number walk-waltzed back to the bar, grabbed the woman who'd first greeted Meeker, and led her out onto the dance floor. As the older couple moved to the big band swing music, the cares of the world disappeared, for at least a few minutes. Helen was glad for the reprieve, even if vicarious.

Chapter 45

It was just past 9:00 on Monday morning when Henry Reese strolled into the office. It had been almost two weeks since he'd found the Packard, and he still had no leads on the man who sold the car or on Marge Hooks. The trail was as cold as a butcher shop's walk-in freezer. A bit amused, he listened as his partner in "The Grand Experiment" assured someone on the phone that she'd take good care of something. What that something was, he had no idea, and he wasn't sure he wanted to know.

As Meeker set the phone in its cradle, Reese sighed. "I'm tired of striking out."

"I know what you mean," Meeker agreed. "That's why I'm trying a new slant."

"Your math must be better than mine," he

cracked. "I can't come up with any new angles. Who were you gabbing with on the phone?"

"Whom," she corrected him.

"Fine, with whom was you gabbing?"

"I think your verb," she teased, "should be *were*."

"Never mind the English lesson, just give me the dope."

"Eliot Ness," she proudly announced.

"The guy who broke Capone?"

"None other."

"He's not with us anymore," Reese noted, "so why did he call?"

"Actually," she explained, "I called him. He's working for the city of Cleveland now. Trying to clean up the police and fire departments."

"So," an impressed Reese asked, "does he have a lead or something on one of our cases?"

Meeker got up from behind her desk and walked toward the door. "Come with me. I'll explain as we walk."

"Where we going?"

"The basement."

As they waited for the elevator, Meeker began to unveil the reason behind her suddenly upbeat mood. "We've hit the wall on the Rose Hall kidnapping—with you unable to track down the Hooks woman, and I've heard nothing from the sheriff in Oakwood on the sketch. So I wanted to do something wild. I got the idea from studying some of Ness's case files."

"When did you do that?" he asked as the elevator doors opened.

"Back when I was in law school," she explained as they moved inside and the doors shut. "Ness and his men actually drove around in some of the bootleggers' cars and trucks for a while. They drove by places the hoods haunted showing off that the feds had the vehicles. Essentially they were rubbing their supposed successes in the hoods' faces, trying to get them angry enough to make a stupid move."

"I've heard something about this," Reese noted, "but I don't see what it has to do with the Hall case."

As the doors opened into the basement, Meeker stepped out and continued her lecture.

"The only thing we've got that we can really use in this case is the Packard. We know it is tied to the case. We know it was the drop point. We know it was stolen and resold. We know it once had the ransom money in it."

"I know we know all that stuff," Reese shot back, "but cars don't talk."

"Evidence does," she corrected him. "And the car is evidence. And there is always emotion connected to evidence. Show a suspected murderer a photo of his victim lying dead at the crime scene and nine times out of ten there will be a reaction. Same thing when a thief is asked to hold something he's stolen." She stopped walking through the evidence room and lab and posed a question, "What is often the only way to find answers when you've hit dead ends in cases?"

"Luck?"

"Well, maybe sometimes," she agreed, "like when you found the Packard. But consider this, in most cases the trump card is the press. If we can get every newspaper in the country involved in this case, then maybe we'll find Marge Hooks or our mystery car salesman."

Shaking his head, the man grimly announced, "Our case is ancient news. We aren't going to push the war in Europe off the front pages. Dead cases generate no interest, and they don't sell any newspapers. Besides, the kidnapping involved a small-town family that has no connections to anyone who is rich or a celebrity. This isn't Lucky Lindy; this is just a poor family who somehow got messed up in something they didn't deserve."

"Follow me," Meeker ordered.

Turning with her, Reese's wingtips matched the woman's pumps stride for stride. As they rounded a corner, he spied her trump card. As they approached the far wall he shrugged. "It's the Packard. I see it's been painted back to its canary color."

As they stopped alongside the car, she announced, "It's just like it was when it was taken. The fender is fixed, and the paint is the factory color. I made sure of that. I got a list from

Carole Hall of the things they kept in the glove box. The maps, a fingernail file, a screwdriver, a few sticks of Doublemint, and a tin of aspirin are just where they should be."

"And?"

"And this is now my car," she proudly explained. "I'm going to drive this everywhere I go. And we are going to put out a nationwide press release trumpeting that the FBI, along with the President's special crime unit, is putting this car into service to track down the man in the sketch. Within hours his picture will be circulated by wire services all over the country. In truth, probably all over the world, too."

"And you think the papers will bite?" Reese asked incredulously. "It's old news!"

"You bet they will bite," she bragged. "They'll bite like hungry fish after a live, wiggling worm. Walter Winchell has already written a piece on it. It will run this weekend on the wire. Lowell Thomas is doing a radio program on the way we are using the Packard, and Universal Newsreels is not only featuring the story, but is offering a reward of ten thousand dollars."

"How did you manage all this?" he demanded.

"After I mapped out the idea," she said, "I made one call."

"Who?"

"Eleanor."

"I keep forgetting about your family connections."

As they continued to study the car, she dropped her voice. "Do you think it has a chance at working?"

"It just might," he admitted. "Having the press spreading the word often generates leads. Maybe one of them will be something we need. But have you considered that this stunt might well backfire? If the girl's still alive and the kidnappers get spooked by this media blitz, they might kill her."

Meeker walked over to the car, opened the door, and took her place behind the wheel. She let her eyes fall on the speedometer and said, "Thirteen thousand, four hundred and seventy-six miles. How many more miles do you think we'll have to put on the Packard to solve the case?"

He shrugged.

Looking toward Reese, she admitted, "I thought of the campaign costing Rose her life. In fact I almost backed out because of it."

He moved to the door before asking, "What changed your mind?"

"I didn't make the decision," she quietly explained. "Carole Hall was the one who assured me she wanted to take the risk."

"If the worst happens," Reese solemnly asked, "and you and I see the worst that can happen every day—can she live with the knowledge that she helped cause her daughter's death?"

"Henry, could you live with not knowing if your

daughter was dead or alive? Was being loved or abused? Could you live looking at every child you saw and wondering if that child was yours?"

"I don't know," he replied. He paused a moment before continuing, "How do you live with it?"

A confused look crossed her face as she looked back at her partner. He only allowed her to suffer for a moment before making the admission.

"I sensed a long time ago that this case meant something more to you. Do you remember that?"

"Sure," she replied, "and I told you every case was special."

"But not this special." He caught her eyes and held them with his own. After taking a deep breath, he continued, "I did some digging into your past. Your sister was kidnapped."

Tears filled her eyes. "You had no right!"

"You're my partner. This thing was eating at you too much. I had to know why. Now I do, and I understand. I've read the case files."

She turned back toward the wall and shook her head. She should have told him. She shouldn't have tried to keep it below the surface. After all, it was why she used her connections to get them the case. Yet he didn't know everything. He couldn't from a case file. That only held the cold and static facts. It wouldn't contain anything of the sister she'd known and loved.

"I was eleven when my younger sister was snatched," she began, as she turned back toward

Reese. "If you studied the file you know that Emily was just three, a few months older than Rose. My dad was a prosecutor who was working a case against a man named Perello. Perello was a part of a New York City mob that was heavily into drugs, bootlegging, prostitution, and gambling. One day my mother took Emily to a city park to play. Emily was there one moment and gone the next." The agent glanced over to her partner. "We got the standard ransom notice, and it was paid. But they didn't give Emily back. We never got her back."

"I'm sorry," Reese whispered.

"I know," Meeker assured him. "But there is more, and you need to hear it. Let me tell you about what not getting Emily did to my parents. That stuff is not in the case files. My father threw himself into his work, but he was never really the same again. Mom? Well, she sleep-walked through life for a while and did her best to be a good mother to me. Yet her spirit was broken."

"I can't imagine," Reese noted.

Meeker nodded. "We never went anywhere that Mother's eyes weren't searching the crowd looking for Emily. I never knew a day when she didn't cry. That was my life. It was completely filled with gloom. When I went to college, Mom retreated into a shell. She spent a lot of time sleeping. One day she took a handful of pills and died. There was no note and I'm not sure she meant to kill herself, but I knew she needed to find a way to end the pain."

The room was a quiet as a tomb. Meeker, who had maintained a strong, deliberate tone through the whole narrative, now turned her head toward the window. Her eyes were moist, and she felt as if someone had pushed a fist down her throat. She hadn't been this wrung out in years. But at least now he knew the whole story.

"What about your father?" Reese softly inquired.

Meeker dabbed her eye as she turned. "Dad soldiered on. He somehow didn't break down until five years ago. He took me out to eat at a place in Manhattan. Who should walk in but Geno Perello! Dad tossed down his napkin, charged across the room, and slugged the thug in the face. What followed next wasn't pretty. Two middle-aged men, dressed in dinner jackets, whaling each other like six-year-old boys. No one tried to separate them as they rolled over tables and staggered around the floor. Dad ended the fight by pinning Perello to the floor and fracturing the man's skull with a champagne bottle."

Meeker allowed the long-buried image to linger in her mind for a moment before continuing, "In front of a shocked crowd, I crossed the room and helped Dad off the floor. His face was flushed, his knuckles bleeding, and he was so mentally and physically spent he could barely make it to a chair. A few seconds later his hands went to his chest, and he fell face forward onto the table. They told me later it was a heart attack that killed him. I still think it was the ugliness of what losing his child had brought into his life that really did him in. He just couldn't live with the anger or the emptiness anymore."

Her eyes met his. "You asked me if Carole could live not getting her daughter back. And the answer is no, she can't live with it. My parents couldn't either. What you do is go on living in spite of it. At least for a while."

Turning away from the car, Reese did something that was almost unknown to his nature. For the first time since childhood, he said a prayer.

Chapter 46

October 3, 1940

The leads started to trickle in the moment the stories started to run on radio and in the news-papers. After the newsreel story hit theaters, the FBI offices were flooded with tips. The man in the sketch had been seen by eyewitnesses in a thousand different places all over the United States, Mexico, Canada, and even Europe. One of the most unique leads came from a woman in Maryland who swore that the man's name was Fritz Schultz and he was a member of Hitler's high command. Another one that brought grim smiles at FBI headquarters identified him as John James, the butler for the British royal family.

"He does look a bit like James," Reese noted as he tossed the Brit's photo back onto his desk.

Meeker didn't bother looking up from the stack of information she was weeding through, but she did manage to quip, "A little."

"How many have been interviewed now?" Reese asked.

"About two hundred!" she said. "I wanted leads and I got them. Something's bound to come out of these in time."

A knock on their door was followed by the entrance of a wavy-haired, blond, blue-eyed man blessed with the shoulders of a weight lifter. His fame as a Golden Gloves boxer was proven by both his muscular arms and his masculine grace. "Here's the latest," Agent Stan Gates announced while carrying a large box into the room. "Hope you enjoy reading them."

"There must be a thousand here," Reese grumbled.

"Actually one thousand two hundred and forty-two," Gates replied, "but who's counting?" After he dropped them on Meeker's desk he shot a grin Reese's way, turned on his heels, and departed, slamming the door behind him.

"Well, you were begging for something to do," Reese moaned.

Most of the leads were easy to dismiss, but occasionally there was a tip that rang with a bit of truth. Each one of those was placed in a special basket. Every hour, Meeker would take the keepers next door, where assigned agents made calls to see if they were worth pursuing in greater detail. Usually only one out of ten was. Those few saw field agents in face-to-face meetings. It was past three in the afternoon when the woman finally came across something that seemed like more than a long shot—something she felt deserved her personal touch.

"Okay," she said, her upbeat tone alerting Reese that she might actually have something worth reading, "this sounds really promising."

She glanced across the room to her partner. Noting that she had his attention, she continued, "This report is from Oakwood. So the location is right. A woman, Nancy Andrews, claims that the man in the sketch lived there until a few months ago. She calls him *spooky*."

"Is that a description or a name?" Reese asked.

"Description."

He raised his chin and grinned. "We are fairly near Halloween. Did she provide a phone number?"

"Yeah, and I'm about to call it. Why don't you get in on the extension and add any questions you feel need to be asked."

Meeker picked up the phone and gave the

dialing information to the switchboard operator. Two minutes later, Nancy Andrews was on the line.

"Miss Andrews, this is Helen Meeker. I'm working with the FBI."

"It's actually *Mrs.*," came the quick, no-nonsense reply. Without taking a breath, Andrews continued speaking in a nasal tone. "I've been married for twenty-seven years to my wonderful husband, Joe. Well, maybe not wonderful, but he does make enough to pay the bills. Wish he made more so we could afford the nicer things. I've wanted a piano in our house since we got married. And worse yet, we never have made that trip to Los Angeles he's been promising for years. He just keeps dangling that over my head like some kind of joke. Well, I've had enough. Next time he mentions it, I'm going to smack him one."

Meeker shot a glance across the room and noted her partner rolling his eyes. This was going to be one of those calls.

"Anyway, I saw the newsreel at the theater just last week. I went there with my neighbor Gertrude Mason. She doesn't get out much. Poor dear, her husband died a few years back, and she has no kids. She has spells, too. She gets dizzy as can be a couple of times a week. I've told her to go to the doctor, but she won't do it. Just don't understand people like that. Do you?"

Seeing her chance, Meeker cut in, "No, I don't.

About this man, the one you said looks like our sketch. You described him as *spooky*."

"Oh, him," Andrews enthusiastically replied. "That's why I wrote to you. I know who he is."

"And that's why we called," Meeker assured her. "Tell me about him."

"Oh, I will. Did I mention that Gertie and I thought you looked so pretty in that newsreel? You could be a model. You have the best teeth. Wish I had teeth like that, but I have two bottom ones that just won't line up with the others. They're kind of pushed forward. Katie Lots assures me I could get that fixed by a dentist in Chicago, but I just tell her I'm going to have to live with it. My Joe just doesn't make enough money for us to spend it like that. So I have learned to keep my bottom teeth covered when I talk or when I have my picture taken. Now if I had teeth like yours I'd never shut up. I'd just talk and talk so people could see them."

"Yes, ma'am," Meeker noted. "Now, about the man . . ."

"Oh, him! Well he must have moved away a few months back because the Lesters, they own the small house he was renting, have rented it to someone else now—a nice family who has three kids." As the woman continued to drone on, Meeker jotted down the name of the family that had rented the man the house.

"The youngest one of the Lesters' kids, I don't

remember her name, is going through that screaming phase. Isn't that the way most girls are when they are five or six? I know my Elizabeth was like that. Well, we called her Lizzie. She'd scream for no reason at all. It drove Joe crazy, yes it did. He could take only so much, then he'd head off for a walk. Sometimes he didn't come back for hours. Guess it became a habit. Even though Lizzie lives in Ohio, he still gets up in the middle of our conversations and just goes out for a walk."

"Mrs. Andrews," Meeker tried again to steer the woman back to the point of the call, "you said the man in the sketch lived not far from you?"

"A couple of blocks. We really don't have street names here, or if we do, they never put the signs up. We just get our mail at the post office. We've been box 47 ever since we got married. I like stability like that, don't you?"

"Yes, ma'am," the agent assured her. "Do you know where the man went?"

"Heavens, no. I don't talk to people who look like that. He was scary. Kind of had a sneer on his face. I never saw him smile. Never saw the reason folks would give him odd jobs, like mowing their yards, trimming the hedges, or painting their houses, but they did. That's how he got by, I guess. But I will tell you this; the picture you ran in the paper was the spitting image of him, except his eyes were a lot more beady and his

271

lips a bit thinner when you saw him in person. He still gives me chills."

"I see," Meeker replied. "What else can you tell me about him?"

"Well, he was about Joe's height, maybe five-nine, kind of stocky but not fat. He drank and smoked a lot. He was at an outdoor concert we had here last year. The Jimmy Martin Band was playing. Have you heard them?"

"No."

"They're pretty good, except for their horn player. He hit some bad notes, but maybe he was just having an off night. I always told my girls to never judge someone until you've met them twice. Guess that goes for musicians, too."

"About the man," Meeker's tone showed more than a hint of impatience.

"Oh yeah, he literally lit one cigarette with another. A chain-smoker, I think they call them. Anyway, he was there by himself and didn't applaud even a single time. I thought that was rude."

"Do you know his name?" the agent cut in.

"Melvin, Marvin, I'm not sure. I remember it started with an *M*. Never heard his last name. But I know someone who'd know. That's Sam Johns. He was Abbi Watling's attorney. That's why he'd know. And the Lesters would likely know, too."

Reese looked across to Meeker and shrugged.

She signaled for him to jump in on the call. He shook his head and mouthed, "This is your baby; you rock it."

"Mrs. Andrews," Meeker said, "who is this Abbi Watling? Do you have her number?"

"Deary, that would *really* be long distance. She died back in 1936, or was it 1937? No, I'm pretty sure it was '36. It was Jean Harlow who died in 1937. Boy, she was a great actress!"

"Why," Meeker pushed forward, "would this Abbi woman have known this man?"

"Mr. Johns?" Andrews asked, seemingly a bit confused. "I thought I told you Johns was the man to contact. He was Abbi's attorney."

"So." Meeker sighed. "The man you sent us the tip on. Why did Abbi know him?"

"Well, why didn't you say so rather than confuse me?" Nancy complained. "Abbi would have known him because he worked for her. Didn't I tell you that? I meant to. You know how it is? When you get a little older, sometimes you forget what you say. I wasn't that way when I was a kid. I could memorize like no one's business. That's why I got the lead in all the plays. By the way, what color was that suit you wore in the newsreel?"

"A pale blue," Meeker said.

"It looked gray. I do wish they'd make those newsreels in color. That would have saved Gertie and me arguing over that and the color of your eyes. Did I tell you that you could have been a model?"

"Yes, you did," Meeker replied.

"Well, you don't have to get in a snit about it," Andrews shot back. "I meant it as a compliment even if I did repeat myself."

"Sorry," Meeker replied, not meaning her apology at all. "Anything else you need to share about this man?"

"Only one other thing I remember, but it's probably not important."

"What's that?"

"He held his cigarettes in a funny way."

The agents' eyes met from across the room. Meeker took a deep breath.

"Mrs. Andrews. How did the man hold his cigarette?"

"Between his pinkie and ring finger of his right hand."

Placing her hand over the phone's mouthpiece, Meeker asked Reese, "Wasn't Johns the man who came in with the local cop and Hall during our first interview here?"

The agent nodded.

"Henry, dig up his number and see if you get the name of our smoker."

As Reese carefully hung up so he could call the switchboard, Meeker got back on the line with Andrews.

"I want to assure you that you've been a huge

274

help, Mrs. Andrews. This might just be the break we need. If it pans out, you'll get that reward the newsreel company is offering. I'm sure that there'd be enough there for you to make that trip to Los Angeles and get your teeth fixed."

"My, my!" The woman excitedly laughed. "I forgot about the reward."

"And," Meeker cut in, "I'm going to send one of our agents to do a full interview with you. He'll call to set things up. You'll love visiting with him. His name is Stan Gates."

"I will make sure and bake some of my brownies for him. Joe doesn't like them, says they are too salty, but I'll bet Mr. Gates will."

"I'm sure," Meeker smiled as she replied. "And make sure he eats several. Thanks."

She didn't give the woman a chance to reply before setting the receiver down. As luck would have it, Reese was just putting his phone back in its cradle, too.

"I can't believe you did that to Gates," the male agent said.

"He deserves it," Meeker shot back. "Did you get anything?"

"Johns was out, but his secretary will be back soon. I figured you'd want to drive down to Oakwood tomorrow, so I set up an appointment with the attorney for eleven."

"Perfect."

Meeker leaned back in her chair and put her feet

on her desk. It had taken months, but they had a break. Now it was a matter of getting the press on the lookout for the handyman. If they did that, then maybe the Halls would get the answers they needed to go on with their lives.

Chapter 47

Just across from the Oakwood post office, Samuel Johns's office was a converted storefront made up of two rooms. The front area where the secretary's desk sat was about ten by twenty. Beside her oak desk were two small bookshelves and a couple of mismatched wooden chairs for visitors with a table between them. A few news-papers and magazines were scattered on the small black bench alongside the front window. Against the back wall a counter held a silver coffee pot. Next to that was a door. Johns was standing in that back doorway when the two agents walked into his place of business.

"Welcome. You made good time," the attorney said.

"Not a lot of traffic leaving Chicago," Reese explained, "but there's quite a bit going on, so we might not be so lucky when we head home."

"Well, good to have you." Johns grinned. He waved toward the empty desk. "Barbara is out right now. She had to go to the bank and post office, but I can invite you into my humble quarters as well as she can. Come on back."

They followed the attorney into a room that was not only larger than the outer office; it was furnished a lot more nicely, too. The man's desk was a massive walnut piece longer than most pool tables. A brass desk light with a green shade sat in the middle of the workstation. Floor-to-ceiling bookcases lined the back and side walls. The shelves were filled with impressive volumes covering every facet of the law, as well as hundreds of books on history, literature, and travel. On the front wall were a half-dozen file cabinets made from what appeared to be cherry-wood. The three large chairs that were positioned in front of the desk sported green leather held in place by bright brass tacks.

Evidently noting his guests' admiration, Johns said, "You should have seen it when I bought it fifteen years ago. This was a corner grocery store at the turn of the century. If you look up, you'll see the pressed-tin ceiling. It's about all I left intact." He paused while Meeker and Reese glanced up then waved toward the chairs. "Now have a seat, and we can discuss whatever questions you might have."

"Mr. Johns," Helen began.

"Miss Meeker."

"There was man who once worked for a woman named . . ." The agent opened a file and glanced through her notes before continuing, "Abbi Watling."

Johns smiled. "Dear sweet Abigale. What a grand dame she was! Never met anyone like her."

Meeker nodded. "So you knew her well."

"I was her attorney for more than twenty years. I handled her estate when she died back in '37. She had a heart of gold."

"And the man who worked for her?" the agent prodded.

"During that time there were a lot of folks who worked for Abbi. She was pretty much a sucker for someone needing a meal or a job. Do you have any idea when this person worked for her or what he did?"

Meeker again checked her notes. "It appears, from what Nancy Andrews told us, that it would have been shortly before Miss Watling died." The agent pulled the sketch from the folder and slid it toward the lawyer. The desk was so large it only made it about a third of the way across. Johns had to rise from his chair to pull it the remainder of the way.

"Hmm . . ." he said, setting the drawing back on his desk and looking back toward his guests. "That looks something like Mitchell Burgess. Looks more like him than anyone else who worked for Abbi. But Burgess's hair is a bit darker, or at least it was the last time I saw him, and his brow is not as pronounced. Has kind of a cleft in his chin, too."

Meeker glanced toward her partner. Reese shrugged.

"I suppose," Johns continued, "that Nancy told you this drawing was the spitting image of Burgess."

"She pretty much indicated that," Reese admitted.

"Nancy's vision is not very good, but she's too vain to wear glasses. She's had three car wrecks in the past year because she simply drove into things. But there is one thing she's very good at and that's talking. She's the gossip queen of Vermilion County."

"We found that out," Meeker assured him.

"When she comes by here," Johns said with a laugh, "Barbara has instructions to tell her that I'm not in."

"Well," Meeker admitted while shaking her head, "we're not really here to discuss Mrs. Andrews. Do you mind if I ask you a couple of more questions about Burgess?"

"No, not at all."

"Is he still in town?"

The attorney leaned back in his chair, closed his eyes, and crossed his arms over his chest. He remained that way for about thirty seconds before his eyes popped open. "You know, now that I think about it, I haven't seen him since sometime last spring. Might even have been in the winter. He usually comes around during the summer asking me to use him for yard work. He didn't this year. So he very well might be gone."

Reese nodded, looked over at Meeker as if to get her approval to jump into the fray. She tilted her head slightly and smiled.

"Mr. Johns," he said.

"Agent Reese, isn't it?"

"Yes. Did you ever see Burgess smoke?"

"All the time," came the quick reply. "If he was awake he was puffing."

"Was there anything strange in the way he smoked?"

"I don't follow you. He pretty much did it the same way I do. He put the cigarette in his mouth, took a draw, and then blew it out. The only thing was he smoked a lot more than anyone I knew."

"What about the way he held his cigarettes?" Meeker jumped back in.

"I guess he held them like everyone else. I don't remember anything unusual about it. Of course I didn't really spend any time socializing with him. When I saw him, the smokes were in his mouth and he was cutting grass or pulling weeds."

Meeker leaned forward and probed a bit deeper, "Was there anyone else that knew him well?"

"I guess you could ask around," the attorney offered, "but he was a lone wolf. He didn't have a friend to his name. I don't remember him ever having a friendly conversation with anyone. But, as I said, you could check around. Someone might recall. He probably bought his cigarettes at the grocery store or Meyers' Marathon station. You could talk to the folks who work there. I would tell you to talk to the Lester family, but they went somewhere on vacation. Supposed to be gone more than a month."

"Thanks," a disappointed Meeker replied. "Do you or anyone you know have a photo of him?"

He shook his head. "No one was close enough to him to take a picture, and no one liked him well enough to ask for one."

"No family?" Reese chimed in.

"Not that I know of," Johns replied. "Of course I never asked. But I never knew anyone to visit him."

"Too bad," Meeker replied. "We'll ask around anyway. Maybe someone in town can give us a bit of information. Thanks so much for your time."

The trio got up, headed out the office door, and moved through the front room. Reese was just reaching for the doorknob when Johns snapped the fingers of his right hand. "So, what did Burgess do?"

"It looks like he is connected in some way to the Rose Hall kidnapping," Meeker informed him.

The news seemed to stun the attorney. He rubbed his forehead, his expression showing that he was having problems processing the information. "Lord, I hope not. My giving him work was probably what kept him in town after Abbi died."

"No one can hold you accountable for that," Reese noted sympathetically.

"Maybe from a legal standpoint," Johns said, "but it's not all about law, is it? And maybe just as bad, I helped George Hall buy that car. Everyone in town but me thought it was cursed. Maybe it was."

"I'm not sure what you mean?" Meeker quizzed, hoping he would explain. She thought back to the unfortunate accident she'd witnessed when the car was being assembled.

Johns's tone seemed troubled as he went on, "That Packard was involved in a couple of accidents—not wrecks, just strange things that cost a couple of men their lives. Abbi bought the car when no one else would touch it. Then she died not long after that."

"Did the car cause her death?" Reese asked.

Crossing his arms across his white shirt, just above his protruding belly, the attorney shook his head. "No, the coroner ruled it a natural death. She was old, too, but she'd been in good health, so I had my doubts. So did Jed, I mean Sheriff Atkins. I probably shouldn't even mention the other strange thing."

The woman glanced over at Reese before demanding, "What strange thing?"

Johns shrugged. "I'm sure it doesn't have anything to do with Rose Hall, so probably not worth tossing out."

"Let me decide that," Meeker replied.

"There was the matter of the missing money."

"Money?" the female agent asked, suddenly even more interested.

Johns nodded. "Abbi converted her bank accounts to cash a few months before she died."

"Was it a considerable sum?" Reese chimed in.

"Yeah, maybe one hundred grand."

Reese dug his hands deeply into his pockets and whispered, "Wow!" He shot a look toward Meeker before asking, "You never found any of it?"

"Not a dime, and we tore her house apart looking."

"Why didn't we know about this before now?" Meeker asked.

"No one knew except me and Jed," Johns explained. "Besides, it didn't apply to your case. I'd almost come to believe she spent it all, because no large bills ever turned up around here."

"Large bills?" Meeker asked.

"Yeah, she had all the cash in hundreds."

"Henry," Meeker noted, "the cash the little girl found that paid the down payment for the store, those were hundreds, right?"

"Yeah," Reese said, his eyes showing that he was on the same track as his partner. "And she found them by the garage."

"This has never been about some old robbery," Meeker explained. "This was never about a few thousand dollars. This was about something much bigger." Meeker looked to Johns, "Did Burgess know about the money Watling pulled out of the bank?"

"He might have," the attorney admitted. "He worked for her. He could have overheard her talking or seen her with it. But he couldn't have taken any. He never had an extra quarter to his name."

"We need to go see Carole Hall," Meeker said.

Chapter 48

The agents walked the two blocks to the shop. Carole Hall was alone when they entered. Meeker didn't bother with the usual greetings.

"Carole, do you know a man named Mitchell Burgess?"

"No, why?" She was obviously confused.

"What about your husband? Did he know him?"

"Not that I know of. Why?"

"Do you know how to get ahold of George?"

She nodded. "He gave me his number."

"I need it, and I need to use your phone."

The shop owner gave Meeker her address book opened to the number. Four minutes later George Hall was on the other end of the line.

"Did you know a man named Mitchell Burgess?" Meeker demanded.

"Didn't really know him," the man answered, "but Rose and I talked to him once."

"Was it right after you found the money?"

The line went silent for a few moments before George, his voice weak, came back on the line. "Yes, it was right after she found it. I was asking around, trying to make sure no one had lost it. Surely that had nothing to do with her being taken. I mean he was a bit strange, but he'd been around town for a while. Should I have told you about him when it happened?"

"I wish you would have remembered him then," Meeker replied. "But that's water under the bridge now."

"I didn't," the man whispered. "Maybe I was too shocked. But I only ran into him once. And I just never thought anyone from Oakwood could . . ." He paused a moment before asking, "Are you sure it's him?"

"No," the agent replied, "but we might be closer. We'll keep you in the loop. Now let us do our job."

Carole looked toward the agent as she hung up. "What's this all about?"

"Maybe nothing," Meeker explained. "And maybe everything. We will have to find Mitchell Burgess to know for sure. We feel confident he was the one who sold your car to the salesman.

And as he knew about the money, that means he was likely involved in the kidnapping. Come on, Henry, we've got to get moving."

The two walked quickly to the door. Just as they were about to leave, Meeker looked back to the shop owner. "Say a few prayers. This is definitely a break, but there is still much to be done."

Carole nodded as the pair charged off down the street on foot.

"So, Helen, what are you thinking?" Reese asked once they were a full block from the shop. "It's like you know something I don't."

"I believe the car has always been the key," she replied. "Yet to be sure I need to ask Johns one more question."

Meeker rushed into the lawyer's office, past the secretary, and without knocking, pushed his office door open. A surprised Johns was sitting at his desk on the phone. As he looked up and spotted his uninvited guests he mumbled, "I'll have to call you back. There are some FBI agents in my office."

"Sorry to bother you, but I need a couple of answers," Meeker explained.

"Okay," he replied while setting the phone's receiver down.

"Did you search the car for the money?"

"You mean her yellow Packard?"

"Yeah."

"We looked in the trunk," he said.

"What about under the seat? Or actually in the seat's cushion?"

"No," he admitted. "Do you think that's where she hid it?"

"I think so."

"That explains something I never understood," Johns whispered.

"What?" Meeker demanded.

"She and her niece took me out to eat one day. Abbi insisted on driving. I let Janet ride up front, and I rode in the backseat. I couldn't believe how lumpy and uncomfortable it was."

Meeker glanced over to Reese. "The gal I brought in to do the lab work on the car, Becca Bobbs, found a piece of a hundred-dollar bill under the seat pushed up into the springs. What we found out from Mr. Johns here, combined with the lab report, tells me Abbi must have hidden her money in the car. So, Burgess likely searched everywhere but there. But he put two and two together when Rose found the money. She probably reached her hand in between the top of the seat and the bottom. Maybe she was playing and lost something down there. The toy dogs maybe. A few of the bills must have worked their way down to that area and she pulled them out."

"But she said she found them on the ground," Reese argued.

"Maybe what she lost was something she wasn't supposed to have," Meeker explained. "I remember being a kid and playing with things I wasn't supposed to touch, like my dad's lighter or my mother's jewelry. If I'd lost one of those things I wouldn't have wanted to show my parents exactly where, because if they found it I'd get in trouble. . . ."

"But why didn't Burgess just take the car? Why the kidnapping scam?"

"Maybe he tried to take the car but between both of the Halls using it and then locking it in the garage at night, he couldn't get to it. So he got impatient. Or . . ."

She smiled as another thought came to her. "Or he wanted to know if they had found all the money. If they had, then coming up with the five thousand would have been easy. The Halls wouldn't have protested at all. But if they seemed concerned about raising the money, if they had to go to extremes to come up with the cash, it meant Watling's loot was still in the car."

Reese nodded. "So when the Halls had to scramble for cash, he had his answer. That's why he wanted the car left at the rest stop. He needed to search it. But that would've taken some time, so he just took the car." He paused. "But why not just destroy the car after he found the money?"

"Because he couldn't resist"—Meeker smiled—"making a few more easy bucks. Every small-time crook who tries to hit the big score still can't let go of who he once was when every dime counted."

"And the kid?" Reese asked. "They were probably spooked that she could identify them."

"And you know what that means," Meeker added.

The ringing of the phone caused three sets of eyes to turn toward the closed door to the entry. Johns's secretary picked up, and they could hear her say, "Samuel Johns, Attorney at Law. How can I help you?" A moment later the door cracked open.

"Are either of you Henry Reese?"

"I am."

"There's a call for you. The party says they are from the FBI."

As her partner moved toward the outer office and to the phone, Meeker cast an accusing stare back at the attorney. "I can't believe you didn't recognize Burgess the first time you saw that sketch in the newspaper."

Johns set his jaw and fired back, "Listen, young woman, in my practice you defend a lot of people. I always try to see the good in them. If I can't, then the case is in trouble. I now wish I had never had any dealings with Mitchell Burgess. But what I'm telling you is that in my mind, the man in your sketch didn't look like the man I knew. I just didn't see it until you finally pointed it out to me."

"Because that man in the sketch was guilty?" Meeker asked. "And you couldn't take knowing that you might have been part of the reason a little girl died?"

Her words cut into Johns with the fury intended. She wanted him to think about it. If he had opted not to get involved for fear he was the reason this happened, then he needed to have a lot of sleepless nights. And he needed to be forthcoming with any other information he had. As she heard Reese end his call, she slyly noted, "We got lucky. Thanks to talkative Nancy we have something concrete to go on, but it might be too late."

"Luck," he wryly laughed, "that's what that car you drove up in brings everyone who drives it for a while. Then, according to what everyone around here believes, the Packard turns on you. Suddenly it cuts you down. If legend is right, you're in for some bad times."

Meeker looked into the man's suddenly sad eyes. "You believe that?"

"I didn't," he admitted, "but since watching what happened to the Halls, I do now. You need to take that car back and park it. You should never drive it again."

"Thanks for the warning," she snapped, "but I'm going to see if there's still some good luck left in that ride for me."

"We've got to get moving," Reese urged as he joined the two.

"Let's roll," Meeker replied. But before she walked out, she added one terse coda to the proceedings, "If I find out you knew that it was Burgess in that sketch and you did nothing, then I'll be back to deal with you personally."

Chapter 49

"Drive 150 west," Reese said as they slid into the Packard.

After starting the car and pulling away from the curb, Meeker glanced to the left and asked, "What's up?"

"Nothing to do with the Hall case or anything you're working on. It was a case I was assigned to a year ago before they teamed us up. You know about Jack McGrew."

"Of course," she replied as she turned right and brought the car up to speed. "You brought him up the other day as having known that Hooks character. He's a one-time small crook that graduated to the big world of bank heists. He's been on the Public Enemy List for a couple of years. If I remember correctly, he's from Wyoming."

"That's our guy," Reese replied. "We got a tip that he is holed up in a farmhouse nearby between two small towns—Ogden and Hope. There's a trooper waiting about two miles south of Ogden on the highway. His partner is watching the house to make sure McGrew, if he is there, doesn't take off."

"So, we need to speed it up a bit?" she asked, pushing the car up to seventy.

"No," he said, "we've got lots of time. We are going to do this one real quiet-like and try not to create any fireworks. And speaking of fireworks, you set a few off today. You were pretty hard on Johns back there."

"Oh." She grimly smiled. "You heard me dig into him when you were on the phone?"

"I can do more than one thing at a time. But why the issue with him?"

"He should have recognized the sketch."

"How do you know? You've never seen Burgess, maybe the sketch doesn't look enough like him to set off alarms."

"I think he might be hiding something," she shot back. "But maybe you're right. Maybe the sketch doesn't look like the Burgess he knew. Time will tell. Now, how did McGrew get the nickname 'Pistolwhip'?"

"It's not a name he likes," the man explained. "He got pistol whipped by a member of the Chicago mob back when he was trying to make their team. He was just a hick from the west trying to impress Capone and his gang. He took one step too many. Unless he's gotten it fixed, his nose is still pretty crooked."

Reese waited a moment before adding, "When

you get about halfway through Ogden, you turn left on 49."

"Got it. What do we need to know about McGrew? Are we going in to arrest the guy or just confirm he's the one in the house and then wait for backup?"

"The latter," Reese explained. "I've seen McGrew. When I get a look I'll know if it's him. If it is, we'll call in a task force with lots of firepower. Then, after we've figured out how many men are in that house, we'll move in. Hoover has stated that he'd like to save the courts the cost of a trial."

"That's grim," she replied, "but I understand. It's not about the banks, it's about the blood he's spilled."

"Three cops," Reese added. "Look up there. That must be the trooper beside that car parked in the ditch."

Meeker eased the Packard to a stop on the shoulder, and the two got out to meet with one of Illinois' finest. As they walked up to the man, the agent noted a bit of dampness in the air. Looking over her shoulder she observed storm clouds gathering. She wasn't looking forward to getting wet, not in her best suit and pumps.

"You Reese?" the trooper asked.

"Yeah, and this is a member of FDR's crime task force, Helen Meeker."

"I've seen you in the newsreels, ma'am. I'm Strickland." He nodded at her.

"How far is the farm?" Reese asked.

"About a mile to the west, down that gravel road over there. We got a tip from a postman about McGrew being holed up in the house. The postman recognized him from a poster that had been pinned up in the post office."

"Yeah," Reese said, "those things work from time to time. Whose house is it?"

"No one has lived there for a couple of years. The man who owned it before sold it to a neighbor and moved to the city to work in a factory."

"Anybody there besides McGrew?" Meeker asked.

"We don't know," the trooper admitted. "My partner, Jim Schwatzy, is up there. Maybe he can tell us. You ready?"

Reese nodded.

"Then get in the Packard and follow my Ford. I'll lead the way."

A few drops of rain spattered on the windshield as they reentered the Packard. By the time they turned onto the gravel road the skies opened up.

"The rain's a good thing," Reese noted as he pulled out his gun and checked it. "It'll make us harder to spot."

"I take it you're expecting trouble?" Meeker noted, her eyes going to the thirty-two.

"We shouldn't have any problems, but you never know. There's no predicting a snake like McGrew. The ones that know they're going to death row are the most dangerous." He lifted his gaze to hers. "Can I ask you something?"

"You can ask," Meeker replied, "but I'm making no guarantees I'll answer."

"You ever fired your gun? Well, you know . . . at something other than a target?"

"No," she honestly replied. "I'm hoping I never have to."

"Neither have I," he admitted. "But if this is McGrew, we might both get our baptism by fire."

The trooper pulled off the road about a quarter mile from a dilapidated, two-story frame house surrounded by a large barn, a corncrib, and a chicken coop. Each of those buildings, just like the house, needed a new coat of paint. Except for one small stand of trees, the remainder of the flat area was completely surrounded by cornfields.

Strickland stepped from the car and glanced over to the small clump of trees. After waving, he walked back toward the two agents. With guns drawn, they waited in the light rain alongside the Packard.

"Schwatzy's over in the trees watching the place," the trooper explained. "I'm sure he'll come over in a minute to give us an update."

Meeker cast a look in that direction. As she peered through the now steady shower, she saw no movement. "You sure he's there?" she asked.

"Yeah," the man replied. "But we can go over and meet with him there."

"Might be better," Reese suggested. "The trees will at least offer us a bit of shelter from this darn weather."

With Strickland leading the way, the trio stepped through knee-high grass to the six or seven trees. "That's strange," the trooper said, "he's not here."

As the two men took a few steps up the fencerow toward the home, Meeker inspected the area where they had expected to find Schwatzy. It was obvious the man had been here—she could see where his shoes had pushed down the grass. There were also three recently smoked cigarette butts that had been dropped by a tree. She studied the field just to the right of the trees. The corn-stalks were brown. Heavy ears, almost ready to harvest, were pulling them down toward the black Illinois soil. Everything looked normal except for a series of broken stalks about twenty feet beyond the woods. It was obvious that some-thing had disturbed them. Moving quickly forward, she ducked in between the rows of corn and followed the channels for almost fifty feet. She stopped dead in her tracks when she spotted the crumpled body in the uniform of a state trooper. The man was lying face down in the black soil, a broken cornstalk resting on his back as if it were a funeral bouquet.

Before approaching the body, she crouched close to the ground. Peering through long rows of corn, she searched for any sign of the person responsible for the attack. Only after she was assured that she was alone did she cautiously head toward the trooper. Moving her gun to her left hand, she reached down with her right and placed it on his neck. He was alive!

Rolling him over, she wiped some mud from his face. His breathing was steady and there were no signs of any obvious injuries. Quickly determining that there was no blood on the uniform, she felt the top of his head. There was an obvious huge knot.

Bouncing up, she moved back to where she'd left the men. They were just coming back down the road. When they got close, she quietly informed them, "Schwatzy's back in the field. He's been whacked on the head and he's out like a light, but he doesn't appear to be seriously injured. Still, we need to get him to a doctor."

Strickland hurried past them to check on his partner. As he did, Meeker looked to Reese. "You find anything?"

"Yeah, the whole place is on alert. I'm surprised they didn't shoot him, but maybe they were trying to do things quietly. There's no way out other than this road, so they're holed up for the moment."

"You said *they?*" she asked.

"I think there are four of them. I can't be sure if that is all, but I did get close enough to the windows to see that many and make a positive ID on McGrew. They've got a big seven-passenger Buick sedan behind the house. I'm also betting they probably have way more firepower than we do. We're going to have to get backup. In fact, we probably need an army out here. Why don't you get the injured trooper into town and notify the bureau that we need some help?"

"Not going to happen," she quickly replied. "Strickland can do that. He knows the area far better than I do. My place is with my partner, and so is his."

"But, Helen—"

"You know better than to argue with me." She smiled. "I'll keep watch here. Why don't you go help get Schwatzy into the car and give Strickland the numbers he needs to get us some help from Hoover."

"You're crazy," he said, moving away from her and into the field.

Maybe she was. In fact maybe they both were. They were no match for well-armed thugs. Yet they had a duty that they'd sworn to uphold, and nowhere did it give them an out just because they were the underdogs.

Chapter 50

As Strickland drove off with Schwatzy, the two agents got into the Packard and followed him until they were out of the home's line of sight. At that point, Meeker turned the car around and pulled into a cornfield that had already been harvested. The still-standing corn in the untouched field next to it kept the Packard from being seen by anyone coming from the direction where McGrew was holed up. The pair then worked their way through the standing corn to a fence, crossed it, and moved through more rows of corn until they came up to the back side of the gang's hideout. Stealing up behind the old barn, they carefully sized up their situation.

The Buick was still parked where Reese had seen it earlier. So at least no one had made a move to leave. Yet there were signs of life as men occasionally peered through windows. They were on watch, there was no doubting that.

There was a small door at the back of the barn. Meeker pointed to it and whispered, "Why don't we at least get out of the mud and rain."

He nodded, and they hurried along thirty feet of wall. The door easily pulled open, and the pair stole into the old, drafty structure. A quick inventory proved they were alone and that the barn housed very little that would have been of use to McGrew.

"What's that?" she asked, pointing to a wood and metal device in the corner.

"A hand corn sheller," he explained. "No one uses that sort of thing around here anymore. Everything has been mechanized."

"Thus all the old wagons with the wooden wheels," she said. "And look up on that shelf. There are a couple of bows and a full quiver of arrows. Wish 'Pistolwhip' was using those rather than automatics."

"I agree," he said. "Let's move over to that window so we can see the house."

The pair stealthily crossed the sagging wood-planked floor and eased down as they neared the glass.

"Helen, why don't you sit for a while. Maybe get some mud off your pumps. I'll take the first watch."

Easing to the floor, she placed her gun beside her and pushed her back against the wall. Her favorite suit had probably had it. She'd torn it in three places on the trek to the barn and now she was resting in years of dust.

"You see anything?" she asked.

"Nothing worth mentioning," he replied. "What're you thinking about?"

"About how much I paid for this suit and how well it fit. I wonder if the FBI would buy me a new one as I ruined this one in the line of duty."

"Don't hold your breath," he said, chuckling. "Hoover would just use it as an excuse to end 'The Grand Experiment.'"

"I hate this," she noted. "If the cavalry doesn't get here in time, I might just make my exit looking my worst. I have three runs in my stockings and my makeup is all over my face. And just look at my shoes."

"You were the one that pulled the strings to get into a man's world," he teased.

"I know," she replied with a smile. "I wouldn't change it either. But something Johns said today does have me wondering about one of my choices."

"What's that?" he asked.

"The car," she replied. "I wonder if the Packard's luck is still working for us or if it has shifted over to the dark side."

His eyes still focused on the house, Reese shook his head. "I don't want to say what I'm thinking on that."

"You know," she said, "we can't afford to die here."

"If you've seen my bills," he chided, "I can't afford to die anywhere."

"No," she returned, "I'm serious. If something happens to us, no one is going to pick up the Hall case. It will fall between the cracks. That family will never know justice. They will never know what happened to their little girl."

He glanced over to his partner. "There has to be more to your life than just work. Surely you do something for fun."

She shook her head. "Not me. Even my leisure reading is research. Ever since Emily was taken, my focus has always been on trying to make my life count for something. Right now that means finding Rose or at least finding out what happened to her."

"You need to learn to do something other than work."

"Might be a little late for that now." She let a shaky grin reshape her face. "But if we get out of this mess and solve the Hall case, maybe I'll let you show me what you do for fun!"

That brought out a smile. "You are in for it now!"

The sound of the house's back door creaking open brought both of them back to reality. Pushing herself to her knees, Meeker joined her partner at the window. With their eyes watching his every move, a tall, thin man walked out, lit a cigarette, and wearily jogged out to the car. Opening the driver's door, he reached in, retrieved something from inside, then hurried back to the house.

"What'd he get?" Meeker asked.

"No clue!" Reese replied. "But I'm guessing they're getting ready to make their move."

She glanced at her wristwatch. Strickland had been gone twenty-four minutes. That wasn't enough time to get reinforcements in place. They needed at least another half hour to get their forces into position.

"You believe in God?" Reese's off-handed question caught the woman by surprise. She considered it for almost a minute, trying to frame it by what was going on at this very moment, before attempting a reply.

"I don't know," she admitted. "I have real problems believing there is a caring God when I see what my parents went through and what the Halls are going through now. This job, dealing with people like McGrew, it doesn't leave much room for faith. Guess I'm just too cynical."

"Makes sense," he replied. As she slid back down to the floor, he kept his eyes on the house. She had just regained her seat when he added, "But because of what I see in this job, it makes me firmly believe there is evil at loose in this world. And if I believe in evil, then I almost have to believe in good."

She'd never thought of it like that. There was no doubt in her mind there was evil. She'd believed that since those who took her sister destroyed her innocence, but what about the good? Could good be a force, too? And if good was alive, did that prove there was a God?

"Helen, you ever read the Bible?"

"I did when I was a kid. I was looking for answers and tried everywhere. You wouldn't

303

believe the books I read looking for answers in college."

His eyes never leaving the house, Reese quipped, "Did you know Gates went to seminary before he became an agent?"

Helen shook her head. "Stanley? The palooka at the Chicago office that kept bringing in those tips generated by the newsreel?"

"Yeah, he believes that he is in law enforcement to touch others the way Jesus did."

"I don't follow you," she admitted. "I just thought Gates was a clown who liked to tease us."

"I'm not sure I get him either," he declared, "but he says it's about people like the Halls. They have been injured, and it is our job to solve the crime so they can experience healing. Gates claims doing that allows them to have some hope again. And he says that each of us who are involved in bringing that hope is doing something noble. In his mind, bringing a lost child home or bringing resolution to a family is like we are carrying a bit of God around in us."

She'd never considered that God could be inside her. It was an interesting perspective and one she'd like to discuss with Gates at some point. But if God was really good and He was all-powerful, as she'd been told so many years before in church, then why did He allow Rose Hall to be taken from her family? Try as she could, Meeker could not reconcile the two.

"We've got movement," Reese announced.

"Are they heading to the car?" she asked, pulling herself back up to the window and watching as an armed man stole out onto the porch. Just then a car pulled into the drive.

"No," he said. "They've got company."

The rain had stopped and the deep maroon Sharknose Graham coupe was pulling to a stop in front of the Buick. A lone man got out of the coupe, pulled a large duffel bag from behind the car's front seat, and walked casually to the back of the house. The car and his hat shielded them from seeing much of him as he opened the back door and disappeared inside.

"What do you make of that?" she asked.

"The fact that they didn't hightail it out of here when they discovered Schwatzy makes sense now," he grimly explained. "They were waiting on a delivery that was so important it was worth the risk."

"What could be worth that kind of wait?"

"Maybe cash," Reese suggested. "McGrew has to have it to buy his path to freedom."

If it was cash or something else, Meeker understood one thing very clearly. The waiting was over. With the delivery made, the gang would be hitting the road in just a few minutes. So even if their reinforcements had not arrived, it would be her and Reese's job to stop McGrew before he got away. That meant they were actually going to have to fire their guns at real people. And as they were going to be outgunned and outmanned, it likely meant she'd never live to have that theological discussion with Gates or let Reese show her how to have a good time.

Chapter 51

"Wish there was some way we could buy some time." Reese sighed. He checked his watch and frowned. "The visitor just carried two Thompson submachine guns to the Buick. We can't fight that kind of firepower and win. They'll blow us to kingdom come in a matter of seconds."

Meeker looked as her partner, who quickly bowed his head, closed his eyes, and mumbled a few words. He was praying. It was beginning to look like that was about their only way out of this mess.

"Maybe we should just let them drive off," Reese whispered as he opened his eyes and once more studied the house. Shaking his head he added, "You need to get out of here."

"I'm not leaving you alone," she snapped.

"It's not about that," he argued. "One of us needs to survive to tell Hoover what happened."

"He doesn't like me," she shot back. "You leave. He likes you."

"You're so darn stubborn," Reese whispered.

"Thought you'd be used to that by now," she jabbed. "So now that we've established we are both too stupid to leave, tell me what's going on."

"I feel like Jim Bowie."

"That makes me Davy Crockett, and that makes this barn our Alamo," she solemnly added. "If I'm going to die, at least it will be with someone I respect."

"It goes both ways," he replied. "By the way, the thin guy has been joined by a guy who could be the heavyweight champion of the world. They're tossing bags into the Buick's trunk. Meanwhile the deliveryman just strolled out, shook the skinny guy's hand, and is moving toward the Graham. Looks like he's leaving now. The others are heading back into the house, probably to get the rest of their stuff."

"Sounds about right," the woman noted while pushing herself up from the floor. She glanced through the glass and observed the coupe start, drive around an old stone well, and head back out to the road. She then looked back to the one remaining vehicle. "How far would you say it is to the Buick from here?"

Reese shrugged. "Forty feet, maybe a little more."

She patted his arm and grinned. "That's about perfect. You might want to say a quick prayer for strings."

"What?"

His question was not answered.

Meeker quickly made her way back toward the door where they'd come in. Moving past the wagons and over to where the corn sheller had been placed, she reached up to the shelf. She grabbed a bow, pulled back its string, but it snapped. Tossing it to one side, she retrieved the other one. This was no child's toy. It was a nice bow, well balanced and crafted from quality materials. At one time it had probably been used for hunting. Saying a quick prayer of her own, she pulled back the string. It was tight. She repeated the action a few more times before chuckling.

Reaching back to the shelf she grabbed the quiver, counted a dozen arrows, and retraced her steps. She leaned over her partner's shoulder and studied the scene. No one was outside the house.

"Where are our friends?" she asked.

"Still inside."

"Good, you keep your eye on things. I'm going to open that corner door."

"Why?" he asked. "You don't need to be a martyr."

"Not going to be. I'm going to play cowboys and Indians, and I'm hoping and praying it's the team with the bow and arrows that wins."

She quickly covered the thirty feet to the small, four-foot-wide door at the corner of the barn. A four-by-four set across braces bolted in place on each side of the entry kept the door locked.

Setting her bow and arrows on the floor, she lifted the heavy piece of lumber, carefully placing it on the ground. Before attempting to open the door, she studied the three hinges. They were rusty. Turning, she hurried back to the shelf to retrieve something else she'd spied there—a single can of motor oil.

When she returned to the door, she used one of the arrows to poke two holes into the thin tin top. She then generously poured the can's entire contents over the hinges. Taking a deep breath, she tossed the now empty can to one side, grabbed the handle, and slowly pulled on the heavy door. It groaned slightly, one of the hinges protesting, before the oil did its job. When she had the door slightly open, she eased up to the opening and looked outside. Everyone was still in the house.

Grabbing the bow and arrow, she threaded the latter into the string, leaned against the doorframe, and slowly pulled back. Using the bow's site, she aimed at the left, rear passenger-side tire and let go. The arrow sped through the damp air landing ten feet short of its target and skidding under the car.

Undaunted, she picked up a second. Repeating the routine, she adjusted her aim and let go a second time. This time the arrow flew a bit farther, sticking in the ground just a foot short of the car.

As no one had appeared on the porch, she still had time for at least one more attempt. Picking up a third arrow, she brought the sharp tip to her lips and gave it a quick kiss. Setting it in place, she pulled back the bowstring and adjusted her aim for the third shot. Pulling back, she let the arrow fly and watched as it sped through the air with a hiss. A second later the hiss was coming from a tire that was quickly losing air.

Smiling, she picked up a fourth arrow. She leaned again into the doorjamb and aimed at the front tire. Taking a deep breath to calm her nerves and slow her heart rate, she again made like Robin Hood. Her aim was true once more. Within a minute, both tires were completely flat.

Putting the bow and quiver over her shoulder, she closed the door, replaced the four-by-four brace, and hurried back to her partner. Reaching down, she picked up her gun and took another look out the window. The tires were now completely useless.

"That was amazing!" he quietly exclaimed.

"And it's not in the FBI manual either," she bragged. "I'm sure they've only got one spare, so we've bought time for our backups to arrive. Now let's get back to the Packard. When they discover what's happened, the first place they're going to look is this barn."

With Meeker leading the way, the pair raced out the back door and into the cornfield. They jogged through the muddy field, crossed the fence, and ran across the second cornfield. Jumping into the

Packard, the all-but-breathless woman inserted the key, turned it, hit the starter, and tossed the sedan into reverse. Pulling back onto the road, she hurried to the corner. Leaving the motor idling, she shifted into neutral and checked the car's dashboard clock. It had been fifty minutes.

"Where did you learn to do that?" Reese asked, his wind just now returning.

"Minnitotoo Camp. I was the archery champion three years running. I did have *some* fun when I was a kid."

"When you asked for prayer," he said, "I gave it a try. I think what just happened qualifies as a miracle."

"Maybe." She laughed. "But a part of the credit should go to Penny Watkins."

"Who was she?" he asked.

"My archery instructor."

She smiled as her eyes picked up a welcome sight. A line of a half dozen cars was coming down the road single file. The cavalry had finally arrived.

Chapter 52

Carole's head spun around when a voice declaring that a special news bulletin was about to air interrupted the dramatic presentation she'd been listening to on her Philco console. Setting the dish she'd been drying on the shelf, she walked closer to the radio, hoping and praying that the report had something to do with her daughter.

WDWS reporter, Alfred Jennings, is reporting that the FBI and the Illinois State Police have trapped one of America's most notorious and elusive public enemies, Jack "Pistolwhip" McGrew in a farmhouse between the small communities of Ogden and Homer. McGrew, who is wanted for a laundry list of major offenses including murder and armed robbery, has so far resisted demands to surrender. At this point law enforcement have not made a move to apprehend McGrew. It seems they are perfectly willing to wait it out. We will break into programming if there are other further developments. Now back to "The Lux Radio Theater."

The phone's ringing drew Carole Hall's attention from the radio. Turning the volume down, she walked into the kitchen and picked up the receiver. She was surprised when the operator informed her that George was on the line.

"Hello." His voice sounded so good to her ears.

She paused, took a deep breath, and replied, "Hello, George. How are you doing?"

"Better," he assured her. "I haven't had a drink

312

in a couple of weeks. I'm eating and sleeping pretty well again, but it still hurts."

She bit her lip. "I know it does. Mr. Mondell called today. He asked about you. Told me he has a place for you when you come back."

The line was silent for a few seconds. Finally George asked, "What did that call mean today? You know, the one from Helen Meeker."

"She's got a lead, that's about all I know."

His voice was shaky as he continued, "And the man, Mitchell Burgess, she thinks he was involved?"

"George, she wasn't real clear on that point. But I think so. Mr. Johns came by later and told me that the FBI seems to be pretty sure that Burgess was a part of it. I still don't know why. Maybe we'll know more when they find him."

"*If* they find him," George corrected her.

"If," she wearily agreed. "You have to admit, it's a lot more than we had."

"Yes," he agreed. "Of course, up until now we've had nothing." He paused before asking, "Carole, do you think Mondell was serious about my having a job if I came back?"

"I know he was," she assured him. "Do you want to come back?" Her voice was tinged with apprehensive hope.

"Maybe after Christmas. I don't think I can face Christmas at home, but maybe I could come back after that. I miss you, sweetheart, much more than you'll ever know."

"I miss you, too," Carole answered. "And I need you, George. I really do. I really need you at Christmas, too. So please don't wait that long. I can't face the holidays alone."

He didn't immediately answer. In fact, the line was silent for so long she thought he might have hung up. But finally his voice came back on. It was so soft she barely heard him.

"I love you. Good-bye."

After she set the receiver back in its cradle, she crossed the kitchen and opened the back door. She made her way out into the cold dampness of the fall evening. Opening the side door to the garage, she switched on the light and looked at the boxes she'd packed away earlier in the year. Walking over to the closest one, she pulled the lid open and looked in. There was a Shirley Temple doll staring up at her. As tears clouded her eyes, she whispered, "I'm sorry that I gave up on you. I'm sorry I tried to close you out of my life. I still love you; I really do, Rose."

Closing the lid, she picked up the box and walked back into the house with some of Rose's most precious things in her arms. She crossed the kitchen to what had been her daughter's room. Then, not really understanding why, she flipped on the light and began to unpack the box. There might not be a chance in a million that her little girl would ever come home, but if she did, this room would be ready for her again.

Chapter 53

It was almost ten on what had turned out to be a cold, clear night. Sporadic shooting had been going on for about fifty minutes. At least one hundred men were involved in the operation—*men* being the operative word. The FBI agent in charge, Alvin Lepowitz, had made it obvious that Helen Meeker was not really an FBI agent, had not been through the bureau's extensive training, and was therefore not prepared to be part of the group that apprehended this public enemy. Meeker didn't protest; there was no reason to. She was, in a figurative sense, outgunned.

So, pulling her coat tightly around her, wishing she could change into something other than the torn, muddy suit she'd been wearing all day, she leaned against the Packard as she sipped coffee and listened to the gunplay from a half mile down the road. Meanwhile, while she had been relegated to waiting it out in the cool, damp air with some of the Illinois troopers, her partner in "The Grand Experiment" was on the front lines trying to drive the gang out of the house. It could have been worse—at least Lepowitz hadn't given her an apron and used her to ferry coffee up to those in the battle.

"Ma'am."

Meeker turned and saw Trooper Strickland's now familiar face. "What do you need, Murray?"

"Could you come over here a second?"

Strickland was standing on the opposite side of the Packard, his arms crossed over his uniform coat. He looked strangely out of sorts. A round of machine-gun fire punctuated the night air causing her attention to drift back down the gravel road to the farmhouse. Then, in a pattern that had become the norm over the past thirty minutes, things were quiet. The strange serenity only lasted a few seconds before it was broken again by her partner's voice on a bullhorn. Reese had never sounded so good.

"McGrew, this is your last chance. Come out with your hands up, or we set the place on fire."

It was nearing the end. With the firepower the FBI had brought, the outcome was inevitable. The sooner the better! Now she just hoped that no one would be taken out in a hearse.

"Miss Meeker."

She'd almost forgotten about Strickland. Spinning on her muddy pumps, she waltzed back to where the trooper was standing.

"It looks like it's almost over," she noted as she approached.

"Not yet," a voice she didn't recognize announced. Stepping out of the darkness, his gun drawn and ready, was a man with a very crooked nose.

"Sorry, Miss Meeker," Strickland said, "he came out of that cornfield and surprised me."

"Don't do anything stupid," the stranger warned.

"I think I already have," she quipped.

"Listen, lady," McGrew snarled, "the trooper here tells me that car is yours. Get in. You're driving me out of here. I'm getting in the back-seat. If you try anything, I'll shoot you. And don't think I've got anything to lose."

"I'm sure you don't, McGrew." Her voice was calm. "But what if I don't get in the car?"

"Then I cut this trooper in half right here."

She saw the grimace on the officer's face, and thought of the wife and two kids he'd told her about earlier in the day. Shrugging her shoulders, she ambled to the driver's door and got in. She watched in the rearview mirror as the public enemy the FBI thought they had cornered brought the butt of his gun down onto the back of Strickland's head, causing the trooper to fall to the ground. Meeker gasped. Satisfied that his victim was out cold, McGrew opened the back door, tossed in a bag, and joined her.

"I'm right behind you, lady, and my gun is aimed at the back of your pretty little head."

As she turned the key and hit the starter, she laughed. "It's a pretty hard head, so you might need to fire twice."

"Stop with the jokes and drive!"

Backing out onto the road, she spun around and

drove up to the trooper manning the roadblock. As she pulled to a stop, she saw McGrew slide down in the seat.

"Bob," she announced, "nature calls. I'm running into town. Can I bring you anything?"

"No," he said, "I'm fine."

Slowly giving the car some gas, she eased down the gravel road toward Highway 49. A few moments later McGrew's ugly face again filled the rearview mirror.

"You did just fine," the hood slyly noted.

She didn't dignify the compliment with a response. Pulling up to the highway, she eased to a stop at the sign and waited for McGrew to give her directions.

"Go left. When you get to Ogden, turn left again on 150. I'll give you more directions after we get a few miles down the road. I wouldn't want to overload your brain with too much information."

"Yeah," she noted sarcastically, "you are a whole lot brighter than me."

Meeker made the turn and slowly pushed the Packard up to fifty. At that point she relaxed and casually watched where her headlight beams met the darkness. After a mile, she broke the silence with a question.

"How'd you get away?"

"While the guys were trying to fix the car, I walked out into the cornfield. I must have beaten the G-men by about two minutes. Then I hid out there until the shooting started."

All she could see in her rearview mirror was the shape of his head. It was too dark to make out anything else.

"So you deserted your partners?" she noted.

"They're the hired help, not my partners," he quipped. "They're paid well to take risks. When they signed up, they knew the score. Life expectancy is limited in our line of work. Okay, lady, we're coming up to Ogden; make a left at the stop sign onto the U.S. highway."

Meeker did as he instructed, pointing the Packard east. She followed the familiar pattern through the car's three forward gears and again climbed to fifty. But this time she didn't allow the car's speed to level out. Little by little, at a pace she was sure her passenger wouldn't notice, she pushed the car harder. Within a mile it was doing sixty. A half mile later she'd gained another ten. As the car hit seventy-five, she glanced into the rearview mirror. He was looking out the side glass, watching the landscape. Sensing she had him where she wanted him, she punched the gas pedal and watched the sudden burst of power push him back into the seat cushion.

"What are you doing?" he screamed as he sat up and put the gun right behind her ear.

"Taking you where you want to go!" she yelled over the engine's roar. "Or maybe I'm providing passage to the place you deserve to go."

"Slow down," he demanded, "you're going to kill us!"

"Maybe!" she shouted.

"I'll shoot you if you don't slow down."

"McGrew, if you shoot me you're sure to die," she explained. "Your best bet is to hope I can hold the car on the road. There appears to be a railroad crossing ahead—you'd better hang on."

The man's eyes grew larger as he peered through the windshield. Pushing the car even harder, she aimed the Packard's long nose down the middle of the road, dissecting the center stripe. They were going ninety, and the vehicle was still gaining speed. She was impressed! A few seconds later, she hit the spot where the tracks intersected the highway. The slight rise in the pavement combined with the rough crossing caused all four wheels to leave the ground. For fifty feet the Packard flew like a DC-3 but it came down much harder, bottoming out, its frame scraping the pavement sending sparks flying in all directions.

Keeping her hands on the wheel, Meeker hit her brakes hard. The Packard's rubber grabbed the pavement, tossing everything in the car forward, including McGrew. Fifteen seconds later, as the car ground to a stop, the agent reached across to the glove box, and yanked open the door, grabbing her extra gun. As her finger found the trigger she whirled in her seat. A stunned McGrew was still struggling to get up. As he looked across the top of the front seat from the floorboard he saw the revolver's barrel. His eyes widened.

Meeker smiled and in an icy tone said, "Drop the gun or greet the devil."

McGrew considered his options for less than a heartbeat before setting the pistol on the floorboard and lifting his hands in the air. Keeping the convict in her gun's site, the agent stepped from the idling car and yanked open the rear door. She grinned and barked, "Keep your hands up and get out. When you get out of the car, lay face down on the pavement." She watched him step out, fall to his knees, and hesitate. All that did was bring another warning from Meeker. "If you want to live another minute, put your nose on the concrete."

He eased forward, catching himself with his hands, before lowering his body to a prone position. It was only after his face was flattened against the road that she spoke again.

"Put your hands behind your back."

He again followed her orders to the letter.

"Now don't move. If you even flinch, I'll end your life right here and now."

She reached to her car, pulled some handcuffs from the glove box, and before McGrew knew what had happened had them locked around his left ankle.

"What are you doing?" he demanded.

"If we had your Buick I'd lock you in the trunk," she matter-of-factly explained, "but I guess I'll have to improvise. Turn over."

Rolling over onto his back, McGrew looked up for her next orders.

"Okay, Jack," she ordered, "snap the other side of the cuffs around your right ankle. Make sure I hear it lock."

The confused and frightened man rose to a sitting position and did as she asked.

"Okay, big man, get up."

McGrew pulled himself to his knees and awkwardly rose to his feet. As he did, he looked to the woman.

"Climb up on the fender and lay on your belly on the Packard's hood."

"What?" he asked, his eyes moving from the smiling woman to the nose of the car and back.

"You heard me!" she barked. "Be quick about it. I want your feet on the driver's side of the car and your head on the passenger side."

It was not going to be easy. With his ankles cuffed, just climbing up on the bumper and clearing the headlights was tough.

"This is impossible, lady," he complained as he slid off the fender and landed hard on the road-way.

"No, it's not," she said. "Now get on that running board and leap up onto that hood. You've surely seen fish jump. So just do it."

With his ankles locked together, the man hopped back to the car using a method usually reserved for sack races at Sunday school picnics. Then, using his hands to gain leverage, he managed to stick a landing on the running board.

"You're doing good, Jack," Meeker assured him. "Now leap like a salmon up on that hood."

He did as instructed and landed with a thud on the metal bonnet. It must have hurt, but he didn't complain.

"Now," Meeker ordered, "work your way toward the nose of the car. I want your body just behind the hood ornament. You got that?"

"Yeah." He sighed. He wiggled forward, his belly and chest on the hood.

"Good job," she said. "Now you just lay still. My gun is trained on you, but I've got to get something out of the trunk."

Keeping her gun trained on the man, she popped the trunk lead, dropped her left hand in, and found what she needed. A few seconds later she was back at the front of the car studying the man lying face down across her hood. Grabbing his secured ankles she jerked him around until his feet lined up with the Packard's driver's side headlamp.

"Hey, that hurts!" he screamed.

"It probably does," she said. She snapped another set of handcuffs onto the headlamp bracket and locked that onto the first set of cuffs around the man's ankles.

"What are you doing?" He used his hands to push up on the passenger side front fender. As he did, a bullet flew just inches over his head.

"Jack," she shouted, "the next one goes through your brain! Now get your belly back on the hood."

He quickly did as she asked. Walking over to the front of the car, she smiled at her handiwork. If only Reese could see this.

"Don't move," she ordered McGrew. She moved to the passenger side of the car. "Now lay your hands down on the side of the headlight." When he didn't move, she stuck the gun into the side of his forehead and cocked the trigger. A second later, the hands fell into place.

She snapped one side of a third pair of cuffs onto his left wrist and the other on the right. She then produced a fourth pair of restraints locking them on the passenger headlamp bracket and the other to the cuffs that were around his wrists. He now looked like a trophy from a deer hunt being transported back home.

"What are you doing?"

"Taking you back to the farmhouse," she informed him with a smile. "The wind might be a bit cold, but at least the motor will heat the hood enough to keep your belly warm."

"You can't do this!"

"Watch me!" she barked.

Smiling, she got back in the Packard, started it

up, turned the car around, and headed west down 150. Ten minutes later, she was back at the road-block. As a stunned trooper looked on, she rolled down her window and asked, "Where's Reese?"

"Still up at the house."

"What's with the guy tied on your hood?"

She ignored the trooper's question. "Are the fireworks over?"

"Yep, they gave up," the still mystified trooper answered, "but McGrew wasn't there. Strickland said he grabbed you and got away. There's a team out looking for you now and another looking for McGrew, but I see we can call off both searches."

"Yeah, call them back in," she quipped. "I'm about to deliver a package to my partner." With no other explanation, she slipped the car into first and headed toward the house.

Fifty members of the FBI's exclusive boy's club watched the Packard pull into the farmhouse lane. Meeker waved as she steered the vehicle to a spot just in front of the Buick. Turning the motor off, she pushed the door open and stepped out. Reese was the first to run up to her.

"Who . . . ?" He then got a good look at the man over the hood. "What . . . ?"

"I think 'when' comes next and then 'where,'" she chided. "It's McGrew. He took me for a ride, and then I took him for one. Here are the keys to the cuffs. I don't think he'll give you any problem now."

"How did you do that?" Alvin Lepowitz demanded as he walked up to the car.

Meeker studied the agent for a few moments. He was built like a fullback, must have had a half a bottle of Wildroot slicking down his black hair, and his face had the pained look of constipation. "You know," Meeker said, addressing her partner, "Lepowitz screwed up. He let one of the guys Hoover has had you dogging for two years slip through his hands." Then she turned to the man whose mouth was hanging open. McGrew was screaming for someone to get him away from this crazy woman. "Let's just say," Meeker went on, "you should be glad this *woman* didn't let your prize catch slip away."

She dropped her hand and smoothed her jacket before adding, "Now get this guy off of my hood."

Chapter 54

Meeker reclaimed the Packard after her prize catch was taken into custody and headed to Urbana, Illinois. The task force was meeting at the police station there, and though she knew that they wouldn't let her in on the questioning, she still wanted to hang close enough to get information from Reese.

The drive took her directly over the spot where

she'd tied McGrew to the hood. She smiled as she traversed the railroad crossing at a much lower speed than she had earlier in the evening. Patting the Packard's dash, she whispered, "Your brakes might have saved me tonight." And that fact was true. Packard's engineered safety and attention to detail, along with the FBI mechanics that reworked the sedan before she began driving it, might well have been the reason the stunt worked. She was sure that once McGrew had gotten far enough from the farmhouse and felt comfortable, he likely would have killed her.

Pulling up to the Urbana Police Department's main building, she got out, stretched, and then, remembering that McGrew had brought something with him when he'd forced her to drive him away, threw open the back door. In the glow of a street lamp she noted the item on the floor—a bag.

Pulling the bag up to the seat she unzipped it and looked inside. What she saw was pretty much what she'd expected: clothes, ammunition, and cash. She grabbed the gun, dropped it with the rest of McGrew's stuff, rezipped the bag and, after tossing it over her shoulder, made her way into the combination jail and police station. She flashed her presidential credentials to the desk sergeant and took a seat. Twenty minutes later, Reese walked in with Lepowitz.

This time the man actually talked to her without snarling.

Making a detour, he walked across the room, stood in front of Meeker, and announced, "You know how I feel about women working with men. It's a distraction. The only reason you're on loan to us is because of your family's long association with Roosevelt. When he's out of office, you won't be anywhere near FBI work ever again. I will make sure of that. Do you get that? You got lucky when you captured McGrew, but that doesn't change my opinion of women in the FBI or any other kind of law enforcement!"

"Yes, sir." Her words were accompanied with a sly grin, which was not lost on Lepowitz.

"You should be dead right now. You know that? But nevertheless, what I heard you did with that bow and arrow, and the way you subdued McGrew shows me that working with Reese has taught you something. When this experiment ends, I'll write you a letter of recommendation to anywhere but the FBI."

"How generous you are, sir," she quipped.

He glanced down at the duffel bag sitting beside the woman. "What's with the bag?"

"This was what McGrew took with him," she explained. "It was in the backseat of the Packard. There's a gun, some clothes, a lot of ammo, and cash."

The station door opened behind them, and four troopers escorted McGrew across the reception area and through doors at the back. The captured man glanced over toward Meeker and shook his head.

"I don't think he likes you much," Reese noted.

"The feeling's mutual," Meeker replied.

"He does make a good hood ornament," Reese added.

"I thought so," she shot back.

Lepowitz cut in, "Reese, you know as much about this guy as anyone here. You come in with me for the interrogation. And, Meeker, why don't you find an empty office somewhere and count the cash in that bag."

"That sounds like women's work," she noted.

"Yes, it does." Lepowitz smiled. "I'm sure you're suited for it."

The desk sergeant escorted Meeker to the conference room and gave her a legal pad and pencil so she could take notes. Dumping the bag's contents onto the table, she went to work. Her first chore was detailing the information on the manufacturer, make, model, and serial number of the firearm. She then recorded the information on the ammunition. She next went through the clothes, searching all the pockets and noting what was in each. Finally she turned her attention to the cash.

The money looked almost new. Though it was not crisp and it had a few creases, it was nevertheless very clean. Pulling off a rubber band, she thumbed through the cash. The bills were all one hundreds; while not startling, it was a bit strange.

Most stores had a habit of carefully examining anything larger than a twenty, and so criminals liked smaller denominations as they drew far less attention when purchasing items.

The bills' serial numbers were consecutive, indicating they likely had been part of a major bank heist. If this was true it would be a snap to link McGrew to that crime. She noted the starting and ending serial numbers on the pad then set about counting the C-notes. There were exactly one hundred bills and all, except for the last one, were in perfect shape.

She set the bills aside, picked up the pencil again, and began to record the information. Then lightning struck. Picking up the final bill, she studied it more closely.

"My Lord," she whispered.

Pushing her chair back from the table, she rushed from the room and down the hall to where two agents were standing in front of a door. Instinct told her who was on the other side.

"I need to see Lepowitz," she announced in a demanding tone.

"He's with the prisoner, Miss Meeker," the taller of the two explained.

"I know that," she quickly replied, "but this is about the case. I have to see Lepowitz now. I have an angle that he needs to ask McGrew about. Let him know I'm here."

"I can't do that, ma'am," the square-jawed man

calmly but firmly replied. "Agent Lepowitz left instructions that no one was to go in until he was finished."

"He did?" She turned on her heel, walked two steps back in the direction she came from then whirled and raced toward the door. Before the agents could react, she'd twisted the knob and charged into the room.

McGrew's eyes found Meeker even before Reese or Lepowitz had a chance to turn around. The hood ornament barked, "Get her out of here! That woman's crazy."

"Meeker!" Lepowitz screamed as he rose from his chair. "You can't be in here."

Her eyes aflame, she shouted back, "I already am!" Shifting her gaze to the other side of the small wooden table, she waved the one-hundred-dollar bill and said, "Where did you get the money that was in your bag, McGrew?"

Lepowitz glanced toward the door and to the two men who had been guarding it. They stood open-mouthed, motionless. "Get her out of here."

Meeker paid no attention. "Where did you get this cash, McGrew?"

As one of the agents laid a hand on her shoulder, she turned to Lepowitz and warned, "Get this guy's hands off me. If you don't let me get the answers I need, the next call you get will be from my friend and boss FDR. Do you understand?"

"You can't do this to me," Lepowitz warned.

"Try me," she dared him. "I had the power to be assigned to the FBI when no other woman in the world could. Every time you've tried to turn me into a secretary, you've had your own personal fireside chat with the President. I want to know just one thing from this goon. That's all! Then you can have him all to yourself, and I'll be on my way back to Chicago. You can even take personal credit for arresting him. You can change the story so you tossed him over the hood of your car and brought him in. But you let me ask him where he got the C-notes!"

Lepowitz set his jaw as he reconsidered his options. Looking back toward the door, he waved the men out. He then glanced back at the prisoner. "Where'd you get the cash?"

"It's not mine," he spat.

Meeker looked over to Reese and nodded. Reese turned back to McGrew. "Was this what you were waiting for, and why you didn't leave sooner?"

The prisoner sighed. "I had to have the ten grand to get to Mexico. There were going to be a lot of people I had to pay off along the way."

Meeker moved quickly around the table, tossed the torn hundred down, and demanded, "Who brought it to you? Who was driving the maroon Sharknose Graham?"

McGrew shook his head. "I won't tell you."

Sensing a moment in which he could regain his

authority, Lepowitz pointed his finger and hissed, "Tell us what we want to know or things are going to get even worse for you!"

"Worse for me?" McGrew laughed. "Excuse me, I'm headed to the death house. The only question unanswered is which state gets to do the honor and whether I'll die using gas or electricity. Your threats mean nothing to me."

Meeker cut in. "What if we could make it easier on you? Maybe we could exert a bit of influence and get you a life sentence. It's been known to happen."

The con shook his head.

"Can I talk to Reese outside?" Meeker asked.

"As long as you don't come back in," Lepowitz growled.

Picking up the bill from the table, Meeker opened the door and strolled back into the hall. Her partner followed along behind her. She led him around the corner where they could not be overheard and, leaning close, whispered, "You can work McGrew over all you want, he's not going to give up the name."

"You mean loyalty of thieves?" Reese asked.

"No," she replied, "he has no loyalty to anyone. I found that out by the way he talked about the others at the farmhouse. He'd have rolled over in a second on them. However, that guy driving the Graham means something to him personally."

"But why's it so important?" Reese asked.

"What difference does it make? We have McGrew."

"I'm taking this bill back to Chicago with me," Meeker explained, "to make sure my theory is correct. But I think the money that man gave to McGrew was a part of what Abbi Watling hid in the Packard."

A look of disbelief washed over Reese's handsome features. "What? How can you be sure?"

"A corner was torn off. I think the missing part was what Bobbs found in the seat cushion. So work your magic on McGrew, do whatever you have to to make him spill, see if he knows anything about the kidnapping, but my guess is he won't open up no matter what tactics you employ. If we can somehow find out who he thinks enough of not to rat them out, we are likely a lot closer to the answers in the Rose Hall case."

Reese stood silently, his hands in his pockets as he contemplated what he'd been told. Meeker gave him a few seconds before announcing, "I'll give everything in the bag and all my notes to one of Lepowitz's flunkies. I'm taking the hundred for our case. If he protests, tell him to call the President. I'll see you back in Chicago."

Chapter 55

Meeker arrived at her Chicago hotel room at four in the morning. She showered, changed, and headed directly to the office. Checking out the evidence file, she pulled the small piece of a bill out and set it next to the one she'd discovered in McGrew's getaway bag. It was a perfect match.

Pulling the sketch made from Landers's description, she studied it again. She was pretty sure this was Mitchell Burgess. But who was Burgess? Except for those who knew him vaguely in Oakwood, there was no Mitchell Burgess. They'd run down every person named Mitchell Burgess in the country, and none was a match. It had to be an alias. So where was he, and who was he before he arrived in Oakwood?

Looking at the drawing, she thought back fourteen hours. The man driving the Graham had worn a hat, and she never really got a good look at his face. Could he have been Burgess? If only she could relive those moments again and spend more time studying the man.

So what was next? Maybe it was her female mind working, but one move seemed obvious. If the FBI couldn't find Burgess in any of the usual ways, then it was time to try something unusual. Picking up the phone, she waited for the bureau's switchboard operator to connect her with head-quarters.

"Helen Meeker here. I need all the information we have in our files on Jack McGrew."

"Not going to be easy. You know he just got captured."

"I'm aware of that," she assured the file clerk. "So where do I have to go to get my hands on it?"

"We won't have it until after the agent in charge is finished processing McGrew."

"I see," she replied and hung up.

A haggard Henry Reese staggered into the office just as she was putting the phone down. His tired eyes reflected the long night he'd been through.

"Lepowitz is not happy," Reese said. "He's vowed to end your association with the FBI. I heard him talking to Hoover on the phone. They're going to try to get FDR to pull you for safety reasons. They're going to spell out that you almost got killed yesterday, and that would have been terrible for the organization's image."

"It wouldn't have done me much good either." Meeker grinned. "Besides, I caught McGrew."

"That's not the way the report will read," the man replied. "I think they've got the power to move you on this time. With what's going on in Europe right now, the President could probably be convinced he needs you in another position."

"I can buy some time," Meeker assured him.

"I'll tell the President about the new lead we have on the kidnapping case. He'll at least force them to give me the chance to follow it up. And I need your help."

Reese forced a smile as he eased back into his desk chair. "What do you need?"

"Everything," she said. "I need the story of McGrew's life. That might help me come to know the answer to who this man is that he wouldn't give up. Let's start with his family."

"They're all dead," Reese explained as he leaned back and propped his feet on the desk. "His mother died when he was about three. His father worked on ranches and moved around a lot. He was killed while breaking a horse when McGrew was about sixteen. Jack was on his own after that."

"No aunts, uncles, cousins?"

"No," Reese said, "when his father died, that was it. No friends either. Barely went to school, never belonged to any kind of organization or church. Fell in with livestock thieves not long after his dad was killed. Spent a little time in jail, but that didn't change him. Eventually came to Chicago with dreams of working for Johnny Torrio's mob, but he just didn't get along or mix well with the immigrants from Europe that ran the gangs. Thus it was not a marriage made in hoodlum heaven."

"What about prison time?" she asked.

"He served two stretches. The first was in the late twenties for bootlegging. That was in Joliet. He made a return appearance at that prison in 1932. That stay lasted eighteen months. He gained an early release for doing some kind of good deed. That fits, too. From what I have found out, he was always a model prisoner."

"Ironic," Meeker noted, pulling herself out of her chair and moving to the window. "He stayed out of trouble on the inside but got into it on the outside. What about since his last release? Did anyone get close to him?"

Reese got up and joined her at the window. "No, he was a lone wolf. He usually put together a gang, used them for a job or two, paid them off, and never saw them again. He had no long-term relationships with women either."

"Then I guess I need to go to Joliet," she said.

"The prison?"

"Yeah, the answer has to be there. As you noted, on the outside he owed no one and no one owed him, so that's the only answer. Someone he knew in one of his stays became the brother he never had. We have to find that man, and we have to do it very quickly."

Chapter 56

Getting into a prison was not difficult; it was the getting out that was the pain. There were tens of thousands across the country that could verify that fact, too. The heavy gate closed behind her.

Meeker had always been a bit claustrophobic. There was nothing in her past that seemed to have triggered this fear, yet it was something that marked her since childhood. Thus, whenever she walked into a prison, her blood pressure rose and her heart rate accelerated. And that feeling of being closed in had been haunting her even as she and Reese drove the Packard from Chicago to the west side of the state.

Meeker had been to Joliet many times, but she had never really stopped to enjoy the community. This trip would be no different. She and her partner would walk into the prison, be admitted into the records section, and with the help of a couple of trustees start digging through files. It would be time-consuming, detailed work, and it would all have to be done behind those high, imposing, and confining walls.

The warden was too busy meeting with a local congressman to greet them at the gate; so one of his assistants drew the task. Greg Bost was friendly enough, in a grim sort of way, but far from interested in the reason for their visit. In very businesslike fashion, he escorted them to the records department, where they were met by two men in prison garb.

"Mr. Reese, Miss Meeker, these are two of our trustees. The man sitting behind the desk is Jefferson Tisdale. The one at the far group of file cabinets is Lee Miles. We call Lee "Babe" because of the way he can smack a baseball around the yard. These men will assist you in any way they can. You can come by my office before you leave if you have any other questions or requests. I will escort you out."

Meeker set her purse and briefcase on the table and smiled at Miles. Babe, as they called him, was built like a moose and had a head full of thick, straight dark hair. His expression matched his nickname, and when he smiled, his eyes lit up. He looked a lot more like a teddy bear than he did a convict.

"How do you do?" Babe announced, proving that his voice matched his size.

"Fine," Meeker replied. "How are you?"

"As good as a long-termer can be," he assured her.

She then looked to the other trustee. While Babe was fair skinned and light-eyed, Jefferson Tisdale was dark with deep-set brown eyes. His smile was slight, and as soon as her eyes met his, he glanced down toward the floor.

"Hello, Jeff," she said. "It is okay if I call you Jeff? Or would you prefer Jefferson?"

"Jeff's fine," he quietly replied. "That's what my mama called me."

"Well, you two can call me Helen, and my partner is Henry. Now if you'll come over to the table, we'll spell out what we're looking for."

The four found places at a large oak table in the center of the room, where Meeker laid out their goal. "We think that in one of his two stretches in this place Jack McGrew developed a very special friendship with someone or did something for someone that left that person beholding to him."

"You talking Pistolwhip McGrew?" Babe asked.

"Sure am," the woman said. "Did you know him?"

The big man grinned. "I was here for both of his stretches. Nobody got close to him, though. He stayed by himself. Don't recall him causing any trouble, and he really didn't even talk to his cell mates. I know because I lived across from his cell for about a year."

"Did he ever have any visitors?" Reese asked.

"None I saw," Babe continued.

"Well then, I guess we go to records," Meeker said. She pulled the sketch of Mitchell Burgess from her briefcase and dropped it on the table. "We are looking for a prisoner who looks like this man. Did this guy serve time with either of you?"

"I don't remember any con that looked like that," Babe said.

The woman looked to the other trustee. He glanced from the sketch to the agent and back before mumbling, "I never saw a prisoner who looked like that."

"Well," Reese suggested, "let's get all the files of all the men who were here when Pistolwhip was here. Let's compare their mug shots with this sketch. If you discover any that come close, toss them my way."

The trustees nodded. They actually seemed eager to help.

"And one more thing," Meeker interjected, just as the men were about to head toward the file cabinets. "The man we are looking for has a deep scar on his right index finger."

Jeff stopped, a flash of recognition crossing his face then moved toward a cabinet. The woman watched him for a moment before crossing to where he was leafing through files.

"Did you know a prisoner who had a bad scar on his index finger?" she quietly asked.

"No, ma'am," he politely answered, "never known a con like that. I'm sorry."

For five hours the men dug through files and pulled a half-dozen photographs that bore at least a small resemblance to the sketch. As Reese got on the phone to check on the ex-convicts' whereabouts now, it quickly became apparent none could be connected to the kidnapping or to the delivery made to Jack McGrew. Three were still in prison, one was dead, one was crippled, and the final one had moved to Australia.

Helen looked back to the big man who was putting the files back in their proper places and shook her head. "Babe, it appears we have struck out."

"That never happens to me," he quipped.

The other trustee had already finished putting the files he had pulled back and had returned to his desk. As Meeker studied him, she noted a perplexed look on his face.

"Something troubling you?" she asked.

"I'm as right as rain, ma'am," he assured her.

She moved toward him. "How long you been here?"

"Eight years," Tisdale replied. "Still got two more to go."

"What'd you do?" she gently prodded.

"They say I stole some money from a man I worked for," he replied, looking her in the eye for the first time all day. "I didn't, though. Just nobody too interested in taking the word of a colored man."

"If you didn't," she said, "do you know who did?"

"Not sure," he sighed, "but I think it was the boss's son. Nobody wanted to hear that."

"I'm sorry, Jeff."

343

"Wasn't your fault," he softly assured Meeker. "Just born the wrong color, that's all."

"We need to get moving," Reese prodded. "Still have a long drive ahead of us."

Meeker stood and studied the two trustees a final time. "Thanks, gentlemen. I do appreciate it."

Following her partner, she stepped out of the large records department room and into the hall. Reese was already three steps ahead when she called out, "Wait a minute!"

He turned. "What's the problem?"

"I just realized something. I'm claustrophobic—" she began but before she could continue, he cut her off.

"We've talked about that. It's hardly news."

"But everybody has something that holds them back. There are things I don't do because of my phobia. I can't go down in a mine or a cave or get into a crowded elevator."

"Makes sense," he agreed, "but I don't see what that has—"

This time she cut him off. "You are scared of clowns."

He rushed up and put his finger to her lips. "You promised you'd never tell anyone that. I shouldn't have told you."

"But that's the reason you don't go to the circus. And you don't go even though you are fascinated by large cats and really want to see a lion tamer in action."

344

"So, what does that have to do with anything?" Reese whispered. "I cheat myself—big deal! I can live without the circus."

"But what if you had a crime scene at a circus? What if the person killed was a clown? Could you go and investigate without going a bit crazy? Would you hesitate taking the assignment?"

He jabbed back. "Would you investigate a murder in a coal mine a mile underground?"

"I think so," she admitted. "And that's why I need to go back in there and ask Jefferson Tisdale one more question."

"What's his phobia?" Reese asked.

"White authority," she explained. "He has been programmed his whole life to not speak up against white people. It has likely been beaten into him. So he'll answer questions, but he won't volunteer anything. He knows volunteering information might well get him into trouble. I just asked the wrong question."

Turning, she retraced her steps and opened the door into the room. The two trustees were still there, Tisdale at his workstation behind the desk.

"Jeff," she said as soon as their eyes met, "you told me there wasn't a prisoner who looked like the sketch. Did you know someone else who looked like that drawing?"

"Sure did," the prisoner replied, slowly, reluctantly.

"Who was it?" she asked.

His gaze flicked to the other prisoner before answering. "A guard who was here for a few years. His name was Mr. Burton."

Reese, standing in the doorway, glanced to Meeker. After their eyes met, he looked from Tisdale over to Babe. The big man smiled. "I didn't know him very well. He always worked in a different part of the prison than I stayed in."

"You got a record of employees that shows their pictures?" the woman asked.

"Sure," Babe volunteered, "right over here. Jeff, do you remember Burton's first name?"

"No, sir, he was just Mr. Burton to me."

"Okay," the big man replied, "shouldn't be that hard. Do you remember when he left?"

"Yeah," Tisdale said. "Right after the big riot. He got taken captive, and a couple of the cons carved on him. He was too scared to come back behind the walls after that."

"Here's the file," Babe announced, pulling it from the cabinet and bringing it back to the central table.

Meeker yanked the sketch from her briefcase and set it beside the small image in the employment record. "Close enough," she noted. "What do you think, Henry?"

"Yeah," he agreed. "And note his first name is Mitchell. The initials match. Probably the same guy. But why would he change his name?"

346

Meeker looked back toward the trustees. Babe shrugged. Tisdale's expression was a bit more hopeful.

"Jeff," she asked, "do you have any ideas?"

The trustee looked to Babe. "Do you remember Merkens and Jensen?"

"Yeah, they were bad hombres," the other trustee said. "Even I was scared of them."

"Well Merkens was killed in the riot," Tisdale explained. "Got taken down by a guard's bullet. That was when Jensen grabbed Burton. He worked him over with his fists during the chaos. When he bloodied him up good, he got a hold of a shiv and started cutting on him. Burton fought back and that really set Jensen off."

"I heard about it," Babe said, "but I was in solitary then, so I never saw anything. Did you see what happened?"

"Yeah," the black man replied. "I was behind a locked cell door, but Jensen went after Burton. After he knocked him out, he vowed he was going to cut off Burton's trigger finger. I guess he thought Burton shot Merkens. He and Merkens had been friends from even before their days in prison. Jensen was just getting started when Pistolwhip rushed up behind him and grabbed him. An awful battle happened. I thought both of them would kill each other, but McGrew finally won out when he slammed Jensen into the bars and knocked him out. He pulled Burton over into

347

a corner and kept the other cons away from him until order was restored."

"So," Reese asked, "Burton's index finger on his right hand was pretty messed up?"

"I heard he never could use it right again," Tisdale explained.

Meeker looked over to her partner and announced, "It's time to go. And, gentlemen, I really want to thank you." She pulled two tens from her purse and said, "Use these any way you want."

"Miss," Tisdale hesitantly added, "Jensen swore he'd kill Burton if he ever got out. I'm guessing that's why he might have changed his last name."

"Makes sense," she replied. "I'll get Burton's file back to you when we finish with it."

Thirty minutes later, the two were out the gates and headed back to Chicago. It had been a good day, but there was still much work to be done. They had to find Burton or Burgess or whatever name he was using now. That wasn't going to be easy, but they were much closer to that than they had been yesterday. They had a real name and a tie to McGrew and the Packard.

"Henry, you know McGrew," she said as she drove out of the city limits. "Do you think he was in on the kidnapping?"

"No," Reese answered assertively. "If he'd have even known about it, he'd have gotten a lot more than ten grand. Burgess was just paying him back an old favor. When you understand what McGrew did for him, the price wasn't too high either. In fact, it sounds like a bargain to me."

"You're the expert on McGrew," she noted. "Why didn't you know about this prison riot?"

"Not sure anyone knew about the incident with Burgess other than Tisdale and those that witnessed it. It wasn't in his files. You know," he added, a touch of admiration in his tone, "I never picked up on the race angle in dealing with Tisdale."

"I understand being the underdog," Meeker said and then shrugged. "Let's just say convincing Hoover and his crew that a woman can add another sensibility in investigations, and that we might notice things his men miss, ain't easy."

Chapter 57

December 6, 1940

Mitchell Burgess might not have existed before his stop in Oakwood, but in just two weeks the agents traced the much more obvious trail of Mitchell Burton clear back to his birthplace in Columbus, Ohio. He was forty-four and had been married three times. In fact, he was still married to all three of his wives even though none of them had heard from him in years and had no idea where he was now. He had no one. His parents were dead, and his lone sibling, a sister in Dayton, Edith Burton Mass, had last seen him in 1928.

Burgess managed to make it through high school, but he never lasted long at any job he landed after that. He'd been a farmhand, was employed as a gas station attendant, then a baggageman for the railroad before landing the guard position at the prison. Those who knew him during his jobs found him rather cold and aloof. The word that kept coming up was *loner*.

"Look at this," Meeker noted. "Our man worked on the assembly line at Packard in 1936. Looking at the months he was employed by the company, he was there when I visited."

"It is a small world," Reese shot back.

Meeker turned her attention back to her research. The man had been arrested about a half-dozen times for everything from petty theft to driving without a license, but he'd never been convicted on any of those minor violations. Thus, because his official record was clean, he was able to get the prison guard job at Joliet.

He appeared in Oakwood just a few months after the prison riot with his new name. During that time he produced bogus documentation under the name *Burgess*, likely obtained through contacts he'd established while working at the prison. Yet when he left Oakwood, the trail ended.

The one hope that had been driving the agents

was finding a connection between Burton and Hooks and using that to track down Hooks' wife, Marge. There was nothing. Thus, five weeks later, after trips across country chasing down several leads, they were no closer to finding the man or the woman he'd lived with in St. Louis.

It was just a few minutes before noon when Meeker wearily glanced up from one of the files and sighed. "Ready for lunch?"

"Sure," Reese said. "With the cold wind and all that white stuff coming down, may I suggest Mac's Chili?"

She cocked her left eyebrow. "It wouldn't matter if it was the hottest day of the summer, you'd still find an excuse to eat at that dive."

"It's the atmosphere," he offered.

"It's certainly not the food." She laughed.

She was reaching for her purse when the door flew open. Walking through unannounced was Alvin Lepowitz. He had a smile on his face so large it gave him a third chin.

"What brings you in from DC?" Meeker asked.

"Important work," he shot back. He studied the woman's face before taking three steps forward and handing her a large folder.

She didn't look at the contents, but by the man's smug demeanor she knew what it had to be. "I'm guessing you didn't fly in to give us a new FBI case?"

"Actually," he grinned, "I rode the train. No, the

folder doesn't have anything to do with the FBI, but it is a new assignment. You're heading back to the White House. 'The Grand Experiment,' as Eleanor called it, is over. As I predicted, it has been labeled a failure. Thus the FBI will remain a boys' club, and no calls from you will change that. Hoover and I have made sure of that. You're out of cards."

"What about the Rose Hall kidnapping case?" she demanded. "I know more about it than anyone. And we now pretty much know who did it. All that's left is finding him."

"It's not important." The visitor was practically giggling. Helen balled her fists. The man went on, "With Europe falling apart and Germany and Japan placing agents in this country to stir up trouble, we have much bigger fish to fry. Now pack your bags, and turn over all your files to Reese. There's probably some typing you need to be doing at the White House."

Meeker was boiling. Her instincts demanded she fight to keep her association with the FBI. Yet if there was any way it could have been saved, Lepowitz wouldn't have made the trip. This was his victory. Just like he'd vowed, he'd finally put her in her place.

"How long do I have to wrap things up?" she asked.

"As long as you need." His tone changed, suddenly seeming to take on a hint of understanding. He smiled before adding, "As long as you're out of the office by five today. You're expected to report to your new job on Monday."

The big man turned proudly to Reese. "Dixon will be your new partner. I know you've worked with him before. Finish up your duties here. Whatever you can't get done by the end of this month, assign to other Chicago agents. You will be working out of Los Angeles."

Lepowitz turned back to Meeker, "You have a good trip back East. Oh, and by the way, turn that yellow car over to impound. This case is dead. We no longer need it as possible evidence. We're going to offer it back to the owners. If they don't want it back, we'll auction it off."

"They won't want it," Meeker shot back. "And this is not over. There'll be women on the front lines of FBI work soon."

"Yeah, right," he snarled, "just like they'll let Negroes play in the major leagues. It's a white male's world, sweetheart. Get used to it. I suggest you settle down, find a husband, have a few babies, and learn to cook."

He was out the door before she could respond. Seething with rage, she grabbed a glass paper-weight and threw it at the nearest wall. It shattered into a thousand pieces.

"Feel better?" Reese quietly asked.

"No," she growled. "What's going to happen to the Halls? What's going to happen to all the other women who need to be working here? Women have instincts and intelligence this bureau could use! You know that!"

"Time doesn't change attitudes very quickly," he said. "We have to accept that, too. But I can assure you of this. I will tell everyone I know that you were the best partner I ever had."

"Seriously?" she asked.

"No doubt."

Chapter 58

It was four thirty when Helen Meeker returned the Packard to impound. By that time she'd contacted Carole Hall. The woman, who was very upset with the FBI for pulling Meeker from the case, assured the agent that neither she nor George had any interest in keeping the sedan. Then, after a soft thank-you, she hung up.

The life she'd loved was over. She'd figured in time it would be. Even though she was being sent packing, she felt good about her work. Yet, the fact that she'd never closed the case on Rose Hall's kidnapping would, as Reese had warned so many weeks before, haunt her for the rest of her life.

"Here you go," Meeker said, tossing the keys to the attendant. "It goes up at the next auction. The owner's address is in the file on the seat. Send the money to her."

"Got it," Jinx Stally replied. Dressed in blue coveralls and wearing a Cubs baseball hat, his eyes moved from the woman to the car and back. He seemed to falter for a moment before clearing his throat and choking out, "We'll miss you. I know what I think doesn't matter a bit to old J. Edgar, but you were one of the best the FBI had."

She glanced back to the sixty-year-old man, noted a bit of moisture in his clear blue eyes and a look of genuine affection etched into his wrinkled face. "Thanks, Jinx. And it might not mean anything to Hoover, but it sure does to me."

Reese was waiting outside to take her back to her hotel room. She had a reservation on the 7:30 train back to Washington, so she needed to get moving. Pulling her coat closer to her body to fend off the strong, frigid lake wind, she nodded at Jinx, stepped outside the garage and into the fading sunset. Fighting tears, she had just about made her way to the passenger side of the agent's car when it hit her. Opening the door, she looked across to the man and said, "I forgot something. I'll be right back."

Retracing her steps, she walked back through the garage door just before Jinx was about to close it. Hurrying as fast as her black pumps would allow, she moved to the Packard's front passenger door, grabbed the handle, gave a twist, and felt the door spring open. Pulling it back, she looked at the familiar interior one more time.

Setting her purse on the seat, she searched through the contents. Below her billfold and gloves, almost hiding under an address book, was something she needed to return to its place. After fishing out the magnetic, toy Scotty dogs from her bag, she snapped her purse shut. She clutched the twin playthings in her fist for a few moments as she said a quick prayer then reached under the seat. Satisfied they had been returned to where Bobbs had found them, she closed the door, strolled back out to Reese's car, got in, but said nothing. She was still as mute as a mime three blocks later.

"It's the Hall case," Reese finally announced. "That's what got your goat and your tongue."

She didn't answer or look his way but instead studied street scenes outside her window. With snow spitting from the sky, stores displaying holiday decorations, and shoppers crowding the sidewalks, it looked like Christmas. It was the time of wonder and magic for children. It was a time of joy and cheer for adults. Yet if Rose was alive somewhere, would there be any wonder or cheer for her? And what would the holidays be like for her parents?

Pulling her arms over her chest, Helen looked toward Reese. The words she wanted to say caught in her throat. So, shaking her head, she turned her gaze back out the windshield to where the wipers were slowly dusting the snow from the glass.

"I won't," the man solemnly said as he pulled up to a red light.

She quickly looked into his eyes. She had to be sure that he meant what she hoped he did. "Won't what?"

"I won't quit working on the case," he vowed as the light changed and he pulled forward. "And I'll let you know if I find out anything. I promise."

That wasn't nearly enough, but it was something. At this moment, holding on to Reese's promise of not giving up was all she had.

"And, Helen," he added, "I am going to find a way to teach you how to have fun someday. Life is much more than work."

Chapter 59

"I wish there was better news," the gray-headed doctor sadly told the two anxious parents. "There is just nothing more that can be done."

Nate Coffman looked from the physician to his thirty-year-old wife, Beverly. She was a small woman graced with great strength. He'd always figured she could support the entire world on her five-foot-tall, ninety-pound frame. But he could see in her almost black eyes that this was too much.

"Are you sure?" Nate's question hung in the air like a foul odor.

The kindly physician pushed his finger through his thinning hair and glanced out a slightly ajar door to the waiting room. There, sitting on a chair playing with a doll, was an energetic blond-headed girl. She appeared healthy, but she was a time bomb waiting to explode. And when she did, her life would be snuffed out in less time than it took to sneeze. Turning his gaze back to the couple, he crossed his arms and leaned up against his desk.

"Nate, I brought you into the world thirty-one years ago," the doctor began, his tone almost fatherly. "I nursed you through whooping cough, the measles, and a half-dozen other illnesses. I fixed your broken right arm, twice. In spite of all that and a number of other things, you grew up into the strapping man that sits before me today. But as much as it breaks my heart to admit it, I can't do anything for your little girl."

Walking over behind his desk, the physician eased down into his chair. After making sure both parents were looking directly at him, he continued, "Two months ago when Angel fell off the monkey bars and hit her head on the concrete, I thought it was nothing more than a concussion. That's all it looked like then. Even when she experienced that mild seizure two days later, it still didn't concern me that much. I figured she'd get over it. But the second one sent me scrambling."

"It was my fault," Beverly moaned. "I shouldn't have let her play on those monkey bars. She is simply too young for an activity like that."

"It wasn't your fault," Dr. Hutton quickly snapped. "Kids are going to play and they're going to fall. That's the way they are. What happened didn't create that mass in her head. It only stirred it up a bit sooner. It was like a monster hiding in the shadows waiting to leap out. There is nothing you could have done about it!"

"But surely," Nate argued, "there is someone out there that could remove it."

"I've shown you the x-rays," the doctor sadly explained. "There is no one in Chicago that can do that kind of surgery. Heaven knows I've made calls. There's a guy in London who is experimenting with a procedure that might work a few years from now, but he's not ready to try it on humans. Beyond the scores of telephone calls, I've written many, many letters, and I've gone through every medical journal I could find. I put out the word begging for someone—anyone —who was willing to try to untangle that ungodly mass from her brain. A few neurosurgeons who have done exploratory surgery in this area have visited with me, but when they see the x-rays they all say the same thing. The operation would kill her."

Beverly pulled out a handkerchief from her purse and dabbed her eyes. She then looked back to Dr. Hutton and forced out a question she didn't want to ask, "How long?"

"She'll make it through Christmas," he assured her, his sad eyes looking toward one of the room's bookshelves. "But as the tumor grows, the seizures will get worse. I could get her some medication that will reduce the pain and might buy her a bit of time, but it is very expensive."

"I'll get the money," Nate assured him. After wringing his hands he gently reached over and caressed his wife's shoulder. "I can take some extra flights. I think the supervisors at American can get me a bit more work. And we have some stuff we can sell. I own a nice, almost new Mercury; I can get some good money for it."

"But, honey," Beverly protested, her eyes meeting his with an expression of hopelessness, "we need a car. What if we have to get Angel to the hospital in a hurry? We can't wait on a cab."

"I'll buy a good-running, older car," he explained.

"Nate," Dr. Hutton cut in, his tone that of a pastor comforting a wounded member of his flock. "That is all well and good, but is having the medicine as important as you being with your daughter in her last few weeks or months?" He paused, rubbed his forehead in frustration, and added, "I can't answer that for you, but please think about that when you're scheduling additional flight duty. Being home with Angel and

Beverly might be more important than anything else."

The father nodded and glanced toward the waiting room at his little girl. She was playing with a doll. She looked perfectly healthy, as if nothing were wrong. "I know. But selling things we don't really need is not going to hurt anything or anyone. There is someone at the airline that wants my car right now. He's already told me what he'd give me for it. And I have a camera and a few other things I can pawn. You just order the medicine for Angel."

Hutton nodded.

"Now," the mother said as she wearily rose from her chair, "if there is nothing else, I'd like to get home. I need to get the Christmas tree up and decorated and . . ." Unable to finish, she hurried out to her daughter.

Nate stood up and shook his head. He couldn't believe the overpowering feeling of helplessness that had invaded his life. Tears ran down the rugged pilot's cheeks as he stood in front of a man who'd brought him into the world. His clouded eyes moved from his wife back to the doctor. "What have you got to heal a broken heart?"

Chapter 60

"What brings you out in this weather?" Jinx Stally asked the stranger.

Dusting the snow from his topcoat, Nate Coffman replied, "Got to have a car and heard there was going to be a couple in your auction today."

"I work on them," Jinx explained, "and we only have one that is really dependable." He pointed. "It's that wild yellow Packard over there. It's a 1936, but it's solid. Doesn't burn any oil at all. The weather is so bad, doubt many folks will make it out today, so you might get it cheap."

"It's a good runner?" Nate asked.

"Like new," the mechanic assured him. "It's the pick of the litter."

"I'd like to take your word for it," Nate said, as he yanked off his gloves. "But I still want to look at each of them. Can you tell me where the others are?"

"They're back in the right corner of the building," Jinx explained while pointing in the general direction. "The keys are in them, so start them up if you want. I wouldn't bother trying that '33 Caddy. That one should be melted down."

The pilot nodded as he ambled toward the vehicles. For fifteen minutes he looked them over and came to the conclusion that the old man was right. Only the Packard seemed worthy of a bid. With that in mind, he strolled back to the front of the building where the auction was starting.

It seemed that the half-dozen folks who braved the storm were much more interested in buying two 1939 Ford two-ton flatbed trucks than they were the cars. So, shockingly, his initial bid of a hundred dollars secured the Packard. As he walked up to give the clerk five twenties, Jinx waved and said, "You won't be sorry."

After signing the papers, Nate drove the car out of the garage and into the snowy Chicago streets. By the time he'd arrived at their home in Wilmette, he was convinced he'd gotten a great deal. In fact, he was so proud of the purchase, he left it in the driveway idling rather than pull it into the garage. A few seconds later, he had his wife and daughter wade out through the snow so he could show off the latest Coffman family vehicle.

"That sure is bright paint," Beverly noted.

"Yeah," he said with a laugh, "won't be any problem finding it in a parking lot."

Sweeping his daughter into his arms, he asked, "What do you think, Angel?"

"I love it, Daddy."

"Well it's yours, girl."

"And, Daddy?" she asked.

"Yes, Angel."

"Can we keep it till I'm old enough to drive it someday?"

Nate looked to Beverly. The tears in her eyes showed she had no answers. Looking back toward the car then toward his sweet daughter, he took a deep breath and choked out, "We'll see."

Chapter 61

"What's wrong?" Nate asked, pulling himself from the bed.

His wife's screams were so loud they sounded almost as if they were right beside him. But she wasn't in her usual spot on their bed. Her calls were coming from down the hall in their daughter's room. "Nate, come quick. Angel's having a seizure!"

Without even flipping a light switch, his bare feet hit the cold wooden floor as he raced down the hall and ran through the door to his daughter's room. Beverly was trying her best to keep Angel's trembling body calm, but the girl's eyes were rolled back in her head and her arms and legs were jerking in every direction. He'd seen seizures before, but none as severe as this one.

As Nate touched his daughter's forehead, he noted her ragged, shallow breathing. She looked as if she were drowning.

"We have to get her to the hospital," Beverly whispered. "She can barely breathe!"

"Wrap her up in a blanket," he ordered. "I'll throw on some clothes and get the car out and warmed up."

After hurriedly tossing on pants, a wrinkled dress shirt, shoes, and a topcoat, Nate raced to the garage. Opening the door, he was rudely greeted by a fierce north wind and a blanket of snow. While he'd slept, blizzard conditions had come to Chicago. Looking beyond the front yard, he noted that the streets were already packed by at least half a foot of the white powder. No one had predicted this.

Stepping into the car, he pushed the gas pedal four times, pulled out the choke, and punched the starter. As the six-volt battery delivered a burst of power to the starter, the engine slowly turned over, but it didn't catch. Taking a deep breath, Nate pumped the gas pedal two more times and once more hit the starter. The results were the same.

"Come on, baby, don't let me down now!"

He'd just finished sweet-talking the car when the passenger door flew open and Beverly eased in with Angel in her arms. Her worried eyes looked to her husband as she slid across the seat toward him. "What's wrong? Why haven't you gotten it started?"

"It's a cold night," he explained, "the oil is thick."

"But, Nate?" She moaned, trying to keep the shaking child in the safety of her arms. "We've got to go now. I think she's dying."

"I'll get it started," he assured her as he pressed the gas pedal two more times and hit the starter. The old motor wheezed. It coughed twice more as Nate continued to press the starter; then it finally caught and began to purr.

"Let's go," Beverly urged.

"It has to warm a bit, or it'll kill when I let the clutch out." He looked at the instrument panel, silently pleading with the engine to heat up. After a minute of idling and the temperature needle still registering *cold,* he pushed in the clutch and backed the car out of the garage and across the snow-covered lane. In spite of the fact that the snow was up to the running board, the Packard's wheels steadily propelled the family to the street.

She pulled Angel even closer to her body. "Can we make it?"

As the car gained traction and eased forward, Nate grimly smiled. "The car's heavy," he explained. "And the motor is powerful. If I keep it in first and second and we don't have to stop much, I think it will get us there. Just say a few prayers."

The words had no more cleared his lips than Angel began to shake even more violently in Beverly's arms. After staring at his daughter in the dim illumination of the dash lights, he glanced down at the car's clock. It was two thirty-five. Even on a good day, the drive to the hospital would take ten minutes. How long would it take tonight?

As he eased down the street, the wipers couldn't keep up with the falling snow. They did their best to push the slush off the glass, but still Nate could only see for a few seconds at a time and then the world was white again until the blades moved back the other direction. Thankfully there was no traffic, so Nate could aim the car right down the middle of the empty streets and ignore all the stop signs. Still, because the snow was so deep and visibility so poor, the best he could do was a top speed of fifteen miles an hour. Even at that speed he felt as if he were trying to control a sled flying down a mountain trail.

Block by block they fought their way through the raging blizzard. Twice the car slid toward a curb only to have Nate reverse the steering wheel, slow down, and regain traction. All the while, Angel continued to shake uncontrollably. A mile became two and then three and finally four and five. What seemed like days was less than half an hour, and somehow Angel managed to hang on.

It was just past three when Nate finally saw the four-story brick hospital through his almost completely snow-covered windshield. He slid like a boat into port into the emergency room's drive-way. But pulling up the slight incline caused his wheels to spin for at least thirty seconds. He thought he was going to have to stop the car, grab his little girl, and race the last one hundred yards on foot. Just as he was about to shift into neutral and set the emergency brake, the Firestone tires caught and the Packard jerked forward. They were going to make it! He had just eased in front of the hospital's doors when Beverly's words caused his heart to stop.

"She's not breathing," she cried out. "Nate, she's not breathing!"

Nate said nothing. With no explanation, he reached over and grabbed Angel from his wife's arms, pushed open his car door, and raced through the snow up the ramp and into the hospital. Charging up to the desk, he screamed, "My baby's not breathing. You've got to do something!"

A middle-aged nurse, dressed in a starched white uniform, got up from her chair, glanced down at the child, ran her hands over Angel's face, and then gently took her. She barked some instructions to another nurse who was sitting across the room at another desk. That woman grabbed a phone and called for a doctor to come down immediately.

"She's got a mass on her brain," Beverly explained as she came up behind Nate. "Dr. Hutton has been treating her."

The nurse nodded, her kind brown eyes catching the couple's for a moment as she quickly moved

368

across the room. "We'll do what we can," she assured them. "You stay here, and I'll get her into the emergency room." Just before she disappeared into a side room she glanced over her shoulder and called out, "When did she stop breathing?"

"Just as we drove up," Beverly said.

"Good."

A second later, the nurse and Angel were gone, leaving the two frantic parents alone in the waiting room. Nate pointed toward the chairs, wrapped his right arm around his wife's back, and gently guided her toward a seat.

Chapter 62

For five long hours, Nate comforted his wife while they watched doctors and nurses coming and going. Outside, the snow stopped falling and the city awakened to an unexpected winter wonderland. It was the kind of scene Angel would have loved and one that would have likely found her up to her waist in snowdrifts making every-thing from snowballs to forts. But that wouldn't happen today. In fact, it might never happen again.

It was just past eight when Dr. Hutton emerged and walked across the room to the where the couple was sitting. While he appeared exhausted, there was also a peace in his eyes.

"Is she . . . ?" Beverly couldn't force herself to

say the words that had been etched in her mind for hours.

"She is fine," the doctor softly replied. "She is sleeping and we are about to put her in a room. But if you hadn't gotten her here at the very moment you did, we would have lost her. How you made it through that storm I don't know. I mean the only reason I was here was because I couldn't get home."

"Thank God she's okay," Nate said with a smile. He looked toward the doctor and then his wife. He knew what the doctor meant was she was all right *for the moment*. Today, tomorrow, or next week, or next month, Angel would be hit again, and when it happened the ending would likely be much different.

"When can we take her home?" Beverly asked.

The doctor smiled. "If nothing else happens and she feels good, I would say tomorrow. Now, Beverly, why don't you go see her right now. It will take a few minutes before the room is ready, but I know you need to hold her."

The woman didn't need to be asked twice. She bounced off the chair, across the room, and into the open door that had been her focus for so much of the night. After she had disappeared, the doctor took a seat beside Nate. After putting his hand on the father's shoulder, he softly said what didn't need to be said, "What you experienced tonight will happen again. There is nothing we can do about that. The mass is growing and things will get worse. So, as a friend, not as Angel's doctor, I recommend that you cherish the good days you have left. Crowd as much into them as you can. Make what life she has left as sweet for Angel and yourself as it can possibly be. Every moment in each day is a gift."

Chapter 63

Nate watched Angel sleep that night at the hospital. Even though he sent Beverly home to rest and get ready for their child's homecoming, he never left the chair beside her bed. The next day, after their yellow car had retraced the route from the hospital to their home, he followed the little girl everywhere she went. He felt as if he were trying to crowd a lifetime of memories into just a few short moments.

As the horrible day of the bad seizure turned into a good day and then a great day, Nate found it hard to leave for his next flight run. Yet he had to work because bills still came in. So to make sure he was always informed on what was going on at their small, brick home in Wilmette they began a new routine. He'd call Beverly from Midway Airport before he got on the plane. He'd then call her from the airport, wherever that was, as soon as he landed. He'd call her again from the hotel and the next morning before he took off. The calls were always the same— Beverly would answer; he'd say, "Hello;" and she'd say, "She's fine." They'd talk for a few minutes, and then he'd hang up.

When he'd get back to Chicago, as soon as he deplaned, he'd race to the employee's entrance and look for the Packard. As long as it was there, as long as his wife was in the driver's seat and his little girl's mitten-covered hand was waving from the back window, it meant he would get to embrace her at least a few more hours or maybe a day or maybe even a week. And that was how life was measured—in moments. One moment at a time.

The days turned into weeks and the weeks to a month and then two, and just as the focus of his life changed, so did his prayers. When they'd discovered the mass in Angel's head, he'd asked for a miracle. That prayer continued until the big seizure hit. The prayer then changed to "Please let me be there when she dies."

He knew it would tear him to pieces to see his daughter take her last breath, and he dreaded that experience more than anyone could begin to understand. But he had to be there, not just for Angel, but for Beverly. He couldn't bear for her to go through that experience alone. With the infertility and all they had been through even before Angel came into their lives, that would simply be asking too much.

A hundred . . . no a thousand times . . . he had thought back over all Beverly had endured during their marriage. It had almost broken her heart when she found out she was the reason they couldn't have children. She felt she had cheated him and even begged Nate to divorce her and find someone who could give him children. It had taken him more than a year to convince her that adoption was something he was excited about. But for reasons he didn't understand and she couldn't quite explain, she didn't want to adopt. If God wouldn't let her have kids, she saw it as a sign that she wasn't supposed to. He'd figured they'd never have children. Until fate stepped in.

An older woman at church, Blanche Ragsdale, was taking care of a little girl from Missouri whose parents had died. She brought the little blond bundle of energy into the Sunday school class that Beverly was teaching. The child and woman instantly bonded. A few weeks later when Blanche died unexpectedly of a heart attack, Beverly immediately stepped in to take care of the little girl. They were told that Blanche had left Angel to them in her will. So, simply because of that one act, Beverly found a way to see God's hand in everything—from her not being able to have children of her own to sending Angel her way.

And then came the fall at the playground.

Now, each time he looked into Angel's eyes, he

knew this would be their only child. Beverly simply couldn't make a leap of faith to adopt again. Thus he had to squeeze every moment out of these last few weeks or days. He had to embrace being a parent now because there would never be another time.

Chapter 64

Nate Coffman sat in the pilot's seat of the DC-3 as he went over his checklist. After completing it, he looked to his copilot. "Collins, did you have a good Valentine's Day?" He didn't really care if the other man had done anything special for the holiday; he just felt the need to make conversation.

"Not bad," the copilot replied. "I got Kathy some perfume. That special French kind she likes. I dropped a lot of money on it, too. Do you know what she got me?"

Nate smiled. "What?"

"She got me a rake. What am I supposed to do with a rake in Chicago in the middle of the winter? You tell me that." Collins looked out the window and studied the scene on the Nashville, Tennessee, tarmac. "Got some weather moving in. Are we all loaded up?"

"I'll walk back and check with Ann," Nate replied.

Moving from the cabin to the passenger compartment of the American Airlines plane, he tipped his head to a couple of elderly ladies and caught Ann Grayson's attention. After showing a ten-year-old boy how to fasten his seat belt, the stewardess walked over.

"You need something, Nate?" she asked.

His eyes scanned the seats. "Is everyone who bought a ticket on board?"

"We're missing one," she replied, "but we are already five minutes behind schedule, so I guess that's his tough luck."

"Okay," he answered. "I'll get things rolling."

Moving back to the nose of the plane, he tossed himself into the pilot's seat. Just as he picked up the radio's microphone to inform the tower that Flight 22 was ready to go, he heard a voice on the speaker.

"American Flight 22. One of your passengers just checked in. The agent told him he was too late. You want to open the plane up for him or just take off?"

The pilot glanced back toward the gate. This trip had taken him out for two days. Two days was nothing to most people, but to him it was a lifetime. The crew had already rolled the steps away, and the door had been latched. So if they left the guy stranded, it wouldn't be their fault. He wouldn't get in trouble with the airline for it either.

Nate glanced over to his copilot. Collins

shrugged. "Won't be another plane leaving for Chicago until tonight. The guy will have a long wait. But it is up to you."

Sighing, the pilot barked into the microphone, "Tell him to pick it up, and have the ground crew get the stairs back in place."

Ten minutes later they were airborne, the pilots flying the metal bird through a light snow northwest toward Chicago. As they climbed, the precipitation grew heavier. At six thousand feet they were in the midst of a full-blown blizzard. Yet the snow was not the main issue of concern for the veteran team; it was the wind. Gusts were hitting them like punches from a heavyweight champ. As Nate battled to keep the crate on course Collins quipped, "God's not in a good mood."

For a full hour they fought weather that often caused the plane to drop fifty feet with no warning. Yet somehow the plane held together. Then, as if a magician's hand had waved, the scene changed and they flew into clear skies.

"One hour to go," Collins said with a smile. "Been a piece of cake so far."

"Whatever kind of cake it is," Nate shot back, "I'll pass next time."

For thirty minutes they flew over a snow-covered Hoosier state with nothing on their minds but setting the DC-3 down at Midway. It didn't take long to realize gremlins had somehow worked their way into the airship's mechanics.

"You seeing that?" a suddenly tense Collins asked.

Nate looked down at the instruments. The right engine's oil pressure was down and temperature up. "What do you see out the window?"

"Not what I want to see," came the answer.

"We have an oil leak?"

"Sure do and it's a major one."

"Okay," Nate replied as the motor's temperature climbed higher, "let's shut her down and fly the bird on one."

Collins reached over to kill the engine in order to avoid a possible fire and set up the DC-3 to fly on a single motor. Nate felt secure in the knowledge that the plane only needed the one to fly. But his sense of security didn't last long. Within minutes the left engine was dripping oil and heating up fast, too.

"What's going on?" Nate demanded. "Things like this don't happen. You don't lose two engines in a whole career, much less on the same flight."

"How long do you think she'll hold up?" Collins asked.

Nate shook his head, leaning to check several gauges as his blood pressure started to rise. "Give me your opinion," he said.

"Why don't we ask the chief mechanic?" the copilot suggested. "He's on this flight."

"Go get him," Nate ordered.

Collins jumped up from his seat and moved

quickly into the main cabin. Less than a minute later he came back with a surprisingly calm Albert Wiggins.

"Do you see what's going on, Wiggins?" Nate barked as he pointed at the control panel.

"Yeah," the veteran mechanic solemnly answered. He casually listened as Collins informed Midway of their issues before he glanced through the window at the one running engine. "I'm surprised it lasted this long."

The man's matter-of-fact tone shocked Nate. Glancing back toward the wounded motor, the pilot demanded, "Don't you realize what we're dealing with here? We're going to have to set this plane down in the next couple of minutes."

"Going to be a bit hard to do that," Wiggins explained. "When you hit the landing gear button there will be a small explosion that will destroy any chance you have at getting it down. You still have a lot of fuel in this crate. So if you try a belly landing, this thing will light up like a torch when you hit the ground."

A thousand questions rolled through Nate's mind as he tried to process Wiggins's cool explanation, but above all the others there was only one question that needed to be asked. "Why?"

"Just tired of living," came the answer. "I'm really good, maybe the best mechanic American has, but the company has passed me over for promotion a half-dozen times because I don't have a college degree. I'm tired of not being appreciated. So I figured if I was going to check out of life it would be worth it to make the airline look bad, too."

"But," Nate forcefully argued, his face growing red, "you're taking twenty-seven people who want to live down with you. That's not just suicide, that's murder."

Wiggins shrugged and smiled weirdly. "I'm putting others out of their misery. Look at you, your daughter is dying. Life is hell—that's all there is to it. So killing the folks on this plane is really doing them a favor. It will end all the suffering they have to deal with each and every day. Won't it be better for you not to see your kid die?"

As Nate fought to keep the motor running and the plane in the air he mumbled, "What kind of sick person are you?"

Collins had evidently had all that he could take of Wiggins, too. With no warning the copilot jumped from his seat, turned, set his feet, and delivered a right hook to Wiggins's jaw. The middle-aged man collapsed like a sack of potatoes. Then, after admiring his handiwork, the copilot sat back down in his seat.

"How much time you think we have?" Collins asked as he snapped his seat belt.

"A couple of minutes," Nate explained. "Maybe five on the outside. If we had the landing gear we could glide her into a field somewhere. We just crossed into Illinois so we're over flat farmland. But if Wiggins wired an explosion to go off when the gear goes down, the bumpy landing might trigger a blast anyway. Getting all the passengers off before the plane erupts might not be possible. And the lakes are not frozen as solidly as we need them to be, so there is really only one option."

Nate unfastened his belt and looked toward the other man. "Collins, pilot this thing; I'm going to get down there and find that bomb and cut the power to it. Get on the horn, and let the passengers know we have an issue but that it's being handled."

"I can't take her in," Collins argued. "You've got more experience. I know you can set her down. Besides, odds are you wouldn't find the bomb before the power goes out."

"Don't have to," Nate shot back. "Take the wheel."

As Collins took over flying the plane, the pilot got up and moved to a drawer containing a few tools. Wiggins groaned on the floor, seeming to be coming to. Digging out a pair of wire cutters, Nate headed for the hatch leading into the bowels of the plane. A minute later he was in the very cold underside of the aircraft. A quick study of the wiring led him to the main lead connected to the landing gear's mechanics. With one swift snip, the power to the gear was cut off.

Then Nate manually opened the bay. As he did, subzero temperatures filled the plane's belly along with hurricane-force winds. Grabbing a huge crank made specifically for events of power or hydraulic failure, he began lowering the gear. He was just finishing when the left engine sputtered and quit. He took a last look at the snow-covered scene below, then reversed his course and climbed back to the hatch. He pulled himself into the plane's cabin and rushed to his seat. Amazingly, even without power the plane was still aloft.

"You take it," Collins said. "You're the one with the most hours."

"Fine," Nate replied. "But inform the passengers of what is going on, tell them to be ready for a hard landing."

As his copilot calmly explained the situation to the passengers, Nate looked out the window. It was a strange sensation to be gliding over the Illinois prairie with only the sound of the wind. The ship was sailing so smoothly through the air that if they hadn't been in a life or death struggle, it would have been incredibly peaceful. And even though this strange sensation begged the pilot to embrace and enjoy this unique moment, he pulled himself back into the role he needed to play. With the wheel in his hand, Nate employed his flaps and rudders to aim the plane toward a long, open field. As the plane drifted below five hundred feet, he shot a look to the stewardess who had just poked her head in the cabin. "Are the passengers prepared?"

"As much as they can be."

"Get yourself buckled. As soon as we get this crate on the ground," he barked, "get back there and get them off this thing. I'm hoping it doesn't burn, but it could; the left engine is still plenty hot."

Ann moved to comply.

As he concentrated on making a perfect, unpowered emergency landing, something he'd been taught back in flight school but had never attempted, thoughts of Angel raced from the deep recesses of his mind and called out to him.

"Don't worry, baby," he whispered. "I'll be home sooner than you know."

Chapter 65

Nate Coffman stood in the snowy field surrounded by twenty-six of the twenty-seven souls who'd put their lives in his hands. They were all well and staring at the silver ship that had somehow landed relatively undamaged on the frozen Illinois prairie.

As the pilot considered what he'd just been through and how much just taking another breath meant to him, Collins strolled up to his side. "That was smoother than your normal landings."

Nate grinned at the verbal jab before whispering, "Where's Wiggins?"

"He's still on board. Tied him up real tight. I'll let the police escort him off later."

The pilot smiled. "He's not as good a mechanic as he thought he was."

Collins laughed. "Or maybe the plane is just better than any of us realized. I'm going to write a thank-you note to the Douglas folks."

"Where's the pilot?" a voice called out from behind them.

Nate and Collins turned as a tall, thin man with salt and pepper hair pushed by the other survivors and toward the flight crew. He was well dressed and moved with the grace of someone who'd played sports in his youth. A dark mustache accented thin lips, a chiseled jaw, and green eyes. He was so striking he looked as though he stepped out of a Clipper Craft clothing advertisement.

"I'm the pilot," Nate announced as the man drew closer.

"Great job," the man enthusiastically announced. "I've been flying planes for twenty years, and never have I ever witnessed anything like that. The way you set her down was simply amazing."

"Thank you, sir. I'm Nate Coffman."

The stranger stuck out a gloved hand. "Franklin Wiles." As their hands met, the man added, "I was the man who caused you to be late. When I saw that engine go out, I almost wished you hadn't waited for me. Fate's kind of a strange thing."

"Yep," Nate replied. "It's funny. I was able to get this piece of machinery down from the sky, and because of what I was trained to do a few lives were saved. But . . ." his voice trailed off along with his thoughts.

"But what?" the man asked.

"Nothing," Nate replied.

The sound of sirens caused both men, as well as the rest of the passengers and crew, to look over to a gravel road that ran beside the field. Police cars and ambulances were on their way.

"Glad we don't need those," Wiles noted.

"No injuries is pretty amazing," the pilot agreed as he stepped away from the stranger and moved closer to the plane. Out of the corner of his eye, Nate noted that Wiles walked over to visit with Collins for a moment. The men exchanged words, and the stranger nodded before he moved slowly back over to rejoin the pilot. As the vehicles parked beside the field, a dozen men got out and began to head in their direction. Wiles quietly voiced what had been embedded in Nate's mind since the successful landing.

"So, it's your daughter that you can't save," he said quietly, meeting Nate's gaze.

Taking a deep breath of the cold air, the pilot shook his head. "I guess Collins told you."

"He did."

"It's nothing you need to be concerned about."

"I'd like to know more," Wiles said, "if you care to share. If not, I will respect your privacy."

Nate didn't answer. Waving to a local sheriff, he called out, "We're fine, but the man that created this mess is tied up in the plane. My copilot can fill you in on the details."

"Thank you," the cop called out. "I radioed for a school bus to haul your people out of here."

"Thanks," the pilot called back. "We just need to get these folks someplace warm. And we need to get their luggage."

The officer nodded.

Nate glanced over his shoulder. "Collins, can you fill the sheriff"—he paused on the name, which the officer supplied as Jed Atkins—"tell him about Wiggins?"

"Sure," the copilot answered.

As the local rescue team went to work helping the passengers across the snow and over to the road where they'd be picked up by the bus, Nate moved closer to his ship. She looked like she was ready to take off. And if the motors hadn't been sabotaged, she could have. But for the time being, the DC-3 was going to have to wait in a wheat field. All things considered, not a bad fate. It could have, and probably should have, been much worse.

Wiles strolled up beside the pilot. "I'd still like to hear about your daughter."

The pilot was surprised the stranger had followed him on his walk to the DC-3's nose. He'd figured Wiles would have been anxious to leave with the other passengers. Why did this man want to concern himself with Nate's problems?

"She's sick," Nate replied. "Got a head injury a few months back and seizures followed. The x-rays revealed a mass in her brain. Doctors tell us surgery isn't an option because of how the mass is tied into her brain. So the seizures get worse, and in the next few days or weeks or months, a girl who has yet to even go to school will die. Kind of funny, I have the skill to save all these people, but . . ."

"Where do you live?" the man asked.

"North of Chicago. A little place called Wilmette."

Wiles stepped between the pilot and his ship and asked, "If there was a neurosurgeon who had the skill to do the work, would you let him try?"

Nate smiled, "I would, but even if that man existed—and Dr. Hutton tells me no one is willing to attempt this kind of procedure—I couldn't afford it. Lifesaving options are for the wealthy. Those without money die. It's a fact of life. Always has been."

"I won't argue," the man replied. "Maybe twenty years from now that'll change. Maybe we'll have a system that will provide medical care on an equal basis."

"Do you believe that?" the pilot asked.

"Maybe not," came the reply. "But it's a nice dream. At this moment I owe you something. You saved my life. And since my specialty is brain surgery—some people call me the best in the world—I'd like to look at your daughter's case."

For a long moment Nate couldn't speak. He stared at Wiles then placed his hands on the man's left shoulder and looked him squarely in his eyes. His words caught in his throat.

"I mean it," Wiles assured. "There are no guarantees, and maybe I can't help her. But I want to try. You've already paid for my services."

"I was just doing my job," Nate said.

"And now it is time for me to do mine."

Chapter 66

Nate Coffman paced the hall outside the surgical waiting room in Chicago's Parkside Hospital. His daughter's operation was now five hours old, and the only word he and Beverly had been given during that time was that it would be a while longer.

Feeling frustrated at not being in control, the father moved back into the room where his wife calmly waited. She'd been with Angel through this whole thing. She held her when the pain was too great to bear and played with her when she seemed completely healthy. During that time Beverly had developed a kind of tranquility he couldn't fathom. Even now her face looked so peaceful it was almost as if she didn't have a worry in the world. He couldn't understand it. Angel's life was hanging in the balance and that fact evidently hadn't pushed its way into his wife's head.

"Why don't you sit down?" she begged him. "Walking is not doing you any good at all."

"They've opened up my little girl's head and are operating on her brain," he said. "Don't you get that?"

She nodded. "Isn't it wonderful? A few weeks ago we had no hope at all. We were waiting for her to have one more seizure and die. Now we have hope. I want to embrace that feeling, Nate. Hope is the most wonderful thing in the whole world!"

He eased down beside her. How simple she was. She wasn't asking for the moon or wishing on a star. She was just giving thanks because she finally had a reason to hope.

And there was real hope, too. Dr. Wiles seemed to believe he could untangle the mass in Rose's head and make his girl all right again. Yes, the surgeon told them it was risky, but it was a risk worth taking. After all, when you had no hope, even a sliver of hope was worth gambling on. There was that word again. *Hope!*

The sound of footsteps on the tile caused him to

look up. Standing in the waiting room's entry was the man who'd once been late to catch a plane. He'd removed his surgical garb and was dressed in dark slacks and a long-sleeved, white shirt. As the couple locked onto him, he raised his eyebrows and smiled.

"Doctor?" Beverly asked as she rose.

"First of all, you have a very strong little girl. Her heart never skipped a beat."

"Thank God." Beverly sighed.

"Second, I was able to cut out all the mass. We'll test it, but it doesn't appear to be cancerous. I would bet my life it won't come back either. I don't think we damaged any parts of her brain in the process. So, if things go well in the next few days, Angel should live a very normal life with only a scar hidden by her beautiful blond hair."

As Beverly's eyes filled with tears of joy, a still-worried Nate latched onto something Wiles had just said. "What do you mean *if things go well?* The surgery is over. Wasn't that the tough part?"

"Yes, it was," Wiles assured the father, "but the big issue now is infection. We have to make sure that doesn't happen, and that means keeping her here until she is completely healed. It will likely be two or three weeks until she's home. But I have no doubt she will get there."

"Thank you," Beverly said, reaching out for the man's hand.

"Amazing," Nate added.

"What I did today will be the norm in years to come," Miles assured him.

"I can accept that," Nate explained. "People put their lives in my hands every time I fly. What's amazing is that if we hadn't waited at the gate, without Wiggins going crazy and trying to use the plane to commit suicide, without that landing in that field, none of this would have happened."

The doctor shrugged. "Maybe there's a plan behind this. Maybe it was mapped out before the events happened. Maybe each one of us is a player, and we all had to play our parts in order to save an Angel. In any case, I'm glad I had a part in it."

He looked each of them in the eyes thoughtfully before he went on. "A mass like this killed my sister twenty years ago. That's why I am who I am, why I have these skills. As Beverly explained to me last week, your little girl lost her birth folks and ended up being adopted by the pilot who would save my life. There's something much bigger than us going on here. None of us knows what that is, but I sense it's not over yet."

His work done, Wiles smiled then turned and left. As the doctor turned the corner and strolled down the hall, Beverly latched onto Nate's arm and whispered, "Hope has turned into faith."

He smiled. *Faith* was another really good word.

Chapter 67

December 7, 1941

It was Sunday, and except for the constant rumors of war, there was no reason to go to her office at the White House, so Helen Meeker opted to sleep in. She got up at ten, fixed some toast for breakfast, and went through a stack of mail that she hadn't opened through the week. One of the nice surprises among all the bills was a Christmas card from Henry Reese. He'd been transferred to Hawaii and used much of the enclosed letter to brag about how beautiful paradise was. Now she was sure he wasn't going to have a white Christmas, but where she lived the verdict was out on that one, and in truth she wanted snow this year. She wanted anything that would bring a bit of cheer into her lonely life.

Even though everywhere she looked signs of the holidays were around her, she was having problems grasping that Christmas was just two and a half weeks away. Yes, the radio was pumping out seasonal favorites, the stores were fully decorated, and Christmas tree lots were sharing space with used car lots, but try as she could, she couldn't get in the mood. Maybe it was because she had no one to celebrate with. In fact, beyond buying gifts for a few of her fellow staff members at the White House, she didn't have a reason to go shopping. Maybe even worse was that no one would be remembering her either. The Christmas card from Reese might well be the only really personal and meaningful holiday message to come into her life this year. And then there was the unsolved Rose Hall kidnapping case that still haunted her. Knowing the pain the Halls were going through coupled with the loss of her own sister so long ago had built a wall between her and others. Deep down she didn't want friends or partners. She didn't want to get close to someone only to have that person ripped from her.

As she contemplated her loneliness, Meeker brewed some tea, poured herself a cup, wrapped her terry cloth robe tightly around her body, and picked up one of a dozen files she'd brought home yesterday. The one she chose was the profile of a fifty-two-year-old German immigrant. Like all the others in the stack, he was suspected of being a spy.

As she opened the folder she immediately noted that there was nothing menacing about his photo. Put a fake white beard on him and Herman Strauss looked like he could have played Santa at Macy's. Yet his dossier held pages of reports linking him to suspicious activities in New York City and Boston. As she weeded through the interviews and eyewitness accounts, she was pretty much con-vinced Strauss very well might be a Nazi plant attempting to form an underground movement in America. At the very least he needed to be brought in and questioned to make sure he wasn't a part of the fifth column.

Five folders later it was not time nor boredom but hunger that finally pulled her from her work. She couldn't believe it was already afternoon. How had that happened? Where had the time gone? Setting the files on a coffee table, she got up, switched on the radio and, while its seven vacuum tubes warmed up, walked through her small apartment's living room to the kitchen. After pulling out some bread, she opened the refrigerator and started searching for something to put on it. Because the radio finally came on, she never finished that simple task. A news reporter's voice made sure of that.

"Reports are flowing in from several sources now confirming that a surprise attack on Pearl Harbor, which is in the Hawaiian Territories, has caused great damage and resulted in great loss of lives. The Japanese struck by air at about eight local Hawaiian time. There was no warning!"

Meeker was so stunned she almost didn't hear the phone. It was the sixth ring before she managed to cross back into the living room and pick it up.

"Hello." She paused as she listened to the words coming from her office before saying, "I just heard about it on the radio." She paused again before adding, "I'll get dressed and be at the White House as soon as possible."

Moving to the radio, she cut it off. Whatever her life had been, it was suddenly much different. Being alone at Christmas no longer was the most haunting thought in her head.

Chapter 68

There was a special potluck dinner after services at the Oakwood Methodist Church, and Carole had somehow convinced George they needed to go. And even though the ache in his heart from losing his daughter was still deep and raw, he did have much to be thankful for. He was home, doing well at work, and he and Carole were expecting again. Their baby was due in April. This child certainly would not fill the hole left by Rose's absence, but it would at least bring life and energy back into their home. They so needed both of those things.

Almost everyone had finished eating their choices from the potluck table and were now sitting around the tables catching up on local talk when an unexpected guest walked into the fellowship hall. His mere appearance at church caused all eyes to turn to the door.

"My goodness," Beatrice Eicker announced, "don't go outside. I don't care how cold it is, lightning might strike you. Sam Johns has actually come to church."

A half-dozen people laughed, but not for long. Everyone was staring at Johns. He simply didn't look like himself. The usually fastidious man hadn't shaved, and he was wearing old, stained, and wrinkled pants and an equally shabby flannel shirt. He wasn't smiling either. His grim posture bathed the room in an uneasy silence. He moved to the head table, stood beside Reverend Morris, and sized up the crowd. Finally, after more than a minute of awkward silence, he spoke, "I come bearing some very bad news." His tone was as somber as his message.

"Is someone dead?" Carole Hall asked.

He nodded. "Many are. The Japanese hit Pearl Harbor today. They bombed our Navy yards."

"Where's that?" one woman asked.

A man yelled out, "California."

"No," Johns corrected him. "Pearl Harbor is a Navy base in Hawaii. Jap planes hit us this morning. Radio reports state that thousands were killed, and there was evidently much damage done to American ships. I am hearing that other Pacific bases are being hit as well."

Johns took another deep breath. "Ladies and gentlemen, we are at war!"

Almost instantly, a host of people picked up

their belongings and headed out the door. One of the first were the Halls. Neither Carole nor George noticed the stiff breeze or the near freezing temperatures as they walked in stunned silence to their home. It was only when they were inside and were removing their coats that Carole posed the question she dared not think, much less speak. "What does this mean?"

George shook his head. "It changes everything. I'm sure I'll end up in the service somewhere. I'm sure, since Germany and Italy are allies of Japan, that we'll be fighting them as well."

"No," Carole whispered. "You can't leave me again."

"I'll put it off as long as I can," he promised. "Hopefully I'll be here when the baby comes. But I won't have a choice. They'll need men like me. I'll have to go when they call. You have to understand that."

She shook her head and sighed. "Why now?"

Chapter 69

Janet Carson had not moved from in front of her radio since she'd heard the first news bulletin. She thought of her late Aunt Abbi, who had visited all the nations involved in what had suddenly become a World War, and how she would have been fascinated by this turn of events.

In fact, that wise old lady had even predicted there would be another war not long after Hitler had come to power in 1933.

Like her aunt, Janet was not blind to what was going on over there; she'd been reading between the lines in the newspapers and listening closely to political speeches. For those who wanted to acknowledge reality, it was obvious America had been inching toward this point for some time. It was just she didn't expect the plunge into war would be due to an attack on an American base. She'd figured it would be the Nazis taking out an American ship. And it was a shame that it had happened so close to Christmas. She would have students whose fathers or brothers would be leaving for war just before Santa arrived. That wouldn't make for a merry anything.

It was two hours after the first report aired that her phone rang. She immediately recognized her cousin Jim's voice.

"Guess you know about what the Japanese did today?" She was surprised there was no sense of shock or sadness in his tone.

"Yes," she replied. "It's horrible."

Jim agreed, "Going to mess up a bunch of lives, that's for sure. Thank goodness I can't pass a military physical. At least I won't be putting my life on the line. But the good news is there should be some money to be made in it, too. I've been looking at which companies will likely be ramping up weapon production, and I think I have figured a way to make some real cash. I just called to see if you wanted to invest some of your savings, too. This could be a real opportunity!"

"You're serious?" she asked. "The world's falling apart, thousands, maybe millions are going to die, this country might not win the war, and you're thinking about making money?"

"You've got to be logical," he explained. "You're a teacher—you know your history well enough to understand that fortunes are made by war. I want to be one of those making the big bucks."

"James, how can you be so selfish?"

"Don't lecture me," he snapped. "Just remember when I come out of this living high on the hog that I gave you a chance to change your address, too."

"You're living pretty well right now," she shot back. "Besides, what makes you think you won't pass a physical? Except for being fat you look pretty healthy to me."

He laughed. "I've got a doctor who'll make sure I don't pass my physical. I'm not going any-where. The men with brains or wealth never go to war."

"Some kind of *man*," she sniped.

"I'm the smartest kind of man," he answered. "I figure out the best thing for me, and I'm going for it. I don't let little things like being a patriot get in my way like you do."

He hung up before she could say anything else. His call had angered her, but it had also given her an idea. She picked up a notebook and started to write down a series of questions. Tomorrow she was going to not just comfort her fifth graders about the devastating effects of the attack, but she would also challenge them to think about the cost of war.

Chapter 70

"I don't want you to enlist," Beverly pleaded. "You've got Angel to think about. This year has been the best in our lives. She's healthy again, and she needs her dad. There are school plays and programs and homework, and you need to be there for all of those things. This is the most important time for you to be the father I know you can be."

As he searched the bedroom for his gloves, he answered, "I want to be that kind of father, too, but this is bigger than us. This war is going to be won by men like me who know how to fly. I can go into this battle as an officer. I'll have good money to send home while I'm also doing my part for this country. You shouldn't want to stop me from doing that."

"But, Nate, there are hundreds of men like you; let them go."

He smiled as he found his gloves on a shelf in

the closet. They were just where he had left them. Stuffing the gloves into his coat pocket he turned back to his wife and explained, "Those men *will* go, just like me."

"But who's going to do the work here?" she demanded. "Who's going to build all those planes and tanks? Who's going to deliver the mail? Who's going to stock the shelves? Someone has to stay home and make the things needed for war and do all the jobs the men are leaving behind."

He gently squeezed her shoulders as he looked directly into her dark eyes. "The women will step up. Across the Atlantic they are working in the factories, at the post office, in shops . . . They are doing the work men used to do while their husbands are off fighting. And retired folks will be going back to work, too. That's the only way we can win."

He grabbed his billfold and began to pull out scraps of paper. One by one he read them before tossing them onto the bed.

"What are you looking for?" she asked.

"I've got a phone number of a major in the Army Air Corps. He was a passenger a couple of months ago. He's the guy I need to talk to. With my background and flying experience, I should be in line to become an officer."

Beverly shook her head. She was beaten and she knew it. There was no use arguing with him.

Nate was going to join. He might even be gone before Christmas.

Why, when everything had become so perfect, did it all have to fall apart?

Chapter 71

March 10, 1942

Beverly had been working at Motl Aviation for six weeks. Before the war started she'd never seen herself as a retail clerk or a secretary, much less a line worker in a factory. But the more she'd thought about Nate's words, the more she became convinced she needed to do her part. Beyond knowing that she was building the very bombers her husband would be flying in Europe, the company took excellent care of the children of employees. A bus hired by Motl took the children to a neighborhood school and picked them up at day's end, bringing all the kids back to child-care facilities right on the plant site. With the school just three blocks away and the child-care program less than fifty yards down a long hall, Beverly felt as though she was never separated from Angel.

It made it easier that Angel loved school and really enjoyed the time after school hours playing with kids her own age whose mothers also worked at the factory. In a very real sense, because the girl was so social, Angel was happier than she'd ever been just playing by herself at home. And though Beverly knew her little girl missed her father, the letters they received always made both of them smile. So things weren't as bad as she imagined they would be.

It was just past five. Beverly had already punched out and was heading down the hall toward the child-care department when someone called her name.

"Mrs. Coffman."

She turned and noted a slightly heavyset, older woman hurrying down the hall in her direction. Though she didn't know the woman's name, she recognized her from the lunchroom.

"Mrs. Coffman," the woman called out again. By the time she was next to Beverly the stranger was out of breath from her sprint down the hall. "I'm Clara Baker. I work on assembly line B. My daughter, Jenny, and your daughter, Angel, play together every day."

"Mrs. Baker, so nice to meet you. I've met Jenny. She is a wonderful young girl. Angel loves her."

"Thank you," Clara replied. "I hate to ask you this, but we had an issue on my line today, and I need to work another four hours so we can catch up. I was wondering, as they don't keep child-care open late, if you could take my Jenny home with you tonight. If you give me your address, I could pick her up later."

"Sure," Beverly replied, "Angel would love to have her over." She pulled a pencil and an old envelope from her purse to scribble down her address and telephone number.

"Thank you," Clara said, tucking the envelope into her uniform pocket once she handed it to her. "I'll walk with you to child-care so I can tell Jenny where she's going."

Jenny seemed genuinely excited as they left the plant and strolled out to the parking lot. She and Angel were giggling as they waltzed along rows of cars. Beverly ushered them to the fourth row and directed them to the right. Halfway to the fence sat their Packard.

Seeing the car, Jenny smiled. "Is that yours?"

"It sure is," Angel told her. "My daddy bought it for us."

Beverly unlocked and opened the front driver's side door, climbed in, and released the lock on the back door. Angel crawled into the rear seat. When the woman looked at her daughter for an explanation, the girl piped up with words that made Beverly very proud. "You always say we are supposed to give the best things to our guests. Jenny is our guest, so she should ride in the front seat."

Beverly smiled and waved her hand toward the front door. Jenny grinned, pushed her dark blond hair away from her face, and climbed in. Closing the door, the woman hurried around to the other side.

The drive home was uneventful. The girls talked about school, clothes, and radio shows. They were three blocks from the Coffman's home in Wilmette, when the conversation moved to dolls.

"I've got a doll that cries," Angel bragged.

"I've got a couple of dolls," Jenny replied. "They don't cry, but one of them has eyes that close."

"That's neat," Angel enthusiastically noted.

"But dolls aren't my favorite toys," Jenny explained. "You know what is?"

"No. What?"

Beverly pulled into their drive. Parking the Packard, she shut off the engine and reached for her purse that was sitting between her and Jenny. Just as she did, the little girl placed her hand under the corner of the seat. The bemused woman watched as their guest felt carefully along the seat's edge. A growing smile indicated she'd found what she was looking for. Jenny pulled her hand up and showed the woman two magnetic Scotty dogs. They were small enough the little girl could hide them in her fist. One was black and the other white.

"Watch what they do." Jenny almost laughed. "See when I put them nose to nose they look like they're fighting."

"Wow," Angel exclaimed. "That's swell! Let's go inside and play with them."

"Okay," Jenny agreed as she reached for the door handle.

"Just a second," Beverly quietly said. "Before we get out, I need to ask a question."

Both girls looked at the obviously confused and curious woman. "Jenny, how did you know the dogs were under the seat?"

"I put them there," she immediately explained.

The woman considered the answer. She didn't know how the girl could have put them there. Yes she'd walked around the car in the plant parking lot, but Beverly had been watching Jenny during that time. She had been standing talking to Angel. Beverly was sure of that.

"Jenny," Beverly asked, "when did you put them under the seat?"

"A long time ago," came the puzzling response. "My real mommy gave them to me."

The woman had no idea what to ask next, so she opened the door and followed the kids into the house. Yet, as she watched the girls play with Jenny's favorite toys, the troubling question as to how they got into her car and on the bottom of the seat frame continued to prick her mind. Try as she could, she just couldn't let it go. This was a mystery that she had to get to the bottom of, and she figured there was one sure way to do it.

Chapter 72

"I hope she wasn't too much trouble," Clara said as she stepped into the Coffman's home.

"No," Beverly assured her, "she was wonderful. The girls are up in Angel's room playing with one of her dolls. Why don't you come into the living room and warm up a bit? It's cold out tonight."

"It sure is," she agreed, following her host across the foyer. "I didn't know the temperature was going to drop like it did. Chicago is just a lot colder than I'm used to."

Beverly pointed to a large, green chair, and after Clara sat down, Beverly eased onto the corner of the couch. As she did, she reached down to the coffee table and picked up the dog toys. Her guest's eyes followed her movement, but they registered no signs of recognition upon lighting on the toys.

"Have you ever owned a Packard?" Beverly asked.

"Heavens, no." Clara laughed, emphasizing her answer with a big wave of her hand. "I've never even ridden in one."

"Have you ever owned toys like this?" Beverly asked, opening her fist to reveal the black and white dogs.

"No," Clara answered. "I've seen them but never owned any. Why do you ask?"

Pulling her fist shut, Beverly explained, "Because your daughter found them in our car. She told us she put them there, and they were hers."

Suddenly the heavyset woman bolted from the chair as if she had been given a jolt of electricity. Even before she was completely upright she hollered, "Jenny, it's almost ten. We have to get home." She then slipped her gloves on and looked toward her host. "Thank you again for taking care of my girl."

"Clara," Beverly softly but firmly replied, "you didn't answer my question. How did your daughter know these dogs were in our Packard?"

"Where is that girl?" Clara said nervously.

"I'm here," came the answer. A second later Jenny appeared. She'd already slipped her coat on and was buttoning it up.

"We need to go," Clara said, grabbing the little girl's arm and pulling her toward the door.

"I have to get my toys," Jenny argued, pointing toward the dogs that Beverly was holding in her open palm.

"Those aren't yours," the woman snapped.

"Yes, they are," Jenny answered, digging her heels into the carpet. "And I want them."

Still holding the girl with her left hand, Clara pulled back her right and brought it sharply across Jenny's face. If it stunned the girl, she didn't show it, nor did she cry.

A shocked Beverly didn't know what to do. She wasn't prepared for what had just transpired.

"You shouldn't have done that!" Angel said.

"Listen, you little brat," Clara barked, "Jenny lied, and she needed to be taught a lesson. Maybe you do, too."

Frightened, Angel rushed past the woman and behind her mother. A second later, the door slammed shut.

Chapter 73

Beverly remained unsettled for the rest of the night and all the next day. She couldn't get the events of the preceding evening out of her mind. They ate at her like a hungry dog gnawing on a bone. The fact that Clara had slapped Jenny was less troubling than the woman's response to the toy dogs. There was something wrong, but Beverly had no idea what to do about it. After all, was it really any of her business anyway? She barely knew the woman or the child. Yet as much as she tried to convince herself the situation wasn't something that should concern her, she couldn't shake it. It consumed her thoughts while she worked that day. At lunch she even tried to find Baker in the cafeteria and ask about the toys again. She later convinced herself that it was good she hadn't found the woman.

As she and Angel drove home, Beverly remained mute, allowing the radio's music to entertain her daughter. Finally, after ten minutes of silence, Angel turned down the volume and said, "I sure wish Jenny had been at school today."

"She wasn't there?" Beverly asked.

"She wasn't at the child-care room either," Angel explained. "Maybe her face hurt too much."

Her daughter's words stung. Yes, this was her business. Making a right turn, she drove around the block and headed back for the plant. Leading Angel by the hand, she crossed the parking lot, entered the main building, and took an elevator up to the third floor. She walked down a hall and into the personnel department, where she flashed her work badge and made a very innocent inquiry.

"I need to have the address of one of the line workers—Clara Baker. I took care of her daughter for her last night, and little Jenny left her favorite toy at our house. I need to return it."

An elderly, white-haired woman with large glasses glanced up from her duties. She studied the badge and then Beverly before asking, "What was that name again?"

"Clara Baker."

Getting up from her desk, she waddled across the room to a file cabinet. She opened a drawer, leafed through the contents for a few seconds then, pulling a pencil from its resting place on top of her ear and a piece of paper from her pocket, jotted down the information. Closing the cabinet, she waddled back and announced, "Here it is. Seems like a lot of trouble for a toy."

"Thank you," Beverly said, grabbing the paper and looking at the address. It appeared to be an apartment house in Evanston. It would only be a few blocks off their regular route home. But even if it had been twenty miles out of their way, she would have gone that distance, too. She was suddenly that deeply troubled.

"Come on, Angel."

"Are we going to visit Jenny?"

"I sure hope so."

It took thirty minutes to get to the red brick complex. There were five one-story buildings, each housing four apartments. Clara Baker lived in 3B.

It was just getting dark when Beverly knocked on the door. No one answered. She tried again.

"I don't think they're home," Angel noted.

Not giving up, Beverly pounded on the entry. As she did, an older man stepped out of the next unit.

"You looking for Clara?" he asked.

"Yes," Beverly replied. "You know where she is?"

"I own this place," he replied. "I'd like to know where she went as well. I was gone, but the folks over in 3A told me she came home late last night, packed up her car, and headed out. Except for some food, a bed, and a couple of chairs, there ain't anything left in that place. She cleared out owing me a month's rent. And the place is such a mess it is impossible to describe. I'll have to repaint every wall before I can rent it again."

"So you don't know where she went?" Beverly asked.

"No idea," he replied. "Sorry about that. Hope she didn't owe you money, too." The short, pudgy man stepped back into his flat and shut the door.

Alone in the darkness, Beverly wondered what she should do now. Something was obviously very wrong, and Jenny finding those toys in their car had triggered it all.

"You know, Mommy."

"What is it, Angel?"

"Jenny never calls her mommy *Mommy*. Why is that?"

Beverly looked down at her child. "What's she call her?"

"Nothing," came the flat response. "That's strange. She's the only kid I know who doesn't have a name for her mommy."

Beverly was now even more troubled. If Clara wasn't the mother, and they certainly looked nothing alike, then who was? Where had the little girl come from?

"Mommy, seeing as how they're gone, do you think we should do something with their mail?"

Beverly turned around and looked at the small metal box beside the doorframe. Tampering with it was likely a federal offense, but she didn't care. She yanked out two envelopes and examined them. Both had return addresses in Koshkonong, Missouri. Stuffing the letters into her coat pocket, she grabbed Angel's hand and with purpose in her step walked back to the Packard. She couldn't do anything tonight, but tomorrow she had a rare Friday off. She just hoped that even with the whole world at war she could find someone who would listen to her strange story.

Chapter 74

Even though Henry Reese wanted to be in the military, J. Edgar Hoover stepped in and kept him and about a dozen other agents from enlisting. It seemed Henry's duties with the FBI were of more national importance than fighting in the Pacific or Europe. That meant, at least for the moment, that he was back in Chicago investigating possible espionage at a local munitions plant. His one-week investigation had not revealed any fire and very little smoke.

In the old office he'd once shared with Helen Meeker, he picked up the phone. It was time to close this case and ask for a new assignment. As soon as someone in the Washington DC office picked up the line, he was going to ask to be shipped back to Hawaii. He knew there was real work to be done there, work that would place him much closer to helping end this war. But a knock on his door kept him from making that call.

He set the phone down, got up, buttoned the middle of the three buttons on his suit coat, crossed the room, twisted the knob, opened the door, and was greeted by the last person he wanted to see—an agitated woman and her smiling daughter.

"May I help you?" he inquired.

"I hope so," the woman quickly replied.

"Come in," Reese said. "There are two chairs in front of my desk. I want to warn you they aren't as comfortable as the ones you will find in firehouses, but hopefully they'll do."

"I'm sure they'll be fine," she answered, moving with a sense of urgency to the desk. As the tiny woman gracefully sat in the chair on the left, her daughter climbed up into the one on the right.

After they were settled, Reese closed the door and strolled over to join them. As he took his seat, a large clanking noise filled the room shocking the visitors and causing them to crane their heads back toward the far wall.

"It's the steam heat!" he yelled. "It'll calm down in a second." As if on cue, it did. "Now, I'm Agent Henry Reese. What can I do for you two young ladies?"

"Mr. Reese, I'm Beverly Coffman. This is my daughter, Angel. I work at Motl Aviation."

He nodded and observed the woman nervously fiddling with her wedding ring before asking the dreaded but apparent question, "I'm guessing you believe that enemy agents are working in the plant."

"No," she answered, her voice filled with shock. "Has that been a problem?"

He shook his head. "But from the number of tips we get, you'd think it was. So what are you here for?"

"It is about a little girl," she began. "Though I really have no proof, I think she has been kidnapped." As he leaned forward, she added, "I know it sounds strange, but I need to explain my story to someone."

"Please do," he replied, glad to be visiting with a civilian who wasn't seeing spies everywhere. Resting his elbows on his desk and staring directly into the woman's eyes, he waited for her to give him the details.

Beverly explained the events that had happened on Wednesday night. She then shared the events that had transpired at the apartment. After she'd finished, she looked to the man for some signs of urgency. There were none.

"Mrs. Coffman," Reese began, "what you've given me would make a solid soap opera script, but there's hardly enough here to link it to some kind of child abduction. Maybe the child's toys represent a bad memory for the woman. And perhaps the little girl stuck those toys to your seat while you weren't looking. Kids move quickly."

Beverly reached into her purse and fished out the magnetic dogs. "Here they are."

"I've seen a lot of dogs like this," he assured her. "You can buy them all over the country. They even sold them at shops in Hawaii when I was there. I almost bought some for my nephew."

"I know that they aren't unusual," she replied, "but Clara Baker was genuinely upset, very nervous, near a fit, when I told her that Jenny found these in our car."

Reese took the dogs and placed them on his desk. He made them move as if they were playing with each other as the woman continued, "I also found these letters with a Missouri return address in Clara Baker's mailbox. I didn't open them, but you might want to. Maybe it will tell you something."

Reese took the envelopes and dropped them beside the dogs. Sensing he needed to say something that would give the determined woman some sense of comfort, he added, "I'll look into this. Write your address down for me and if I find out anything, I'll contact you."

"You really will check on where she went?" Beverly asked.

415

"I promise," he assured her. "Now did you take a bus or a cab?"

"No, we drove."

"Where are you parked?" he asked.

"We found a place on the street about a half block from the front door."

"Weren't you lucky," he observed, pulling himself from his chair. "I need to stretch my legs, so let me ride down on the elevator and walk you to your car."

Strolling from the office, they quickly stepped down the hall and punched a button. A second later, a bell rang and the doors opened.

"Where to, Agent Reese?" the young elevator operator asked.

"First floor." After the elevator started moving, the agent reopened the conversation. "Mrs. Coffman, is your husband in the service?"

"He's on his way to England," she proudly replied. "He's a pilot. He'll be flying bombers."

"Brave man," Reese noted, a bit of envy evident in his tone. The door opened, and the trio stepped out into a lobby that was alive with activity. After passing a barbershop and newsstand, the woman and child entered the revolving door. He followed behind. The wind was brisk, and the gray skies suggested another blast of snow was on its way. Suddenly Hawaii called out to him, and he couldn't wait to get back to the office and make that request.

"We're right up here," she announced.

The woman walked with a determined step. He sensed she would have been going even faster if her daughter's legs had been a bit longer. As the sounds of honking horns and screeching tires filled the morning air, a bus eased up to the curb and dropped off a dozen passengers, forcing the trio to stop for a few seconds. After the bus patrons had headed off in three different directions, the woman picked up her pace. It was only then that Reese saw it. Fifteen steps and twenty seconds later, she was pushing her key into the door lock.

"This is your car?" he asked, a sense of urgency now filling his tone.

"Yes," Angel assured him. "My daddy bought it."

"Where did he get it?" Reese demanded.

"Why?" Beverly asked. "Is that important?"

"It very well may be," he assured her, his eyes still glued to the Packard.

"He bought it at an auction. In fact, it was at an FBI auction."

"My Lord!" Reese exclaimed. "She's alive."

"Who's alive?" Beverly asked.

"If I'm right," he shot back, yelling over the commotion created by another passing bus, "a girl we've been trying to find for almost two years." Sweat suddenly appeared on his brow as he asked, "So this is the car she found the toy dogs in?"

"Yes!" the woman replied. "They were held in place by the magnets. She said she'd put them under the front seat when she was with her real mommy."

"Okay," Reese hurriedly said. "We need to get back to my office right now. I've got to make some calls, and we've got to track down this Clara Baker woman. The fact that she might be from Missouri, where the car you are driving was once sold, or the fact she has contacts there says more than you can ever believe."

As the woman and her daughter turned and headed back toward the office building, Reese took a final look at the Packard. Meeker had been right again. The car had been the key all along.

Chapter 75

Meeker had just stepped back into the White House's office wing after a lunch meeting with a supervisor in the OSS, when one of the clerks, Victoria House, waved and cried out, "Helen, an FBI agent called from Chicago. He needs you to call him as quickly as possible. By the way, love that suit."

"Thanks," Meeker said as she passed in front of House's desk. "I picked it up last week at Woosters. They've managed to get in some new things in spite of the war. Did the agent leave a name?"

"Yes," the twenty-four-year-old brunette replied, "Reese. Henry Reese. He said he was calling from Illinois." She handed her a slip with the phone number.

"So he's back in Chicago," Meeker remarked.

"What's that?" the clerk asked.

"Nothing," Meeker assured her. "Have the switchboard make that call and when they get Reese, patch it through to my desk."

"Patch it through." House laughed. "You're starting to sound like a spy."

Ignoring the comment, Meeker made her way down a long hallway and into her small, ten-by-ten, windowless office. It was that lack of window that she most hated. She loathed not being able to see what was going on outside. Doing so just helped her think.

As she moved through her door, the phone rang. It was the switchboard alerting her that Reese was on the line.

"How you doing, Henry?" she asked.

"Except for the cold weather in Chicago, fine. Let me assure you, I do miss Hawaii."

"Gee, it's good to hear your voice. When did they transfer you back to the States?"

"About six weeks ago," he explained. "But I didn't call to catch up. I've got something you need to know about, and I'm hoping you can work with me at least one more time."

"What is it?" she asked, suddenly intrigued by the possibility of reuniting with the FBI agent. "You have something the OSS needs to look into?"

"No. Is that who the President has teamed you up with now?"

"This week anyway. I kind of freelance. But the spy guys use gals, too, so it is much easier to fit in at the OSS than with you G-men."

"No doubt," he agreed. "It is long overdue. Now give me your ears! I've got a really good lead on the Rose Hall kidnapping."

She took a deep breath, got up from her chair, and leaned on the corner of her desk. "Define good lead." She followed that with a question she didn't want to ask. "Have you found the body?"

"No," he quickly shot back. "I am pretty sure she is alive and living with a woman who up until a couple of days ago worked in the Motl Aviation here in Chicago. As soon as she found out someone might be on to her, she bolted with the girl. This woman's name was Clara Baker. I'm thinking she might be the Clara Hooks woman we couldn't find in St. Louis back when we were looking for the owner of the Packard."

"She and her husband owned the place where Burgess lived when he unloaded the car?" Meeker asked.

"Yeah, the same one. I had a couple of folks who knew her in Missouri look at the picture we got from her Motl Aviation personnel file, and they were sure it was her."

"Where did she go?" Meeker asked. "Any idea?"

"My best guess is southern Missouri. Or at least that is where the answers are going to be. In case she is there with the kid, I want to go down there myself. Could you fly into St. Louis? I could pick you up, and we could drive down there together."

"I don't think Lepowitz would like that," she replied.

"I don't think it matters," Reese assured her. "The big guy has fallen out of Hoover's inner circle. Besides, this woman worked for one of our biggest suppliers of bombers—it could be a matter of national security. And in times like this, when it comes to matters of national security, all branches of the government and the agencies within those branches must work together. You say you're OSS this week?"

"Yeah."

"I'll put in a request that you help me clean this up. After all, you never know what this woman stole from the plant. Could have been plans for a proposed bombsight." She knew he was making a joke, but the scenario did give her probable cause to be involved in the case.

"I'll pack my bags," Meeker informed him. "But before I do, I've got to ask how you found this woman and discovered she might have Rose."

"The car," he explained. "The little girl rode in

the yellow Packard. It seems the family who reported her brought her to their house to play. They had bought the car at our auction. This girl they knew as Jenny reached under the front seat—"

"And found two magnetic dog toys." Meeker didn't let him finish.

"How'd you know?" He sounded more than a bit amazed.

"I knew they were there," she whispered. Moving off her desk, she sat down in her swivel chair. Her eyes fell to her calendar. There was nothing in DC that she couldn't put off for a few days. Plus there was an investigation she needed to do in Chicago concerning a possible group of German sympathizers in the city's west side. Justifying the trip would not be a problem. And if anyone protested, she'd just call Eleanor.

"Henry, when can you get to St. Louis?"

"I can drive down early tomorrow morning and be at the airport by noon."

"I'll catch the first plane out. And if I beat you, I'll wait."

"I'll check the schedules," he assured her, "and I'll make sure I'm waiting at the gate."

"Thanks," she said softly.

"It will be good to get the team back together. Maybe 'The Grand Experiment' can be revived."

"I just want to close the case," she replied. "Bye."

"Good-bye, Helen."

She placed the receiver back in its cradle. Getting up quickly, she marched out the door, down the hall, and into Gladys Termane's office. She waited for the fifty-year-old secretary to finish jotting down some information while she was on the phone before lightly tapping on her desk.

"What is it you need, honey?" Termane asked as she hung up.

"I've got to get to St. Louis as soon as possible. Can you book me out on a flight in the morning?"

The woman smiled. "I'll do it even if I have to bump an admiral off the plane."

Chapter 76

As promised, Reese was at the gate waiting for her. After quick greetings and grabbing her two bags, they hurried off to his car.

"You got one of the new ones," Meeker noted as she slid into a 1942 Ford Coupe. "How did you rate not getting stuck with one of the older, well-worn members of the FBI's mechanical fleet?"

"When they jerk you out of Hawaii," he said with a laugh, "and back to winter in Chicago, they feel they owe you. Now, let me catch you up on what I've found out since we last talked. After all, you'd rather talk about that than cars."

"Let me have it," she anxiously replied.

After they'd pulled out of the parking lot and pointed the maroon sedan south onto the highway, he gave her the scoop. "A local sheriff did a bit of legwork for me, and based on my description he was able to confirm that a woman who looks like Clara Hooks or Clara Baker is staying in a farmhouse about a quarter mile outside of Koshkonong."

"Koshkonong?" she asked.

"A little town in the south central part of the state. Not far from the Arkansas border."

"Koshkonong," Meeker said again.

"The locals call it Kosh," Reese informed her. "Now back to what I know. A little girl has been spotted with this older woman. The car in the drive matches the one Beverly Coffman saw Baker bring when she came to her house—a black midthirties Dodge. It has a large dent in the front fender."

"That information sounds solid," Meeker said as she nodded. "Do we know who lives at the house?"

"The man's name is Mike Burtrum. He's middle-aged and is somewhat a hermit. Moved to town about a year back. Bought the place where he lives with cash. Doesn't get out much. Goes to the grocery store about twice a month, and along with food he buys lots of cigarettes."

She lifted her eyebrows. "Same initials as the handyman in Oakwood and the prison guard. This guy's not very imaginative."

424

"Mr. Burtrum also holds his cigarettes the same way as Mr. Burgess, according to our source."

Meeker checked her watch. "How long will it take us to get there?"

"We'll be there by five."

"And we are sure the local cops haven't spooked them?"

"The sheriff has his mouth taped shut for two reasons. One, he's scared of the FBI, and the other is the reward's still out there, and he doesn't want to share it."

She glanced at a two-story Victorian home along the road. As she studied the gingerbread pattern on the porch railing, she posed one final question, "Are we going in alone?"

"No," the man answered. "I hope that doesn't disappoint you."

She turned her attention from the house back to the driver. "No, I'm fine with that as long as no one is trigger-happy. I don't want Rose to get hurt."

"I've read about the cases Melvin Purvis handled. He always went in with more firepower than he needed just in case something unexpected happened. So I have Austin Ross and J. P. Adams coming in from Little Rock. They were down there working on a bank robbery case."

"I remember Adams," she said. "I trust him."

"There is a part of my plan that requires a woman," Reese continued.

"Really," she said with a grin. "What do I do?"

"Not you," he shot back. "The guys are bringing along a gal from the secretarial pool. She's had some experience on the stage in high school and college, and we need those skills."

"We do?"

"Let me hang on to one of my secrets for a while," he quipped, a twinkle in his eyes.

As they left the St. Louis city limits heading south on Route 66, she eased back against the Ford's Bedford cord upholstery.

"Finding Rose Hall sure would put Hoover in his place," Reese noted, as if reading her mind.

"I really don't care about what old J. Edgar thinks," she softly replied. "I don't care about 'The Grand Experiment.' It's not nearly as important as giving that child back to her parents. You have no idea what that would mean to me."

"I think I have a better idea than you realize," he assured her. He paused for a long time before adding, "What was your sister's name?"

"Emily," she said softly. "I don't really even remember what she looked like."

"Don't you have pictures?" he asked as he reached over to turn the heater down a bit.

"No," she sadly answered. "Dad destroyed them after Mom died. He got rid of everything that was hers. It was as if he were trying to wipe out every facet of her existence. And he was success-ful except for one place." She grimly shook her head. "He couldn't wipe her out of his mind, and that killed him as surely as it killed Mom."

"I can't imagine," Reese proclaimed. "I really can't imagine that kind of pain."

"It's with me every day." She sighed. "That's why I pushed Eleanor into getting me a job with the FBI. You all are the ones who deal with kidnappings. I wanted to be there and help bring some-body's kid home."

"Looks like you're about to do that," he assured her.

"Maybe," she said, "but let's not get excited just yet. Let's hope she's still there and this wild goose chase is about over. When Carole Hall gets her kid back, then I will celebrate. But not until then."

Chapter 77

In Rolla, Missouri, they got off Route 66 and took U.S. Highway 63 to Koshkonong. As they rolled past the WELCOME sign, she sized the place up. There must have been two hundred people living in the city limits. There were a couple of stores; a filling station, a garage claiming to work on trucks, tractors, and cars; a post office; and a bank. Along the road on each side of the buildings that made up downtown were unassuming frame houses. Judging by the age of the cars and the size and condition of the homes, Koshkonong's citizens had experienced some very tough times during the Depression.

It was just past five when Reese piloted the new Ford into the parking lot of a small, native-stone Baptist church. A 1939 Ford was already there. Leaning against the hood, seemingly unconcerned about the cold north wind, was J. P. Adams. Meeker guessed the woman barely visible in the backseat was their actress, and Austin Ross had to be the man inspecting the gravestones at the cemetery on the north side of the old church.

After Reese set the parking brake and switched off the ignition, the two travelers got out and walked to Adams's position. As they strolled over to the spot, the woman opened the door, and Ross made his way across the cemetery to the parking lot. He was the last to arrive, and no one spoke until he did.

Sensing all eyes on him, Reese began, "This is Helen Meeker with the OSS. She worked this case with me from the get-go, and she deserves to be in on the finish."

Adams, a man of average height and build, nodded at her. "Nice to see you, Meeker. Wish they'd kept you around. Though we were all jealous Henry drew you as his partner."

"Thanks," she said, returning his smile. "If we can close this case up, I'll consider my time with the FBI worthwhile."

"Helen," Reese continued, "this young feller is Austin Ross."

Ross chuckled. At fifty-two, he was one of the oldest men in the bureau. Though he might have had some years on him, his hair was still jet-black, his body firm and fit, and his dark eyes filled with energy and life.

"Nice to meet you," he said in a deep voice that would have been welcomed for the bass part in any quartet in the country. Ross turned his gaze back to the woman they'd brought with them.

"This is Judy Asher, but today we can call her Bette Davis."

Asher was not beautiful, but she was kind of cute in a girl-next-door way. The sparkle in her hazel eyes and the shine in her honey blond hair exuded Southern charm. Yet it was her cute figure on her barely five-foot frame that men would have found alluring.

"Hi," she squeaked, accompanied by a quick wave.

Reese winked at Asher before turning back to the men. "Did you all drive by the house on your way in?"

"Yeah," Ross volunteered. "It's a frame home, maybe a thousand square feet. It has a small porch on the front and kind of a stoop on the back. Those are the only two entries or exits. There are no outbuildings, but there are some large cedar trees growing very close to the house. There's a pretty thick woods on the back and sides of the place. That should give you lots of cover as you work your way in from the south side—"

"So," Reese interrupted, "you are thinking the south side is the best way for Helen and me to get to the back of the house."

"Yeah," Ross said with a nod. "Based on the placement of the windows and doors that would likely be the path where the folks inside wouldn't see you."

From his spot leaning on the car, Adams picked up the conversation. "Austin's right on the mark. If we can get the adults in that house separated from the kid, you should be able to grab her without putting her life in any kind of danger. It'll be Judy's job to grab their attention and hold it. By the way, do we know how many adults will be there?"

"The sheriff told me there were never more than two," Reese explained. "I had him scope it out yesterday, and he swears it's only the woman, Clara Hooks, and our guy, Mitchell Burgess, aka several other names with those same initials."

The agents nodded. Reese turned his attention to the woman.

"Miss Asher, do you understand what you need to do?"

"When we get everyone in position," she quickly explained, "I walk up to the front door of the house and knock. I'll be crying. I'll explain that my car broke down a few hundred yards up the road and I need to make a call. As the house doesn't have a phone, I'll try to get the man to come look at the car with me to see if he can fix it."

"And if that doesn't work?" Reese quizzed her. "What do you do then?"

"I cry even harder and do everything in my power to at least get him to step out on the porch."

"Okay." Reese grinned. "We've got about an hour before it's dark enough to pull this off. Did you see a place anywhere near the house we could hide the cars and ourselves until that time?"

"Yeah," Ross replied. "There's a lane that leads to a farmhouse not too far away. We checked. The house is vacant. No one has lived there for a decade or more. The lane is passable, and the house and barn sit about a half a mile off the road. We can hide the cars behind those buildings. No one should see us."

"Lead the way," Reese said.

After they'd gotten back into Reese's FBI-issued car, Meeker remarked, "That's your big surprise? That's the master plan you were so tight-lipped about?"

"Yeah." He sounded a bit wounded. "What's wrong with it?"

"Nothing," she said with a laugh, "but the way you were hush-hush about it earlier, I was expecting something a bit more dramatic."

431

He shook his head as he eased his Ford behind the other agents' car. A mile down the road, when they were just beyond the city's southern limits, Ross tapped his brakes twice. Meeker knew the code.

Glancing to her left she saw the frame house.

"There's the old Dodge," Reese pointed out. "Looks like she is there."

"Yep," Meeker replied.

It was shabby, its white paint cracked and peeling, the roof patched with three different types of tin. The porch was not level, and the porch's roof was leaning forward. It looked as if a strong wind might take the whole place down. There was a large dirty window facing the highway. Meeker's heart stopped as she noted a small figure with blond hair staring through it. A few seconds later, the little girl and the house were out of view.

Chapter 78

For the next hour, all Meeker could picture was that face peering through the dirty piece of glass. She had been too far from the child and the window was too dirty for Helen to make out any details, so maybe it was her mind playing tricks on her, creating an impression of a sad, mournful expression. But in her mind the pain was there.

And it was that pain that was now eating at her and making time feel as if it were standing still.

As the minutes slowly passed, as the light gave way to dusk, and then darkness, Meeker felt more apprehension than elation. Even if they did get the child back, would they be returning the same little girl the Halls had known and loved? In Rose's time away from her family, what kind of damage had been done? Would her wounds heal?

As those questions shook her soul with questions she couldn't comprehend much less answer, she forced her thoughts in a new direction. The Halls had no idea what was going on. They didn't know that Rose has been found. They couldn't guess as they sat down for supper on this evening that what happened in the next few minutes would impact the rest of their lives. But what if the raid went south and Rose didn't make it out?

No, Meeker wouldn't allow herself to think that. She knew all too well what it meant to not have a child come home. So this case couldn't end that way. There had to be a happy ending that saw the parents wrapping their arms once more around their little girl.

"I'd trade my life for hers."

Looking over from his seat behind the Ford's big steering wheel, Reese said, "Hope it doesn't come to that. I have spent hours planning this out. I don't want any shots fired. I want Burgess or Burton or whatever his name is to be taken alive.

I need to know if he did this on his own or if he had help. After all, this case is more than just a kidnapping; it is a possible murder of an elderly woman and stolen money in the amount of a hundred grand. That makes this case the trifecta."

He was right. If they could get proof that Abbi Watling was murdered, then someone was going to go to the chair.

"Did you ever consider if there was anyone you'd die for?" Meeker asked Reese.

"That's a loaded question," he replied. Glancing her way and smiling, he asked, "Are you wanting to know if I'd die for you?"

She shook her head. "No, it wasn't until tonight that I'd ever thought about the question."

"And you've decided you'd die for the kid."

"Yes, I think I would."

His expression serious, Reese softly said, "Well there are a lot of preachers and at least one agent I know out there who'd say that you just suddenly understood a bit about what it is like to think like Christ."

"I don't think that's it," she answered. "This isn't biblical. At least not in my mind."

"I disagree," he replied. "I think everything is."

"You'd better explain that," she said.

"I don't understand my own faith," he admitted. "So there is no way I can begin to understand or explain yours. It is pretty personal anyway."

Personal was a good word. From the beginning,

this case had been personal. For Helen it was about healing old wounds and defining the price of life. And contrary to what a world at war seemed to be saying, life was not cheap. Each life mattered. Maybe that was biblical.

Reese glanced down to his watch. "It's time."

Chapter 79

They all piled into Ross's car for the short trip down the highway to the rickety farmhouse. Ross and Adams were in the front, Meeker sat against the passenger door in the back, Asher in the middle with Reese on the far side. Needing to size this up one final time, they slowly drove by the place. Once they'd rounded the curve and were out of sight, they turned around and did it again.

"There's another car there now," Ross noted.

"Did you note the make and color?" Meeker asked, as if already knowing the answer.

Reese beat Ross. "It was a dark Graham Shark-nose coupe."

"We've seen it before," Meeker noted.

Snapping his fingers, Reese said, "That was the car that delivered the cash to McGrew."

Meeker nodded. "So we were right about the identity of the man Pistolwhip wouldn't give up."

When they were about a quarter mile beyond

the home, Ross pulled the sedan off the highway and into the ditch. Popping the hood, he got out and jerked the wire loose from the coil. That way, if Asher could convince Burgess to walk to her car with her, he'd find it not working.

"Everyone know what they're doing?" Reese asked, as he stepped out into the cold night air.

They all grimly nodded as they checked their weapons. Meeker and Reese had FBI-issued handguns. Adams and Ross yanked Thompson submachine guns from the trunk and snapped in the ammo. Trying to lighten the mood, Asher pulled her compact from her purse and dabbed a bit of powder on her cheeks.

"My weapon is loaded," she nervously announced.

"You'll never be out of sight," Ross assured. "If he makes any kind of move, it will be his last."

"Check your watches," Reese ordered. "Asher, you make your move to the front door in ten minutes. When we see you engage the man, we'll sneak in the back door."

"What if it's locked?" Adams asked.

"It's an old house," Reese said. "I've got the hardware to pick old locks right here in my pocket."

"Good luck," Ross said.

"Be smart," Reese added. "A little girl's life hangs in the balance."

The trio from Little Rock headed down the road toward the house while Meeker and Reese cut across the highway and into the woods. The trek through the brush was not easy until they finally stumbled onto an animal path. Following it, they quickly made it to the edge of the woods by the house. Leaning against a large oak, they waited.

Two minutes later, they spotted Asher. She took a deep breath and then clumsily jogged up to the house. As she was wearing pumps, it wasn't easy to traverse the rocky ground. Getting to the porch, she noisily clomped up the steps and began to pound on the door. As she knocked, she yelled, "I need some help." She screamed it four times before the door cracked open.

"What's going on?" a woman asked.

"My car broke down about a hundred yards back up the road," Asher breathlessly explained. Her performance was first rate. She sounded hysterical, or maybe by this time she actually was.

"I need to use your phone to call someone," she begged, her voice ragged.

The door was still only halfway open, and the woman behind it didn't seem inclined to open it any wider. In a firm voice, she announced, "We don't have a phone."

"But I need help. Maybe your husband could help me."

"I'm not married," the woman answered. "And Kosh is only a half mile down the road. You can find someone with a phone there."

The woman tried to shut the door, but Asher stepped in to block the move. "Isn't there someone here who could look at it? Or give me a ride to town? I'm scared to walk in the dark. I'm just a helpless woman who needs a friend."

"What's going on here?" a man hollered from inside the house. His voice was edgy and coarse.

"This woman's had car trouble," the woman snapped. "I told her we can't help, but she won't leave."

Asher made her move. "I need a man. Would you please help me? I'll make it worth your time and effort."

The hint of a reward must have motivated Burgess; a few seconds later, he pulled the door open and stepped out onto the porch. "What's your problem?"

"It just quit running," she explained. "It's about a hundred yards up the road. Would you take a look at it for me?"

"Let's go," Reese whispered to Meeker. "This is as good a chance as we'll get."

The two stole up the side of the house. Hiding between a bushy cedar and the home, Meeker peeked into the living room window. The woman was standing at the door, looking out to where Burgess and Asher were still talking on the porch.

"The girl's not in here," Meeker whispered.

Moving to the next window, they looked into a vacant kitchen. There appeared to be another room beyond it, but that window was on the back side of the old house. So she signaled for them to move on. A few steps later they were in a very ill-kept backyard. A few dozen empty tin cans had been thrown out just beyond the back door, and two broken chairs leaned against the wall alongside a barrel spilling over with trash.

After quickly surveying the scene, Meeker pointed to the window in the nearest wall. Fortunately there was a light on. While Reese kept his gun aimed at the back door, Meeker sneaked up and looked in. The room was tiny, not more than six feet by eight. It contained a small bed and a chair. Sitting on the bed talking to a sad-looking doll was a little girl. From all the times she'd stared at her pictures, studying even the most minute details, Meeker was quickly convinced it was Rose Hall. So this was it. They had to move now!

Ducking away from the window, she pointed to the room and nodded. Reese's affirming look was all she needed. Crouching down, she hurried to the back door. With the man at her side, she climbed up the two wooden steps and tried the handle. It was locked. She pulled her gun and stepped out of the way as Reese crouched down and examined the keyhole. Yanking a couple of tools from his pocket, he went to work. It took him sixty seconds to complete his mission.

"Try it now," he whispered.

She twisted it to the right and it clicked. Inch by inch she eased it opened. As she did, she heard the voices of Asher and Burgess coming through the house from the front porch.

Meeker silently stepped into a room containing a cot and an old wooden chair. There were four dresses hanging in one corner, a few magazines tossed on the lone end table, and some women's shoes pushed under the cot. This must've been where Clara slept. To the left was a door that led to Rose's room. Halfway up the door was a large bent nail pushed through a hook that held the latch in place. Helen grimaced. When they put Rose to bed, they made sure she stayed there.

Meeker pointed it out to Reese. He nodded and moved soundlessly in the other direction. Pushing past Meeker, he slid beside the archway leading into the kitchen. He kneeled there, aiming his gun at the lone figure in the living room. Then when he was set, Meeker stole the rest of the way through the back room to Rose's locked door. Silently she yanked the nail out, dropping it into her pocket. She eased the latch back and pushed the door open. As she stepped into the tiny room, she touched her lips with her left index finger and whispered, "I'm here to take you back to your real parents."

"My parents?" Rose whispered back. "Clara said they didn't want me."

"Clara lied," Meeker said. "She's a bad woman. Your parents want you more than you can imagine. Now, we have to be very, very quiet."

Slipping her gun into her own coat pocket, she found the girl's shoes and managed to get them on her feet. Just as she did, chaos erupted in the front room.

"Mitch!" Clara screamed. "Someone's in the house!"

The man cursed while slamming the door shut. A second later, gunfire broke out. Three shots sounded, one from close range and the others from the front of the house. Scooping the girl into her arms, Meeker pulled the door open and stepped out. The first thing she saw was her partner face down on the floor. Filling the archway leading to the kitchen was Mitchell Burgess.

Chapter 80

"Who are you?" Burgess demanded.

"Federal agents," Meeker barked back.

As the man glared, his eyes burning with rage, Meeker placed the girl on the ground and gently pushed her behind her own body. When she was sure Rose was shielded, she turned her gaze back to the man with the menacing and very lethal thirty-two pointed straight at her.

"I'm taking this girl back to her parents," she boldly announced. As she spoke, her hands went into her coat pocket where she found her own firearm.

"No, you won't," Burgess said. "I knew we should have killed her."

"I'm walking out that door with this child right now," Meeker hissed. "You aren't going to stop me."

Gripping the gun, she aimed at the man's gut and pulled the trigger. There was no fire or recoil; the gun had jammed.

"You're dead," Burgess growled. But even as his words hung in the air, he staggered. He suddenly seemed confused and disoriented. The gun in his hand began to tremble as his face filled with a blush of color. Dropping his right arm to his side, he pulled his left up to his chest. A second later he moaned and fell to his knees, the gun falling from his hand to the floor.

Meeker quickly stepped over the stricken man and retrieved his gun. A second later she grabbed Rose's hand and led her out of the house. Scooping her up in her arms as her feet hit the grass, Meeker raced around the side the house. When she reached the front, she saw Asher standing in the drive and the two other agents running up.

"This is Rose," Meeker barked. "Take her down to the car right now."

After pulling the girl to her chest, Asher asked, "What happened?"

"Reese is down!" Meeker yelled. "Break down that door, and take care of that woman. I don't know if she's armed."

As Adams leaped up on the porch and kicked in the front door, Meeker raced to the back of the house. With Burgess's gun in her right hand, she hurried up the steps. Burgess was still on the floor where he'd fallen. Leaning up against the wall, his gun trained on Clara, was Reese. When Helen looked his way, the agent shrugged.

"I thought you were dead," she quipped.

"No real damage," he said. "When I was ducking out of the way of his shots, I hit my head on the side of the wooden frame of the archway. I must have knocked myself out."

"Likely saved your life," Meeker observed. "If he'd thought you were breathing, he'd have shot you for sure."

"I'll take this one off your hands," Ross announced, as he made his way into the kitchen. A few seconds later, Ross pushed a sobbing Clara out the door. As he did, Adams joined them in what had been the woman's room.

"Who got Burgess?" Adams asked.

"Not me," Reese admitted. "Must have been Helen."

"Not me, either. I think he had a heart attack."

She bent over and touched the man's neck. He was very dead. She glanced back to the two men and nodded. "Can't help him. Why don't we get the woman to the local jail, and I'll take care of the girl."

"Where is she?" Reese asked.

"She's with Asher and she's fine," Meeker assured him. "But we need to get her back to her parents."

"Not so fast," Reese cut in. "It will only take a couple of hours for us to take this house apart and see if there is any money left. If there is, we need to find it now. For the moment, Miss Asher can take the child into town and take care of her. Ross and Adams will be right back to help us once they get Clara checked in at the local jail."

Chapter 81

Meeker was anxious to get back to Rose. She felt responsible for the girl and didn't appreciate the fact that it was Asher watching her in town instead of her. But just because she was miffed at having to dig through the house didn't mean she wasn't doing a thorough job. She even double-checked everything the men did. Yet the only thing she found of interest was a phone number on a scrap of paper in Burgess's billfold. As there was no phone at the house, she slipped that into her pocket. She'd find out whose number it was later.

"There's nothing in the house," Adams said as he sat down in a threadbare living room chair. "We've been all through it. That includes the tiny attic. Ross even got his flashlight and checked the crawl space under the house."

Meeker grimly added, "When I questioned the woman, she claimed she didn't know anything about any money. Strangely, I believe her. I think she was too shocked and frightened to lie. Maybe she took Rose in an attempt to make up for the daughter that was killed."

Reese shook his head. "Well, if there is any money left, he might have buried it. We can get a full team in here to search the property, so there is no reason for us to do that."

"Has anyone looked in Burgess's car?" Meeker asked.

"I looked through the trunk and the glove box," Adams answered. "There was nothing there."

"How about under the backseat?" she asked.

Reese's eyes caught hers. Grabbing a flashlight, he led the way to the Graham. Opening the passenger door, he flipped the front seat forward and reached for the back cushion. It wouldn't move.

"Let me see the light," Meeker demanded.

After sliding it on, she aimed the beam down toward the floor. There were two latches, similar to the one that had been rigged on the door leading to the small room where the couple had hidden Rose. The only difference was these two were secured with small padlocks.

"This is a job for our locksmith," Meeker announced. Stepping back, she handed the flashlight to Reese who immediately kneeled down and examined the locks.

"My tools of the trade won't work on these," he explained. After standing and yanking out his gun, he added, "So step back and cover your ears. I'm doing this the old-fashioned way."

One shot was all it took for the first lock to give up. The second one was a bit more stubborn. The agent used three rounds to "unlock" it. Replacing his weapon in his shoulder holster, he reached down and flipped the lower part of the backseat. Shining a light on the upside-down cushion revealed at least a part of what they were looking for. "Let's take the cushion inside and see what we have."

Back in the house the four agents sat around a wobbly wooden table and pulled the money from the cushion. After splitting it four ways, they started counting. As the loot was all one-hundred-dollar bills it took less than five minutes to tally.

"I have five thousand four hundred," Adams announced.

Ross tapped his pile and said, "Four thousand three hundred."

Reese chimed in, "Six thousand even."

All eyes fell on the woman. "Eight thousand two hundred." She did some quick mental math and said, "That's twenty-three thousand nine hundred. Even taking into account that ten grand he gave McGrew and the fact he bought the Graham, this house, and likely some other things, that's well short of what was missing from the Watling estate. There should be a lot more left."

"We'll have to get a team to search for places he might have buried it," Reese repeated. "Someone needs to question the woman, too. She might know more than we think."

"We through here?" Adams asked.

"I guess so," Reese said. "At least the searching part. When are the other agents going to get here?"

"In about two hours," Ross said. "Some treasury men from Springfield."

"Okay," Reese said with a sigh. "This place has to be guarded until we are sure we've found all the cash. I'd do it, but I know that Helen feels we need to get Rose back to her parents. And I agree with her. Can you guys stick around until backup arrives?"

"Sure," Adams chimed in, as if he had a choice.

"And, Ross," Reese said, "as you are the veteran, you're in charge until I get back in a couple of days."

"You got it," he replied.

"We'll drop your car off on our way back to town."

"You can give us that new coupe." Adams laughed. "We won't complain."

"No way," Reese shot back.

Gathering up the cash, Reese led the way to the car that someone had pulled into the driveway.

He already had it started when Meeker slid in and closed the door.

"At least we got the kid," he said. "And some of the cash. I wonder what he did with the rest."

"He never had it," Meeker stated.

He looked at the woman, her face illuminated by the dash lights. "What do you mean?"

"He didn't have the brains to orchestrate this complex deal. There was someone working with them. That person either has the rest of the cash or had it."

He grinned. "I'm thinking you have an idea as to who it is."

"I've got a lead," she admitted, "but I need some help to figure it out. After we get Rose back to her parents, I want to gather everyone who was associated with the Packard in one place and lay out what I think happened. With everyone there, I believe we can figure it all out. Can you help me arrange that?"

"I think so." He laughed. "And by the way, I understand you stood between Rose and Burgess. So you did offer to lay down your life for that little girl."

"You offered your life as well," she quickly replied. "So now we both know what we are made of."

Chapter 82

Thanks to counting games with playing cards and the alphabet countdown with road signs, as well as reading through the half-dozen books they had purchased at a store in St. Louis, Meeker and Rose had fully bonded on their trip from Koshkonong to Oakwood. During those long hours of games and stories, the child opened up, and from her own young perspective, she told Meeker about her life clear back to the day she was taken.

The little girl remembered two men. One was Burgess or Burton. He'd taken her from the shop. But she'd only seen the other man a couple of times. She couldn't remember what he looked like, but she did recall that his words hurt. She couldn't put it any clearer than that, so Meeker didn't fully understand what she meant, but whatever he'd said, the tone he'd used had obviously had a profound effect on the girl.

Rose said Burgess was the man who had given her to Hooks, the woman she had been told to call Mommy. But Rose wouldn't do it.

"She hit me," Rose announced, "when I wouldn't call her Mommy. But I didn't care. I just kept saying, 'You're not my mommy.'"

And she seemed to understand where she was going. She remembered her parents. She could describe them in detail. She also remembered her room and a laundry list of other facets of her life. Best of all, she was excited to be going to Oakwood. Even though Oakwood was where the nightmare had begun.

Reese parked the '42 Ford in front of the flower shop. The motor was still idling when Meeker opened the door, stepped out into the sunshine, and then turned and reached for the little girl's hand.

Rose took in the sight of the flower shop. She smiled and hopped out into the street, tugging on Meeker's arm as they headed to the front door. They didn't have to open it; Carole did that for them.

The next moment was like nothing Meeker had ever witnessed. The fact that it happened at Carole's Flowers was so appropriate.

As quickly as Meeker let go of Rose's hand, the child jumped up into her mother's arms. There was no hesitation. Rose knew she was home. As the child and mother drew each other close, Helen saw her own mother longing for a moment like this that never came. And as Carole began sobbing, it was the child who offered words that summed up the whole episode.

"It's a happy time," Rose scolded her, wiping her tears. "Mommy, it's a happy time."

Kissing her daughter's cheek, Carole whispered, "Yes, it is. Yes, it is!"

Standing at the counter, his eyes filled with disbelief, was a man in an Army uniform. He was just days from being shipped overseas. The little girl lifted her head from her mother's shoulder. No one had to tell her who he was.

"Daddy!" Rose screamed.

Rushing to his wife and child, George wrapped them both up in his arms. "My baby," he whispered.

"I'm not a baby anymore," Rose corrected him.

After stepping through the open door and into the shop, Helen Meeker stood to one side silently watching the reunion. She didn't know what to do or what to say. It was all so overwhelming. The moment she never actually believed would happen had happened.

She sensed her partner's presence behind her. Leaning close, he whispered in her ear, "Look outside."

Meeker glanced over her shoulder and out the window. A hundred people where watching through the glass. Many were crying, some were praying, and no one was saying anything. Maybe it was because, like Meeker, they couldn't figure out what to say.

"With all the uncertainty in this world," Reese quietly said, "with so many of their husbands and sons fighting in a war, these people needed to know that someone could safely come home. You've given them that."

"We have," she corrected him. "Even if J. Edgar never admits it, 'The Great Experiment' worked!"

He nodded and whispered, "And everything's set for tonight. Everyone will be here. Are you sure you won't tell me what you have planned?"

"No." She smiled. "Let me have my moment and put the cap on this case and my career with the FBI in my own way."

"I owe you that much," he assured her.

"Are the technicians going to be able to hook up the special equipment I need?"

Reese nodded. "They'll have it ready. Listen, I need to get into Danville and make sure everything you and I need has come in."

"You've got my list," she whispered. "This is my show. What do you need?"

"That's *my* surprise," he answered. "Consider it a thank-you for a couple of times you saved my life. I'll see you later."

Reese opened the front door, the bell rang, and he stepped out. As he disappeared, Meeker turned her attention back to the reunited family. In a short while she was going to have to push that little girl into a place where at least one more bad memory was going to bubble to the surface. She prayed that not only would Rose be strong enough to handle it, but that she would be strong enough to help her uncover the complete truth.

Chapter 83

It was almost eight when nearly everyone who had had any kind of a connection to the Packard was gathered in Carole's Flower Shop. Rose and Angel were playing jacks on the floor in a corner, while most of the others had found places to stand, sit, or lean as they waited for the final invitee to arrive. Though most of them knew each other, it was not a comfortable scene. No one understood why the meeting was called, and each of them fidgeted as if they were standing outside the principal's office waiting to find out what they had done wrong. None of them made eye contact with each other, and except for a few whispers between George and Carole, no one spoke. Thus, beyond the children's play, the only real noise was the uneasy breathing of those waiting for the party to start.

Henry Reese, dressed in a black suit with white shirt and black tie, had spent enough time getting ready for this unique moment in his personal history to appear very much Hollywood's proto-type of an FBI agent. Unlike the others, who were tense, he was relaxed, casually leaning up against a display case that stood beside the front door. He seemed to sense that the final curtain call of

Eleanor's Grand Experiment was going to be very special indeed.

As the flower shop's clock struck the hour of eight, Meeker glanced out the window. A single streetlight illuminated the 1936 Packard Beverly Coffman had driven down to Oakwood from her home in Wilmette.

"When are we going to get started?" Sheriff Jed Atkins asked. "Mabel doesn't like to be left alone at night."

"I was waiting on the arrival of another guest," Meeker answered, "but I guess I can get started. Let me start by telling you I brought each of you here tonight because of a connection to that yellow Packard sitting on the street just outside this shop. It has made an impact on every life here in some way or another, and I believe it is going help us solve not just one but three crimes."

Her eyes shifted from the sheriff, to Sam Johns, to Landers, who'd come up from Arkansas, to the Halls and Beverly Coffman, before landing on Henry Reese. She winked at her former partner, and then she shifted her gaze to the salesman from Arkansas. Landers reached up and rubbed his throat with his right hand.

"You have a question, Bill?" Meeker asked.

"You said three crimes? I thought there were only two."

She nodded, spun on her heels, took a long look at the front glass, and then explained, "Everyone knows about the kidnapping. Everyone here also knows about the money that was stolen from Abbi Watling. But I think only one person in this room is aware that there was a murder."

"A murder?" Sheriff Atkins's voice was laced with a mixture of confusion and shock. "Are you talking about Abbi? I always had the gut feeling someone killed her."

Meeker looked from the sheriff to the man standing beside him. Samuel Johns caught her gaze then diverted his eyes to the floor. He was really uneasy, and why not? This case would have been a lot easier if the attorney had just taken a closer look at the sketch of Burgess.

"Mr. Johns," Meeker broke into the silence. She caught him and everyone else by surprise. "I still don't fully understand why you didn't recognize Burton, the man you knew as Burgess, from our sketch."

The lawyer awkwardly shrugged. "I guess I should have. I just didn't think he was capable of doing anything like that."

"That shows bad judgment in at least two ways," Meeker calmly explained. "I'd expect more from a member of your profession. As a member of the bar, I might be inclined to believe you were keeping quiet to protect yourself."

"I've heard the gossip," Johns shot back. "There are a lot of folks who seem to think I had a hand in the missing cash."

"And," Meeker continued, "even if you didn't help plan her murder, you might have been after Abbi's money. Even lawyers struggled in the Depression. The year Abigale Watling died was about as tough as any in the 1930s, so maybe you needed to get your hands on that cash. Janet Carson trusted you. It wouldn't have been that hard to pull the wool over her eyes. And you seem to be a pretty big spender. That desk in your office probably costs more than most cars."

"Are you serious?" the man roared. "How dare you question my integrity!"

She smiled. "Well, when I visited with you in your office you did expose something that would put any professional investigator on alert. It sure set off warning bells." Glancing over at Reese, she paused.

As Meeker considered her next words, Johns was deflating like a balloon on a winter's day, and though he surely wanted desperately to defend himself, he seemed at a loss for words. Finally he asked, "What did I say or do?"

"You knew which seat in the car the money was stored under," she explained. "When we gave you that scrap of information, you told us it was the backseat that was uncomfortable. We hadn't told you that our lab found the evidence in the backseat. We just said a seat."

"But," he argued. "I tell you I'm innocent."

"We'll see," Meeker replied. She paused for a

moment, her eyes falling on George and Carole Hall, before noting, "Of course it seems even more strange that a trained officer of the law like Sheriff Atkins missed indentifying Burgess."

"I thought the sketch looked something like Mitchell," he admitted. "But I wasn't sure. I'd have looked stupid if I was wrong."

"You look pretty stupid now," Meeker solemnly noted.

"You know what many at the FBI are saying?" Reese added.

"Yeah," the sheriff mumbled as he folded his arm. "Some folks in town are, too. They're saying I worked with Burgess or Barton or whatever his name is and I took some of Abbi's money."

"It's not that far-fetched," Meeker said, "that you and an old friend like Sam Johns would be in this together. After all, you were the ones who supposedly searched the Packard after Abbi died."

"I swear—" he said.

"Not right now," Meeker cut him off. "Save swearing until your hand is on the Bible in the courtroom."

The dinging of the bell over the door caused everyone to turn. Dressed in a gray coat, Janet Carson stepped in, clutching an envelope in her hands. Her gaze moved from person to person in the room until her eyes finally locked onto Meeker.

"Are you Helen Meeker?" Carson asked.

"Yes, I am," Meeker replied.

"Here is what you asked for."

As Meeker took the envelope, Janet unbuttoned her coat, revealing a nicely tailored olive-green suit that matched her pumps. She pulled the coat off her shoulders and laid it down on an empty bench.

"If you're going to point fingers," Atkins barked, "then you need to look at her."

"Miss Carson?" Meeker asked.

"Yes," he growled.

"Why?"

"Well," the sheriff said, "she must have money. Look at the suit she has on. I bet it cost a pretty penny. Doubt if she could buy that on a school-teacher's salary."

"But her aunt's money was going to her anyway," Meeker pointed out. "What reason would she have to take it?"

"Maybe she wanted to avoid paying taxes on it," Atkins said.

Meeker cast an eye toward the late arrival before moving to the center of the room and pulling a small scrap of paper from her pocket. "The missing piece might be right here. It's a phone number I found in the billfold of Mitchell Burgess. It's pretty old, as you can tell by the faded ink and worn paper. But it was important enough that he kept it. Why?"

She gave the paper to the sheriff. "Does this number mean anything to you?"

He glanced at it and shook his head. "It's not a local exchange."

"No, it's not," she agreed. "For those of you who can't see what is written here, does Jupiter 7-2673 mean anything to you?" No one answered.

"What about the rest of you?" she asked.

After a few moments of silence, Bill Landers spoke, "I know of a Jupiter exchange in Ohio, but it wasn't that number."

"That's the problem we have," Meeker noted. She took the paper back and waved it in the air. "Whoever wrote this number down didn't add what city or state it was in. Since Burgess knew whose number this was, he didn't need to record that information. Yet we need it. Without it, we can't arrest the person that I'm pretty sure was behind the theft of the money from the Watling estate and the kidnapping."

"It could have been Burgess working alone," Johns interjected.

Meeker crooked her right eyebrow. "Do you think he was smart enough to do all that was entailed in this deal?"

"I don't know," the attorney admitted. "But to me, that is what makes the most sense."

"Of course that's what you want us to believe," the sheriff snapped. "You're afraid they'll link this mess to you."

"Jed!" Johns barked.

"Well," the sheriff yelled, "if I didn't do it, then you seem to be the next logical choice! You were Abbi's lawyer. You knew about the money. Burgess worked for you after Abbi died. Your tie to him is stronger than anyone's! Maybe our search was just to make you look innocent and throw suspicion elsewhere. Maybe you already had the cash safely tucked away. Maybe you knew that others knew about the money and you were just covering your trail."

"I don't know why I ever voted for you," Johns shot back. "You're an idiot!"

Meeker smiled, waved her hand, and cut the men off. "Let's get back on track—what about the number? Does it mean anything to anyone?"

No one answered.

"Rose," Meeker gently said, moving over to where the two children were playing. The little girl looked up. "You said that there was a second man who was involved in taking you. Would you stand up and look around this room?"

The little girl pushed up from the floor and took the agent's hand. "You take a very close look at the men in this room. Are any of them the other man you told me about?"

Rose slowly moved her eyes from Atkins to Johns to Landers. After she studied each of them, she shrugged, "No, the mean man's not here."

The trio of men breathed collective sighs of relief.

"Of course," Meeker said, "there could have been a third man—the brains behind this deal. So you men don't need to relax too much yet."

"That leaves me out," Atkins barked, "because everyone here seems to think I'm stupid."

Meeker wryly smiled before turning back to the little girl. "What did you tell me the man looked like?"

"He was kind of fat and frowned a lot. He had a whiny voice. He was not as old as those men."

"That could be a hundred people I know," George noted.

"Yeah," Johns added. "That description fits several people I've represented. We could go to Danville and see ten people who fit that description in five minutes."

Meeker nodded in agreement. "And because I don't know where the telephone that goes with this number is, the one Mitchell Burgess had in his billfold, I can't connect a man fitting that description to this number. And besides, it might not even be a working number. I've called it in every Jupiter exchange in about a dozen different states and have gotten nothing. The office is still checking the states I haven't called."

"So this is a colossal waste of time," Atkins growled. "I'm going home."

"Not yet." Reese held up a hand to stop the man. Meeker motioned for the agent to talk privately outside. They stepped out the door. It was time to up the stakes.

Chapter 84

For almost two minutes no one moved. Except for the two playing children, all eyes were locked on the front door. They each had to be wondering where Reese and Meeker had gone. What were they doing? What surprise did Meeker have next?

When the door opened and the bell rang, those gathered saw a complete stranger walk through the door. The small, slight man with the crooked nose was dressed in a prison uniform. He had shackles on his feet and hands. He looked anything but happy to be a part of the proceedings.

"Ladies and gentlemen," Meeker said, "this is our special guest for the evening. His name is Jack McGrew."

"Pistolwhip?" the sheriff asked.

"Don't call me that," the newest guest growled. "My name's Jack."

"Why is he out of jail?" the lawyer nervously demanded.

"I had a friend"—Meeker smiled—"who made this possible."

"You must have friends in some pretty high

places," Landers said, awe evident in his tone.

"If I told you how high," Reese chuckled, "you wouldn't believe it."

Shaking her head, Meeker turned to face the convict she had single-handedly captured. "I trust you understand the need to give the complete truth here tonight."

"As long as you don't throw me over that yellow car," he replied, "I'll pretty much do anything. You are one scary broad."

"I'll take that as a compliment. Jack, you don't know these people, and none of them know you. But you were good friends with a man those gathered here all had contact with at one time or another. They knew him as Mitchell Burgess, but when you met him he was a prison guard at Joliet named Burton."

"Yeah," McGrew quickly admitted. "I knew him."

"He was your friend," Meeker continued, "wasn't he?"

"Sure, he was a good friend."

Meeker took a step toward McGrew, cutting the distance between them to five feet. "I know the last time you saw Burton was at the farmhouse on the night you were captured. In the couple of years before that, did you see him at all?"

"A few times. We met, had drinks. Nothing big, just two friends getting together."

"And did he talk about his life?"

463

"Yeah," McGrew replied. "Friends tell each other what's going on. I told him about my deals, and he told me about his."

"Did you know about the kidnapping and the reasons behind it?" Meeker asked.

"Sure, he told me. It was all about the money. They wanted to get their hands on the old woman's loot."

Meeker smiled. "You said *they*. Did he tell you who *they* were or how many there were?"

McGrew nodded. "Since he's dead, guess it doesn't matter if I squeal some. It was a two-way split."

"Who was his partner?" Meeker demanded.

"He didn't give me a name. Just said he was a louse he had to deal with. He also told me the guy was heartless and ordered him to kill the kid. But he couldn't do that. He might have been a bit strange, but murdering a kid was not his game. He didn't have the stomach for it. You have to be pretty sick to do that. So he gave the kid to some woman who had lost her own daughter."

"That all adds up," Meeker replied. "Clara's daughter had been killed. In fact, the girl had been murdered. You have any information on that?"

The con shrugged. "I only know that she saw something she shouldn't have when her dad was dealing with the mob. It was to teach the old man a lesson about crossing them on a deal. I heard it tore him up so bad it killed him."

"That gives us a bit more information about that unsolved crime. But let's return to this one. Did Mitchell tell you anything else about the partner?"

"No, but that's not unusual. I never told him about the guys who worked with me, either. It's safer that way. What I didn't know couldn't come back to hurt him." He shrugged. "Now if you don't need anything else out of me, I'd rather not be here."

"Only a couple more questions," Meeker assured him. "Did Burton, as you knew him, or Burgess as the others called him, mention Samuel Johns?"

"Yeah, he told me that guy skimmed money from people whose investments he held."

Meeker turned around and stared at the attorney. "Maybe that's why you didn't want to recognize the sketch. He knew too much about you."

"But I didn't take Abbi's cash," Johns quickly replied. "Jed and I looked . . . we looked hard, but we never found it."

"But what about your dealings with Miss Watling?" Meeker asked. "I think we can prove you"—she glanced back to Jack—"what was the word you used? Oh yeah, *skimmed* some from her during her regular business dealings. Maybe she found out. Maybe you needed to get her out of the way."

"I'm not saying anything more without an attorney," Johns replied.

Meeker nodded and looked back at Jack. "What about Sheriff Jed Atkins? Mitchell say anything about him?"

"Oh." McGrew laughed. "He talked about him a lot."

Meeker glanced over to where the sheriff was standing. The color had completely drained from his face.

"What did he say?" Meeker asked, her eyes never leaving Atkins.

"He said he was stupid. I remember his words exactly, 'Dumb as a rock but honest to a fault.' "

"Thank the Lord." Atkins sighed.

Reese opted to get in a quick jab, "Never heard a man take being called dumb so well."

"Might be why he didn't recognize the sketch," Meeker added. "Reese, you can take Mr. McGrew out to the boys for his ride back to the Big House."

"Can't wait to get out of here," the convict replied. "I hope I never meet you again. You are one scary lady."

Chapter 85

Meeker waited for Reese to return before she picked up her questions. As soon as her partner had settled into his place against the wall, she waved the large envelope Janet Carson had brought with her. With absolutely no fanfare, Meeker opened it. After pulling out a single photo, she set the folder on the rolltop desk and walked over to show the black-and-white image to Rose.

"Is this the guy?"

"That's him," the girl sneered as she replied. "He's mean!"

Meeker put the photo back in her pocket and studied the faces around her. "The man in this photo was the man Burgess called."

"But you said the number didn't work," Carole noted.

"As it's written here, it doesn't," Meeker admitted. "But if you dial Jupiter 3-7627, it does."

"I may be dumb," Atkins cut in, "but I can memorize almost anything. That's not the number you read a while ago."

"You're right," she agreed. "The number I just called out is the number on Burgess's piece of paper reversed. To protect the identity of his partner in this crime the number was written backwards. It was a pretty clever code, too. Everything would have worked if we hadn't found Rose and if we hadn't discovered that piece of a one-hundred-dollar bill in the seat springs in the Packard."

She moved to the counter and pointed to a phone connected to a large speaker. "We installed this special line tonight. You'll be able to hear the call, but the party on the other end will only be able to hear the caller. Nevertheless, I would like to ask each of you to remain quiet. It is vital that this seem like a private call."

As she picked up the receiver and dialed, Reese moved out of the showroom and into the office.

"Operator." Her voice came through the speaker and filled the room.

"This is Helen Meeker. I'm working with the FBI. About an hour ago I asked you to be ready to make a call for us."

"Yes ma'am. I believe you wanted Jupiter 3-7627."

"That is correct. And I gave you the city."

"Yes, ma'am. Connecting now. Speak when your party answers."

Meeker waved at Janet. The small woman moved quickly across to the counter and took the phone.

"Hello." A man's voice on the other end of the line now had everyone's attention.

"It's Janet. I called to warn you. You're in trouble. The FBI caught Burgess. He talked, and they know you were a part of the kidnapping and taking Abbi's money."

Everyone in the room watched the speaker box, waiting for his answer. It took the man on the other end almost thirty seconds to come up with a response.

"Why are you warning me?"

"I want the money you've got left. How much is it?" she demanded.

"What good would giving cash to you do me?"

Janet looked to Meeker. After the agent nodded, she continued with the script Meeker had prepared. "I can provide you with an alibi for the kidnapping. I can say you were with me that day."

"I've only got ten grand left. Is that worth you lying for me?"

"I need the money," she quickly replied. "There's a house I want to buy. But you've got to tell me one more thing."

"What?"

"How did you kill Aunt Abbi?" Meeker figured he would balk at answering the question, so she was not surprised when the line went silent.

"Tell me," Janet demanded. "I can't begin to trust you if you don't level with me."

Those in the room could hear the man taking several deep breaths before his voice came back on the line whispering his response, "I'm kind of proud of that. I think it was a stroke of genius on my part. After all, I fooled everyone. I have a friend who is a pharmacist. One night he was telling a group of us about drugs that mimic heart attacks. I took notes."

As the morbid explanation hung in the air, Reese stepped back into the room and waved at Meeker.

"So you gave it to Burgess, and he gave it to her?" Janet asked. Helen could see from the expression on her face that she was mortified at the news he was delivering.

"Heavens, no," he replied. "I couldn't trust him to mix the right dosage. I drove into town and surprised her. I gave it to her at dinner. After she took it, Burgess and I searched the house. We didn't find the money. He figured out it was in the car years later. That's why we had to kidnap the girl. I figured it would be the easiest way to get the cash without directing suspicion my way. Besides, the guy who owned the car never left it anyplace where we could get to it without someone noticing."

"I can't believe you did it," Janet said, shock ringing in her voice.

"I should have cut you in from the beginning, but I didn't think you'd go for it. The only person who figured it all out was Johns. He put it together a few months ago. I had to give him ten grand to keep quiet."

All eyes went to the attorney. Before he could speak, the voice came back on the line, "I need you to hang on, someone's at the door."

"I'll go ahead and hang up," Janet replied. "The folks at your door might take up too much time for me to wait."

Janet handed the phone to Meeker who put it back in its cradle. As she did, Reese strolled into the shop's back office. Thirty seconds later, he popped out into the main room and announced, "We have him in custody."

"I'm sure," Carole volunteered from behind the

counter, "that the man on the line was the guy who called giving us the information on the ransom money and where the drop point was. I'm just sure of it. It was the same voice."

"So am I," George added. "What's his name? I'm guessing several in this room know."

Meeker looked from the Halls to Carson and then to Johns. It was the lawyer who spoke first, "Jim Watling; Abbi's nephew."

"You mean," Atkins cut in, "his greed was so great he'd kill and kidnap just to get his hands on the hundred grand?"

Janet Carson nodded. As she did, the sheriff pointed his finger at the attorney and leveled a verbal barrage that hit the bull's-eye, "Samuel Johns, you're a snake! You mean to tell me that you found out and then were bought off for a few thousand dollars? Even though this family was missing their child?"

Meeker looked over to Johns. He shrugged. There was no covering his guilt now. "I had nothing to do with Abbi being killed or the kidnapping. You need to know that."

"But you didn't let us know Rose was alive either," Meeker said.

The attorney took a deep breath before continuing to try to justify what he'd done. "Like I said, I didn't have anything to do with taking Rose or murdering Abbi. I never figured out where the money was. I only put everything together after the visit with Meeker and Reese." He glanced toward Meeker. "I was talking to him when you burst back into my office on that day. After you left and I was sure you were out of town, I drove down and confronted Jim. He offered me the ten grand as a bribe. I couldn't do anything to bring Abbi back, and he assured me the girl was dead, so I took it. It was wrong and so was I."

George Hall rushed across the room. Before anyone could reach him, he delivered three sharp blows to the lawyer's gut. Reese and Atkins pulled George back, but the man spat, "You could have gotten our daughter back to us!"

After slowly pulling himself upright, Johns sadly shook his head. "I swear, Jim Watling told me she had been killed. He swore that Burgess had taken care of her. If I had known she was alive, I'd have turned him in. I swear."

"I hope," Meeker said, "for your sake, you did think Rose was dead."

"Why the circus?" Atkins asked, turning to Meeker. "Why not just arrest Jim Watling and Johns and not bring us all into this? Is that information from the phone call admissible in a court?"

"It was a legal wiretap," Reese assured the sheriff. "We had Carole's and Janet's permission, as well as a court order, to listen to all of Watling's calls."

"And you are not so dumb, Sheriff Atkins,"

Meeker added. "We could have locked Jim Watling up for a long time without the call. We already had enough evidence with the phone number and Rose's identifying him in the picture to prove he was at least involved in the kidnapping. But we needed to get him to admit he killed his aunt. We had no proof of that. The bonus was getting him to talk about Samuel Johns's role in this. Thus the need for the circus. And, might I add, the show has closed for the night."

Reese waved his hand. "Unless Helen objects, everyone except Mr. Johns is free to go home now."

"Except for Mom and me," Angel announced. "We're staying with the Halls tonight."

"That's right." Rose laughed. "I can't wait for you to see my room. It's just like it was when I left."

"Sam," the sheriff announced as he put his hand on the attorney's left wrist. "As soon as I get these cuffs on you, you'll be going with me. They've got a nice warm cell for you down at the county jail."

Johns said nothing as the group looked on, and his old friend slapped what some called *bracelets* on his wrists. Once they were locked in place, Atkins gently pushed the man toward the door. Just before he walked outside, the attorney took a last look at those who were witnessing his fall from grace. It appeared as though he were trying to come up with something to say, but this time words failed him. So when the sheriff placed a hand in the middle of his back, Johns moved silently out into the darkness.

As he disappeared, Meeker put her arm around Janet Carson's shoulder. "I'm sorry."

"I'm not surprised about Jim," Janet answered. "But I can't believe Mr. Johns was in on it."

"He just let his greed overrule his common sense," Meeker explained. "That happens all the time. If you don't believe it, come visit me in Washington."

Carson nodded.

"And you'll get back some of the money," Meeker assured her. "Sorry we couldn't get it all."

Janet smiled. "I'll be giving it to a children's home that Aunt Abbi loved. So whatever is left will go for something pretty special."

Carson picked up her coat, slipped it on, and headed toward the door. As she did, the Halls and Coffmans moved from the main room into the office. Reese walked back in.

"So I hear you bought the Packard?" Reese quipped, as he strolled over to Meeker's side.

"Sure did," she answered. "I felt I owed that car."

"You probably paid too much for it."

"Probably," she agreed. "But I'm not worried about resale value. I'm keeping it forever."

"Where you staying tonight?" he asked.

"I've got a room at the Regis in Danville."

He smiled. "Get a good night's sleep. And I hope we can work together down the road."

He then surprised the woman by leaning forward, looking deeply into her eyes, and bringing his lips to hers. He let them linger there for a moment then pulled back just enough to whisper, "I still need to show you how to have fun."

"I'm ready," she whispered back. "You name the time and place."

"It will be soon." After leaning forward for a final soft kiss, he turned and strolled to the door.

Chapter 86

"I'm checking out," Meeker announced, setting her bag down in front of the main desk in the Regis Hotel's lobby. She was studying the counter's green leather padded top when the older gentleman dressed in black slacks, a white shirt, and red vest moved forward from his station behind that desk.

"Hope you enjoyed your stay."

"I had a good night's sleep," she assured him. "In fact, it might well have been the best I've had in years."

"What was your room number?" he asked.

"Four-thirteen," she announced as she handed him her key.

"If you're Miss Helen Meeker," he replied,

reaching for what looked like a shoe box, "then someone left something here for you." He set the small package on the counter. "Wonder what it could be."

"I have no idea," she answered. She met his eyes. "And as I have more enemies than friends, do you have the name of the person who left it?"

He glanced at his notes. "No, but I do remember he was young, good-looking, and the maid said he was very charming."

"That narrows it down." Meeker smiled.

"Well, miss, you paid in advance, so do you need help with your bags?"

"I only have two," she replied. "I can handle it."

"Thank you. Please stay with us the next time when you're in town. And I hope what is in the package will bring you a great deal of happiness."

Meeker placed the shoe box under her arm, put her purse over her shoulder, and picked up her bags. She waltzed through the small lobby and pushed out the door where she was rudely greeted by a relentless, cold north wind. Turning to her left, she quickly marched the half block to the hotel's parking lot. Among all the gray, blue, black, and cream colored cars, her bright yellow Packard was easy to spot. Unlocking the door, she reached around, popped the handle on the back door and scooted her bags onto the backseat. Closing the back door, she tossed her purse into the front seat and slid in. Taking her place behind the wheel, she closed that door, slipped the key into the ignition, pulled out the choke, pumped the gas pedal twice, and hit the starter. After the motor roared to life, she slipped it into neutral, lifted her foot from the clutch, and adjusted the choke. It was time to examine the surprise.

There was a single red ribbon holding the lid onto the box. She untied it and set the top to one side. Inside was a white business envelope with her name written in pen. She recognized the handwriting. Taking the envelope, she carefully opened the flap to discover a single piece of typewriter paper. She unfolded it and read the short message.

Dear Partner,

When you told me you had nothing of your sister's, not even a photo, I did some quick digging. Your father didn't destroy everything, simply because he didn't have everything. I had these things pulled from the case box on Emily's kidnapping. I don't know if it will bring you any peace, but at least you have something.

Henry

She was filled with a mixture of apprehension and curiosity. Taking a deep breath, she placed the letter on the seat and looked into the box. On the top was a rag doll large enough to fill the small cardboard container. As soon as she saw it, she could picture Emily dancing across the floor with it. Grabbing and clutching the doll to her chest, Meeker closed her eyes and, as if by magic, a wealth of lost memories flooded her mind. The instant they reached her heart, the tears began to flow. Both the memories and the tears continued relentlessly for five minutes.

As she sat alone in the Packard, she remembered a dollhouse, a trip to the zoo, presents under a spruce, a Christmas tree, and hot dogs at Coney Island. There were birthday cakes and matching Easter dresses and eating apples after climbing a tree. She could remember scores of forgotten elements of her life with Emily, including the way she laughed and talked, but no matter how hard she squeezed the doll she simply couldn't see her sister's face. Finally regaining enough composure to set the doll aside on the car's seat, she pulled a handkerchief from her coat pocket. After drying her eyes, she looked back into the box.

The only other item was a four-by-six-inch photo. Her hand shaking, she carefully lifted it from the box. Staring back at her was the face she had forgotten. What a beautiful face it was! She had dark, straight hair, and a cowlick at the top of her forehead. Her smile was so natural and a bit lopsided; her eyes, large dark eyes, were so very expressive. And it was those eyes that seemed to call out to her. It was the eyes . . .

"My Lord," Meeker whispered. "My Lord," she said again.

Setting the photo back in the box. She pushed open the car door, locked it, and raced back to the hotel. Running over to a phone booth, she dumped her purse and began counting out change. When she was convinced she had enough, she called the operator.

Chapter 87

The drive to Chicago took over two hours, and for one very intense and personal reason it was the longest trip of Helen Meeker's life. It was just past noon when she parked the Packard in a lot on Jackson, picked up the shoe box and her purse, paid the attendant, and with a determined step made her way to Michigan Avenue. After taking a left, she waited impatiently for a light and crossed the street. A half block later she opened the door to Foster's Café.

"May I help you?" a finely dressed older woman asked.

"I'm meeting someone for lunch," Meeker quickly explained. "I don't know if she beat me here or not."

"How old would this person be?" the hostess asked.

"In her early twenties and she's pretty."

"Is she a brunette?"

"Yes," Meeker whispered.

"If I'm right, she's in the side booth all the way to the back, on the street side. Would you like me to lead you?"

"No," Meeker hurriedly answered. "I'll find her."

As she swept by the coat check stand and into the restaurant's main room, she didn't notice any of the other people dining at one of the city's hottest lunch spots. She was barely aware of the smell of the food or the plush feel of the carpet. Her eyes were locked onto a single booth. Nothing else mattered.

The trip across the congested room took only thirty seconds, but to Meeker it seemed hours. She was literally breathless when she arrived at that booth and got her first real glimpse of the young woman sitting in that tall-backed bench seat.

"Hi," came a crisp, happy greeting. "I guess you're Helen."

Meeker was too busy studying every feature of the face that was now just a few feet in front of her to respond. She didn't speak or take her eyes from that face, even as she awkwardly pushed her body into the bench opposite her guest.

"You must be Helen," the now confused woman noted again. When Meeker didn't respond, she shrugged. "When my supervisor at Marshall

Field's told me that someone from President Roosevelt's office wanted to meet me for lunch, I couldn't understand why. It was even a little bit scary. But I wasn't going to turn down a chance to eat at Foster's. I can't believe I'm here. The menu is amazing!"

Meeker nodded.

"Hold it!" the young woman noted. She tilted her head to the right as if trying to summon a memory and carefully studied Meeker with those dark, expressive brown eyes before continuing. "I've seen you before. I think I recognize your face. Was it at college?"

"No," the agent finally found her voice, "it was in St. Anne's. You were waiting tables."

"Yeah, that was it. I was staying with my friend Marie. I was working for Mrs. Thornton, trying to make enough money to pay for tuition and room and board."

"Did you?" Meeker asked.

"Did I what?"

"Make enough money for college?"

"No," she sadly replied. "I fell short. So I haven't finished yet. I'm working at Marshall Field's. Of course you know that. After all, you called me there. Sorry I couldn't come to the phone, but they don't allow us to take personal calls."

"What about your family?" Meeker asked. "Can't they help you with college?"

481

"No family," she explained in a matter-of-fact manner as if she'd told the story a hundred times. "I was raised in an orphanage. A woman dropped me off there and told them my parents had died. The woman claimed to be my aunt, and she said she was too poor to take care of me. The staff thought I was about three. Because the woman didn't have any proof as to who I was and she disappeared before she could sign any papers, they couldn't put me in the adoption pool. At the time I didn't even have a name. I called myself by one letter—*M*. They had enough Marys and Marthas there, so they gave me Alison. And, at some point, when they gave up trying to find where I came from, I got the last name of Ward. You know, like ward of the state."

As Meeker digested the information, she sadly nodded. "That had to be tough."

"Well," Alison replied, "it was no walk in the park. But the staff was really nice. I did well in school. Christmas was a little lonely, but I'm fine now."

"I guess you don't even know your birthday?" Meeker observed.

"Well I have one," she smiled. "It's August 17, 1918. They figured I was about three, and that was the date I was dropped off at the home."

Meeker nodded. The timeline fit. That was about three weeks after Emily had been abducted.

"I am so sorry I spilled out my life story," Alison

said. "I'm sure you aren't interested. In truth, my life has been kind of boring. So why do you want to speak to me? The note I was given by my supervisor about meeting you for lunch said your name was Helen Meeker?"

"That's right," Meeker quickly assured her. "And your life is anything but boring. I want to know all about it."

A waitress set two glasses of water in front of the women and asked, "Do you know what you'd like to eat?"

"You can have anything on the menu," Meeker assured her.

"I always wanted to try one of their steaks."

"Then we'll do it." The agent smiled. "Bring us two T-bones."

"We only have sirloin today," the waitress explained.

"How do you want yours cooked?" Meeker asked.

"I've never had one," she replied. "I don't know."

"Two steaks, medium, with baked potatoes and some of your incredible homemade rolls."

The woman jotted the information on her pad. "And to drink."

"A Coke," Alison quickly answered.

"Me, too."

After the waitress left, the young woman looked back at Meeker. "Why did you want to see me?"

Opening the shoe box, Meeker pulled out the photo. Holding it with the back side to her guest, she asked, "Would you smile for me?"

The question was strange enough that it evoked an involuntary smile followed by an obvious question. "What?"

Meeker looked from the picture to the woman on the other side of the table and returned the smile she'd asked for. Handing the photo to Alison, she watched as the girl studied the image. Looking up for a moment to Meeker, she tilted her head as if to pose a question she was probably too tongue-tied or confused to voice.

"I think you called them dents," Meeker softly said. "But our father always called them dimples. I didn't remember that until this morning. Your dimples are on the top side of your cheeks."

"You said *our father?*" the shocked woman whispered.

"Yes, I did."

Alison shook her head and looked back at the photo. "You're not just playing with me, are you?"

"No," Meeker assured her, "you and I are sisters. I was eight when you were kidnapped. And the reason you called yourself by a letter was that I called you 'Em'."

Meeker reached back into the box and pulled out the doll. As soon as it emerged, Alison dropped the photo onto the table and reached for it. Tears filled her eyes as she whispered, "Molly."

"I'd forgotten you called her 'Molly,' " Meeker whispered back, trying her best to keep her composure. "But I remember now. Molly Bee."

"Molly Bee Good," Alison corrected her as she pulled the doll to her body. "We're sisters!" She met her gaze again, wonder in her face.

Meeker nodded.

"And my real name is?"

"Emily Ann Meeker."

"And our folks?"

"They're dead, but I'll help you get to know them. I can tell you so much about them. We can look at pictures." She paused, bit her lip, and sobbed. "It would mean so much to them to know that we found each other. They loved you with all their hearts."

"I have a name!" Alison quietly said.

Meeker nodded and added, "And I have a sister!"

About the Author

Ace Collins lives to write! His writing career spans over two decades with more than sixty titles to his credit. Ace has won numerous awards for his writing including three Golden Quills, an America's Writing Award, and the Angel of Excellence Award. An Arkansas-based writer, Ace has been married for thirty-five years. He and his wife Kathy have two sons. Ace's hobbies include restoring classic cars, collecting movie memora-bilia from the Golden Age of Hollywood, and following college basketball.

Center Point Large Print
600 Brooks Road / PO Box 1
Thorndike ME 04986-0001 USA

(207) 568-3717

US & Canada:
1 800 929-9108
www.centerpointlargeprint.com